DANGEROUS BOYS
RENT BOYS

Two New Collections of Erotic Tales

Plus One Complete Novel:

Matthew: One of Lenny's Boys

Edited By
JOHN PATRICK

STARbooks Press
Herndon, VA

Books by John Patrick

Non-Fiction
A Charmed Life: Vince Cobretti
Lowe Down: Tim Lowe
The Best of the Superstars 1990
The Best of the Superstars 1991
The Best of the Superstars 1992
The Best of the Superstars 1993
The Best of the Superstars 1994
The Best of the Superstars 1995
The Best of the Superstars 1996
The Best of the Superstars 1997
The Best of the Superstars 1998
The Best of the Superstars 1999
The Best of the Superstars 2000
The Best of the Superstars 2001
The Best of the Superstars 2002
What Went Wrong?
When Boys Are Bad
& Sex Goes Wrong
Legends: The World's Sexiest
Men, Vols. 1 & 2
Legends (Third Edition)
Tarnished Angels (Ed.)

Fiction
Billy & David: A Deadly Minuet
The Bigger They Are...
The Younger They Are...
The Harder They Are...
Angel: The Complete Trilogy
Angel II: Stacy's Story
Angel: The Complete Quintet
A Natural Beauty (Editor)
The Kid (with Joe Leslie)
HUGE (Editor)
Strip: He Danced Alone
The Boys of Spring
Big Boys/Little Lies (Editor)
Boy Toy
Seduced (Editor)
Insatiable/Unforgettable (Editor)

Heartthrobs
Runaways/Kid Stuff (Editor)
Dangerous Boys/Rent Boys (Editor)
Barely Legal (Editor)
Country Boys/City Boys (Editor)
My Three Boys (Editor)
Mad About the Boys (Editor)
Lover Boys (Editor)
In the BOY ZONE (Editor)
Boys of the Night (Editor)
Secret Passions (Editor)
Beautiful Boys (Editor)
Juniors (Editor)
Come Again (Editor)
Smooth 'N' Sassy (Editor)
Intimate Strangers (Editor)
Naughty By Nature (Editor)
Dreamboys (Editor)
Raw Recruits (Editor)
Play Hard, Score Big (Editor)
Sweet Temptations (Editor)
Pleasures of the Flesh (Editor)
Juniors 2 (Editor)
Fresh 'N' Frisky (Editor)
Taboo! (Editor)
Heatwave (Editor)
Boys on the Prowl (Editor)
Huge 2 (Editor)
Fever! (Editor)
Any Boy Can (Editor)
Virgins No More (Editor)
Seduced 2 (Co-Editor)
Wild 'N' Willing (Co-Editor)

Published in the United States
STARbooks Press
PO Box 711612
Herndon VA 20171
Printed in the United States

Many thanks to graphic artist John Nail for the cover design. Mr. Nail may be
reached at: tojonail@juno.com.

Book and text design by Milton Stern. Mr. Stern can be reached at
miltonstern@miltonstern.com.

Library of Congress Card Catalogue No. 94-066680

CONTENTS

EDITOR'S NOTE

Most of the stories appearing in this book take place prior to the years of The Plague; the editor and each of the authors represented herein advocate the practice of safe sex at all times. And, because these stories trespass the boundaries of fiction and nonfiction, to respect the privacy of those involved, we've changed all of the names and other identifying details.

INTRODUCTION: THE TOUGH AND THE TENDER
John Patrick

"In America the boy must also be a rebel.
America is doomed to love boys,
precisely because they play hooky,
cuss, steal in a mild sort of way,
and dream of violence."
– *Leslie Fiedler*

We love danger. It draws us like the moth to the flame. And the more dangerous the boy, the more we like it. Good bad boys can be tough and tender at the same time. They all seem to have dirty smiles and hard-guy eyes. Sometimes the nastiness goes out of their eyes and something is exchanged that is harder than a kiss but softer than the going legal tender. And then they seem to shine in the dark like fireflies.

The sex tends to be quick, furious, often anonymous. But always thrilling. Some of the most dangerous boys are found on the street corners of both big and small towns, peddling their wares. Or down some dark alleys. In a story in Gay Review, Rodney Hamblin succinctly describes this phenomenon: "He was visiting relatives in the city while also keeping alert for a new boy of the type he preferred: one who had spent time in alleys, bedrooms both clean and dirty, with men both tall and short, handsome and plain. Ejaculations bathed boys like that. Youth is invulnerable and it did not matter to them. Some men were kind and some were cruel. That did not matter either. What mattered to them was that there be many."

In his book of poetry, Orpheus Descending, William Bory expresses perfectly our attraction to boys whose wares are for sale:

I think 1 like prostitutes, because 1 could never be one. They are always unsatisfactory.

My metier is love, not sex.

They know, after all, the sex is secondary, and so they like me, the gifted amateur.

But the prostitute, high-priced or low, beginner or veteran, commands, even demands, our respect. Coleman Dowell once made up a ditty to describe this need:

I'll lick your boots If you tell me to, I'll lick your boots And even higher

But if you rent me out to other mens, baby, I'll cry a boo hoo hoo hoo hoo hoo

I fear when it comes to renting, I speak from long experience. And, luckily, I have been afraid of a rent boy only once in my life. Curiously enough, it was in the so-called City of Brotherly Love, in a luxurious hotel room in Philadelphia. It was a Sunday night and in those days the bars were closed. I took to the streets. As I recounted in my book What Went Wrong?, in 1975, I found a very young blond, enticing me with his bulging basket and mischievous smile:

"What's up?" he asked as our eyes connected. He was one of several leaning against a brick wall near the intersection of Fifteenth and Spruce, the youths of the night, kids with nowhere to go, ever alert to opportunity.

"Nothing much," I replied, "it's Sunday " The bars are shut on the Sabbath in Philadelphia. I knew this from my several visits to the city on my public relations junkets for a Fortune 500 company with strong Bicentennial tie-ins. My client, like me, was a married man with children, and, I discovered, we shared a desire for exploring many forms of eros. He taught me where to find gay men. My first visit to a gay bar was in Philly, the Allegro. By this time, I had settled into a pattern. My attitudes had formed early on. My brother, six years my senior, had used my body for sexual release from the time I was ten until he went off to college. Because it seemed I was being rewarded by him for this, with treats and special favors, I saw nothing wrong with paying for someone's company. My best encounters had been with those I had paid. I began to prefer it because I felt I was in control of the situation. As a married man, I sought a refuge from the emotional control of my wife. I felt it was unfair that sexuality be a slave to relationships. I sought the freedom to pursue eros where I could find it.

I had used services and met boys in bars in Philadlephia but on this particular night, with the bars shut and not having made any advance calls, I was attempting my first street pick-up. Whatever I said to the scrawny youth over the next few moments seemed to have worked because we struck a deal. When we arrived at my room at the posh Latham Hotel, the kid ducked into the john. As I listened to him urinating, I stood in the middle of the room, on unfamiliar ground, wishing I hadn't gone through with it. Picking up street trash suddenly loomed as a dangerous new experience. Remembering my client's horror stories about how such boys beat and robbed their tricks, I stashed my wallet in the refrigerator.

When the kid came out of the bathroom, I was pouring myself a drink. I offered him one but he declined and quickly shed his clothes, bounced on the bed and started stroking himself. I blanched at his vile smell and I remembered what someone once said of French boys: "They should never remove their socks." My eyes roamed the rail thin body and settled on the pimply face. He wasn't ugly but he wasn't cute either. As he lackadaisically played with himself, I made up my mind: I had done the wrong thing after all. There was no romance to this. It was commerce, pure and simple. Too quick.

Too dirty, even in the splendor of the Latham suite. I wanted no part of it. "I'm afraid I've changed my mind," I said.

"Oh, no ya don't," he spat. "Ya give me my money or I'll call downstairs and tell 'em ya got a 16-year-old here in the room bare-ass naked." I had only sipped my drink. I was stone cold sober. When I was under the influence, the innocent were as much at risk as the guilty.

Calmly, evenly, I tried to reason with the youth: "Oh, I intend to give you your money."

He snarled, "Then why'd ya stash your wallet in the refrigerator?"

I was dumbfounded. He must have sneaked a peek at me while he was in the bathroom.

"No reason." I began stammering. "I...I really don't know. All I have is traveller's checks anyway."

"Don't trust me, eh?"

"I'm sorry."

"Ya, sure, asshole." He jumped up from the bed and tugged his jeans back on.

I was angered but I remained calm. "But, look, I wouldn't start making trouble if I were you." I swallowed hard. "My client's in the next room," I lied, "and all I have to do is start pounding on the wall."

"You look, asshole," he said, pulling his shirt on over his head, "just give me my money and I'm outta here."

I took my wallet from the refrigerator and handed him a fifty. "Just fifty?"

"You wanted thirty. That's all I have. The rest is in traveller's cheques."

"Let me see ..." he screamed, yanking the wallet from my hand.

The trembling seemed to start in my hands and knees, waves of quaking fear, too long suppressed, running uncontrollably through me. I lunged at him, wrestling for my wallet. He pushed me away, hard. I fell against the bureau, then lunged at him again as he made his way to the door. I grabbed at his shirt. He turned and hammered my face with his fist. Around the edges of my vision, I saw a door open and close. Then I saw black.

I awoke on the floor. Dazed, I struggled into the bathroom. The mirror reflected a ugly red welt on my cheek and a black eye but I was lucky to be alive.

I met a lot of boys during my days of constant travel and have never regretted the chances I took. Indeed, one of our favorite themes in our anthologies is the fact that you to leave home to find paradise, as far as boys are concerned. Alfred Chester, who was having his period of greatest fame as a writer in the early sixties, with Esquire praising him, and editors calling him day and night to write reviews and essays, threw up all his success and went off to live in Tangier, Morocco, where expatriate Paul Bowles, the daddy of

gay authors, held court with his lesbian wife, Jane. Edward Field recalls, "Morocco was paradise for Chester from the beginning. Paul Bowles said he never saw anybody melt into Moroccan life as quickly as Chester. I and my friend Neil were there when he picked up a tall, fierce-looking fisherman on the beach, Dris, who was happy to give up the fishing boats and move in with him.

"Alfred wrote a fascinating story, 'Glory Hole,' about the young men of Tangier discussing their foreign lovers, whom they call Nazarenes. This story should be required reading for anyone going to Morocco. The Moroccan boys, it turned out, had a fear of oral sex, worrying that their pricks would be bitten off, though Alfred's own boyfriend, Dris, soon overcame this fear. Dris repeated a story about an old queen blowing one of the boys, who held a large rock over the Westerner's head, in case he bit off his cock. But it was not all oral sex. After living with Dris for a few months, Alfred wrote me that his asshole was so large a family could move in. He said that Dris knew he was not Marilyn Monroe, but if the one in his arms felt good, that was good enough for a Moroccan. And Dris certainly seemed happy with him.

"Some of the resident foreigners complained to Alfred that their Moroccan boyfriends wouldn't kiss them and make love, just wanting to fuck, so Alfred went to bed with them and reported back that the boyfriends were very tender lovers. So perhaps this problem had to do with the foreigner's attitude. But these street boys do have their own traditions and hierarchies, Alfred reported. Between good friends, sex is all right, but no more than the head of your friend's cock must penetrate your asshole. Another rule is that the older one fucks the younger, and pays the younger – when youths don't want to be fucked anymore they grow a mustache. The exception to this, Alfred said, was the Nazarenes, for the Nazarene always pays. Naturally enough, since the local boys are usually poorer than the foreigners.

"When Neil and I visited Dris's family, the women stayed in their own quarters. One time, we were sitting with all the men, when Dris, who was holding his little nephew on his lap, grabbed the boy's crotch and said in his gruff, Arab voice, 'He grow up and make money fucking Nazarenes.' But when Dris's teenage brother ran away to hustle foreigners in Tangier, he went looking for him and sent him home. Alfred also said that in their love affairs, the Moroccan never leaves the Nazarene, but vice versa. One Moroccan youth I talked to said he would never go with a Nazarene again because they always went away.

"Alfred's Moroccan paradise was only tarnished by recurrent poverty, and the mental problems brought on by indiscriminate use of drugs, especially kif, the local form of cannabis. He could live on very little, and writing reviews and essays brought in almost enough money, but not quite. He also had a major disappointment when his book of stories, Behold Goliath, did not do well when it was published in 1964. This perhaps lay behind his first

breakdown, when he panicked over being surrounded by 'murderers.' For, after all, Jane Bowles' friend, Libby Holman, had shot her husband. William Burroughs had shot his wife. And Bowles himself, under the influence of kif, bragged that anyone could be rubbed out in Tangier. This boast seemed threatening to Chester, since Paul, after a fight with him, had written a friend that he was planning to have Chester rubbed out.

"Chester recovered his sanity, and went on to write his brilliant novel, The Exquisite Corpse. He even stopped wearing his ridiculous wig, after it caught fire in the kitchen, and showed his bald head for the first time. But in the late summer of '65, an old friend, the accomplished and beautiful Susan Sontag, came to visit him in Tangier, where she checked into El Minzah, the classiest hotel in town, Susan was now world famous after publishing her essay, 'Notes on Camp.' Moreover, with her beauty, Alfred was terrified she would turn the head of his boyfriend, Dris, who like many Moroccans was bisexual. Though Dris was awed by her, this did not happen.

"On Sontag's arrival, Chester simply flipped out, and started hearing voices, and suspecting people, especially 'the authorities,' of tuning in on his bald head, so recently de-wigged. He refused to have sex with Dris anymore, and following the instruction of the 'voices,' even tried fucking a whore. His behavior became so antisocial that the Moroccan government had him expelled and flown back to the States, where he arrived at the beginning of 1966, unimaginably loony."

Speaking of Burroughs, he frequently travelled to find new boys to play with, as well as write. From Lima, Peru, where he had travelled in 1953, he wrote his friend, the notorious poet Allen Ginsberg:

"(This is) the promised land for boys. I never saw anything like it since Vienna in '36. But you have to keep an eye on the little bastards or they'll steal all your fucking valuables. (I lost my watch and $15 in the service.) Oh well the watch didn't run anyway. I never had one that did. I have not seen here any queer bars (hope I don't see any), but in the bars around the Mercado Mayorista – Main Market – any boy is wise and available to the Yankee dollar. Last night I checked into a hotel with a beautiful Indian to the great amusement of the hotel clerk and his friends. (I don't think the average U.S. hotel clerk would be amused at such an occurrence.)

11- Lima also has an extensive Chinatown, good restaurants, pleasant climate, the cheapest living I hit in S.A. In short I wouldn't mind settling down here, but I still like Mexico better."

A week later, he writes:

"Woke up with an honest boy and my valuables – or what's left of them – intact. Found him without a lamp too. That was lost in the service a week ago.

Thought of writing a story about a sage who returns from the mountain a lecherous drunken old man chasing young boys. The story is flash-

back from jail where sage is languishing for indecent exposure. Point is some old bum in jail for molesting a child may be "the Sage." Quien Babe? Not me. The older I get the less I Babe, the less wisdom, maturity and caution I have. "A few self flashes. Shadow boxing with a young kid in a louche Peruvlan bistro (Haven't you any dignity at all? Obviously not), making a pass at a 13-year-old Indian boy right in front of his father, brothers and uncles, dragging home two ragged brats. All I remember is they were young. Woke up with the smell of youngness on my hands and body.

"Now if I was wise and listened to a psychoanalyst, I would give up young boys and be an assistant professor somewhere sitting around hatching a cancer of the prostate ...and accepting reality.

"Instead if I live to 80 will be demonstrating judo to some young boy in some louche bistro. Like the Poet says: 'God keep me from ever being a wise old man praised of all.' Yeats, 'Poet's Prayer.'"

Later, he writes Ginsberg to discuss "an average, non-queer Peruvian boy" he has met:

"They are the least character-armored people I have ever seen. They shit or piss anywhere they feel like it. They have no inhibitions in expressing affection. They climb all over each other and hold hands. If they do go to bed with another male, and they all will for money, they seem to enjoy it. Homosexuality is simply a human potential, as is shown by almost unanimous incidence in prisons, and nothing human is foreign or shocking to a South American. I am speaking of the South American at best, a special race: part Indian, part white, part God knows what. He is not, as one is apt to think at first, fundamentally an Oriental, nor does he belong to the West. He is something special, unlike anything else. "

A year later, Burroughs was in Tangier and he wrote his friend Jack Kerouac:

"...The one time I met Bowles he evinced no cordiality. Since then he has made no effort to follow up the acquaintance. (Under the circumstances it is his place to make advances once he knows that I am here and who I am). He invites the dreariest queens in Tangiers to tea, but has never invited me, which, seeing how small the town is, amounts to a deliberate affront. Perhaps he has some idea that trouble might result from knowing anyone associated with narcotics. Since Tennessee (Williams) and (Truman) Capote, etc., are friends of Bowles, I, of course, don't meet them when they come here.

"... Kiki has confiscated all my clothes and intends to cure me of the habit. I also have various new, substitute preparations prescribed me by a good, German Jewish, refugee doctor. So I have hopes of success with Kiki here to care for me, and to provide the appropriate amenities when I start coming off in my pants (I have no pants) – spontaneous orgasms being one of the few agreeable features of the withdrawal syndrome. And not limited to single orgasm, one can continue, with adolescent ardor, through three or four

climaxes. Usually you are too weak to go out and find a 'love object' as the analysts call them. (When you are coming off the junk, I mean, you don't feel up to looking around for sex.) Sounds so passionless, like, 'I found a pretty hot 'object' last night.'

"I find myself getting jealous of Kiki – he is besieged by importunate queens. In fact I am downright involved, up to my neck in Maya. He is a sweet kid, and it is so pleasant to loll about in the afternoon smoking tea, sleeping and having sex with no hurry, running leisurely hands over his lean, hard body, and finally we doze off, all wrapped around each other, into the delicious sleep of a hot afternoon in a cool, darkened room, a sleep that is different from any other sleep, a twilight in which I savour, with a voluptuous floating sensation, the state of sleep, feeling the nearness of Kiki's young body, the sweet, imperceptible, drawing together in sleep, leg inching over leg, arm encompassing body, hips hitching closer, stiffening organs reaching out to touch warm flesh.

"...I would think twice before giving up sex. It's a basic kick and when it's good as it can be it's good."

Some men unfortuantely, give up on sex before they even get started. Consider in world traveller who shared his experience in Thailand with the readers of RFD magazine. This anonymous contributor told of meeting a boy from L.A. who had gone to work in Thailand and what happened one night when the boy invited him to go out to the bars with the boy's boss_

Standing between my legs, unneraingly close to my face is a boy. "What yo name?" he demands. "Where yo come from?"

1 tell him.

"You like me. We go hotel," he says.

"Whoa now scooter!" I blurt as my companions burst into laughter. He looks at me wildly and defiantly like Grace Jones in Conan. His nostrils flare, he is handsome. Proud with his baseball cap backwards. He's about 13, 1 judge.

"You want him?" the boss asks.

"No, man. He's too small, too young," 1 say.

"Come on, look at him. He'd be like a little monkey all over you," the boss says.

Suddenly, one of the Thai boxers on stage lands a solid swack of a blow on his opponent. The blood splatters on my glass. He hits the mat like a roasting chicken dropping onto the kitchen floor. The Jagermeister liquor is warm in my gut. The crowd sort of half cheers and johns, whores, bartenders and boys turn back to drinks, clients and hazy visions of the dreams they're chasing.

The boy between my legs is gone. Flashing a quick smile, he cruises the reef of barstools like a little shark sniffing for the horniness that equals

blood in the water. He sees himself as the predator. Maybe it's easier that way. "What a strange scene," I say. "It's all so taboo."

"Yeah," the boss man says. "That's part of the rush. They're so young."

"Sexually what's in it for them?" I ask. "Can they even get hard?"

"Yeah, most can," he says. "But mostly they just do what they're told."

The L.A. boy shakes his head sort of disapprovingly. I order another Jagermeister. There has been this sweet little person giving me the puppy dog look all night. It's a girl I find out. She's so small that she can perch on top of the barstool. Mini drag queens have mock cat fights and do silver screen diva pantomime. The sea breeze blows in and the ritual continues. A ritual of lust, loneliness, power and life and death. On my way out I give the little girl a dollar. "They really appreciate that," the boss nods approvingly.

I met lots of beautiful boys in Pattaya. Most were for rent. Even as I write this I wonder why I didn't go through with a transaction. And I come up with a few things: I'm afraid that it would be awkward, and that the sex would be no good; I'm afraid of AIDS; and when I get down to it, well, there's just very little adventure in the rent boy paradigm. I would go after some of them if it was an open forum. I would love to seduce them, run away to an island with them, make love and laugh. It's the thrill of the chase, really. The not knowing is the excitement. The unfolding of the drama. Besides the cash, what's in it for them, anyway? How long can they live doing this? What future?

There was a lot of safe sex info around the go-go boy bars. They say that the boys are trained well and insist on safe sex. What about the little ones? Who teaches them? I was getting a massage when they dragged the body of a 17-year-old boy past me. Heroine overdose. I watched as they hoisted him onto a motorcycle. They sort of sandwiched him between the driver and a passenger holding his limp body up. They crept off. Just then, a rent boy with perfect white teeth and a babyface flashed me one of those unforgettable Thai smiles and said, "Hello, handsome man."

A reader who wrote Advocate Men magazine also had unanswered questions regarding male prostitutes, beginning with, "Why do male whores charge so much more than female whores? The prices go from $150 an hour up to $500 an hour. In these hard times that is a pretty steep price! Is it because males have more to offer than females? I have always had a penchant for 'working boys' and am fascinated by the mind of the male prostitute. When in a guy's life does he make the decision that his genitals are going to be his ticket to a free ride in life? Is it the money? Or is it that he's too lazy to work?

"I have spent thousands of dollars on male prostitutes and have always been amazed at what some guys will do for money. One time I was sucking a hustler's dick and licking his nuts. I raised his buttocks so I could eat

his asshole, and he said, 'That's extra.' This guy was selling parts of his anatomy by the piece! I'm just curious about his motivation."

The magazine's editor tried to answer: "Sex is like any other commodity. The people who sell it will charge whatever the market will bear. Scarcity also drives up the cost. If local law enforcement makes it more difficult for male hustlers to find clients than their female counterparts, they will be more expensive. Then there's the personal factor. Some clients get charged more because they are obnoxious, difficult to deal with, and have a negative attitude about hustlers or prostitution in general.

"Sex workers are anything but lazy. It's a difficult, demanding, and dangerous job. You have to be competitive, punctual, a good communicator, attractive, and imaginative. People who are not self-starting don't last long in the field."

And those who do last long in the field seem to lead charmed lives. The porn performer and callboy Taz Action, for instance, who, Dave Kinnick says, "seems to be one of those rare few who lead charmed and absolutely surreal lives. Taz is currently living with a daddy who is not his father somewhere out past Pasadena. But, as he told us by phone the other day, he had expected to be in South Beach, Fla., where he had gone recently to 'make some money.' The trip ended prematurely.

"It seems the Miami-adjacent pseudo mecca didn't prove as friendly or lucrative as Taz had hoped. After arriving in town and making some quick cash through methods known only to Taz, he swooped into the Boardwalk, a popular dance bar and stripper venue. He sort of announced to the manager that he had arrived and expected to make some money that very night. He was met with less than the star treatment he has come to expect. In fact, Taz was told he'd be working strictly for tips by way of audition and was scheduled 15th in the dancer lineup! About this Taz was indignant: 'I'm a professional prostitute! To have the nerve to ask me to auditionT Taz has a good deal of professional pride. He describes the manager as 'nice and very professional. But the other boys he's got working there are largely straight and look like they think the place is called Steroid Alley. They were rude, and not one of them spoke a single nice word to me. But you know what? They were just trying to protect their $20 tricks!"

Defending his honor and lamenting the prevailing demeanor of these plush ponies of the footlights, Taz says, "I may be a little blond bottom, but at least I can get a hard-on! All those big steroid guys tie up their balls in their pants but can't get it up. I can come three, four, or five times in a row!' Feeling rejected by the local titty teamsters, Taz hopped on the next plane home."

In addition to the many books on the subject of male prostitution available these days, you can get a helluva education just reading (and often acting upon) the classified ads run in most gay magazines. Gary Indiana,

(author of Rent Boy), in his short story "Dreams Involving Water," keeps a fascinating diary of his "dates" with rent boys – and, incidentally, doesn't bother with capitalization:

Uncut Latino. Rico: 24, 59': 158#, 30W; hung 9" thick, very friendly, 5 mins to Manht. 24 hours. Rico is a fraud like his accomplice Chico, potbellied not very clean – the cock's about 2-3 inches, stands there expecting you to give him a hard-on which he's never able to achieve, tries sort of pushing his limpness into you – then grunts a few times – he's out again. Some of these guys change their names from month to month, reword the ads, invent new bodies faces, cocksizes for themselves and show up with the same unsavory swindle. You can tell by checking the phone numbers against the old ads, for all they get ripping people off they're too cheap to change the numbers.

Slim's a vigorous and conscientious fuck, nine thick inches and he's cute, he'll get you into four or five positions whatever feels good and nice and slow sometimes he likes it. Tony from uptown, big frame, huge cock, pleasant face but nothing special: good if he's got poppers with him. Nice-tasting meat. European gymnast's half-Greek half-German, looks mainly German. Competent fuck, but mechanical, no initiative. Earns the money but it's no fun for either of you.

...his voice sounds too sanc, too ordinary. didn't ask what do you like, didn't talk dirty, didn't describe himself probably 'he's really good. giant ants on the TV, radiation nightmare from the fifties. losing: time in your life, energy, friends, the will to continue, hopefulness. never meet anyone, nowhere to meet them.

...this one's name's tom. he just got home from the gym. 20, nice firm shape, dark eyes, black hair, a face good enough to eat. strips casually, gets on the bed in his briefs, lies on his back and lights a cigarette. I touch his cock through the brief, he's already hard: substantial. where are you from. what do you do, I mean besides

...play with his fingers, stroke his palm. its hot outside. lick me, okay?he peels off his underpants and rubs his prick. pulls up his balls.

I lick down under his balls, his ass rises slightly and he shifts his weight around until I can get my tongue into his asshole, spread his cheeks apart with my thumbs and suck his rectum and work gradually up across his balls and up and down his prick, a nice wide piece of work with a large sensitive head, nibble around the rim, and flick the cordlike tissue just under it with the tip of my tongue, slide my mouth down over the whole thing, ease my head up and run my open lips down his cock bone and up the middle of the vein and then let him pump it in and out of my mouth kneeling on top of me he inches forward on his knees and then sits down on my mouth, his asshole centered on my tongue and I make love to his cock forcing my tongue deeper and deeper into him. we stay like that for a long time and he leans back until

he's lying down stretches out his legs and I kiss him everywhere ... he's fucking me with my legs around his neck he pushes my legs away, gripping my ankles until my knees are behind my head and my ass is sticking up and now he's lying straight on top of me balanced on his toes like he's doing pushups in and out of my ass pulling all the way out and slamming himself back in on every stroke. it hurts I love him he turns me over and fucks me lying flat on top of me.

....his legs inside my legs pushing my legs wider and then slides his legs over mine and pushes my legs closed fucking my hole as if he wanted to make sure he's fucked it every way he can think of and after that he carries me to the chair sits down and arranges me with my back to his chest and slips his cock back into my ass and fucks me foran hour so slow we're hardly moving and he pulls it out just an inch or so and slides it back up inside me and out again an inch and back in as far as he can and every so often pulls out three or four inches or five inches and holds it there like that for a long time and slowly slowly pushes his hip bones forward just a little just a little till its all inside me again and then its almost imperceptible again for a long time and when I feel like he's part of my own body he pushes his ass back drawing out the whole nine inches except for his cockhead he leaves inside then slips the head out and pushes just the head back in, lets it out with a pop and slips it in, just the head five, ten, fifteen times and then it slides back inside me the whole thing I feel his balls against my hole and him breathing against my neck... .

Burroughs and his pals aside, child prostitution is an area where many NAMBLA members don't seem to see the potential for abuse, researcher Brent Hartinger finds. "The Readers Digest implicated NAMBLA in southern Asia's ghastly child-sex industry," he says. "In Thailand, Sri Lanka, and elsewhere, children ten years old and younger are sold or abandoned by poverty-stricken parents into prostitution, and scores of pedophile tourists from around the world gather to take advantage of cheap, young flesh.

"But sex tourism is a very complicated issue. It's not the story that gets played out in the media. Boys who are involved in prostitution in poor countries – and this is characteristic of young male prostitutes everywhere – they're their own operators."

Research indicates otherwise. According to Mic Hunter, author of Abused Boys: The Silent Victims of Abuse, at least in the U.S., boys involved in prostitution and other sexual relationships with adults typically come from dysfunctional families and have absent or emotionally distant fathers.

"If [sex with men] is such a good deal, you'd think kids would be out looking for it," Hunter says.. "But kids who are in happy homes, kids who are getting attention and getting a nurturing touch that isn't sexualized, aren't interested in doing this."

Police statistics are particularly damning. Detective Patrick Flood of the Sacramento County (California) Sheriffs Department has worked on

numerous child molestation cases. According to Flood, NAMBLA members often exchange home-made child pornography and other pedophile information: informal guides on how to evade United States authorities, for example, or details about sex tours. In some cases, Flood says, NAMBLA members have even exchanged boys. One NAMBLA member was arrested for running a "boys' school" in Bangkok, which was actually a front for a prostitution ring where foreign men could "sponsor" a boy in exchange for receiving sexual favors at a later date.

Nevertheless, a lot of people, both straight and gay, are troubled by criminalizing sexual relationships between adults and older teenagers who obviously are more capable of consent.

"If a 16-year-old gay teen wants to have a relationship with a 25-year-old man, is that something we ought to criminalize?" asks David Finkelhor, director of family research at the University of New Hampshire. "Still," he adds, "if there were evidence that adults tended to be responsible (in relationships with boys), it'd be a lot easier to argue for decriminalization. My sense is the opposite."

AIDS, of course, raises the stakes of adult-child sex higher than ever before. If, as NAMBLA maintains, children really are as capable as adults of making rational decisions about sex, one would assume that safe-sex practices would be as common in adult-child sex as they are between consenting adults.

Unfortunately, it isn't so, says Elliot Ramos, youth intervention coordinator at the San Francisco AIDS Foundation. "There is a high percentage of unsafe sex that occurs between younger men and older men," Ramos says, a fact he attributes primarily to "control and [mental] abuse" on the part of the older partner. In fact, both Ramos and Abused Boys author Hunter point out that, based on their interviews of same-sex pedophiles and their underage partners, many of the men are even more interested in adult-child sex now because they assume the child isn't infected with HIV so they won't have to use condoms.

Dangerous boys appeal to all strata of society. In Obsession, his biography of Calvin Klein, Steven Gaines talks about a boy the designer became obsessed with, Alphonso. "With his chiseled, rock-hard swimmer's body, curly hair, monosyllabic answers, and the swagger of a street kid, Alphonso was a sexy enigma," Gaines recalls. "Friends remember that Calvin met Alphonso through Giorgio Saint D'Angelo, who passed Alphonso along after having a brief affair with him. The sketchy biographical information about him – which he evasively would neither confirm nor deny – was that he was a New Jersey or Brooklyn working class kid who married and fathered a child, then five years old, with his high school sweetheart. They lived in a shack of a house in the marshlands of Queens, waiting patiently for the day he returned. Giorgio's friends also remember going to a squalid apartment in Spanish Harlem to visit Alphonso. Alphonso was the most significant and

tortured in a series of unrequited love affairs that Calvin embarked upon with allegedly straight boys, relationships that strained the patience of his other, more prescient friends. Alphonso was tolerated by Calvin's friends, even though he was supposedly as dumb as a post. 'He had a nice, hard ass,' remarked one of Calvin's staffers, 'but not as hard as his head.' Alphonso seemed available to wealthy gay men, although quite clearly he was filled with disdain about it. He was archetypal homosexual 'trade,' a straight boy who would allow himself to be had in exchange for gifts or money. Whatever the motive in Alphonso's mind, he was given prominent modeling jobs in Calvin's menswear collection, and he was Calvin's constant shadow. 'He seemed to me to be a guy,' said one of Calvin's design staff, 'who was looking at Calvin as a cow to be milked. He was a hustler, you know, the worst kind, because Calvin seemed quite smitten and I heard rumors that Calvin gave him a car.' Calvin might not have given Alphonso a car, but he did loan him his own when Alphonso said he had an errand to run. Calvin didn't realize, however, that Alphonso was going to pick up drugs, and driving the car home high, Alphonso badly dam-aged it in a traffic accident. Calvin was furious, but he could never be furious with Alphonso for too long. One look from those dark eyes and Calvin was lost. When Chester would tell Calvin that Alphonso was only trouble, Calvin would say, 'Who am I going to settle down with? A thirty-year-old author with patches on his sleeves?'

"Indeed, Calvin's romantic fixations seemed to inevitably revolve around the most unobtainable straight men. Calvin would have sex with gay men, but the only boys that he really seemed to fall in love with were straight. Perhaps this was the paradox Jean Genet wrote about, that the homosexual's search for an ideal man is doomed to defeat, because as soon as another male returns his affection, he is no longer ideal. And that is what Calvin was after, a real man with whom he could fall in love. 'The real truth,' said his assistant Zack Carr, 'is that underneath, Calvin is a very romantic man. And to meet someone and to fall in love and to give [his] heart away ...is something that Calvin would like very much to do...I remember... people who Calvin thought he loved – I think he did love – that didn't turn out to be as loving to him and only hurt Calvin that much more because they made Calvin terrified that he would only be loved for money.'

"Naturally, his pursuit of men most likely to reject him proved frustrating. Worse, he was ill suited to his role of aggressor and still felt uncomfortable in his gay status. One summer day in Central Park, Calvin by chance ran across a heterosexual but naive aspiring model named David Chapman who had just come to New York from Ohio to find fame and fortune. The blond, blue-eyed young man was surprised to get a message from Calvin the next week inviting him to bring his modeling portfolio for Calvin to see at his Sovereign apartment. 'We were sitting on the couch,' remembered Chapman, 'and I showed him my portfolio, but he didn't really seem that

interested in it.' Chapman let it be known in the course of conversation that he was heterosexual. 'We started talking about where I was from and how much we both liked Key West, and then he began telling me how good-looking he thought I was, and I started feeling very uncomfortable. I said to him, 'The one thing I don't like about the modeling business is that I don't like being hit on by gay photographers and people.... I don't like feeling pressured.'

Well,' said Calvin, stumbling for something to say, 'I think that in New York, in this day and age, I don't think you should think of yourself as being gay or straight. You ought to think of yourself as doing what you want to do and be your own man. Flesh feels good no matter what it is '''

David France, in his fascinating exposé Bag of Toys, about art dealer Andrew Crispo, says that "sexually, Crispo ...remained politely distant from his young staffers. Instead, he preferred to sate his urges by foraging the city's darker terrain for the overripe, feral youths he craved. There was something dangerously exciting about bringing untamed toughs into the splendor of his Upper East Side apartment.

"Arthur Smith had decorated it, and his own adjacent apartment, and had each one laid out in Architectural Digest as examples of his work--without mentioning that there were no borders between them, or that there was any relationship between the one called Andrew Crispo's apartment and the one called his. (Of course, Crispo was listed as the owner of the prized art works in both layouts, and Smith was called the decorator; such mentions are worth gold to decorators and dealers.) Both apartments were as luxurious and for fending as velvet-roped showrooms. As severe as Andrew's tricks could appear on the street, or in the sex clubs or subways, once they entered his home, the intimidation of his possessions alone would hammer them into docility and awe, magnificence taming the beast.

"But not all the time. Crispo left his apartment one Saturday morning after a frolicking evening with a leather-clad street kid he'd picked up downtown. The kid stayed behind. Smith was in Europe on business. With no discernible motive, the visitor went on a violent rampage, and ransacked both apartments.

"Ronnie Caran, at home in his apartment just a few floors below the Crispo-Smith duplex, began to notice familiar pieces of debris floating past. 'Andrew! My God,' he screamed into the phone at his friend, whom he reached at the gallery. 'I just saw the pillows from your sofa go flying out the window! And Jesus! There goes your Franz Kline!'

"An incalculable amount of damage was done to several masterpieces, some of which Andrew owned personally and some of which were the property of the gallery (this was always a fine line). Antique statues were overturned and original Art Deco vases were shattered. Andrew's prized piece, a 'veil' painting called Beth Feh that hung over his downstairs sofa, was scratched and misshappen; the Kline work was crumpled and soiled. Stuart

Davis's Rue Lippe, a lighthearted work valued at three hundred thousand dollars, was knocked off the dining room wall, battered about on the hefty sideboard, and left in a corner, wadded up like a stiff towel.

"But the damage was worse in Arthur's bedroom, which the designer considered a masterpiece of his work. The theme was deep red. A diamond-shaped red painting by Roy Lichtenstein (from his famed 'Red Series') hung over a red-draped Russian antique bed, which grew majestically out of a plush red carpet. Even the walls were red – a glazed Oriental lacquer red, giving the room an erotic, gorgeous richness. But this was no ordinary brush-and-roller job; it was achieved with no less than twenty-two coats of hand-rubbed lacquer on a canvas-and-gesso base. The total cost for the finish alone: $22,000.

"By the time Andrew arrived home, Smith's collection of avant-garde Russian knickknacks had been hurled around the room with such force that the red paint had been dented and marred beyond simple repair. The Lichtenstein was destroyed, having been slashed repeatedly with a knife.

"Police officers arrested the young man, whom they found sitting dispassionately on the window ledge, dangling his feet out of Crispo's apartment, and Crispo set about making everything right before Arthur's return. The bedroom was relacquered from scratch. The vases were replaced with similar ones; the paintings were patched by a restoration company in Queens. (The diamond-shaped Lichtenstein, after patching, was sold to an unsuspecting Steve Martin.) What couldn't be immediately salvaged was taken off to a storage garage Crispo rented. Several gallery employees were enlisted in the hush-hush endeavor, all of which was charted in two file folders buried deep in Crispo's personal file cabinet back at the gallery. One, labeled PERSONAL, chronicled the expenses Crispo fronted from his own purses; the other, CORPORATE, measured the hit to his business. The total added up to nearly a million dollars (one employee ventured) – and none of it was ever mentioned to Arthur Smith."

Such scenes might have been avoided had Crispo used the services of reliable escort service or used a trusted friend as pimp. Victor Hugo filled this capacity for his friend, the designer Halston. In the case of Halston, Hugo's ability to fill those needs gave him tremendous power over the designer. "Besides," Steven Gaines says in his biography Simply Halston, "Halston liked the abuse.

"While Victor filled the emotional abyss in Halston's life, the physical was being taken care of by Robert Rogers, an unassuming black man of medium height and build in his late twenties who was one of Manhattan's most successful male prostitutes. Originally from Gainesville, Florida, Rogers held a day job with the New York State Unemployment Insurance office. By night, Rogers was known as "Cuelar" and made $150 an hour with a call boy service named the Black Kings, which specialized in black men. Cuelar had achieved some modicum of fame as the model for a perennially popular line of

greeting cards sold in adult bookstores and sex shops which bore the tag line, 'Everything you ever heard about black men...is true!' As Cuelar's reputation as a courtesan grew, he opened his own call service and began advertising in two gay publications, the Advocate and the New York Native."

"Halston was very into black guys," said Rogers. "If he was prejudiced, he didn't discriminate when it came to sex. He had a strong sexual appetite, and he started giving me money without me even asking, two hundred or two hundred and fifty dollars." Cuelar says he saw Halston personally sixty or seventy times, but as the years went by, Halston wanted to up the ante. "He asked me if I knew of anybody else who was like me, a nice black guy who's well endowed. And I said I did. I sent that guy to him and he started to see him, at least once a week, sometimes twice a week. The guy would get one hundred dollars and I'd get fifty dollars for my referral. Between 1980 to 1983, I sent him many, many guys. Sometimes during the week, usually on a Wednesday, I'd go see him myself, but only for about an hour or so – he had a very tight schedule."

Halston's ultimate fantasy, according to Cuelar, was to have sex with a heterosexual black man, a blue-collar worker, if possible right off the street, and he was willing to pay dearly for it. Cuelar claimed to have waited at the 125th Street train station in Harlem and picked men out of the crowd at random whom he thought would be amenable to the suggestion that they earn up to $500 for performing a carnal act with a wealthy white man. Cuelar claimed it was surprising how many takers he could find at a subway station.

"I would say that Halston was eccentric," said Cuelar. "When you entered his place he would buzz you in, but he would be upstairs on the top floor and he would call from upstairs and say, 'Have a seat, I'll be right down.' He would come down always all in black and these silver clogs. He would descend the stairs very slowly and say, 'Welcome, would you like a drink?' A lot of guys couldn't hold a conversation, but Halston would just talk about current events, sports, and he would ask them questions about themselves. Then he would say, 'Would you like to go upstairs?' You were never in bed more than ten minutes. Several times we were in the bedroom watching TV and Elizabeth Taylor called for Halston's advice about her love life. I remember one time she was on the phone and there was a Burger King commercial on TV, and Halston's advice to Elizabeth Taylor was, 'Have it your way.'"

One night Cuelar got a call for his services from a man with a thick accent who gave his address 101 East Sixty-third Street. "I was shocked when he gave me the address. I said 'What's going on here?' It turned out it was Victor Hugo and he had heard about me from Halston. Halston was away in Montauk, so I went over there. Victor was always coked out of his head, so he wasn't interested too much in sex. He said, 'Don't tell Halston that we know each other.' I guess he had his reasons. I don't think Halston ever knew.

"He was a kind man who always wanted to help somebody. He helped a lot of people, there's no question about it. I don't think he had a mean streak in his body. I always worried about him because nobody was ever in the house with him to my knowledge. It was dangerous, I think. I used to wonder about that because he used to call up other escort services and they would send street guys over, and I was always curious if there was a bodyguard or somebody in the house in case somebody tried to rob him or hurt him. It was very, very dangerous for him to be in the situation that he was in."

But it is not always prostitutes that are the most dangerous boys to know.

In Tallahassee, Florida, in early 1994, Raymond Keith Roberts, a 28-year-old music teacher, wrote a note, carefully locked his car and stepped onto the tracks in front of an oncoming train. His death came one day before his sentencing for the sexual assault of two former students, police said.

Roberts was on a leave of absence from his job at Satellite High School, where he taught music theory and chorus. He faced a sentence of 3 to 5 years in prison, followed by stiff probation for pleading guilty to sexually assaulting two youths, 17 and 18, at his home in Melbourne the previous summer, State Attorney Paul Brockway said.

The engineer and two other workers aboard the train told Leon County sheriffs deputies that Roberts simply stood on the tracks as the train approached him Tuesday morning off U.S. 90 west of the city. He didn't lay down on the track. He just stood there," said sheriff's spokesman Dick Simpson.

Roberts had lived in Tallahassee and was on break from graduate classes at the University of South Carolina, according to police records.

The death was termed a suicide. The contents of a handwritten note he left in his car, parked on a dirt road near the tracks, were not disclosed. 'There is no evidence or facts that would indicate anything other than his intentions were to step in front of that train and end his life," Leon sheriffs Sgt. John Schmidt said. The prosecutor said that in both criminal cases, Roberts gave the youths alcohol and performed oral sex on them after they passed out.

After Roberts was arrested last July, the parents of one victim said they reported the incident only so Roberts would get counseling. They didn't want Roberts to go to jail because he was talented and had a promising career, Brockway said.

"He was a very popular teacher," said Ann Mittman of the Brevard County School District.

And it isn't always the teachers that have problems with the boys at their school. Sometimes the students themselves can find a classmate a dangerous temptation. And it doesn't matter if you have sex or not, there can be problems. In his heartfelt memoir, Stand Before Your God, Paul Watkins recalls his days at Eton:

"...Now he had his eye on a boy called Hewlett, who lived in another House across the school. He had fallen in love with Hewlett and could no longer deny it. He didn't talk to Hewlett. That would have been too obvious.. He just liked to watch him from a distance. It was as if he had fallen in love with the reflection of himself three years before.

"I knew half a dozen people who were in love with Hewlett, and if anything had happened to the boy, I don't know what they would have done. They cared for him like guardian angels, and never laid a hand on him. Most knew that when they left Eton, they would go out and find girlfriends and eventually find wives, but I doubted if they would ever love their wives the way they loved Hewlett. It was a harsh thing to say and never to be said out loud, but for some of them it was the truth."

A BREAK IN THE WEATHER
Ken Anderson

"And you really think Miranda's going to hell just because she's wearing overalls? What about the women with their corn-cob pipes?"

Alex did not know why he was surprised when Malcolm, his fundamentalist student, sided with the "bad-tempered old crones" in Porter's *The Grave*. Alex was usually calm, but it was eleven forty-three and the last class of the day, the last day of the week, and he was already feeling the even deeper calm that engulfed him when home alone on Friday.

"When Miranda and Paul skin the pregnant rabbit, is the rabbit still female?"

"Uh, yes," Malcom puzzled.

Alex leaned on the lectern, holding his chin in his hand.

"And if we stripped Miranda, wouldn't she be, too?"

Alex had a gruff, starkly Anglo-Saxon look about him with thick, blond brows and thick, blondish hair brushed from his forehead in a big, cresting wave. He also had a big, determined jaw, straight, pale lips, and piercing, ice-blue eyes. Though most of the faculty had figured out his personal situation, from quarter to quarter various young women in his classes had been attracted to him – his restrained manner, his sober looks – and, though at present he was not, he had always informed them, in his own discreet way, that he was attached. Malcolm, however, had not fallen for his charms.

"So what's the cause and effect relationship?" Alex asked. I mean, between the overalls and her, as you contend, damned spiritual state. Explain it to us."

The room was a typically austere, contemporary space de-signed, Alexguessed, tominimize distractions. The cinder-block walls were a dreary institutional green, and fluorescent lights glared from the acoustic ceiling. A third of the exterior wall was glass, though, and Alex felt lucky to have it, even if it did overlook the administrative parking lot. A heavy rain was falling on the cars, and beyond them, newly planted, pinioned trees struggled in the wind.

"The cause and effect relationship is that, as the women tell her, it's against the scriptures."

"The same with Maria riding the horse?"

While engaged with Malcolm, Alex could not help noticing another student, Kip, squirming in his seat, tugging at his sweater collar, glancing at Malcolm, then him.

"I'll explain it to you," Alex said, straightening up. "If Maria rides bareback, she may break her hymen, and according to Deuteronomy 22:20, her husband would have the right to stone her to death on their wedding night."

Malcolm fumed. Alex had mentioned sex.

"If you found out your bride wasn't a virgin, would you really bash her brains out with a rock?"

Malcolm clasped his hands on his desk, Alex assumed, to rein in his anger. Kip leaned forward, intent on the exchange.

"As I've pointed out, the story alludes to Deuteronomy 22:6-7, and further down in the chapter, there is also an injunction against commingling fabrics. You may wish to check your labels. Verse 23:1 says a man whose member is cut off should not enter church. I'm sure we all see the usefulness of that prohibition."

Malcolm gasped, but most of the class snickered. An appropriate moment, Alex thought, to go for the throat.

"You refuse even to consider that Homer Barron may be gay. Then you see a nine-year-old girl as a latent lesbian just because she's wearing pants."

Alex glanced at his flock of drowsy, sniffling, overheated students. Three women were wearing pants. It was getting on in March, and that morning, going to his car, he had felt a touch of vernal warmth in the air, which surprised him by buoying his spirits. But the weather was still cold by Southern standards, and he figured the women had worn pants because the pants were warm and, like Miranda's overalls, comfortable.

"Don't you see how inconsistent you are?"

"What I see is someone who keeps bringing up sex all the time," Malcolm snarled, "who keeps promoting attacks on religion, who keeps trying to corrupt impressionable young people. That's what I see. A bad influence."

Kip turned to look at Alex, but as he did, knocked everything off his desk – textbooks, clipboard, notebooks, pen.

"I appreciate your frankness, I suppose, but not your insolence. It's not open season on teachers, despite your apparently indulgent high school experience."

Kip gathered his books, glancing tentatively at Alex.

"I don't know where you're from," Malcolm snapped, "but if you can't abide by the customs of a Christian community, then maybe you should go somewhere else."

"Maybe you should, too. As in now."

Malcolm gathered his books as well, then rose, lurching toward the door. Alex was sure Malcolm was headed straight for the dean. The dean, however, had worn the same checked, polyester suit as long as Alex had known him, and Alex certainly was not truckling to him.

"I don't know why some people are in college," he mused, checking his watch. "They're obviously not here to learn any-thing." Focusing on the class, he added, "If you're the same coming out as going in, why bother?"

Once his books were stacked, Kip glanced at Alex, then slumped in his desk, gazing at the scuffed linoleum, absently folding and unfolding his bottom lip with his thumb and index finger.

"Well," Alex sighed. "A good assignment for the weekend would be to study the allusion to Deuteronomy."

He wrote the scriptural reference on the board.

"Especially the verses about the mother and the young. Try to apply them to the story. We'll write on it sometime next week. Any questions?"

Half the class groaned.

Alex closed his text, then his manila folder, then said, "Have a safe weekend."

After class, Alex returned to his office, a sterile, claustrophobic "closet," as he thought of it, with the usual academic furnishings: a desk, a swivel chair, a couple of book cases, a filing cabinet, and a couple of armless chairs for students. Since there was no window, a fern or an African violet was out of the question, but he had tried to add some color to the room with a museum poster of Caravaggio's Bacchus, two Thai temple rubbings, and over his desk a framed American flag. He sat at the desk, sliding some papers into his briefcase, then snapped it shut and tilted back, staring at the flag.

"Dr. Alden."

Alex turned: "Kip, come in. Have a seat."

Kip slipped his backpack to the floor, taking the chair by the door.

"Uh," he stammered. "I just wanted you to know I think I understood what you were saying, and I – Well, I thought it was great. Man, that skinny blond's a jerk."

"Malcolm's not one of my more sensible students, no. I'll talk to him on Monday. We're near the end of the quarter, and with the war and all, I'm sure he won't drop. Besides," Alex smiled, "what does he know? He has peach fuzz on his lip."

Kip blushed, then stared at the brown carpet.

"But seriously, thanks," Alex said, speaking up. "Nothing like a little support."

Anyone's first impression of Kip was that he looked pretty butch. He wore his hair in a dry, bristly flattop cropped so close on the sides his jaw line ran straight up his head. His flat, pinned-back ears added to the effect. The haircut also gave him a square forehead. He had flat, smooth cheeks and a blunt, slightly crooked nose, which Alex figured had been broken. He rarely smiled, but held his mouth open in a blank, sensual way, and his chin was notched with a fairly pronounced dimple. He was short, about five seven, and

his shortness made him look boyish, but he had broad, man-sized shoulders, the kind, Alex knew, only hard work could mold.

Despite his tough appearance, though, he was obviously high-strung. He had vulnerable, vivid-green eyes and a moody, self-conscious manner as if always on the point of doing or saying something he was not sure of. From the very beginning, Alex had sensed how nervous he was and responded sympathetically, giving him plenty of time to answer in class.

"You must feel wasted," Kip said, "trying to teach a bunch of goobers like us."

"Kip," Alex said, scolding him gently, "I don't have to put anyone down to think highly of myself. That's what racists do. That's what homophobes like Malcolm do."

"Homophobes?"

"People who hate gays. Except in his case, it's not just gays. It's sex."

For a number of reasons, Kip had been a major distraction that quarter. He sat on the front row and kept shifting positions in his desk, and some of the positions were suggestive. At times, he would spread his legs, casually cupping a thigh, or prop a foot on the bookrack under the desk, cocking a leg to the side. He also seemed to light up after Alex had suggested that Homer Barron was gay, Miss Emily's "lover" in Faulkner's "A Rose for Emily." Kip occasionally stopped him in the hall after class, fidgeting and sighing, and the one time he had dropped by the office to go over a paper, they sat very close and, leaning on the desk, were practically breathing on each other. Sitting that close, Alex could not help becoming acutely aware of the light-brown hair on Kip's arm, the mesh of veins in his hand. Or so he told himself. Though Alex knew that a lot of his students were naive, Kip seemed to be more restless lately, and Alex sensed some imminent collision. Boating on the flood last spring, Alex had kept an eye out for debris, and that was the way he felt about Kip. Under the flood of Kip's nerves lurked some huge log.

"Man, it's hot in here," Kip grumbled.

Alex thought of getting up to adjust the thermostat just above Kip's head.

Instead, he said, pointing, "Turn it down, would you?" Kip did, then eyeing Alex, resumed his seat.

"We're finally having a warm spell," Alex remarked, "but it's always too warm in here."

Then Alex found himself confiding in him.

"A student like Malcolm can do a lot of harm."

"Don't worry about it."

"'Twenty-four students will write me a good evaluation ...'" "You bet I will."

"But my chairman will pick out Malcolm's and include it in –

"I'll write something to offset 'im."

Alex rocked the chair a couple of times, then caught himself. "I've had a couple of articles rejected lately, articles I thought were shoo-ins. Part of my evaluation is publications." "What were they on?"

"Anne Sexton and Sylvia Plath. Familiar with them?"

"Man, are you kidding?" Then out of the blue, he asked, "You're gay, aren't you?"

Alex swiveled slowly, planted his feet on the floor, and rested his arms on the chair. So there it was. Bam! The log.

"Why do you ask?" But as Kip was about to answer, he said, "Wait a second. Close the door."

Kip closed the door, then asked, "You have a lover? What are you doing tonight?"

"Nothing actually, but I don't think I should be seeing students, if that's what you have in mind."

"Why not?"

"The ethics of the situation are incredibly complicated."

Kip leaned forward, his elbows on his knees. He clasped his hands and, lips parted, gave Alex one of his restless looks. Alex propped his face on his left hand, the tip of his index finger near the corner of his eye.

"Kip, look," he said, staring. "You're not doing well in my class. Why don't you just let me pre-date a drop slip? You can try it again next quarter, and next time, come to me, or whoever you have, for help."

"I can't drop the class," he explained. "I'd have to pay back all my veterans' benefits."

"This isn't the way to ..."

"That's not what I had in mind," Kip groaned, sitting up. "The class, macht nichts. I don't care about the class. I mean, I do care about it. I was just wondering ..."

He leaned back, staring at the beige walls. He seemed to be gathering his thoughts.

"Look," he admitted, "this may be my last quarter. I'm not cut out for college."

Alex knew that such an intense person would have trouble concentrating on class discussion, let alone homework, that such a skittish colt would shy at an academic bit.

"Your work does seem a little confused, but I don't think it's – ' He floundered, choosing his words carefully. " – a matter of skill. Once you get yourself in order, you can organize an essay, I'm sure."

"If I could get myself in order," Kip said, giving Alex a wistful smile. "Why don't you help me?"

Kip stood, facing the temple rubbings, one red, of War driving a chariot, one green, of Peace playing a flute. "I just thought we could get together and pop a few brews.

You're gay. I'm gay. What's the harm?"

"No," Alex decided, yet he spoke in a tempered tone of voice. "You don't have a vote in this. I don't think it's a good idea, and that's that. You see, just talking about it's already spoiled our teacher-student relationship."

"Teacher-student relationship? OK, sorry," he said, facing him. "Don't worry about it. Doesn't hurt to try."

He picked up his pack, then took hold of the doorknob, but stopped, looking over his shoulder.

"You won't use this against me, will you?"

"Of course not."

"Maybe we can talk next week."

"I'd like that."

Kip stared, then left.

That night, Alex lay in a pair of gym shorts on the couch, reading Mann's The Magic Mountain. He had been reading that and Maugham's Of Human Bondage on and off for years, among others, but decided to make a run at finishing Mann that weekend. Most of upstairs consisted of a large, vaulted, L-shaped space with a dozen windows, and occasionally, when lightning flashed, he would look up and listen to the rain and the militant thunder rumbling across the lake. Framed in the windows, silvery trees would glisten for a moment, then vanish.

Around ten thirty, someone knocked, and Alex set down the book, swinging his legs off the couch.

"Who the hell ..."

He had no neighbors. He lived at the end of a gravel road in a wildlife-management area.

He rose and rounded the corner into the kitchen, where, through the panes in the door, he could see someone waiting in the portico. There was an ice-blue security light on a telephone pole near the barn, as well as a couple of amber floodlights at the corner of the house, and when the man brushed back the hood and started unbuttoning the army jacket, Alex recognized him. Kip made a duck-like motion, wiping his feet on the mat, looking at Alex rather penitently.

"Wait a minute," Alex called. "Let me find the key."

When he returned, Kip had the jacket off and was shaking it, and when Alex opened the door, Kip stepped inside, and a wave of cool, moist air washed into the room. Alex leaned out the door, looking around. Water was sluicing down the drive, and the overflow from the gutters looked like a waterfall from underneath.

"Where's your car?"

"Don't have one."

"You hitchhiked?" Alex locked the door, then said, taking the jacket, "Here. Let me have it."

"Thanks."

"Were you warm enough?"

"That's one thing I learned in the army. No matter what the temperature is, if you're doing something, you're warm."

Alex took the jacket to the bathroom and hung it on the shower head, then brought Kip a towel.

"Who knows you're here?"

"Not a soul, I swear. I walked all the way from Wilderness Camp Road."

Kip began wiping his face and hair. He was wearing hiking boots, baggy jeans, and a T-shirt, all of which were soaked. "How'd you find the place?"

"You're listed. I got a map. Hope you don't mind." "What good would it do?"

Kip lay the towel on the table, then knelt to unlace his boots. He kicked off the boots, toe to heel, then began peeling the drenched socks from his feet.

"This place yours?" he asked, glancing around.

Alex smiled. The place was a cross between a large cabin and a house. The floors were laid with various widths of pine stained to a dark gloss, and the walls were covered with rugged planks from a barn. Except for the TV, sound system, and some contemporary paintings, Alex had furnished and decorated it with handsome antiques, handmade quilts, and braided rugs, along with wicker baskets and earthenware jars of dried herbs and flowers. He had worked toward what he thought of as a spare rural style.

Kip started to stuff the socks into the boots, but Alex said, "Let me take those."

He set the boots in one of the two basins in the bathroom, then wrung out the socks and hung them on the curtain rod, but when he returned, Kip had pulled off his shirt and was just stepping out of his jeans.

Thirty minutes later, they were lying embraced, face-to-face, with their legs wrapped around each other's, their mouths so close their breath intermingled. One breathed out, and the other drew the air into his lungs. Then that one breathed out, and the other drew it into his, as if they were deep underwater, sharing the mask to an oxygen tank.

"Sorry," Kip whispered, caressing Alex's face. "Lost my head."

"Shout all you want. No one here but us bears."

Alex kissed him, then rolled supine, staring at the pitched ceiling. The room had the same rustic interior as the rest of the house, and Alex had

furnished it with an infirmary bed, a night stand to either side, and a cedar chest of drawers, as well as, along one wall, a pine table and bentwood chair he used as an office. On top of the chest stood a brass candelabrum with three white candles, a white porcelain pitcher with a clump of purple statice, and a small alabaster bust of Whitman. Before they had slipped into bed, Alex had lit one of the candles, then turned off the lights. The room glowed with a warm honey yellow, and rain was pattering steadily on the roof. Outside, at the north-west corner of the house, a downspout was dripping slowly, ticking off the seconds like a clock.

"Think I blacked out," Alex chuckled.

He was trying to play the scene over in his mind – First the shorts went, then, like the shorts, his inhibitions. After that, all he remembered was literally a vast, starlit darkness.

"Covers?" he asked, turning on his side, facing him.

The sheet and spread, like the rim of a nest, had bunched at the foot of the bed.

"Uh-uh," Kip grunted. "In fact, next time we're up, let's turn down the heat."

"I'll do it."

"No, don't," Kip insisted, pulling him back. "I'm gonna get up in a minute and get some water."

Alex gazed at the tiny beads of sweat on Kip's upper lip, then, on impulse, licked the divot under his nose.

"You're different," Kip smiled. "You were taking care of you, but you were taking care of me, too."

"Isn't that what it's all about?"

Alex ran his hand over Kip's body – the ridge of his pectoral, the armor-like grid of his abdomen. He cupped his genitals and, as Kip raised his knee, caressed his cheek. Kip was still somewhat tan from summer except for his groin and buttocks. Alex had tan lines, too, but nothing as marked as Kip's. Having a fair complexion, Alex was not a sun worshiper.

"You're in great shape."

"You're in great shape, too," Kip remarked, squeezing Alex's right nipple.

"In summer, I swim to the buoy at the mouth of the cove every day. In winter, I do laps in the school pool."

"I know," Kip smirked. "I watch."

Swimming, Alex knew, had kept him trim mentally, too, especially over the last year.

"I'll get the water," Alex volunteered.

When he returned, he stood by the bed while Kip took a drink. Then Alex set the glass on a coaster. He went around the bed, but when he got in, Kip faced away, wrapping Alex's arm around his chest.

"It was very nice the other way," Alex murmured in his ear.

"It's nice like this, too," Kip said, snuggling.

Alex slipped his left arm under Kip's neck, and as they lay there, flush like spoons, he noticed the freckles scattered on Kip's shoulder, the discreet tattoo on the mound of his deltoid. He caressed the shoulder, gently thumbing the small rosebud. Then he reached the shiny rectangles of Kip's tags.

"Why do you wear your dog tags?"

"I don' know," Kip said. "Just like to."

"Kipling O. Gunter," Alex read.

"Kipling Oliver Gunter," Kip scoffed. "You can see why I go by Kip."

Alex noted Kip's religion (Methodist), social-security number (436-72-2151), and blood type (B+).

"Why two tags?"

"One around your ankle," Kip explained, "and one in your mouth."

"Your mouth?"

'They make you bite down on it. The metal's soft, and it takes the shape of your teeth."

"I don't understand."

"When you're dead."

Alex let the tags slip to the sheet.

"I noticed you were wearing a chain," Alex said. "In class, I mean."

"I could never really tell whether you liked me or not," Kip said. "At first, I thought you were sarcastic. Then I realized you just have this deadpan way of cracking jokes. Once I caught on ..." he trailed off. "They're giving you a hard time over there, aren't they? The college."

Alex rolled onto his back. A beam ran across the ceiling. He followed it to the wall, then down the wall to the bloom-like flame of the candle.

"Well, one," he began, "I'm against the war. Two, they know I'm gay. And three, I'm not a card-carrying Baptist." He rested his head on his right wrist.

"But it's not so much I'm a trouble-maker. I'm clear on that. Most of my colleagues just don't have the slightest idea how to respond to – Oh, God," Alex laughed. "Let's change the subject. Burke College is the last thing I want to think about on Friday night."

The rain sounded as if someone were walking around on the roof, and when the gutter flooded, the clock-like drip became a choked gargle.

"Let's take a shower," Alex said. "You first."

"Take it with me."

"I don't think so."

"At least, sit in the bathroom and talk to me."

Alex shook out Kip's jacket, then draped it over the chair at his desk. Then he lowered the toilet seat and sat there, talking to Kip and watching him shower. Through the plastic curtain, Kip looked as if, because of the tan lines, he were wearing a pair of Jockey shorts. When he turned off the tap, he shook the water from his hands, then shoved back the curtain. He reached one of the towels on the rack.

"His and hers?" he asked.

Alex gazed at the play of muscles in Kip's thigh, the sheen of water on his slick body.

"No," he corrected him. "His and his."

Kip turned, smiling, drying himself.

"Let's keep our pronouns straight," Alex said, "if nothing else."

Kip set his right foot on the side of the tub to dry that leg, then the left, the tags clinking faintly against his knee, and when he had finished, he stepped onto the mat, then bent over to rinse the tub.

Alex took about ten minutes to shower, and when he turned off the tap, he could hear First Take, the Roberta Flack album. When he stepped into the bedroom, Kip embraced him, and they kissed, then danced contentedly to "Angelitos Negros." At the end of the number, Kip reached a joint and matches from the jacket.

"Looks too green to be good," he said, sitting on the bed, "but, man, it'll rip your head off."

"Just what I need," Alex joked, "my head ripped off."

Alex brought a brass, leaf-shaped ashtray from the living room, then lit another candle. He turned off the lights, then sat next to Kip, and they smoked the joint, filling the room with its herbal smell.

When it was down to a roach, Alex tamped it out, then suggested, "Why don't we reverse roles?"

He felt as if the bed were floating off effortlessly, like a raft. "I have something else in mind," Kip grinned, taking a pair of handcuffs from the jacket.

Alex was uninitiated into the kinkier side of sex, yet curious, willing to explore. He also wanted to see what Kip would do, how far he would go. Or so he told himself, standing, taking the cuffs. Kip rolled onto his stomach, and Alex clicked the rings around his wrists, then gazed at him skeptically. Kip reminded him of a callow bird, his bound arms unfledged wings.

"You're a prison guard," Kip said in a strange, new voice. "And it's okay if you're rough."

But Alex was not rough. As he thought of it, besides making love to Kip, he was simply getting some good exercise, about as much as he would have on a leisurely swim to the buoy and back. One stroke led to the next. He was home.

When he started to pull away, Kip said, "No. Stay on. I like the feel of you on me."

"You must like being crushed." He mussed Kip's flattop, then said, "I don't understand why someone hasn't snapped up such a willing slave."

Despite Kip's protest, Alex slid to the side, then pulled him halfway on top so that Kip's head rested on Alex's shoulder. Kip was light to begin with but, under the influence of the grass, felt weightless as cork.

"What about you?" Kip asked, speaking into Alex's neck. "You have a]over, don't you? Prob'ly gone for the weekend or lives in Atlanta."

"He does live in Atlanta," Alex said, pulling Kip's knee across his waist. "We're just not lovers anymore."

"Since when?"

"Since fall a year ago."

"How long were you together?"

"Seven years," Alex said, cupping Kip's buttock.

"I could tell you're the type who likes to settle down." "I am settled down. I don't need a lover to do that."

"You know what I mean." Kip rested his chin on Alex's clavicle, then asked, "What happened?"

"Todd's a little older than I am. I figure about the difference between you and me. What are you, twenty-five or so?" "Twenty-five," Kip smiled.

"Breaking up with him was like going off heroin," Alex admitted. "Not that I've been on heroin."

He stared into the green request of Kip's eyes, then at the square, basket-like light fixture on the ceiling.

"You walk through the part you play every day," he said. "You prepare lessons, grade papers, meet classes."

"How'd you meet?"

"At this smart little bar in Atlanta." Alex heard the stereo click off, then asked, "Hungry?"

"Yeh," Kip blurted. "Munchies would be nice."

Alex got up and cleaned up in the bathroom, then cleaned up Kip with a wash cloth and towel. He draped the towel across the footboard, and as he tossed the cloth into a basin, Kip asked if he would turn off the heat.

"Can you believe this weather?" he exclaimed.

In a few minutes, Alex returned with a bottle of Rioja, napkins, and a plate of sharp Cheddar, water crackers, and cold, moist grapes. He set the bottle on a coaster, then slipped into bed and settled the plate between them. He cut a couple of pieces of cheese and broke a cracker, slowly feeding Kip, then himself. All of his movements, he noticed, were taking a little extra effort. He felt as if he and Kip were trying to eat underwater.

"This is absurd," he laughed.

"You're learning your role," Kip claimed.

"What?" Alex scoffed. "Master of Discipline? Thanks, but no thanks. I don't see my goal in life as dominating people." Then seriously: "I do enough of that as it is."

Alex smiled, yet the smile was edged with concern. He reached for the wine.

"Forgot glasses," he realized. "You can't use one, anyway, can you?"

He sipped some wine, then kissing him, let it run into his mouth. He put a slice of cheese into his own mouth, then transferred it to Kips.

"Grapes?" he asked.

"Peel 'em for me."

They laughed.

"The master peeling grapes for the slave."

Alex crushed a grape between his teeth, then, with it glistening on his tongue, let Kip devour it.

When Kip leaned back, the tags clinked, and Alex asked, "What was the army like?"

Kip snorted, "I wasn't cut out for it."

"Thought you liked being abused," Alex replied, cutting an-other piece of cheese. "How long were you in?"

"Couple of years. One more piece. I'm fine."

Alex fed him another slice, then set the plate on the night stand.

"Stationed in Germany."

From the advertisements in his gay guide, Alex figured that Germany was where Kip had learned about B and D, bondage and domination. In several of the pictures, the men, like giant insects, were wrapped in a carapace of leather and chains.

"What did you do?" Alex asked.

"My job? I was an orderly at the base hospital at Bad Windheim. Near Nuremberg."

Kip faced him, and Alex ran his finger down the ridge of Kip's nose, then dropped it onto his lips. Kip kissed the tip of it.

"And what does an orderly do?" Alex asked.

"Set up, clean up, prep patients. In other words, I came out of the service with no skills."

"You shouldn't deprecate yourself," Alex said tenderly. "At least you came out."

Kip smiled. Alex drank some wine, then held the bottle to Kip's lips. Purple trickled down his chin.

"How did someone as wild as you ever make it through two years of service?"

"I don't know. Just kept Private Gunter on base and my private life off."

"How did you pass on Nam?"

"Guess they needed someone in Bad Windheim."

Alex set the bottle on the stand, then wiped Kip's mouth. "How did you?"

"Asthma," Alex replied. "Never thought I'd be glad I had asthma. Why I swim every day. Lung power."

"Grass bad for asthma?" Kip asked.

"Actually, no. Kills the bacteria."

They lay there, silent, listening to the restful, leaf-like rustle of the rain.

"All those boys killed," Alex remarked.

"And how they're killed," Kip added. "Walking into trip wires, falling into spike pits."

"Sorry," Alex said. "That's the second to last thing I want to think about on Friday night."

"Got just the thing to lift our mood."

"Oh, no," Alex smiled.

"Reach inside the inside left pocket," Kip suggested, indicating the jacket.

Alex got up and groped inside, pulling out a small plastic bag with a white, crystalline powder. He clicked a lamp on, and Kip swung his legs off the bed, sitting up. When he did, the muscles in his abdomen meshed like pleats.

"Ever done coke?"

I'm afraid so," Alex confessed. "My Atlanta connection." "Thought we'd do a line," Kip said. "To stay awake. I don't wanna sleep. Do you?"

With each little surprise, Alex was beginning to realize that the rules were slowly, but surely changing. In fact, the game was.

"Guess not," Alex decided. "You're a little more accessible than Hans Castorp, a character in this novel I'm reading."

Alex chopped up, then laid out four lines on a clip board. He snorted one, then holding the straw to Kip's nose, helped him snort one. Leaning back, Kip coughed, and Alex gave him some water.

Kip rolled onto his stomach and asked, "How 'bout a back rub?"

"What?" Alex grinned, straddling his hips.

"How 'bout a back rub, sir?"

Alex's nose and throat were numb, and the cocaine left a slightly aseptic taste in his mouth. Kip's neck muscles and the contours of his shoulders, however, were pleasantly firm and warm, and Alex could feel himself succumbing to the tingling, effervescent rush. Because he was tired, he had literally felt as if he had been descending, but as the rush crescendoed, it was as if an elevator had stopped mid-floor, then rose.

"Seeing anyone?" Kip asked, his face toward the light. "No," Alex said, massaging him.

"Why not?"

"Just not ready for the single scene."

He squeezed Kip's deltoids and thought of the healing power of touch. To him, it was the sensual equivalent of a spiritual laying on of the hands. All some people needed to be happy, to be cured emotionally, he thought, was a simple touch.

"What about you?" he asked.

Kip smiled: "The lifeguard at the pool at night."

"At school?" Alex asked.

Alex tried flipping through a certain file of faces in his mind, overwhelmed, all at once, by the tiny bubbles of energy coursing through his veins. Though he was sure there were several, he could not think of anyone at the pool during the day whom he suspected of being gay. The lifeguard must have been strictly a night person.

"You meet there?" Alex asked.

"I hung around till closing one night. He showed up with this nine-inch wrench in his trunks."

Alex did not know if the change were due to the subject matter or if Kip had, in fact, relaxed into a deeper, huskier tone of voice. In any case, his voice now had a sexier, more provocative sonority.

"I'll have to find out who he is." Kip smiled wistfully, and Alex leaned over to whisper, "But not for the reason you think."

Alex made what he meant to be an intimate, reassuring gesture. He breathed the subtle smell of Kip's neck, then licked the sweet-salt taste behind his ear.

"Tell me about him," Alex said, sitting up, going to work on Kip's triceps.

"I met 'im every Thursday night in the john off the locker room."

"Why Thursday?"

I don' know. His night to lock up."

Alex's eyes seemed to focus even more clearly, in sort of a mentally super-sharp focus, and with a sudden, grateful access of well-being, he took in the broad, shadow-etched shoulders, the chain like tiny beads of mercury snaking across Kip's neck.

"What's he look like?" he asked, leaning on Kip's back so that his fingers dug into the skin.

"Nice pecs," he moaned.

"What's he like to talk to?"

"He doesn't. Could be a deaf-mute for all I know."

"So you had sex with him last night," Alex concluded, clutching him, kneading him. When Kip grimaced and groaned, Alex said, "Sorry."

"Feels great," he gasped. "And I didn't have sex last night," he swore. "Someone else took his place."

Alex sat up, and Kip craned to look at him.

"But it worries me you might give me something," Alex said.

"I haven't seen 'im in a couple of weeks," Kip insisted, "if that's what you mean. Look, Alex," he began. "What do you want?"

Despite the last few hours, it seemed strange to hear Kip call him by his first name.

"What do you mean?" he asked, crawling onto the bed beside him, lying prone, resting on his elbows.

Kip faced him.

"What do you want more than anything else in the world?" "What everyone wants, I guess – just to keep my head above water."

"Come on. What do you want?"

"A good job, friends, someone to come home to. Why?" "What I want more than anything else is you."

Alex smiled, "You don't even know me."

"I do," he claimed. "Enough to know I could be happy here with you. Man, I'm happy now, and you are, too. I can tell." "How?"

"You're smiling."

"Kip, you don't have to cling to whoever you just happen to be with at the moment."

"You're talking about yourself."

"I'm talking about you," he smirked. "The choice isn't Alex Alden or no one."

"It is." His voice quavered, "I've always felt like a freak 'cause I'm queer."

"Gay," Alex corrected him.

"I'm not going to meet anyone nice as you," he stated. "If I can't have you, I don't want anyone."

Alex looked at him askance, yet curiously.

"I believe you believe it, but it's way too soon. A decision like that takes a lot of time, not just one night. Maybe if we'd been seeing each other awhile, say, six months. Kip," he scoffed, "where's your head?"

"The guy in the gym," Kip stressed. "Something happened. I don't know. When he finished, he bumped me real hard, and I hit my head on this pipe over the toilet. I – I don' know. He was hot, yeah, but after that, I just couldn't see 'im anymore, and then it didn't matter if I saw 'im or not."

Alex smiled pensively, then said, "Maybe he knocked some sense into you."

He caressed Kip's face, thumbing the two moist petals of his lips. Kip sniffed, and Alex withdrew his hand.

"He laughed at me," Kip said. "He just pulled up his trunks and laughed."

Alex stared at the wall through the bars in the headboard. Kip, at Alex.

"Gets you excited, doesn't it?" Kip asked. "Knowing you've got me whenever you want me, can do whatever you want with me – out here. Huh? Come on, admit it."

"Look," Alex confessed, rolling onto his side. "I'm all grown up "

"So am I," Kip whispered. "So am I."

Alex was amazed. No sooner had they extinguished the flame than it flared up again. It was like one of those trick candles that, blown out, comes back to life.

Kip rolled onto his stomach, and Alex crawled on top of him, coupling with him again.

"How 'bout a hit?" Kip suggested.

Alex leaned over the clipboard, and joined at the hips, they snorted the lines. Alex realized he was simply drowning his sorrows in sex and drugs, but he was a willing victim. Turning himself on, he knew, really meant turning himself off, but turning himself off for a night might be just what the doctor ordered.

"Gag me this time," Kip urged, sniffing.

"Suck on your tags," Alex said, switching off the lamp.

Alex slipped the tags into Kip's mouth, and when the rush came on them, instead of a leisurely swim, Alex plunged into more of a race. Bubbles of power rose through his body. A champagne bottle of rapture popped.

"Sorry about that," he said, gasping. "Got a little carried away."

"Man," Kip blurted, "you can carry me away anytime."

Alex rolled onto his back, laying his hand on the crease between Kip's cheek and thigh. He glanced at the clock. It was three.

"Thirsty?"

Alex got up and cleaned himself, then, gazing at the sequins of sweat sparkling on Kip's body, he cleaned the boy. He gave him a sip of water, drank some himself, then lit the third candle.

"I'm wide awake," Alex said, plunking into bed.

"We'll sleep like logs when we crash."

"When will that be?"

Kip struggled onto his back, then draped his leg over Alex's. "I have a lot of trouble sleeping," he said.

"I could tell," Alex remarked. "You're drowsy in class."

"I don't know how to describe it.. Sometimes this pressure starts building up in my chest, and I feel as if I've got to explode or scream or something, or I really will go crazy. If only I could make it stop. If only I could sleep."

"How do you sleep?" Alex asked.

Kip glanced at him sheepishly, then said, "Grass knocks me out. For a while."

"Maybe you should lay off the coke," Alex suggested.

They stared at the patterns in the ceiling, the knots and swirls in the pine.

"Man, it's perfect here," Kip claimed. "Wish we could end it right now."

"What?"

"Everything."

"There's nothing to do after a perfect Friday but have another."

"But I had to practically break down the door, and now that you know me a little better…"

"You mean, now that I've had you."

Kip's passive-aggressiveness did, in fact, worry Alex. What if, next time, he didn't let him in?

"I'm happy here," Kip repeated. "Why go back to ..."What?"

"I don' know. To not being here."

Kip raised his knees, planting one foot on the sheet and one on Alex's knee.

"I don't wanna go out there," he said.

"Who does?"

"As soon as I step out the door," Kip claimed, "something'll happen. I'm telling you, man. By Monday – And this'll be all I'll have, one night. But here, we're safe. I know we're OK here." He looked at Alex, "Nothing makes any difference here, does it?"

The rain came down harder, and somewhere above them, in the hiss of a gust, a limb hit the roof.

"I don't wanna trick anymore."

"Kip, listen ..."

"I don' wanna trick anymore, man. Let me stay here. Please." Then he added, smiling, "How many guys have offered to be your slave, huh?"

"You're not desperate, and you certainly don't have to be anyone's slave. Slaves are roles in fantasies, Kip."

"I just wish we could end it – now," he repeated. "What a perfect place."

"Out of curiosity, how would we do it?" Alex asked, turning, propping his face on his hand.

"Got a gun?"

"No."

"You live way out here without a gun?"

"Let's see," he said, counting on his fingers. "I'm not up to swallowing Lysol. I'm not up to slashing my wrists." "What about running a hose to the car?"

"But that would mean going outside," Alex joked. "It's raining. Nope, I'm afraid we don't have any way of doing it even if we wanted to."

"Guess I'll have to do it on my own."

"Please don't do it around here," Alex smiled.

Alex knew that, at best, he'd never teach again.

"If you're not thinking of yourself," he added, "think of me. Kill yourself somewhere else."

All around them, the rain plashed and gurgled.

"And you wonder why no one wants you."

Alex sighed, then thought for a minute.

"Sorry," he said. "I know I should take you seriously. At first, I thought you were just being weird, like a game, like the handcuffs. Guess you're not."

"No," he said, "I'm not. I'm not kidding about the cuffs either."

Alex looked puzzled.

"I must admit," he confessed, "it's a pleasant thought. No more loneliness. No more hurt – either way. No more anything."

Kip faced him, and Alex held his face, brushing his cheek with his thumb. Alex sensed that, with the mood he'd been in lately, some emotional weight had just shifted inside him, tipping him off balance, but then, as he often had in the canoe, he righted himself, gliding on, slipping quietly across the rain-pocked waters of the night. Part of him was willing to toy with death, of course, out of curiosity, as he had with the drugs and cuffs, but despite his various setbacks, another part was very much content.

"Brahmans admire a man who voluntarily frees himself from the chains of the body," he said deliberately. "I do, too. At this point, however, I still prefer being bound."

"What do you mean?" Kip asked.

Alex had many reasons to live. First of all, he believed in love. He had been in love with Todd, his only lover, and to a great extent still was; but since he was, he knew, ironically, that he could and probably would fall in love again. His mind knew his relationship with Todd was over. His heart and body simply had not accepted the fact.

Secondly, he understood loneliness and did not let it depress him. He knew that he was supposed to feel lonely when alone too long. Loneliness was a natural phenomenon like gravity that drew people together, an instinct necessary for survival, and after a year of keeping his distance from people, he felt like a satellite that had reached the zenith of its orbit and was just beginning to swing back to earth. In short, he was ready to meet someone, but was that someone Kip? Kip was not what he had had in mind.

The simple pleasures, too, counted for more than he had thought – sitting in the canoe on the lake, listening to the rain on the roof, lying next to a young man....

"You never know, Kip," he said. "Everything may work out. That's why you shouldn't even consider – Besides," he stated, "there's nothing straights would like more. Don't give them the satisfaction of finding another fag hanging from the ceiling:"

"Gay," Kip said, mimicking him.

Alex smiled.

"Your arms must be sore."

"I'm fine," Kip muttered. "Just wish I could prove how I feel."

"You don't have to prove anything to me. We've had a very interesting evening. Let's worry about tomorrow tomorrow."

"You'll dump me, like everyone else, won't you?" Kip snapped. "You probably can't wait till I'm gone."

Alex glanced at him calmly.

"Sorry, man," Kip apologized. "You're one in a million. I know that. It's just that ..."

"You're tired," Alex said. "We both are."

He noted how unhappy Kip seemed in the midst of their intimacy, despite what Kip had said. Then Alex realized he may have been thinking about himself.

"Going to the bathroom," he said, rising slowly.

Though his nerves were lit up, every move seemed in slow motion – latching the door, flushing the toilet, taking out his contact lenses, and by the time he had slipped on his glasses and opened the door, Kip had managed to turn on not only the lights in the living room, but also the tuner.

"Kip," Alex groused.

"What?" he blurted, standing in the middle of the room. "Just tell me. You don't like Mick Jagger."

"I need something soothing, if anything. I'm sort of wired," Alex said, making a wired face.

"I forgot which station it was on," Kip said.

"Even better."

As a private joke, Alex turned off the tuner and turned on the stereo, putting on Wagner's "Liebestod."

"Tristan and Isolde."

"Who are they?"

"Famous lovers."

"Didn't know you wore glasses."

"Let's go to bed."

Alex flipped off the lights, then, with his hand on Kip's neck, directed him into the bedroom.

"Have a fan we could set up? Maybe we could open a window."

"I have a fan," Alex said. "I'll plug it in."

Alex set the fan on the floor near the foot of the bed, then aimed it away from them.

"Have another joint in that magic jacket of yours?" he asked.

"Sure," Kip beamed, and they smoked half of another, then finished the glass of water and crawled into bed. Alex took off his glasses, hoping the grass would put him and Kip to sleep. "I feel as if I'm floating on a cloud. I am a cloud," Kip claimed.

They cozied down, Kip's back to Alex's front, with Alex's arms around him, Alex's genitals cupped like chicks in the nest of Kip's hands.

"Nice if we could hold each other," Alex suggested. "But we are."

"You know what I mean."

"Tomorrow night," Kip promised.

"What if I have plans?" Alex said, teasing him.

Alex could feel Kip's body heat. He breathed in the balm of his smell.

"What about your friends?" Alex asked softly.

"What about 'em?"

"Have anyone to talk to, really talk to about things?"

"Not really, no," Kip said. He adjusted his head on the pillow, then added, "Most of my friends don't even know I'm gay. The lifeguard knows me better than they do, and you know me better than he does."

"'No man is living, no comrade left,'" Alex murmured, quoting The Wanderer, "'To whom I dare fully unlock my heart.' What about your family?"

"My mom's dead. My dad – uh-uh. As far as he's concerned, faggots – sorry, gays – don't exist."

Alex listened to the drip in the gutter. He thought of the cold rain, the dark woods, all the foxes, deer, and rabbits huddled for warmth in their warrens and dens, wherever they hid at night. Then he fell asleep, and in his dream, he was hiding, too – crouched in a storm drain under a highway. Shafts of light, like lasers, penciled the dark, and a narrow stream snaked along the floor. He could hear the muffled roar of cars and trucks, the cackle of laughter, the indistinct prattle of men speaking German. Above, a manhole cover ground open, revealing a crescent moon, then a searchlight, and he retreated to the shadows. In the midst of the glare, a man's feet appeared, then the legs, torso, and head as he was being lowered, then dropped into the pipe. He landed on his feet, and a cowbell clanked around his neck. Then he lost his balance, buckling to a sitting position against the curved wall. The cover slid into place with a clank, and Alex approached the man cautiously. First, he realized that the man was Todd. Then he realized that his arms were not tied behind his back, but hacked off.

Alex sat up. Kip coughed, rolling onto his side. Though the living room was full of light, the bedroom was dark with the curtains closed, and Alex switched on the lamp, then squinted at the clock: twelve thirty.

He plunked against the pillow, and Kip swung a leg over his waist, teasing him, "Come on. One more time."

"Go to sleep," Alex smiled, pushing Kip's head onto the pillow.

He switched off the lamp, and they snuggled again, front to back.

Alex was aware of Kip turning. He heard the tags clink and opened his eyes, squinting at the clock, but could not quite make out the digits. He sat up, then slipped on his glasses. It was three in the afternoon.

He stood and stretched, then lingered, gazing at Kip asleep with his head to the side on the pillow. Despite the cuffs, he looked as innocent as a child. Alex thought of finding the key and releasing him, but decided to let him sleep. He wandered into the bathroom and took a shower.

When he turned off the faucet, however, he could hear the TV. He dried off, combed his hair, and put in his contacts. Wrapping a towel around his waist, he stepped into the living room.

"What's that?" he asked.

"Don' know," Kip said, gazing at the screen. "Just turned it on."

They watched a smoking plane dive into a ship and explode.

"You know the Japs had a piloted glide bomb they used against ships?" Kip said. "During the final dive, it went over five hundred miles an hour. Man, hitting a ship at five hundred miles an hour."

He sprang to his feet and, backing up, turned off the set. Lumbering toward Alex, he said, "You should've let me take a shower with you."

Alex could imagine where a little lather would have led. "You're incorrigible."

"I don't know what that means," Kip admitted, "but I think I like it."

Alex stepped into the bedroom, feeling inside the jacket for the key.

"You shouldn't, you know," Kip said, turning.

"Take a shower."

Kip's arms moved to his sides in slow motion. He began flexing and massaging them gently. Alex noticed the wing-like bruises at the base of Kip's back. For a second, he thought they were a tattoo he had missed, a chevron or a fleur-de-lis to go with the rosebud on his shoulder.

"Take a look at those bruises while you're in there. On your back."

Alex handed him the key, then strolled into the kitchen to put on a kettle for tea. He peered through the window at the thermometer on a post of the portico: 66. To the right of the post hung a large spider web strung with tiny diamonds of rain. He looked through the trees at the overcast sky – so over-cast, in fact, the hour seemed much later than it was, an early twilight. It was still drizzling, and the clouds, he noticed, had swung from the southwest to the northeast. A cold front, he figured.

After dinner that night, they cleared the table, rinsed the dishes, and set them in the dishwasher. Alex settled at his desk, grading papers, and Kip stretched out on the couch, watching "The Titanic" on TV. He was using an

earphone, and all that Alex could hear from the living room was Kip's changing positions at times. Alex had grown used to the perfect calm that often fell on the cove at night, and having someone else in the house was a little disconcerting, but pleasant. Did he want the peace or the companionship? He wasn't sure. Then he remembered that for three years, he had enjoyed both.

After a couple of hours, Kip turned off the TV, then ambled onto the south deck and sat in a chair under the overhang. Alex could hear the long lisp of the drizzle. Propping his chin in his hand, be leaned to check on Kip, who was kicked back with his feet on the rail. Beyond the rail was matte black. The wind chime rotated quietly.

After about a half an hour, Kip came in, kissed Alex, and reached into the jacket, He sat on the bed, lit a joint, and, after taking a hit, nudged Alex's shoulder.

"Guess I'm not grading any more papers," Alex said, laying down the pen.

Kip exhaled the smoke, then declared, "It's Saturday night."

Alex took the joint, and Kip stood behind him, massaging his shoulders, and they remained in those positions, taking hits.

"Man, that deck's nice," Kip exclaimed, his voice all smooth and quirky with grass. "Been cooped up all winter."

Kip braced himself on the arms of the chair, blowing smoke into Alex's ear. Alex could feel the tags brushing his back.

Kip nuzzled his neck, then whispered, "Instead of cuffs, what about chains? Got any chains?"

"So it's chains tonight," Alex smiled, tilting his head to look at him. "What about nothing? What about just the two of us in a nice, clean bed?"

"Please," Kip cooed, unbuttoning Alex's shirt. "Just this once, I swear."

He fondled Alex's left pectoral, and his constant attention, along with his pliable kinkiness, had its predictable effect. In a few minutes, Alex found himself squatting beside Kip down-stairs in what he called the boathouse, a storage room he had added to the north side of the house. He had preceded Kip down and was sorting chains when Kip showed up undressed with a red, woolen blanket over his shoulders, like a poncho. He spread the blanket on the floor, then did a push-up to it, the tags touching, then his face. And now Alex was wrapping about a two-foot piece of a small-gauge chain in a figure eight around his wrists.

When he hooked it, he asked, "See if you can get out of that?"

Kip struggled, then grunted, "Uh-uh."

Alex hovered over him, taking him in – his crossed wrists, the firm, white cushions of his hips. He marveled at the paradoxes of his body, at once both soft, yet hard; supple, yet strong – the moment of his and Kip's wonderful oneness hot, yet wet.

"Hell, Kip," he murmured. "I think your plan's worked. I'm already addicted to you."

But when Alex caressed his cheek, Kip said, "No, not here. On the boat."

"The boat," Alex snorted, withdrawing his hand. He thought for a while, then said, rising, "Guess we have enough gas. Let's see if the battery's charged."

The cove was dead-still, but when Alex shifted gears and the pontoon inched forward, a stream of cold air began flowing over them, and Alex scooted over, motioning for Kip to move to his side. Alex put his arm around him, squeezing his shoulder through the damp blanket. They kissed. Then Kip snuggled against him, his head on his chest, and Alex faced for-ward, a hand on the wheel. The motor chugged. The mist parted. The buoy, like a night porter, nodded as they passed.

To starboard, a rocky reef slowly emerged, studded with skeletal Christmas trees and crowned with a hazard marker. Next, rose the giant, black iceberg of an island. Ahead, Alex knew, two points of land framed the main channel, but he could not see them. He figured the direction by angling off the island and eventually pulled even with the one to starboard, a rocky strand rising to a pile of boulders with a marker. He applied the slightest pressure to the wheel and soon was rounding the marker, sidling onto open water. The huge dam gradually swung into view, lit up like an ocean liner.

Alex shifted into neutral, and the motor gurgled. Then he killed it, and rocking gently, the boat quietly drifted to rest. All around them, strips of mist dangled like gauze, lazily twisting and swaying on the flat, dark gloss of the lake.

Alex glanced at his watch, but could not read it. He figured it was after ten. He had been on the lake late at night, but never that early in the year. Even without a breeze, the temperature was much colder than at the dock.

"Frozen?" he asked.

"Fine, sir," Kip breathed, switching to a terse, yet subservient military tone of voice.

"Tell me if you get too cold."

Alex glanced around. To the north stretched the murky blotches of wooded hills, a vague silhouette against the soft overcast. To the east, the nightscape dimmed to that of some other, somber planet. He felt how small and isolated they were, and yet, despite the miserable weather, also strangely happy, sensual, snug. He sighed, and in the bleak silence, the sigh seemed magnified and profound.

"What is it, sir?"

"No point trying to anchor. Too deep."

He could smell the cold vapor directly off the water. "Think I'm in the mood for coke, sir."

"You give a lot of orders for a slave." He felt Kip shivering, then said, "You're freezing, aren't you?"

"Warm me up, sir."

"I'll warm you up, all right," he repeated, at once both playful, yet bored. "The joint first. Guess I can get us in," he added, meaning back home.

Without a word, Alex seemed to know his role in the ritual. He had brought a bottle of Taittinger's, and though he had for-gotten glasses again, he popped the champagne, drinking off the fizzy gush, then holding it to Kip's lips,

"To spring."

"To spring, sir."

Alex lit the joint, and they smoked it the way they drank the champagne, huddled behind the helm, with Alex holding it for Kip. A cloud of smoke, like sandalwood, hung in the air.

"Champagne's for celebrations," Alex stated, "What are you celebrating, dogface?"

"Getting laid by Dr. Alden, sir, You, sir?"

"Forgetting Todd in the throes of sex."

The palest shapes were drifting across the boat, flowing through it, like ghosts,

"Champagne, sir?"

Alex slugged from the bottle, then deliberately slid it too far into Kip's mouth.

When it spilled, Alex said, "Don't gulp champagne, Kip. Sip it."

'Yes, sir," Kip coughed, rubbing his feet together,

""Draw it out like a ..."

"Nice, long fuck, sir?"

"It's one of the great joys of life,' he affirmed, 'one of the major reasons for being."

"Champagne or fucking, sir?"

"Both."

Alex flicked on a flashlight, then flipped up and secured a small, built-in table, where they did the last two lines of coke. When Kip leaned to do his, he was careful to drape the tags over the edge. He licked up the last few crystals, then sat up, sniffing hard and swallowing. Alex faced forward, waiting for the coke to kick in, watching the mist off the bow-- tinted green to starboard, red to port. Kip stood, and the blanket slipped to the deck.

"Unclip my leash, sir?"

"Why?"

Alex had clipped a chain to the one around Kip's wrists. "I love you, sir. I mean, really love you. Just came to me." Kip's response was a non sequitur, of course, but at that point Alex was so stoned he was not sure.

"The coke just came to you, Kip, not love."

"No, sir, love. Ready to show you, sir."

Alex turned off the flashlight, then stood and stripped.

Touching Kip's elbow, he stated, "On your stomach."

He had indicated the bow of the boat, the deck not under the canopy. Kip kneeled, and the tags touched the carpet.

After Alex finished, he stood, but, since his legs were shaky, held on to the windshield. Standing there, he noticed what looked like an glacier – the grey blur of a massive fog bank trundling toward them steadily from the east. He stepped to the stern and, picking up a towel, flopped onto the bench.

"Huh!"

The hoarse sound tore the silence open, and Alex immediately recognized it for what it was, a primeval grunt not only of passion, but also extreme fear. When he looked up, Kip took one step, then, twisting his body, threw himself over the bow. His right calf banged the gate, and he plunged headfirst into the water, the leash rattling over the rail, like a snake. Alex lunged, grabbing it, but when he had pulled Kip, face down, to the surface, it broke, and swinging on the rail, he jumped over-board, bumping Kip's thigh in the splash.

Once, while traveling alone, Alex had stopped at a small motel in Tennessee. It was a mild December night, and there was a lit swimming pool across from his room. So he changed into some shorts, then went to the pool and dove. The spring-fed water, however, was icy cold, so cold, in fact, his body clenched. The life in him had retreated to his chest, crouched there like a turtle in a shell, and only by iron will could he force himself to swim to the edge and climb out.

When he hit the water this time, his body clenched as well, and there was a second in which, stunned, he considered just sinking with Kip. A vast silence closed in on them, a silence even thicker, even more dreadful, than the one above. The water became icier, and Alex's eardrums ached. He could sense the horrible void beneath them, the clammy touch of the lake bottom. Then fear took over, and he forced himself, as he had in Tennessee, to start kicking.

By then, Kip was kicking, too, churning the water. Alex found an arm, then followed it to Kip's wrists, but when he, groping with the chain, unclasped it, he realized that it was the leash. He felt for, then unclasped the other, and when he broke the surface, gasping, the pontoon appeared, nestled in the fog, and Kip began flailing about, choking and coughing.

The next morning, Alex was sitting in a chair by the bed, his face propped in his hand, watching Kip asleep. Kip's head was turned away, cradled in the pillow. His hands lay crossed on his chest.

Again, it struck Alex how strange it was to be looking after someone other than himself, yet he could not help feeling that in Kip's suffering he saw his own over Todd. He himself had become Todd, and the thought saddened

him. He could do better than that, a lot better. All Kip wanted, he knew, was what he himself did, to salvage a little happiness from the sunken wreck of his life. He saw how brave Kip was to jump from the boat, to reject life without love, to demand the best or die, and if love were simply placing a high value on someone, then, Alex realized, in that sense, he loved him. He admired his valiant, if reckless, struggle for love.

All at once, Alex felt bound not only to Kip, but also to any man who had struggled for love. His friends, even Todd – they were comrades in arms in the fight for human dignity. He felt a sense of community with them, with America itself in its faltering quest for human rights, with the reasonable, decent spirit in people that insisted on their humanity. Kip's humanity had literally been brought home to him, and the least he could do, he mused, smiling to himself, was not only forget about Todd for a while, but himself. Suddenly, it was no longer clear who had saved whom.

The wind was tearing through the woods, whistling around the corner of the house. Alex reached the cup of tea on the night stand, and Kip began squirming and groaning, then sat up, dazed.

Alex set down the cup, then taking Kip's hand, asked, "Know where you are?"

Kip nodded. His body looked heavy with sleep.

"Know who I am?"

Kip looked at him, then squeezed his hand, "Yeh." Alex let go, then handed him a glass of orange juice. Opening a plastic vial, he said, "Here, take this."

Kip put the blue and white capsule into his mouth, then sipped some juice.

"An antibiotic," Alex explained. "And these," he said, opening a second bottle. "A couple of aspirin won't hurt. We're covered with bruises and scratches. You can hide the others, but I don't know how you'll explain the ones on your wrists."

Kip's wrists were so bruised they looked stained.

"How do you feel?" Alex asked, his voice calm, soothing. "Fine."

"Your chest?"

Kip coughed to see if his chest were congested, but shook his head.

"We're supposed to take four a day. Let's use up both prescriptions just in case."

Alex set Kip's glass on the stand, then sipping some tea, swallowed one of the capsules. He set down the cup, then glanced at his watch: ten thirty.

"I …" Kip quavered. "I'm sorry for all the stupid things I did last night. Last night, hell. This weekend. I'll just get out of here," he said, turning back the covers.

Alex had dressed him in a pair of boxer shorts and an under-shirt. Kip sat on the side of the bed, then continued.

"I'll drop. I'll drop everything. I was gonna drop out of school, anyway – money or no money. I can't believe I tried to force myself on you like that."

"Lie down."

Kip hesitated, pressing his eyelids with his fingertips. Alex did not know if he were pressing them because they were sore and swollen or because he was trying to press back tears.

"I want to talk to you. Lie down," Alex insisted, and Kip did, blinking, then brushing back his hair.

Alex rose and performed the slow ritual of letting light into the room. First, he drew the curtains and sheers of the west window, then the north. He lingered at the window, staring at the splotched boulders, the carpet of leaves, the nude trees exposed to the sky. A wind rose, and the trees began to sway.

"I shouldn't let you blackmail me like this," he began, turning toward the room. "The fact is I could live with your death."

He strolled to the foot of the bed and, fingering the railing, faced Kip. He surprised himself. In the new light, he realized that what he had said was true. Kip's desperate threats had not really touched him. His need for love had.

"I don't even know you," Alex stated, moving to the chair, taking his seat. "Let's put it this way. I haven't known you long, and what little I do know about you almost killed us." When Kip started to say something, Alex cut him short, saying, "But – let's see how we feel today. If we're not coming down with penumonia, we'll drop by your place tomorrow and pick up your things."

Kip stared at him, then, smiling, promised, "You won't regret it. I'll do anything you say. Just say it. I'll do it."

"I don't want you to do anything I say," Alex remarked. "But what if I said cut the drugs?"

"OK."

"To be perfectly honest, I wouldn't mind a little grass on Fridays myself, but the coke and whatever else you do have to go.'

"Macht nichts."

"I also think we should cut a lot of this fantasy crap. We need to try to relate to each other as each other. Not that I mind left field."

"Yes, sir."

They smiled.

"And no more suicide attempts. You haven't committed a crime. So there's no need to punish yourself, right?"

Kip nodded, biting his lip. Alex finished the tea, then set down cup.

"How would I have explained the chains," he asked, "let alone a certain other well-placed specimen of evidence?"

Despite what he said, he basically did not care what anyone thought of him, just what he thought of himself. He knew the truth. What others thought of him was a practical matter. Even a murder charge.

"They could tie us together?" Kip asked.

"In a second."

Alex could barely hear the leaves brushing against the wall, clutching at the screen to get in.

"What was I thinking of?" Kip asked himself. "Well, that's it. I wasn't. My wires were down from the snow."

"Snow? Oh."

Alex glanced at Kip. Kip stared at the ceiling dreamily. "About school..."

"You'll help me."

"I'll grade papers, and you'll do your lessons, and if you need help, I'll help."

"Thanks," he stammered, facing him. "I can make it with you. I know I can."

Alex smiled, "What's your major?"

"I don't know."

"We'll work on that. We'll find out what you're good at besides sex."

A hush fell on the woods, and Alex glanced through the door, across the living room, across the porch, to the glistening trunks of the trees. It was a great day, he thought. Finally sunshine.

Turning back, he asked, "How are you doing in your other classes?"

"Take a guess," Kip grinned.

"Who's your advisor?"

"Dr. Birch."

"Birch," Alex laughed. "I'll have you switched," he punned. "'To me, I mean. If we have any luck at all, and apparently we do, I'll have you for a student, an advisee, and a lover all in one quarter."

Kip smiled, displaying a perfect set of teeth. He sat up and embraced him, and Alex rocked him gently like a child. Then they gave each other a strong, deeply involved kiss.

"I love you," Kip swore, hugging him.

"Lie back," Alex murmured.

Kip reclined, and Alex slouched in the chair, resting his chin in his hand.

"I don't know if I believe you really do love me," he began. Again, Kip started to speak, but Alex interrupted. "No, don't say anything. Let me finish."

Kip lay still, staring at him.

"I don't think you know what love is. At least, you don't seem familiar with what I think of as love. Not that I have all the answers. But," he

remarked, staring back, "I don't think anyone's really loved you. You don't even seem accustomed to anyone being nice to you. Of course, I understand that all too well. But I wonder if someone had to at some point so you'd know what it is. I don't know. Maybe love comes to a person naturally, but sometimes I think it's like sharing the fire in that Welty story. Someone has to bring it to you, or you have to go get it. Then you have to keep it going to share it with someone else. Maybe that's what you've done," he concluded, "gone and gotten it, demanded it, claimed it as your rightful share of the basic necessities. But," he emphasized, "even if you don't, I think you could grow to love me."

"I do."

"There isn't that much difference in our ages," Alex plunged on. "Todd's seven years older than I am. Todd," he repeated. "What I'm trying to say is that I think in time I could love you, too."

Time, he felt, would surely thaw his heart, freeing him to love him.

"I don't love you now. Let's face it. At least, not in the sense you mean."

Alex could see the hurt in Kip's eyes, the psychic paralysis.

"But there are certain practical things I can do for you, that is, as long as you want me to, certain things that anyone could do for someone else. I can give you a place to live, a sense of stability. God knows your self-esteem needs some work." "I understand."

"Despite teaching, I'm not doing anything better with my life. At least, with you, I'm really helping someone."

He would love him that way, he told himself. He could wait for the other, and even if it did not come, he still would have given him a lift partway.

"On my part," he said, "I'll try to get along with my col-leagues. I can polish chapters of my dissertation and send them out. I really don't need to change jobs just now. Despite the rednecks, I like it here. This place, I mean. I like it here a lot."

He rested his face in his hand.

"I can also get over Todd. I think it may take awhile, at least one day of clear thinking, but I have to. I have to, and I will. There's certainly no point in not getting over him."

Alex moved to the bed, settling beside Kip, facing him, and this time, Kip took his hand.

"Romantic love isn't the only kind," Alex claimed.

Kip's hand felt good. It did not cling to his. It held.

"There's a deliberate, practical love as well. Just plain caring for each other. Romance is fun. It's wonderful. What Todd and I had. But I think the other kind of love is really of more use to people. See what I'm saying?"

Kip nodded, "There's hope."

"I know I sound – well, I sound like a father. It's not what I want."

"Lover'll do," Kip smiled.

"Lover it is."

They kissed lightly. Then Alex noticed that something was missing.

"Where are your tags?"

Kip felt his throat.

"Must've lost 'em in the lake."

"I'll buy you something else, if you like. Something gold." "Would you?" Kip asked. "Man, that would be great." Alex smiled with his eyes.

"I'll get you something," Kip blurted, beaming.

"Not yet," Alex said. "When we see how we are."

A gust hit, and a branch thumped on the deck. Then the house fell silent, so silent, in fact, Alex could hear their breathing. He thought of all the nights he had lain awake alone there, listening to his heartbeat.

"Sure you won't find domestic tranquility a bit dull?" Alex asked.

"Don't see how it could be with you."

Alex smiled. From the lull came the chime-like chirping of birds.

"Well," Alex said, "I finally got to sleep with you the way I wanted to."

He had read about the Nazi experiments in which inmates from concentration camps were held in tanks of icy water for extended periods. The "studies" were supposed to increase the chance for survival of German pilots downed in the Arctic Ocean. According to a certain Dr. Rascher, a blanket was about as effective as a person in warming up the TP, the test person, but Alex found that conclusion hard to believe. Besides, he could think of nothing better than sleeping embraced with a lover.

"The way you and Todd slept?"

"The way I'd like to sleep with anyone," Alex replied, "anyone, that is, with whom I'd like to sleep."

Alex could hear the rush of the wind, the tremulous click of leaves skipping over the deck. He gave Kip's hand a good squeeze, then stood.

Arms akimbo, he asked, "What about a big bowl of chicken-noodle soup?"

WAITING FOR LEFTY
Leo Cardini

When I awoke in the middle of the night, I was sweating my balls off and I had a raging hard-on. The sweat was the result of this incredibly humid, August heat wave that just wouldn't go away. And as for my hard-on; well, I always wake up with one. Usually I just lie back, spread my legs wide apart so my sensitive, low-hanging balls have lots of rising-and-falling space, recall one of my more recent adventures (typically in some dimly lit, late-hour Village haunt, but sometimes right here in piss-proper Lyndon, New Jersey), grab my eight inches of cut, rock hard man meat, and jack off.

But tonight... well, I'd expected I'd wake up like this. In fact, I'd been anticipating it all day long, so impatient for this moment to arrive, I had to shoot off four or five loads of cum during the course of the day just to siphon off the excess that kept on building up inside me. But now the time had finally come. And I knew exactly what I planned to do. I jumped out of bed, acutely aware of the bounce of my cock and the swing of my balls, so ripe for sensual contact that even the air felt good against them. I slipped on a pair of Levi cutoffs that were so worn out as to be practically obscene, being as they were ripped across each asscheek and practically threadbare where the cotton stretches against the bulge of my cock and balls when I'm not wearing any underwear.

Then I threw on a loose white tank top and sat down on the edge of the bed to pull on the same white sweat socks and sneakers I'd been wearing all day long. I was, in fact, dressed in the exact same clothes I had put on when I woke up around this time last night.

And just like last night, I stepped out the back door of my house, no keys or wallet to encumber me, crossed the street, and headed for the deepest, most neglected section of the Sideriver Park. At this hour, I knew it'd be cooler by the river. Sure, conspicuous signs at every entrance warn you that the park closes at sundown, but I always figure they don't apply to dedicated night prowlers like myself. Rather, their purpose is to ward off the sexually timid and unimaginative. In minutes I was strolling down one of the most secluded paths in the park. The nearly full moon and the occasional lamplight plunged me into a black-and-white world where the threat of danger lurked behind every bush, and the promise of passionate encounters patiently waited for me just beyond every bend in the path.

As I walked on, I thrust my hands deep into my pockets. They were both worn through, so I had total access to my cock and balls. I wrapped the fingers of my left hand around my cock, carelessly yanking on it, while I used the "o" of my right thumb and index finger to tug on my balls. Almost instantly I had a hard-on that was begging to be liberated from the confines of

my cutoffs, right then and there, and stroked until another release of cum brought me once again to a more restful state.

But I resisted its demands and continued to walk on until I found just the spot I was looking for. This was several yards past the darkest curve in the path, where the lamp on the left's always out of order.

And just beyond that lamp a park bench borders the path, a bench half-hidden by the overgrowth of bushes surrounding it on three sides. I had reached my destination, the same spot where last night...but that's another story.

No one here yet. Good.

I inspected the deep, dense bushes on the opposite side of the path, satisfied that they would suit my purpose. Then I slowly stripped myself of all my clothes, including my sneakers, and carefully deposited them into the nearby trash can. A cough coming from out of sight down the path told me I wasn't the only nocturnal trespasser about. If it was who I thought it was, his timing couldn't have been better! I quickly stepped over to the bushes I'd just examined, got down on my hands and knees, and snaked myself feet first in between two of them until I judged myself to be completely concealed. Resting on my stomach, my cock pinned to the ground beneath me, I raised my head, supporting it in the palms of my hands, and peered out like a little kid watching television. But what I longed to witness was like nothing you'd ever expect on TV! Ah, it was indeed who I'd hoped it would be – the kid I'd nicknamed Blondie last night in lieu of knowing his real name. Down the path he came, that tall, lean, tight-muscled adolescent with the arrogant, abusive attitude. His blond hair, short on the sides and in back, and long on the top, spilled across his forehead in a mess of defiant, unruly curls that completely concealed his left eye. As he nonchalantly approached, he gave his head a characteristic, unconscious toss, throwing his hair back for the few seconds it would remain off his face. He, too, looked like he was dressed the same as last night. Shirtless and dirty-sneakered, his tank top swayed out of the rear left pocket of his loose denim cutoffs that hung tantalizing low on his waist and shifted from hip to hip with every step he took. As he neared the pack bench opposite me, he slowed down, coming to a complete stop when he was in front of it. Placing his large right hand over his crotch and tugging at himself through the worn denim, he looked down the path in both directions. Seeing no one was about, he sat down, stretching his long arms along the top of the bench back, his broad, long-fingered hands hanging down limply on either side of him. He slouched forward and planted his feet wide apart on the ground, which I now realized was one of his favorite poses (the show-off!), and slowly fanned his knees in and out, in and out, drawing my attention to the loose denim in his crotch, where I knew an enormous cock lie hidden. Looking in both directions a second time, he returned his right hand to his crotch, fondly massaging it. Ah, he wasn't wearing any underwear again, for in no

time his cock had snaked far enough down his right inner thigh for his plump, cut cockhead to emerge from his cutoffs like a sleepy monster that's been awakened in its lair and peeks outside to see what the hell's going on. Twisting his hand until it was palm outwards, he moved it down to his cockhead, encircled it with his thumb and forefinger, and gently tugged more of his cock out into view. Such a fat cock on such a lean adolescent!

He let his head fall back and, now reversing his grip to make a fist around his cockshaft, he slowly stroked himself towards erection. His cock lengthened, in no time rebelling against the confines of his cutoffs in an attempt to stand straight up between his legs. All business now, he sat forward to pull all of his cock and both his big balls out of his pants' leg, forcing the material high up on his thigh. He leaned back again. Lost in his own self-gratification, he slowly ran his fist up and down his substantial cockshaft, mesmerizing me with the steadiness of his cockstrokes. By now I had repositioned myself, balancing the weight of my body on my right hip and elbow so I could mimic his cockstrokes with my own left hand on my own demanding cock. I was as lost in my pleasure as he was in his. But his was self-contained. Mine drew me towards him as if his rock hard, over-sized cock exerted some powerful influence on me I was helpless to resist. I was tempted to come out of hiding, sneak up on him, and kneel between his legs so I could lick those two big balls of his. To approach an adolescent in a dark, deserted park could spell danger. But to announce your presence by creeping up on him and planting your moist tongue on his succulent balls...? No, I couldn't.

But there was that broad-handed, long-fingered fist of his, traveling up and down that huge cock. Jesus, I swear I could even see the glisten of pre-cum oozing out his piss slit. How could I resist?

Fuck!

Just as I was about to creep out of the bushes, he suddenly jerked his head up, wide-eyed and alert. His body tensed, his hand froze mid-stroke on his cock, and he apprehensively looked down the path to his right. There was someone approaching. I could hear it now for myself. Blondie quickly readjusted himself, stuffing his stiff, uncooperative dick and his two big balls back into his cutoffs, pulling the pants leg down over them again. Then he resumed his usual slouched back, knee-fanning position. You'd never have known that a matter of seconds ago he was in the middle of a major, self-indulgent jack off session, the type adolescents are such masters of. Just as I expected. It was his friend whose name I also didn't know from the night before and had dubbed The Stallion. He was about as tall and lean as his friend, Blondie, but with slightly broader shoulders, dark Italian features and a thick, flowing mane of black, wavy hair.

To complete the symmetry of the evening, he too seemed to be dressed the same as last night – a tight-fitting white tank top, and blue sweat pants, cut off slightly higher than mid-thigh, that could not conceal the

enormous bulge of cock and balls he held captive inside. Could he possibly be wearing the same jockstrap as the night before? Imagine the rich odor of teenage crotch sweat that would have built up inside its elastic and cotton pouch, not to mention the savory blend of piss, cum and pre-cum stains where the underside of his cockhead rested against that privileged material! "Hiya," said Blondie.

"Hi yaself," replied The Stallion.

Randy young men with big fat dicks, I thought to myself, don't need great conversational skills to attract the interest of others. "Move over," The Stallion ordered with a sideways nod of his head. Blondie slid down the bench, freeing up the left half of it for The Stallion, who then sat down.

"So where's the brew you said you'd bring?" Blondie asked his friend.

"Fuck. I'm in so much hot water with my Pa, no way was I gonna chance ripping off any more of his beer."

"Shit." Blondie pondered out loud. "All this trouble began with that damn circle jerk in the locker room. Now you can't make a fucking move without your parents giving you the fucking third-degree." "Yeah."

"Maybe we could blackmail Coach Douglas into buying us some beer."

Ah, good old Coach Douglas, still one of my favorite fuck buddies. If they only knew when I first met him he was in the Mineshaft on his hands and knees wearing nothing but white sweat socks and a jockstrap, his face dripping with the jack off cum of the dozen or so guys surrounding him.

"After all," Blondie continued, "I figure it was his fault in the first place, the way he's always talking about how he understands our needs, and joking about if lockers had eyes and ears..."

"Yeah, yeah, yeah ...just drop it, huh?"

Stunned to be cut off in mid-sentence, Blondie turned to his friend and stared at him open-mouthed.

"I mean, it's too hot to get all riled up about it. Besides, look what I did manage to lay my hands on." He pulled a hand rolled joint out of his left sweat sock, holding it up for Blondie's inspection.

"Right! I knew you'd come through."

"Bet your fucking ass," The Stallion said, producing a matchbook from the same sock and proceeding to light up.

They proceeded to pass the joint back and forth, the red-hot ember flitting between them like a stoned firefly, erratic in its movements as it journeyed between their lips.

"Good stuff!" Blondie exclaimed after several tokes, talking over the inhalation he was holding in at the moment.

"Yeah. Got it from Bobby. And guess who he got it from." "Who?"

"His uncle!"

"No kidding?"

"No kidding! He says they turn on together all the time." "Cool. Wish I had an uncle like that."

"Yeah. I guess they're like really close."

Ah, if they only knew how close Bobby and I really were, let alone that Bobby's uncle was the same man who sucked them off last night in this same spot! The conversation paused and you could tell they were soon floating in a stoned euphoria. Believe me, if I hadn't gotten this grass from a trustworthy source, I'd be suspicious about just what was in it. That's how strong it was.

"Yeah," the Stallion mused out loud after a pause, "'That Bobby sure is lucky...in more ways than one."

"Fuck," said Blondie, "Good looks and good grades ain't everything."

"I wasn't talking good looks and good grades."

"Huh?"

"You ever see him in the shower after gym class?" "Oh, yeah, I know what you mean, man."

"He's gotta have the biggest dick in the entire school. Hell, maybe in all of Lyndon."

"Why, you made a survey, or something?"

"Fuck you!"

"In your dreams!"

They fell into another stoned silence.

"Still," The Stallion started up again a few seconds later, "It's pretty fucking enormous. And you know what I think?" "What?"

"It ever occur to you he's always the first out of the shower?"

"No. Why?"

"I think he gets a hard-on and he doesn't want anyone to notice." " Sounds like you sure noticed."

"Fuck you! I mean, take a look sometime. You'll see what I'm talking about. And another thing, you ever find your jockstrap missing?"

"Yeah. Come to think of it, a couple of times. Why? Do you think..."

"That he steals them? Yeah, I do."

"Jesus. What would he want with them?"

Then he fell silent, presumably to ponder the possibilities. What would Bobby want with his classmates' worn athletic supporters, steeped in the odor of crotch sweat? Oh, the stories I could tell you about Bobby and his obsession with his classmates' jockstraps!

"Fucking good grass, huh?" The Stallion stated rather than asked as he held up in front of his face the tiny roach of it that remained.

"Yeah!"

The Stallion put it out on the tip of his tongue and then tossed it into the air, tilting his head back and skillfully catching it in his mouth. The two of them lapsed into silence again. Blondie returned his outstretched arms to the back of the bench, slouching forward and once more slowly waving his legs in and out, in and out. The Stallion had slouched forward also, wrapping his arms around his chest. He spread his legs wide open, extending the left one straight out to the side, and bending his right leg at the knee, shaking it up and. down on the ball of his foot. "You think he'll come again?" The Stallion asked a moment later, reviving their conversation.

"Who? Lefty?"

"That his name?"

"That's my name for him."

The Stallion turned his face towards his friend, his brow wrinkled in a question mark. "Hmh?"

Blondie moved his right hand down to his crotch, imitating a few jack off strokes. "Ohhh," The Stallion replied in knowing comprehension.

Then he added, "Now who's the one who notices other guy's dicks?" Blondie threw him a frown to kill and repositioned his arm along the back of the bench.

"Still wouldn't mind him sucking me off again, though." Blondie continued. "I've been so fucking horny all day long. And every time I thought I could get the chance to jack off, something came up."

"Hell, that's nothing," The Stallion bragged. "I've jacked off four or five times today and I still get horny every time I think about last night. I mean, he was really into it."

"Yeah."

The powerful effects of the grass once again steered them into silence. There they sat, Blondie fanning his knees in and out, and his friend The Stallion shaking his right leg up and down. And I just watched, lazily stroking my cock and savoring the sight of these two young studs with their legs spread apart, unknowingly presenting me with a prolonged view of their bulging baskets, both of them stoned as could be, getting hornier by the moment as they waited for me to show up and suck them off. After a few moments, Blondie's knees slowed down and finally came to a stop. His face was rigid with apprehension as he stole an anxious sidelong glance at The Stallion. He cautiously moved his right hand down to his crotch, unzipped his fly and pulled out his long, floppy, half-hard cock. He shot The Stallion another glance and then made a fist around the middle of his cockshaft. The Stallion's right leg came to a halt as a turned his head to gawk at Blondie's crotch. "You don't mind, do you?" Blondie asked cautiously as he began to slowly run his fist up and down his cock.

"Uh, no! Course not!" he replied, unsuccessful at sounding cool. He did manage to turn his head forward again, though his eyes immediately

returned to where they really wanted to be, focused on his friend's jack off activity. "Like I said, I've been so fucking horny all day long."

"Yeah. And the heat."

"Right. Heat always makes you horny."

"Not to mention the grass."

"Yeah. Sure is fucking good grass."

"Umm, sure is. Uh..."

"Yeah?"

"Do you mind if I join you?"

"Course not."

The Stallion tugged at the drawstring around his waist, successfully unknotting it, and maneuvered his cutoff sweats down to his ankles. When he say up and spread his legs apart again, I beheld that wonderful, up-curving nine-incher that I recalled so well making its way down my throat last night. As he repositioned himself on the bench, his cock impatiently twitched upwards, as springy and responsive as a trampoline artist, until he finally gave in to its demands and started stroking it. The two of them fell silent again, each ostensibly lost in his own grass-enhanced jack off session. But from my hiding place beneath the bushes, I could see was that they were each sneaking as many glances at each other's activity as they thought they could get away with. "Aw, man," Blondie said, breaking the silence, "I got such a fucking load to shoot, if Lefty ever shows up, it'll take him a dozen swallows to get it all down his throat."

"Umm," The Stallion concurred.

And then after a few more cockstrokes it was his turn to break the silence with a "Hmh," clearly aimed at attracting Blondie's attention. "Hmh, what?"

"I was just thinking, like, how many times I've jacked myself off. Like maybe hundred of times..." "

Probably thousands."

"Yeah, probably thousands, and not always alone, you know?"

"Yeah," said Blondie with a knowing smirk.

"And yet I've never touched another guy's dick in my entire life."

Blondie's fist came to a stop. "So?"

"So nothing."

"Oh," Blondie said as he resumed his cockstroking. "Just seems funny, doesn't it?"

"Yeah. Guess so."

"Maybe it's the grass makes me think of something weird like that." "Yeah... though, if you wanted to touch mine...just so's you'll know what it's like..." Their fists suddenly froze in mid-stroke like they'd become glued to their cocks. Blondie closed his eyes and tilted his head back, his body tense

with anticipation. Then he slid his fist down to the base of his cock holding it straight upwards in a most accessible position. The

Stallion slowly reached over with his right hand, replacing his own cockgrasp with his left and wrapped his fist around Blondie's cockshaft. Blondie's cock was long enough that even with his own hand still wrapped around it at the base, there was enough for The Stallion to clutch without touching either his friend's hand or his cockhead. "Ahh," went Blondie as he untensed, slowly removing his hand from his dick, resting his arm along the back of the bench again. He slumped down a little more while spreading his legs father apart. All during this, the Stallion watched his friend's face, intent on gauging the effect of what he was doing, and the extent of the permission granted him, as he began to stroke his friend's cock with long, slow strokes. Blondie let his head fall all the way back, and began issuing one slow, low-pitched "ahhh!" after another. The Stallion lowered his gaze to his friend's cock, staring at it transfixed. After several minutes of cockstroking, Blondie's ah's took on a staccato urgency until it was clear he was close to coming. But instead of shooting his wad, he leaned his head forward again and opened his eyes. "Fuck! I sure hope Lefty's shows up now! You've got me so horny, I can practically feel my cum shooting down his throat just thinking about it." The Stallion looked into his friend's face again, ceasing his cockstrokes but keeping his fist wrapped around Blondie's dick. "You ever wonder what it's like?" he asked.

"What what's like?"

"Putting your mouth on someone's cock."

Blondie let out a silent, nervous laugh.

This shut The Stallion up for a second.

"I was just wondering, that's all," he finally added.

After another pause, Blondie asked, "Why? Would you ever suck someone's cock?"

"Would you?"

"I asked first."

Silence.

"Well?"

"I'm ... thinking about it."

As The Stallion continued to think, he finally released Blondie's cock and studied it. Was Blondie's cock twitching involuntarily, or was it a deliberate attempt to lure his friend into action? Whichever the case, Blondie clearly understood

where things might go and helped them along the way by standing up and making a quarter-turn to his left, facing his friend. But The Stallion just continued to stare at Blondie's crotch. Ah, such a huge, heavy-hanging cock, a

king among cocks, with a luxuriant mane of blond pubic hair. And yet a slave to the force of gravity. Even when it twitched, which it did repeatedly now, it never rose above a ninety-degree angle to his firm, flat abdomen. "Go ahead," Blondie coaxed. "Fuck, you've already touched it, which is probably what got you to thinking about putting it in your mouth."

"Hmm."

"And it's not like anyone's here to see you.

If they only know!

"That's true."

"I mean, if you're that curious it's probably not good to keep it all bottled up inside. Besides, it's cool with me." The Stallion leaned forward, resting his forearms on his knees, staring at Blondie's ever-twitching cock. Blondie put his right hand on the back of the Stallion's head to coax it towards his dick. "And I'd never tell anyone. You know me."

Well, that broke the mood. The Stallion shook his friend's hand off the back of his head and stood up, facing him. Ah a double silhouette, their two cocks so close to touching and so opposite in direction; one hanging down, the other pointing up. "Yeah, I know you. So suck on mine first."

"What!"

"That way we'll be even. You tell on me; I'll tell on you." "Yeah, but..."

"But what?"

"You're the one who's so curious about it."

"And you're the one – if you really want to get down to it – who started all that trouble in the locker room in the first place, no matter how much you mouth off about Coach Douglas this and Coach Douglas that. Boy, if I only told the other guys how..."

"Okay, okay."

Blondie got down on his knees, took The Stallion's now half-hard cock in his hand to inspect it first as it quickly rose again to full erection. I recalled the wonder details I had observed the previous night when Blondie had pushed me off his cock and ordered me to suck his friend off. But I had stared in admiration; Blondie was staring an attempt to procrastinate. "This is fucking blackmail, you know."

"Yeah. Like you're above such things."

"Okay, but let me warn you. You tell anyone about this and I'll knock your fucking head off."

"It'll be our little secret."

Not!

Blondie opened his mouth and wrapped his lips around The Stallion's cockhead. "Good. Now go down on it."

Blondie consumed another inch of his friend.

"Yeah. More," he ordered, putting his hands on the sides of Blondie's head and pulling him onto his cock. Blondie gagged, but made no effort to withdraw. The Stallion coaxed his head up and down.

"Yeah, that's it."

He let go of Blondie's head. Blondie compliantly continued to suck on the first five or so inches of The Stallion's fat, upstanding dick. The Stallion stood there, his sweats down around his ankles, leaning forward at the hips. His eyes were tightly closed now, and his mouth hung open in a long, silent "aah" as he slowly shook his head back and forth in response to the presumably unpremeditated pleasure his friend Blondie was giving him. I'll tell you something. This kid Blondie might be a major prick, and not really into cocksucking, but he sure gave his all to taking care of his best friend. I'd expected no more than two or three token suck strokes. To my surprise, though, not only did he continue sucking his best friend off, but he got so far into it as to take his own dick in his hand and stroke it. The Stallion finally put his hands back on Blondie's head and pulled him off his cock. "What's the matter?"

"I'm going to come if you do that any more."

"Good. So start sucking me off," Blondie ordered, getting up off his knees and placing his hands on his hips, once more assuming his accustomed dominant role in their relationship, his long, heavy cock quivering in front of him like a diviner's rod. The Stallion wasted no time getting down on his knees. Clutching his own dick, he was about to take Blondie's into his mouth, when Blondie grabbed his cock and pulled it up, hoisting his two big balls into unobstructed view just inches from The Stallion's mouth. "Lick my balls!" he brutally commanded.

Astonished, The Stallion looked up at him.

"I said lick 'em!"

Far from objecting to his friend's one-uppance ploy, The Stallion went into a frenzy of self-stroking as he opened his mouth, stuck out his tongue as far as it would go, and eagerly began lapping Blondie's balls. "Yeah. That's it. Lick 'em nice and good. Now take them in your mouth. Um-hmh. Now the other one. Sure you can get them both in, if you really wanted to. Yeah, I thought so. That's it, give 'em a good tug. Um, feels real good. If Lefty shows up..."

The perfect cue for my entrance, but for the someteenth time that evening, I decided to hold off. Things were going too well without me. "...maybe I'll let him lick yours so you'll know what it's like. Keep that tongue moving. Yeah. Good boy." Blondie stroked The Stallion's mane of abundant hair like you would an agreeable pet, saying over and over again, "Yeah. Good boy, good boy."

Suddenly, he pulled his balls out of The Stallion's mouth. The Stallion looked up at him wide-eyed and open-mouthed. But only for a second

before he faced the ground and began dry-coughing and spitting. "What's the matter?" the Stallion asked, truly alarmed.

"Fucking hair all over your balls."

Once he was assured his friend was okay, Blondie went back into character. "So what do you want me to do? Fucking shave them for you?" A smile came over my face as I recalled Coach Douglas at the Mineshaft once saying to somebody, "I shave my balls once a week – whether they need it or not."

"Anyhow," Blondie continued, "you want to know what it's like to suck on some guy's cock, huh?" The Stallion nodded eagerly like an obedient puppy dog.

Blondie took the heavy log that was his cock and rubbed it against The Stallion's left cheek. Then the right. Next he started slapping him with it, several slaps on one cheek, several on the other, going back and forth. The Stallion just closed his eyes and submitted. "Now, open your mouth. Wide!"

He pressed his cock against The Stallion's outstretched tongue. "Okay. Now you can suck on it."

The Stallion enthusiastically went down on his friend with an eagerness that betrayed his intense interest in cocksucking. Maybe a little bit too eagerly, since he immediately started to gag. Not that it stopped him. No, he just went at it with an abandonment that surprised me in one so young, all the time vigorously stroking his own dick. As I watched, I wondered what it felt like to suck cock for the first time – assuming it actually was The Stallion's first time. It had been so long ago for me that, although I can still remember the time, place and person, now, so many years and encounters later, I can no longer recall the impressions of that first occasion. In no time they were going at it lost in a sweaty frenzy, captive to their own oncoming orgasms as they rushed towards ejaculation. If there ever was a time for me to jump out of hiding and have my way with them, this was it. But I just lay there on my side, stroking my own cock and watching their fine performance. Besides, there was always tomorrow night. By now Blondie was going "Ah! Ah!" in a choked, tortured voice. He raised his hands to his chest and started rubbing it slowly up and down while The Stallion reached up with his free hand and grabbed his friend's balls. "Ah, shit!" Blondie exclaimed to his friend's unexpected grasp, encouraging The Stallion to give his balls a good, hearty yank, which he responded to with a violent jerk that coursed throughout his upper body. "I'm gonna come!"

The Stallion accelerated his cocksucking as he held onto Blondie's balls, pulling on them with all the effort he could manage. After another dozen or so suck strokes Blondie grabbed The Stallion on either side of his head and held him in place as he took control over his orgasm, shoving his cock in and out of The Stallion's mouth with long, violent strokes. Finally, with one loud "Ahh!" he thrust his cock deep down into The Stallion's throat. The Stallion

gagged, emitting a muffled, cum-stifled sound while swallowing the sudden spurt of his friend's cum as best he could. But Blondie needed more than one cock thrust to work out all his cum. Still holding The Stallion's head so he couldn't move, he repeatedly rammed his dick down his friend's throat. The Stallion, for his part, rode his friend's orgasm-driven dick like a bronco buster at a rodeo. Finally, Blondie came to rest. But instead of withdrawing his dick, he left it The Stallion's mouth, burying his friend's nose in his pubic hair. It was now The Stallion's turn to come, which he did in a frenzy of cockstroking, as if inspired by the sensations of Blondie's fat cock softening in his mouth and the tickle of pubic hair against his nose. In no time his cum spurted out all over the pavement between his friend's legs. His body shook, his balls bounced out of control, and his cock spewed jism like he had an endless supply. Yet he made no attempt to dismount his friend. He, too, finally came to rest, and Blondie carefully withdrew his cock until it plopped down heavily in front of him. The Stallion gave it one final admiring look and then stood up, holding his softening cock in his hand, a final drop of cum stringing down from its tip until it fell free to the ground. "Whew!" Blondie said, tossing the hair off his sweat-soaked forehead. He bent over to pull up his cutoffs.

"Fuck! You got cum all over the inside of my shorts!" "Tough shit. If I can take your cum down my throat, you can deal with mine sticking to you fucking balls," he said pulling up his sweats.

"I didn't really mean to cum in your mouth."

"Like hell you didn't, you asshole."

"You sure didn't seem to fucking mind."

"That's just because I didn't want to ruin it for you." "Yeah, yeah, yeah."

By now they had their shorts in place and sat down again, no longer open-crotched and randy, but leaning forward, forearms resting on their thighs. After a pensive pause, Blondie asked apprehensively, "Does this mean you're....?"

"Yeah, I guess so."

"What do you mean, you guess so."

"Just lay off, okay?"

After a pause.

"Besides, you had your mouth on my cock, too."

"But that was just because you threatened me, and because I was stoned out of my mind. I didn't really enjoy it." After another pause, The Stallion said, "I did. A lot." "That's cool."

"It is?"

"Yeah."

But you could hear in his voice that he still needed to work it out. "Well, good. Just don't think I'm gonna go down on you every time you get to feeling horny.

"Yeah. "

"And, uh, let's just keep this between us. You know, what I said about being...you know."

"Sure."

"I'm not ready to tell the whole fucking world, yet." "Okay."

They lapsed into silence, looking forward, each lost in his own thoughts. "Shit," Blondie finally said, rising and looking down the path, "I thought for sure he'd come."

"Maybe we scared him off last night."

"Nah. He was really into it."

"Maybe he couldn't."

"Umm."

"Maybe he'll be here tomorrow night."

"Yeah, maybe. I sure wouldn't mind sneaking out of the house again to find out. C'mon, let's go."

"Okay," The Stallion said, rising and readjusting his sweats. "And, uh, remember. Tonight is our little secret, okay."

"You got it," Blondie said slapping him on the back as the two of them started down the path. As they disappeared around the bend, the sky in the east was just beginning to blaze with the advent of another scorcher of a day. I stepped out of my hideout, brushed myself free of the dirt and bits of twigs and leaves that stuck to my sweaty body, and walked over to where Blondie and The Stallion had sucked on each other's cocks. The Stallion's cum glistened in a series of precious, milky white pools. I got down on my knees and stuck my left index finger into what appeared to be the largest. I moved it up to my mouth and tasted the salty, gooey substance. Ah, the precious product of an over-sexed adolescent who'd just jacked off a load of cum while holding his best friend's cock in his mouth. Was it really his first time, as he led Blondie to believe? I might never know.

Or maybe I'd learn more about him tomorrow night.

I dipped my index finger into another pool of his cum, this time rubbing it against my piss slit, causing my cock to jerk upwards. I wrapped my left hand around my cock and in no time my own abundant release of cum joined The Stallion's, the mingle of our jism on the pavement seeming to me as blatant as a billboard in advertising what had happened in the darkness and solitude of the night. As I got up, pulled my clothes out of the trash can and put them on, I thought of how any moment now other people would be walking by. Would they notice this dual discharge splattered on all over the pavement? Would curious dogs go sniffing at it, dashing off at their masters' call with a sticky souvenir of last night's activities glued to their wet noses? Well, nothing to be done but to get through this day – another hot one, to be sure – anticipating, and perhaps planning and providing for another nocturnal

encounter with Blondie and The Stallion, the boys who so successfully managed to fill up their time while waiting for Lefty.

JIMMY
Thom Nickels

Jimmy no longer had to run away to New York to smoke dope in photomatic machines. He could knock on my door and be invited inside to listen to the Moody Blues – his favorite – and then casually suggest if we could smoke. Smoke, of course, was a big thing with him, as it was with everyone I knew that year. But I was tiring of it; around Jimmy it made me too romantically aggressive, and I was afraid of "pulling" too strongly, for Jimmy was pulled easily when stoned, having once been a Hare Krishna monk who'd pale at the head monk's instructions to go up to people in the street and force a stick of incense on them.

Our conversation was filled with long gaps of silence that could not be filled. When I was with Jimmy I saw myself with the older men I used to attach myself to. Marvelous conversationalists who could always steer a conversation into new areas of talk. With Jimmy, I got a chance to steer, one night actually digging into an old folder of manuscripts I had and pulling out some pages entitled "My Religious Autobiography." Jimmy offered to read them, and in his stoned condition, the stories, though written as serious tracts, sounded quite ridiculous.

The silent gaps came and went. Pretty soon Jimmy was adept at steering things himself. He would suggest walks, and during those autumn days it was nice to walk through Cambridge, going by the old stores and buying pipe tobacco and then going into cafeterias and sitting down and looking out the glass windows. Jimmy, his blond hair and pale skin and army boots laced up over his ankles, smoking, not saying a word, but suggesting maybe, a walk over to a frat house...

"...A frat house!" I'd say.

Yes, a frat house, where he wanted to play Chopin on a piano there, which he did, not a soul in the lobby of the house, it being the Thanksgiving holiday. Watching him play, he told me of the times he'd come here as a tot and sit on the same piano stool to play for frat members. "Every Saturday," he said, and I thought it sounded rather sad, because it was as though Jimmy had used these practice sessions as an escape hatch leading out of the alcoholic "control realm" of his father.

Jimmy was standing alone in Harvard Square the night I met him. He was on the subway island, staring into traffic. I had seen him before, namely on the porch of our little apartment building, reading a book by Alan Watts and looking very depressed. It had been a strain for him to say hello to me when I greeted him. He had his army boots on, and he had a severe case of acne – something which I sympathized with, since, having been the syringe

and gauze victim of dermatologists myself, I knew how bulbous acne could force one into a sluggish depression.

Acne victims learn to rise above their skin, however, as did Jimmy the night I went up to him in Harvard Square and re-introduced myself. He was very glad to see a familiar face, and responded with enthusiasm when I suggested we go back to my apartment and smoke "to ashes" a hashish cube I had.

We smoked in the living room, watching Tihailey, the cat, breath in the smoke and loll on her side.

Afterwards, we sat and talked. The lights were on, but Jimmy was in no hurry to leave. Soon the sound of rattling keys and the peculiar 'thud' of the rear door entrance to the apartment brought Chip into the living room. Chip looked wide-eyed at Jimmy; Jimmy smiled. I introduced them formally, though Chip had seen Jimmy on the porch of the house about the same time I did.

"Glad to see you again," said Chip. "Have you two been smoking?"

I met Chip in a bar one Saturday night. I had gone out, not to cruise, but to sit and be idle and take the evening as it came. Across from me sat a guy in wire-frame glasses, nursing a beer and keeping perfectly still. Every so often his glasses would reflect the ceiling lights, so it was hard to tell whether he was looking at me or engaging in some kind of transcendental meditation. I considered it. It took a few beers to get us to smile at one another, and to hurry Chip along in his decision to come and sit next to me.

"I have a friend who owns an apple orchard," said Chip, his arm around my waist, his pronunciation of 'apple' lingering in my mind because he said it as if pronouncing it in the juice of an apple he had actually swallowed. "Tomorrow I'm going to pick..."

Later, we stumbled into the apartment. It was not neat, by any means, but littered with buckets, pails and S.O.S. pads. Chip turned the kitchen light on. "See there," he said, pointing to a pure white refrigerator and stove. "It took me four hours just to clean them..." The air was heavy was disinfectant. A skinny kitten scampered across the room.

On the days that Jimmy would come to visit, he would leave at 5 p.m. and go down to his own place for dinner. That was when Chip returned home from work, so sometimes they'd meet and have a short talk in the hall. Entering the apartment, Chip would look to see if I had done the little things he'd list in notes he wrote when he got up mornings. Peel three potatoes, three onions, and buy a cucumber. "What did you do today?" Chip would then ask, kissing me on the lips but giving me that old Mother Superior stare that suggested that no matter what I had done, I should have done something else.

"I wrote," I said. "Then I went to the Harvard pool for a swim."

"Wonderful," he said. "Can I read what you wrote?"

I went into my little writing cubicle and brought out a three-page manuscript. It was a half-story about a failed relationship with a woman. I read it to him.

"I didn't understand some of it," Chip said when I had finished.

I looked at the manuscript. "What didn't you understand?"

"I'll tell you while you peel me three more carrots," he said.

One night, out of money, we had horsemeat. Chip had chopped it into inconspicuous cubes and included it in a stew. He waited until I was finished before he said what we had eaten. I gagged. "Will we have horsemeat tomorrow?" I wanted to know. "The leftovers," Chip said, "but I'll make you a batch of cornbread to hide some of the flavor."

After dinner, Jimmy would come back to the apartment, and the three of us would talk.

"Who is Alan Watts?" Chip would say, and Jimmy would explain, going over to the bookshelf and getting his books. "Listen to this..." Jimmy would say. Then he'd start reading aloud.

"I'm going to bed," Chip said finally, stroking Tihailey.

Meanwhile, Jimmy prepared to light another pipe. He mentioned walking to Harvard Square. "Are you coming to bed?" Chip asked, lifting the Native American blanket we had draped over the bedroom doorway. "I don't know," I said, "maybe a walk would do me good. I really feel stoned." Jimmy inhaled and held his breath; his green eyes sparkled, he exhaled as his whole body slouched down in the chair, his corduroy trousers rising above his boot tops and revealing his hairless legs. "Let's sit here awhile." I said.

"Goodnight," said Chip, disappearing behind the blanket.

"EEEErggh! You little bitch!" Out came the cat from behind the blanket, scampering like a pathetic rat to the kitchen where she knew lots of hiding places.

"Jesus!" said Jimmy. "Here Tihailey, here Tihailey..."

I went into the bedroom. The phone rang. Jimmy answered it. "It's for Chip," he said, sticking his head under the blanket. Chip collected himself, unraveled the sheets from around him and made his way to the phone. Tihailey appeared on the edge of the bed, gnawing at the top quilt.

It was Chip's friend, Bob, who had been calling a lot lately and whom Chip mentioned a couple of times in connection with an invitation to dinner. Bob lived on Beacon Hill, was a gourmet cook, and was, as far as I could tell, now officially making the dinner invitation.

"He wants me," Chip would say, "but I'm hedging because I don't know what that would mean..."

"...And you too!" came Chip's voice from the telephone. "What? Do I? Mmmmmmmmm!"

I went into the living room, sat down while Jimmy got up and put on his jacket. I asked him where he was going. He said to the Square where he

hoped a girl he knows would be hanging out. I sounded casual – Oh!" – and watched him from my chair, standing in the center of the room, now on his haunches playing with the cat. I noticed his acne was almost gone. "I might stop back if I don't get back too late," he said. I said that I would probably be up, and asked him one more time if he was sure about leaving. Chip hung up.

"Bob's invited me to dinner tomorrow night. He said to bring my Frank Sinatra record and said we're not gonna be able to see much on account of the candlelight..."

I followed Jimmy to the back door. I waited up for him, watching an old late show movie. Then I went to bed, suppressing a desire to walk to the Square in hopes of finding him. I slept with my back to Chip, who woke earlier than me, and who was gone when I opened my eyes to Tihailey, who rested where Chip had been.

YOUNG WRITER WILL HOUSEKEEP FOR ROOM/RENT.

So ran my ad in the underground press when I realized I'd be out of a job in four months time. The hospital was not renewing my alternative military service contract. A number of reasons were cited for the termination: you go home without checking first with the head nurse, you disappear frequently. I didn't argue. I pictured myself cooking for a small family who'd keep me in their attic room. A very fashionable-sounding lady did call, who, as it turned out, had to check with her husband before she could employ a live-in housekeeper.

"Can you handle a ten-year-old child?" she said, "Volleyball, sidewalk baseball, Frisbee on the lawn?"

I never took the job because Chip invited me to come live with him. Three weeks after our first meeting he was helping me move. We went out and bought burlap curtains, a Japanese paper lantern, lamps, a stereo, records, books, posters of Huey Newton and Walt Whitman. Later, we celebrated the move over dinner in an Italian restaurant, Chip drinking Old Fashioneds.

One night, after a walk through Cambridge, Chip and I made our way up the stairs in the foyer of our apartment building, when Chip spotted a note tucked inside the crack of our door.

What's this?" he said, unfolding it, then quickly handing it to me. "It's for you."

I WAS HERE AT 8 O'CLOCK. I LOOK FOR YOU I MUST SEE YOU – RAUL.

"I read it," said Chip.

"He's a friend of mine. He's from South America and I'm one of his few American friends. I met him just before I met you. "And he's coming back?" Chip asked.

"He's really persistent; he'll be back."

"Have you had sex with Jimmy?" Chip asked me point blank one night, the lasagna thick on his fork and held in mid-air while I prepared to answer.

"Have you?" I asked him, thinking of the time I had left the two of them alone for two days with a cube of hash a friend of mine had given me.

"We got stoned one night and undressed and held each other, but nothing happened," Chip said.

"Well," I said, afraid to recount in detail what I thought were wonderful experiments on the sexual stage, "We did it."

"I don't know what you see in him," Chip said, "he's not even cute, really, and he's not even gay."

"He's not a Rosicrucian, either, Chip!" I said. "Do you think I shouldn't have sex with him?" I asked.

"His parents live right downstairs," Chip said; "he's only seventeen, and you know what kind of a man his father is...we have to live here, remember that!"

Jimmy, stoned again, had put the stereo headphones on and was moving to the secret music. Tihailey hopped about his legs as he caressed and cuddled her to his undershirt. "Chashaw!" The light was fading in the room. Somebody in the building was cooking a roast. Through the burlap curtains a few falling leaves could be seen.

Suddenly, Jimmy took off the headphones. "Wow," he said, turning around, "I got this police radio in the middle of Hendrix, a voice saying '37 Garden Street right away ...burning bush! Wow!" He put the phones back on, lying on his back and taking Tihailey in both hands in the air as far as his arms could reach. He brought her down to his chest, clasped her to his belly and then shot her straight up again, where she hung as loose as a wash and dry exhibit, her gold eyes mesmerized from the smoke and the motion.

"You're going to make her sick," I said.

"Not Tihailey," said Jimmy, raising his voice to a pitch, "not Tihailey!"

Without warning, Tihailey scampered into the kitchen. The headphones fell over Jimmy's face as he sat up. "She bit me," he said, "God!" He got up to scout her out. Tihailey's eyes could be seen under the bureau Chip and I had covered with a cloth to suit the kitchen. She extended one paw out as if to defend herself. Jimmy knelt down and stuck one finger in at her. She leapt at it and ran across the hall and back into the living room. "Geez," Jimmy said, stung into slow motion because of the dope. Tihailey attacked the bookshelves, clinging to a large volume six feet above the ground. She lost her

- 67 -

grip and fell over backwards. She ran into Jimmy's legs as he walked in from the kitchen.

"Now I got you, you little monster!"

"Lock her in the cubicle," I said.

"You want to go into the cubicle, Tihailey?" said Jimmy. "In the cubicle? Ah, not Tihailey..."

Tihailey was limber again, letting Jimmy squeeze and fold her legs up around her abdomen. She open and shut her eyes and purred contentedly as he brought her over to the sofa bed. Stretched out on her back, she let Jimmy perform a massage operation. She rolled over, Jimmy's hands going over the full length of her body.

"Cats are sexy, don't you think?" he said. "Tihailey turns me on. Just look how sleek she is, and the way she moves." "Yeah," I said.

"Hey," he suggested, "do you mind if I play that Schubert symphony that sounds so much like an orgasm?"

"Well, I was going to write a letter this afternoon – um, I guess it's night now – but, well, sure. There's always time for the sound of an orgasm." Jimmy's orgasms were mostly silent, although he had a tendency to move around a lot.

Chip entered through the rear door. The sound of packages and keys, and Chip's familiar exasperating "Ah," brought Tihailey into the kitchen. "Get down!" said Chip, "Oww!"

Jimmy stood mute with the record album, unable to make a decision about playing it.

"Who's out there?" asked Chip. Jimmy went into the kitchen; I followed.

"Want to hear an incredible symphony?" Jimmy asked, "...that'll remind you of an orgasm?"

"No," said Chip, "I already know what an orgasm sounds like."

"Ahh, Chip!" Jimmy said, looking at me. "Shall I play it

anyway and liven you up? Do you want to get stoned?" "Listen to that!" Jimmy said, the record on its merry, uphill

climb to crescendo, "you can almost taste the sweetness!" Chip handed me a note as he brought two cantaloupes to the refrigerator. It was the same handwriting as the other one.

I BE HERE WEDNESDAY AT 8 O'CLOCK PLEASE BE HERE – RAUL.

"I want to meet him," Chip said. "I'll let you two have the apartment to yourselves, but I want to meet him."

Jimmy's mother telephoned Chip and asked if he'd mind driving Jimmy to the airport. Chip said that he didn't mind at all, that Jimmy had said

something similar to that awhile back. On Wednesday morning, Jimmy appeared at the apartment with two duffle bags; dressed in army greens, he looked a little ridiculous after two weeks of lounging around in dungarees and talking revolution, pot, Alan Watts and Hari Krishna. His acne had acted up again, and he had the same sleepy-eyed look as when Chip and I first met him.

"Let me see you, turn around," said Chip.

"If you get a knock on your door late one night, it's me running away," Jimmy said, taking the coffee I handed him. "Or I'll go to New York again..."

"Don't you dare go AWOL!" Chip said. "Think of the trouble you'd be in."

We piled into Chip's yellow MG, barely making it with the duffle bags. The ride was tight; I was crushed against the door, with my arm around Jimmy. We passed the cafeterias and the tobacco stores of Harvard Square. Chip sped over the Charles River.

"I'll tell them I'm a Communist before I'll go to Vietnam," Jimmy said.

"Shut up and enjoy the ride," Chip said.

The three of us stood in line at the ticket counter. Jimmy straightened his hat and bent over to pick up his bags. The khaki uniform hid the shape of his body.

We headed for the runway. A group of soldiers clowned and shoved their way towards us.

"I'll go on alone now," he said, "Luxury Vietnam Airlines is down this way."

Jimmy shook our hands, and we let him go.

Chip was dressed and ready to leave for another shopping spree when there was a small knock on our door.

"That's him," I said.

"Get it," said Chip, "he's your friend."

I opened the door. "Hi, Raul," I said, and Raul laughed, following me into the kitchen, carrying a paper bag filled with fruit no doubt, for that was his habit, always bringing bananas and oranges. "This is Chip," I said, pointing to a silent figure in the corner of the room laden down in mustache wax and one of my heavy sweaters.

"Hello," said Chip, obviously impressed with Raul's handsomeness. "I've heard a lot about you."

Raul laughed. He was wearing too much cologne, as usual, but that was part of his charm.

"Well," said Chip, "I have some errands to do, so I'll leave you two.... This is Tihailey," he added. The cat managed a polite meow. "She's a bitch most of the time," he said.

When Chip had left, Raul said, "You live with him, huh? He's nice." I shook my head, beckoning him to the living room.

"Do you want to listen to some music?" I asked.

"What kind of music?" said Raul. I thought of the Schubert symphony, but said I didn't know as I sat on the edge of the sofa bed. Raul opened the paper bag and took out three long bananas.

"You want some bananas?" he asked. I peeled one and ate it, forgetting to thank him. "I bring you fruit all the time ...you don wan fruit anymore?"

I apologized. "Do you want to smoke grass, Raul?" I said. "I never smoke grass before – maybe," he said.

We passed the square pipe back and forth, Raul going through the novice's coughs and chokes. "No more," he said. I extinguished the pipe.

Raul stood up, pretended to yawn, bringing both hands to his shoulders where he started to caress himself. I went over to him. We embraced, Raul leading me backwards in the direction of the bedroom.

"You don wan to make love?" Raul said, lying naked on the bed. He was nestled against the pillows, swaying his right leg so that it constantly nudged his more than adequate hard-on. Without a doubt, he was the most spectacular boy I had ever called a boyfriend.

"I want to, Raul, but for some reason..." Raul gazed at me. I made an attempt to straddle him, then lay on top of him before rolling off. "Here," I said, getting an idea. I put a towel on my head, tying it under my chin. I mimicked a Spanish mama. In Spanish I cried for my white house and my los ninos. Then I was an Arab chieftain, with the towel bandaged across my forehead. "El burro y los ninos es mucho bonito en El Camino Real." Raul howled.

I put the towel on him. "Muy bonita, muy bonita," I cried.

Raul discovered Chip's boy magazines under the bed. We flipped through them, one by one. Raul admired certain boys. "Look at him!" he'd say, holding aloft photographs of skinny black Irish kids, ten inch phalluses in-hand. With others, he was scornful. "I would never do that!" he'd say, referring to an Iowa boy who chose to pose nude while stepping out of his milk delivery truck.

The phone rang. It was Chip. "Has he left yet?" came the hopeful voice.

"No," I said.

"I'll call again in half an hour," said Chip.

"What's this?" said Raul after a long silence, picking up a white envelope that had toppled down from a shelf above the bed. He opened it, as I suggested, then quickly flung it aside.

"It's hair!" I said, reopening the envelope, taking out the thick tufts of white hair that magically stuck together. "It goes like this ..." and I proceeded

to show him the style of the Hari Krishna pony tail. He was horrified. Then I chanted the Krishna chant.

"Whose hair?" he asked.

"A friend's," I said.

"Put it away."

"Does it really scare you?" Tihailey jumped on the bed and began sniffing Raul's underarms.

"I'm allergic!" he said in perfect English, sitting up and holding Tihailey at arm's length. Tihailey got down and went to the sofa bed. I fingered the discarded underpants among the blankets and magazines.

"What time will Chip come?" asked Raul.

"In a half hour, maybe more," I said, pacing myself with Raul's movements towards our pile of clothes.

"Look," he said, "I can see you live with Chip, and so now I think I will not come again for a long time, maybe never..." I flinched; I was not expecting this.

PACO
Peter Z. Pan

I'll never forget the first time I made love to another boy. I lived in an old apartment building in Little Havana, Miami's version of Spanish Harlem. The boy's name was Paco and he lived next door. Paco was beautiful: if you took the best features of all the boys in Menudo and put them together to create one perfect Latino hunk, that would be Paco.

He lived with his divorced mother, who was always busy either waiting tables at Los Cubanitos Restaurant, or on her back with her many boyfriends. Unfortunately, like many inner city youths, Paco was neglected and always getting into trouble with the law – perhaps to attain his mother's attention. He had just been released on probation when our "relationship" began.

My mother and father didn't get home from work until six o'clock. Since I got home from school at three, I had the house all to myself for three hours every afternoon. I usually did my homework or watched reruns of "Leave It To Beaver" and "Dennis The Menace." Once in a while I would go into my old man's underwear drawer and look through his collection of dirty magazines. He had all of them: Playboy, Penthouse, Hustler. My favorite was Hustler because it had pictures not only of naked women, but of naked men having sex with them.

I was quite confused by my attraction to nude men. Every time I saw one, I would feel warm all over and pop a boner. Kind of the same feeling I got every time I saw Paco.

I was in the process of whacking the of boner with the Hustler in front of me, when I heard a loud knock on the front door. I jumped to my feet and pulled my shorts up. The horrid thought of my mother coming home from work early and walking in on me just as I was about to shoot my wad crossed my mind, sending a cold chill down my spine. I quickly shoved the magazine back in the drawer, then ran to the door. After taking a deep breath – and looking down to check if the bulge in my shorts had gone – I opened it.

There stood Paco in nothing but shorts and a smile, holding a ripped towel and a bar of soap. What a sight for my horny young eyes: he had a gymnast's build and was as tanned as they come, with long black curls and big brown eyes.

"E'cuse me, man," he said in his broken English. 'They caught our wator and I estink. Can I juice your chower?"

I thought for a moment I had died and gone to heaven. This gorgeous specimen of a Cuban male – who always ignored me since I was two years younger and therefore of no consequence – was standing there half naked and asking to "juice my chower." The word "yes" escaped my mouth so fast and

so loudly that it brought an amused smile to Paco's face. God, it was so embarrassing!

When he walked into the apartment, I noticed he did "estink," for he had been playing basketball in the schoolyard all afternoon.

"Come this way," I said as I led him to the bathroom; trying my damndest not to let on that I was melting inside. "Are jew alone?" he asked.

"Yeah, my mom and dad are working."

"I never see jew at da eschooljard. What jew do all alone here all afternoon?" he asked with a mischievous grin.

"Nothing!" I blurted out. Again I felt embarrassed and wondered if he had a peephole in the wall between our apartments or what!

Suddenly he grabbed my right hand began feeling my palm. The impish grin again appeared on his face as he said, "Man, jew need a chave." With that, Paco laughed hysterically.

I didn't know whether to laugh or cry. So instead, I blushed like a Catholic schoolgirl caught masturbating.

"It's okay, man," Paco said, holding his palm to my face. "I need a chave too." He winked at me, then walked into the bathroom.

Even though he'd put me at ease by saying that, I was quite perplexed. Was I crazy or was this macho stud really coming on to me? I decided to play it safe and not push it. So when he left the door wide open and began pulling down his shorts --instead of just standing there, blatantly ogling his delicious buck-naked body like I really wanted to – I turned away, telling him to call me if he needed anything.

I went into the living room and tried to concentrate on Tony.

Dow as Wally and Jerry Mathers as The Beaver. But when I heard the water running, it took every ounce of will power I possessed to keep me from sneaking a peek into the bathroom. And then, just as Eddie Haskle was about to say something obnoxious to Mrs. Cleaver, it happened.

"Hey man, com'ere please!" Paco bellowed.

Fuck Wally! My heart skipped a beat as I jumped to my feet and ran to the bathroom.

The shower curtain was closed, so I asked him what he wanted. With a quick jerk he opened the curtain, and there stood Paco in all his teenage glory. Jesus Fuckin' Christ, what a piece of meat that boy had between his legs! I mean, he made the guys in Hustler look like three-year-olds. He was all lathered up too – water bouncing off his broad shoulders, then trickling down his hard torso, firm buttocks, and hot loins. As hard as I tried, I couldn't keep my wandering eyes off his Cuban longaniza. And it was pretty obvious, too.

"Man, jew got any Champoo?"

Speechless, I reached in the cupboard, giving him a bottle of Prell.

"Gracias, man," he said as he poured some in his hand. He then began to lather up his hair.

"Joey," I said. "My name is Joey." By that point, my eyes were glued to his cock.

"Gracias, Yoey."

I looked up and met his eyes. They seemed to be studying me. I immediately thought he was going to beat the shit out of me for being a queer. But then, to my surprise, he asked:

"Yoey, jew like?"

My head nodded instinctively before I could stop it.

"Jew can touch it if jew want, man," said Paco. "It no bite." Again instinctively, my hand reached over and took hold of his enormous meat.

"Jeah, Yoey, that's it. Yerk me off, man."

Since I always did what I was told, I jerked him off. I didn't think it was possible for it to get any bigger, yet his eight inches quickly erected itself to ten glorious inches of Latino cock. Just as I was getting into it, he pushed me away and went under the shower.

"Did I do something wrong?"

He laughed and then said, while the water washed away the lather from his body, "I don't want jew to get soap in jour mouse when jew eat my pinga, man."

Before I could figure out what "pinga" meant (okay, I was a slow W.A.S.P.), he had turned off the water and grabbed me by the hair, forcing me down on my knees.

"Chupame la pinga, maricon!" he stated with authority. Still holding me by the hair, he then shoved his pinga in my mouth.

I choked on it at first, gasping for air. But after a while, instinct again took over and I was able to take it all down my virgin throat. He grabbed my head with both hands and we developed a steady rhythm as he fucked my mouth.

"Si, papi, si! Chupame la pinga!" he kept grunting.

After several minutes of oral delight, he pulled me up and kissed me full on the lips. He thrust his hungry tongue in my mouth like a ravished beast, tasting everything my young mouth had to offer. Then he looked me in the eye and said something I'll never forget as long as I live: "I want to fuck jour boy-pussy!"

Paco pushed me down on the bathroom floor, face down, and climbed on top of me. I was frightened, yet at the same time titillated, filled with ecstasy. He ripped my shorts off with one tug, doing the same to my T-shirt. I then felt something probing my ass. When I looked over my shoulder, I saw it was his index finger.

"Nice y tight, yust the way I likey it," he said while he finger-fucked me, with that familiar grin chock-full of mischief. "Get ready, baby, 'cause here come Paco's pinga!"

Paco dribbled spit into my asshole, then penetrated me with one hard thrust. Excruciating pain was an understatement: it hurt like a motherfucker! I screamed as tears ran down my face. I tried to get away from him, but he held me down like a cheap whore while he fucked me hard.

"Jew no go nowhere, bitch! Not till Paco shoots his hot cum up jour acehole!"

After a few minutes, the pain turned to pleasure, the screams turned to moans – his throbbing joystick began to feel good up my tight, little ass.

"Harder, Paco!" I grunted. "Fuck my ass!"

The Cuban buck's rhythm increased as he rammed his meat in and out of me. "...Jeah! Jeah! JEAH!" he groaned, shooting his cum up my ass.

I thought it was going to be wham-bam-thank-you-gringo and he was going to take off; however, he surprised me by turning me over and sucking my cock until I came in his mouth. And he swallowed! Then he snuggled up next to me on the file floor and tenderly kissed me.

"I love jew, Yoey," he whispered.

I loved him too, and we were lovers for over three months – until he got a knife plunged into his heart in a gang fight. In a way, that knife also pierced my heart.

A DANGEROUS BOY
Terry Cross

It seems to me that some gays are born and some are made, and yours truly falls firmly in the first category. My first sexual memory is from age seven, when I was trying to butt-fuck a friend in a little cave we had dug. I wasn't doing boners in those days and remember trying to push my dick up his tail with my finger. At eight I had discovered the thrills of tickling my wiener in a fast-moving current of water, though nothing much happened. About the same time I developed a crush on a neighbor boy, and at nine I began to discover the thrills of enemas. The image is still clear fifty years later: the enemas were done with a garden hose in a friend's doghouse set under some beautiful crepe myrtles.

At ten, I took it into my head to take it in my head and started blowing a hot and handy nine-year-old who could already deliver a watery load. By the time I reached thirteen there were three notches in my belt, so to speak, with the addition of a couple of fellow 7th-graders to my tally. One was in the Safety Patrol and the other was a neighborhood bad boy with flaming red hair. I was also smooching with another classmate ("practicing for girls") but since nothing further happened it didn't count.

Once I entered the 8th grade, things began to happen quickly. Especially I remember Pat, a lanky classmate with a great shock of warm brown hair who was a wonderful friend. He was a rock hound with a remarkable collection for someone so young. And he loved playing cards; many an afternoon we spent on his porch playing canasta which was all the rage at the time. Then one night we were walking somewhere and the moment of truth arrived when we decided to suck one another. Pat did it to me first, then I tried him but failed. His big hooded dick was just too cheesy for me. I really, really wanted to suck Pat and assured him that I would deliver once he had solved his personal hygiene problem. It turned out that Pat's long uncut dick would just fit in a milk bottle – the glass kind with an inch and a half cardboard cap – so we'd fill up a milk bottle with water ("for something to drink") and take off for the patch of woods behind my house for fun and games. After a bit of wash-up using the milk bottle, I was down on Pat like hell wouldn't have it. There's just something about an 8-inch cock on a junior high student who was into delivering big loads....

We started off by swapping blowjobs, but soon Pat suggested 69. This had never occurred to me and I thought it downright perverted, but after trying it soon saw the light. That year of sex with Pat ended when he moved away. I was crushed, but was soon looking for a replacement.

About this time I discovered sailors as sex objects. Norfolk, Virginia, where I grew up, had plenty. One night my brother and I plus a friend of his

went to a movie at the Colley, a neighborhood theater about four miles from home. By the time we got out the busses had stopped running so we decided to hoof it. While walking along Granby Street, the main drag leading to our neighborhood, I noticed a young sailor walking sort of aimlessly. So I fell behind my two companions and soon they were out of sight on the other side of the bridge over the Elizabeth River. This bridge had a platform underneath for fishermen that was reached by a flight of stairs and soon I was following the sailor down them.

He was not much bigger than I, though a few years older. We started making small talk – he was about as green at pickups as I was. He was at loose ends, he said, because his wife had left him and taken his car with her. Once we had decided that I was going to blow him, I remember asking if it would take him long to cum (ah, the fear of getting caught). He replied that he'd never done it before and didn't know. So down came the flap of his thirteen-button blues and down I went to drain the load from his cut 6-incher. That kept me happy for days! He didn't reciprocate, but after years of blowing boys with no return action it was what I expected. In my mind, this event seems to mark the time I had completed "The Discoverie of Cocksucking," to paraphrase the title of Reginald Scot's 1584 book The Discoverie of Witchcraft.

When I moved to Boston in the mid-'50s, fresh out of college, I really slutted it up for a number of years. Given my background of living in small Southern cities, moving to Boston was an eye-opener. I guess you could say I was like freshly-opened champagne, fizzing all over everyone!

I first moved into a little flat atop Beacon Hill. Every night I'd be out prowling the streets until after midnight, except on weekends when it was usually dawn before I called it quits. "Free love" was my game. That is, there was never any charge for my favors and the one time someone offered me money I actually turned it down. Small-town virtue rears its useless head.

In addition to the expected parade of servicemen of all branches, I indulged in a wide variety of civilians, often picked up at the Greyhound or Trailways bus depots. After a few weeks I began to develop a certain amount of carriage trade – people who came over on their own, occasionally with their own tricks in tow. One of the latter was a fourteen-year-old with a really big uncut dick. His name was Alan and he was from a good Catholic family. His parents had discovered his gayness and thrown him out of the house. Fortunately, an older gay had taken him in and, as I understood it, they had a loving though "open" relationship. Because of this relationship, Alan and I had sex only once in that period. Swinging on his big dick was glorious! Thereafter I saw him around town, especially on Queen's Row, the section of the Public Garden that fronted Beacon Street.

While doing time in the Army, I lost track of many people, but I did run into Alan a few years later when he was settled in a good job. At this point I was living on Boston's waterfront and he knew one of my neighbors who

was something of a fag-hag (as we called them in those politically-incorrect days).

Alan's dick hadn't grown in the intervening years, so what had been spectacular on a fourteen-year-old was generous but truthfully unremarkable on someone twenty-one, about six or seven inches. We had one trip to the "workbench." His cock was a bit cheesy so I had it in mind to take it up the ass but Alan would have none of it – he didn't want to "do that." So I made do, but didn't encourage any rematches.

At that point I shared my apartment with someone I had met when I first arrived in Boston. We weren't lovers, more like sisters, though I do remember one morning when we were both horny and Johnny decided he had to have his dick up my tail.

He was really getting into it when the phone in the bed's headboard rang. It was his mother and he proceeded to have a conversation, all the while continuing to fuck me furiously.

One day, Johnny brought home a cute little sixteen-year-old, or at least that's how old he said he was. Where Johnny found him heaven only knows, though it was most likely at the Trailways. The kid said he was on the lam from the youth services people in Maine, having run away from a foster home. His older brother, about twenty-one, was due to join him in a few days and they were heading to western Massachusetts. They were of French-Canadian extraction.

We soon discovered this sixteen-year-old was sexually adventurous though not widely experienced. He was all for getting fucked and wanted my eight inches up his butt, so we worked on it for about three hours. It was like fucking a vise, with long periods of just letting it "soak" while his asshole tried to get used to my big cock. It was mentally stimulating but something of a physical trial. How I kept hard for so long is still a mystery, but perhaps his desire, coupled with his slender, hairless body and bubble butt explains it.

A day or two later our house guest, who was uncut and not well-hung, screwed Johnny. "It was like being fucked with a ball-point pen" was my roommate's verdict.

Having "chicken" around the house made me nervous, to understate the matter, so I was quite happy when the older brother showed up and I was able to drive them to their destination.

Some of my nervousness might have been attributed to what had happened about a year before that. While I was attending Army summer camp, I became involved with another "dangerous boy." A good friend met someone named Bill he thought I'd like, since he was a motorcycle fan and I had one (a big black Ariel Square Four that I gave myself for my twenty-first birthday). Bill and I met and I liked him well enough. Bisexuality was the name of his game; he'd screw anything that walked. In addition to having a wife and two

kids he had also managed to knock up some other girl, plus he and I were fooling around.

One night he invited me to his apartment for dinner with his family and his younger brother, seventeen, came by to watch television. The brother, Little Chief, as I came to call him, was simply adorable. Later Bill told me that Little Chief had fooled around with one other gay guy before, so I importuned Bill to make me a date with his little brother, which he did. Little Chief and I got on swimmingly and soon I had thrown Bill over for him. LC was slender but muscular, with open good looks, and had what we called a "parlor-sized"' dick – about six uncut inches. He liked to get blown but also let me fuck his cute little ass a couple of times.

He liked women too, and when I got back from a stint of Army active duty, courtesy of President Kennedy, I found him married and reproducing. We still fooled around a bit, but it was pretty awkward and I didn't think I would ever see him again. Imagine my surprise when some months later he called looking for a place to live – he had left his wife. So he moved in with me and we were together for several months.

We parted company over the fact that he was screwing a girl in my bed when I was away and I didn't cotton to the stains this activity left. He later remarried and then the cycle repeated again and we were living together once more, though by this time the sexual part of our relationship was pretty well over. I like to say that he lived with me "between wives." Little Chief was – and is – one of the nicest, "basically straight" guys I've ever known.

SILENT CONSENT
Adam Starchild

Ed liked his job at the gas station, and since it was a typical neighborhood of ranch houses, convenience stores, and low crime, being the only attendant from six until midnight never really worried him. Although the station full mechanical services during the day, during Ed's shift only gas was sold, so his duties were minimal. About the biggest problem he had were a couple of customers driving off from the self-service pumps without paying, but after that he had convinced the boss to start a pay-in-advance policy after dark.

Even when there was a series of gas station robberies in a nearby city Ed gave it little thought. It seemed to him that the crime problems of the big city meant little more than a passing news story on television. The police said they had evidence linking a number of the robberies, but that others were unrelated. Nothing the news media developed in interviewing victims gave any clue as to what the common link was.

Apparently the robbers eventually ran out of inner-city gas stations to hit, because they hit a few suburban stations on the other side of town. Ed had not even heard of these robberies, although he probably wouldn't have thought much about it if he had.

So the police could see into the station while he was working, Ed had been told to turn the lights off as he was going out the door. The night he forgot something and stepped back inside for a minute without turning the light back on was the same night that he hadn't spotted a car that had parked quietly amongst the cars left overnight alongside the station for service in the morning. The two men were inside the station just moments behind Ed. While it was impossible to see in from the street, there was enough light that Ed had no problem seeing the guns. The guns were about all that he could see. His mind wouldn't function and he was like a robot as he handed over the pouch that he was to drop in the bank's night depository on his way home.

The men ordered him to walk into the mechanic's section of the garage, saying he wasn't to worry – they weren't going to hurt him, just tie him up so he couldn't call the police right away. At the back of the garage one of them started to raise the lift, which didn't have a car on it at the time. They told Ed to lie down on the floor. The spot that they indicated, Ed realized was under the lift and he was terrified they were going to crush him. He started to scream. One of the robbers slapped Ed across the face and told him to cooperate or he would be hurt. "All we're gonna do is use the lift to pin you down to the floor, stupid," he growled.

They brought the lift slowly down until one of the metal arms was across his back just above the waist line. It was pressed down firmly enough

that it hurt, and he couldn't move, but there weren't any permanent injuries and no ribs were broken. Once Ed was firmly anchored, one of the robbers pulled Ed's wallet out of his pocket, and read Ed's name and address out loud. He then laid the wallet on the floor where Ed could see it, and said, "Look, kid, we haven't touched your money, but we know who you are and where you live in case you give us any trouble later."

The robber then said to his accomplice, "Take his belt off and use it to tie his hands – I don't want him trying to crawl out of there."

Ed felt a hand squeeze in under him and start unbuckling his belt. The other robber lifted Ed's thighs a little to make it easier to unfasten. The first move that really startled Ed was after the belt was unfastened and suddenly his pants were jerked down to his ankles. Then his work boots were taken off, and the pants were taken the rest of the way off.

He really began to worry when his under shorts were pulled off, and a hand began to slide over his ass, squeezing the mounds and fingering the crack.

Ed cried out, "Hey, what the fuck -

Before Ed knew it, one of the robbers was taping Ed's mouth with a heavy duty tape he found on a shelf. The man said, "We've decided to take your virginity as well as your boss's money – this is just to make sure you don't wake the neighbors when you scream on the first plunge."

"I'm going to explain something to you now, because you might not be thinkin' too clearly in a few minutes," the second robber said. "Right now only you and we know, and the police will know when they find you. If you want to keep it that way, make sure you don't remember too much, because if you describe us well enough that we get caught the whole story will come out in court. Then the whole town will know that you've been somebody's pussy, and you won't want to show your face anywhere."

One of the robbers got the waterless hand cleaner out of the bathroom and began to rub it around Ed's asshole. Soon he was shoving in his slick fingers. With the pressure of the lift on his back, Ed hardly felt the additional weight as one of them climbed on him, but he certainly would have screamed if he could have on that first plunge. His attacker wasn't wasting any time on a gentle entry, and when he was finished the second robber used him just as roughly. Mercifully, both men came only moments after they stuck their puny cocks into Ed.

Tears streaming down his face, Ed lay there worrying about what would happen when he was found. His parents were often in bed when he got home from work so it was quite likely that he wouldn't be found until the station opened in the morning. Then, he reasoned, a whole lot of people were going to know what happened.

But two hours later, Ed's boss showed up, to check on a report from the alarm company that the door hadn't been locked at midnight. Ed had never

known that the door lock was monitored and his boss had known each time Ed snuck out five or ten minutes early.

The boss quickly sized up the situation. As he had long had an unspoken interest in Ed's ass himself – Ed's cuteness was one of the reasons Ed had been hired – he immediately began to see an advantage to himself in the present situation. He pulled the tape off Ed's mouth, and turned on the air compressor to start building up air pressure for the lift. 'When Ed started asking about getting the lift up, the boss reminded him that the pressure needed about five minutes to build up before it could be raised. Meanwhile, he turned the lights off again so that Ed wouldn't be embarrassed by someone looking in, and used the time with his captive audience for some fast negotiating. He let Ed describe the crime, found out the cash loss was only about $200 as most of the sales were on credit cards, and told Ed he might as well wait to get cleaned up and get his pants on before calling the police, since five minutes wasn't going to matter anyway. In an empty suburb at 2 a.m. they would arrive within seconds once they were called.

He knew he didn't have much time to manipulate Ed the way he wanted to, so he sat down next to him and started speculating on how the investigation would go, what would happen when the robbers were finally caught, and how Ed would do in court.

Ed started weeping again. The boss squatted before Ed's face. "You know, there is a way out," he told Ed. He went on to explain that, in his view, the loss was really so small that he was willing to absorb it to protect Ed's reputation. Of course, for this "generosity" he wanted something in return.

"Yeah?" Ed said.

"Yeah, I want a little myself."

Ed didn't answer, just stared at his boss.

"Look, I think you knew the story when I hired you. And let's face it, Eddie, you ain't a virgin anymore."

The boss told Ed to think about it while he went to raise the lift, but he had a pretty good idea of what Ed was thinking. In the city the police might keep the details covered up, but in this small suburb such a good story would travel in no time. He was pretty sure that Ed would rather be fucked again rather than have the story spread around town. After he raised the lift, he picked up the jar of hand cleaner unobtrusively with one hand, while using the other hand to help Ed get up. Ed was pretty shaky on his feet, and without making any move to pick up Ed's pants, the boss silently began guiding him towards the office. He sensed that Ed wouldn't mind if he did it, but knew that it would be psychologically very difficult for Ed to say, "Yes, fuck me."

A gas station office doesn't have a lot of comfortable spots to have sex, but the boss didn't want to take Ed home and probably break the mood that was making Ed give in. Thinking fast as he entered the office, he gently told Ed to bend over the back of his desk chair so the boy could support

himself with his hands on the chair arms. Stand up sex wasn't what he really wanted, but it would have to do.

He unzipped his pants and pulled out his slender, cut seven-inch erection. He dabbed a bit of the hand cleaner on the head of his cock. Spreading the boy's hairless asscheeks, he saw the robbers had left quite a mess. It excited him to think he was part of a gangbang, but he entered Ed as gently as he could, stabbing in the head, then the first couple of inches. Ed groaned and gripped the arms of the chair. 'The boss' cock slipped in easily and he worked slowly and carefully. Once he was all the way in and had got a good rhythm going, he reached around and began rubbing Ed's tender young cock.

Gritting his teeth, Ed stayed limp for quite a while, but eventually his cock stiffened. His cock stayed hard all through the fuck and even began throbbing when the boss came in Ed's ass.

After he pulled out, the boss sat Ed in the chair, wiped the hand cleaner off Ed's cock with some tissues and started sucking Ed. At first Ed protested, but it soon became apparent he was enjoying himself as much as his boss and, after about five minutes, he allowed his boss to take his load in his mouth.

In the coming week the boss would give Ed a raise of $50 per week, figuring that would be good for at least one fuck a week. And occasional parts and service for Ed's car would help lubricate the relationship. It was going to be a good year.

BOYS OF THE CORN
Frank Brooks

I pulled the Harley off the county highway and into the wayside park. The late-afternoon sun on this late-August day in 1975 had me dizzy and dazed. I'd been riding through forests of corn for hours and I was feeling oppressed by the giant green plant, even spooked by it. There's something sinister about a plant when it's the only kind growing for hundreds of square miles. It seemed the smell of it had permeated every cell of my being.

When I cut the engine, the afternoon went dead silent for a few moments, but then a sound broke in, a low, background noise: the papery rustle of corn in the wind. Despite the heat, the sound gave me a chill, as if the corn leaves were tickling the nape of my neck. I pumped some icy water from the park well and splashed it on my face and noted with disappointment that my Harley was the only vehicle at the wayside.

I'd suffered a pulsing hard-on all afternoon and was hoping to find some cock-hungry traveling salesman here, or anybody else, to relieve my need. Usually a wayside park like this, even here in the heart of corn country, had a resident cocksucker on duty. I swallowed a few gulps of water, pulled off my T-shirt and wiped my face with it, then headed for the men's outhouse.

The outhouse was small and primitive, containing one stall with door, and outside it, a urinal trough. A large glory hole had been cut in the stall partition, allowing someone sitting on the toilet bench to view the urinal. Standing at the urinal, doing my best to piss with a hard on, I read the graffiti: FARM BOYS STICK IT IN HERE FOR A JUICY SUCK. An arrow pointed to the glory hole, showing farm boys where to stick it.

I knocked the piss off the end of my cock and went into the stall, then dropped my jeans and sat on the stool to beat off. My eight inches of uncut meat felt extra thick and extra hard after my hours astraddle the vibrating motorcycle. I peeled my foreskin back and worked it up and down while noting that the outhouse reeked of corn above all else.

I was getting a good slide going on my foreskin when the sudden opening and banging shut of the screen door startled me. I hadn't heard a vehicle drive up. Through the glory hole I watched a boy step up to the urinal. He was a beauty, with shoulder-length yellow hair, bound with a turquoise headband, and a freckled, upturned nose. He was naked except for a pair of very short cutoffs, which he unsnapped, unzipped, and let slide down his smooth, tanned legs. His cock sprang into view, seven inches long, cut, and as stiff as my own. I smacked my lips and the kid grinned and swung towards me. He stretched luxuriously and flexed his cock.

"Beautiful!" I said.

He grinned again and turned away from me. Bending forward, he spread his asscheeks, revealing a gorgeous tight, hairless asshole. He backed up, close enough for me to sniff him, but staying just out of reach of my tongue.

"Let me lick it," I begged.

"You got a ten, man? You can lick it for a ten."

I almost laughed. Teenage trade out here in the middle of nowhere? I couldn't believe it! You were supposed to meet only horny farm boys out here who'd let you do anything and want no reward other than a smile. I took my wallet out of my jeans and extracted a bill. I shoved the ten through the glory hole and inserted it between his asscheeks. He chuckled and clamped his buttocks together, taking the bill from me.

"Thanks, man." He leaned forward again. Pulling his asscheeks apart, he pressed his ass to the glory hole as the ten fluttered to the floor. "Lick my butt hole, man."

"Jesus God!" I said, and began to slurp away at the sweet teen asshole and up and down the sweaty cleft. The kid rotated his butt and moaned and I shoved my tongue inside him.

"Yeah, lick out my ass!"

I wondered if I had I died and gone to heaven. Or had this corn scent gone to my brain and made me hallucinate? I swear, the kid's asshole was corn-flavored.

After I'd rimmed him and tongue-fucked him nearly to orgasm, he pulled away. Turning to face me, he squatted and showed me his armpits, from which rivulets of sweat trickled. My tongue strained for a taste.

"Got another ten, man?"

I shoved another ten through the hole. He had me, and he knew it.

"Thanks." He fed me his right armpit, then his left.

I lapped greedily, getting high on the scent and taste of his pungent sweat. After I'd licked his armpits clean, he stood up and shoved his right foot into the glory hole.

"Suck my toes, man. No charge."

For his size, he had huge, beautiful feet, which I licked and sucked while pounding my cock. After I'd satisfied his right foot, he fed me his left.

"Nice!" he sighed, wiggling his toes in my mouth and jerking off. "I dig it."

He pulled his foot away at last and let his cock throb just out of reach of my tongue. A clear pearl of cock lube oozed from his piss hole and perched at the tip of his fat purplish knob. His dick throbbed with every beat of his heart. "Twenty lets you taste this big fucker, man."

With shaky hands, I took two more tens from my wallet, shoved them through the glory hole, and wrapped them around his cock. As he took the bills, my hand gripped his rod naked. I thrilled to the incredibly hard, hot,

silky-smooth feel of it. I pulled until he was pressed smack up against the partition and his dick and balls were inside the stall with me. Holding his stiff cock vertical, I licked his hairless nuts. His ball-sweat tasted of corn.

"Man, suck them big mothers!"

The kid's balls were swollen hugely. I took them into my mouth one at a time, gently tonguing and sucking them. I licked down under his balls and tasted his hairless perineum. I wanted to suck it, but the angle wasn't right.

He hung by his hands from the top of the partition and squirmed against it. "Pleasure me, man! Lick me all over!"

The sound of his sultry young voice alone would have been enough to get me off, but here I had hold of his naked cock and balls. It blew my mind. I squeezed his cock at the base, making it swell even more, its veins bulging, its knob mushrooming, its piss hole wide open and bubbling lubricant. As the sappy lube leaked down the back of his knob and down the supersensitive strand just below it, I slurped it up and the teenager gasped.

"Lick it right there, man! Yeah! It gets me off."

I kissed the most sensitive spot on the back of his cock and his cock glued itself to my lips. Holding his cock by the base, I banged it back and forth across my face, getting off on the feel of its weight and hardness, smearing my face with his dick lube. He started moaning, begging me to suck. I swallowed his cock to the balls.

"Ahhhh!" He pressed hard against the partition, forcing his cock even farther down my throat. "Suck me!"

His entire cock pulsed in my mouth and throat, so hard and hot and boyish-tasting that I could have enjoyed for eternity the feel of its throbbing length buried in my face. But he had other ideas. I could sense he was aching to get off. He started to screw, to fuck hard and fast.

I let him go at it, ramming away. The uncontrolled thrusting and whimpering of a teenager in heat really turns me on. I let him use my mouth as a cunt or an asshole. I'd had my face fucked by so many teenagers over the years that I'd learned long ago how to relax and enjoy the assault.

"Oh man, yeah! Suck! Suck!"

As his cock plunged, I churned my tongue at: the back of it. As he withdrew, I sucked his knob. His naked toes clutched at the floor. My right hand jerked up and down my own hard cock and I had to keep letting go of it to keep from blasting my load against the stall wall before the kid shot off in my mouth.

He was so carried away that I thought he would knock the stall down. His cock felt like a torpedo in my mouth, swelling more and more with each thrust. When he started to whimper, I knew it was all over.

"I'm coming!" he wailed as his cum exploded down my throat. He jerked like a rag doll against the partition, gasping and whimpering and spurting.

I closed my eyes and exploded against the wall, my cum making splatting, splashing sounds as it hit the plywood. I reveled in the rhythmic bursts of pleasure, several of my spurts matching the boy's, and I swallowed rapidly, eating his every ejaculation. His cum tasted sweet and alkaline, and was as corn-flavored as the rest of him. A gust of hot:, corn-scented wind blew in the screen door and whirled through the outhouse. My lips smacked as his cock popped out of my mouth and I swallowed the last few gobs of jism my lips had extracted.

"Far out, man," he said, catching his breath. "You really know how to give head, man." He turned around and pulled apart his asscheeks and my deflating cock immediately reversed course and swelled again. "You wanna corn hole this tight ass, man?"

My cock became hard. "I'd love to, sweetheart."

"Twenty bucks," he said. "But first you buy me supper in town." He pressed his ass to the glory hole and I licked the cleft up and down.

"You got it, baby."

He sat behind me on the Harley, his arms wrapped around me, his bare chest pressed to my bare back as we rode through hot wind. He said his name was Sandy and he directed me towards town and the diner where, he said, they had great fried chicken.

"Where'd you get this chopper, man? It must've cost a lot."

"It's not mine," I shouted back, over the roar of the engine. "I picked it up at the Harley factory in Milwaukee and I'm riding it out to Lake Tahoe for this rich guy who bought it. I don't think he'll ever ride it. He just wants to own it and look at it."

"Crazy, man." The boy lifted his bare legs and wrapped them around my hips. He pressed his bare feet to my crotch. "Take out your uncut weeny, man, and I'll jack you off with my feet. I can get uncut dicks off real easy with my toes."

A car passed us from the opposite direction.

"Thanks, sweetheart, but I'll save my load for when I corn hole you later. I can't come ten times a day anymore like you teenagers."

"How old are you, man?"

"Twenty-seven."

"Far out. I thought you were twenty-two. How much is this rich dude paying you to deliver his bike?"

"Nothing," I said. "He's putting me up in Lake Tahoe for a week in exchange."

I was lying. I didn't want the kid to know how rich I was and have him up his price for the corn holing.

The truth was I'd met Clark, the rich guy whose Harley I was riding, at a health club in Milwaukee where I was working as a masseur. My wages were shit but my tips were good, especially the tips I got for "extras": hand

jobs and blowjobs mostly. Clark came in one day for a massage and extras, and during our conversations he asked me if I was a biker. He was crazy for bikers, he said.

Thinking I'd get a bigger tip if I fed his fantasy, I told him I was. He said he was a "motorcycle aficionado," in town to visit the Harley-Davidson factory and to buy himself a new bike. Then he offered me a thousand dollars to ride his new Harley to Lake Tahoe and deliver it to him there. I was not to wash during the entire trip, he told me, and when I arrived he would strip me, then worship, lick, suck, and fuck my "sweaty biker body" as it lay draped over the Harley in various lewd positions. I could stay in his Lake Tahoe "chateau" for a week, during which he'd wine and dine me, and after which he'd fly me anywhere I wanted to go. I gave the health club notice that very day.

The forest of corn grew right up to the edge of town. We roared past the population sign, then past a large but ramshackle bar called Cobbs Tavern with a sign showing three naked yellow corn cobs dripping melted butter. The parking lot of the bar was crowded with pickup trucks and beat-up cars despite the early hour, as was the parking lot of the diner nearby where Sandy directed me to turn in. Dust devils rose from both parking lots in the oven-hot, corn-saturated wind of late afternoon.

A sign in magic marker tacked on the front door of the diner warned: NO SHIRT, NO SHOES, NO SERVICE! I put on my t-shirt, but Sandy, who couldn't have looked more naked if he'd been wearing nothing but a jockstrap, said it was all right, he knew the owners.

Country music blasted on the jukebox inside. We hadn't taken three steps past the door when a burly redneck in a sweat-stained T-shirt shouted at us from behind the counter, "Can't you read, dum-dum! No shirt, no shoes, no service! Outa here!"

In my saddlebags I found a T-shirt and a pair of old sneakers for Sandy. Back inside, we got scowled at by the redneck, but he didn't hassle us as we found an empty booth. After a long wait, a gum-chewing teenage waitress in a mini-skirt finally showed up and Sandy told her he wanted chicken, fries, and a Coke. I asked for ice water. The waitress scowled at us and left without a word.

"Friendly place," I shouted over the wail of the music.

Sandy, across the table from me, kicked off the sneakers I'd loaned him and planted his bare feet on the seat between my legs. He stroked my swollen crotch with his toes. "Ain't so friendly, but they got great chicken. Ain't you eating?"

"I had my chicken at the wayside," I said. "And later I'm having some more. Don't want to spoil my appetite."

The boy wiggled his toes against my crotch, grinning.

Five new diners walked in and squeezed into a booth across and down the aisle from us. The ugliest hetero couple I'd ever seen in my life sat on one side of the table, and three of the most-beautiful boys I'd ever seen in my life sat on the other side, facing them, and me. The youngest was exceptionally beautiful and sexy, rating fifteen on a scale from one to ten--way off the chart.

The oldest of the three boys, the one seated deepest in the booth, nearest the wall, wore no shirt. The boy in the middle, about a year younger than the first and probably Sandy's age, was barefoot and wore a fishnet t-shirt. The youngest boy, the raving beauty on the aisle and maybe two years younger than the oldest, was dressed exactly as Sandy had been before he'd been thrown out of the diner for failing to meet the dress code. I could see the pink tip of the youngest boy's cock – his legs were spread wide – peeking out the leg of his cutoffs, which were little more than a faded denim rag around his loins.

"Them's the Cobbs," Sandy informed me as I gawked at the three brothers. "Own the tavern up the road. Eat here every meal, everyday. You ever see such an ugly old lady and ugly old man? They claim ma and pa Cobb, both of 'em are drunkards, made a pact with the devil when they were young to drain off all their beauty into their offspring. Now they're uglier than hell itself."

I could believe it. What else could explain such physical beauty springing from such ugliness?

Each Cobb brother had shoulder-length hair that was a shade of blond different from the blond of the other two brothers. The oldest – whom Sandy informed me was named Mike – had hair the color of dark honey. Tim, the middle brother, whose eyes were a chilling blue, was a platinum blond. Ben, the youngest, had hair like ripe wheat during the most golden hour of the late afternoon. All three boys had been in and out of reform school too many times to count, Sandy told me. The whole town feared the Cobbs and avoided confrontations with them, which was why the boys were never hassled about their lack of dress in the diner.

I had to admit that the three brothers, in spite of their beauty, had a sinister, dangerous quality about them, a quality that might have been part of their attraction, for I couldn't keep my eyes off them. Ben in particular held my attention, and my loins throbbed as I gazed upon his fine-textured, golden-brown skin, his large boy-feet, his kissable lips with their coquettish pout. Ben knew I was staring at him and he stared right back, his expression cool and unfathomable.

The Cobbs hadn't been seated for more than a minute before the teenaged waitress hurried to their table with three plates of burgers, fries, and corn on the cob, and three Cokes--for the boys--and two cups and a huge pot of coffee for the parents. As the girl served them, Ben shoved a bare foot up

under her miniskirt. She giggled uneasily and squirmed away. Ben's brothers snickered, but the parents seemed oblivious to Ben's behavior, puffing on their cigarettes and dumping black coffee into their cups. The waitress hurried off.

"Bitch don't wear nothing under that skirt," Sandy said. "Everybody knows it, man. Ben's had a toe up her twat more than once, right here in front of everybody."

"I thought Ben might be gay," I said.

Sandy laughed. "Gay? You can't use words like that to pin down the Cobb brothers, man. They'll fuck anything that moves or don't move. Human, animal, vegetable, or mineral – it don't make a difference to the Cobbs. Ben's got a pecker big as your own, and uncut to boot, and it's been everywhere: down my throat and up that bitch waitress's twat hole for starters."

Ben's dick, as if on cue, poked its head out the leg of his cutoffs. It was moist, maroon-colored, and huge, its foreskin pulled well back. I licked my lips and Ben stared at me, chomping on his hamburger. His two brothers were looking at me too, and Mike nudged Tim.

The waitress brought Sandy his chicken and fries. I asked again for a glass of ice water and got a scowl. As Sandy ate, I watched the Cobb boys wolf down their food while their parents guzzled coffee and smoked. Each time a country song wailed to a conclusion on the juke box, a new one took its place.

"This chicken's giving me an appetite for a good corn holing," Sandy said.

I nodded, hardly hearing him. Two inches of Ben's thick cock now protruded from the leg of his cutoffs, and I stared, salivating.

Sandy pressed his toes against my crotch. "Hey, man, you still there?" He glanced over his shoulder at Ben, then back at me. "Them Cobbs are trouble, man. Mess with 'em at your own risk."

Ben gnawed the corn off a butter-dripping cob, gulped Coke, wiped his hands on his cutoffs, and got up. His cutoffs slid down over the head of his dick, barely covering it. He glanced at me as he walked past, then turned down the hallway towards the restrooms and glanced back again. Without a thought, I was on my feet and following him.

"Hey, man!" Sandy called after me, but Ben had me now.

I hardly knew where I was or where I was going. My throbbing cock, aimed at Ben's young ass, was drawing me after him like a missile homing in on a target. Ben stepped into the men's room and I stepped in behind him. It was a small room with one toilet and a sink. Ben wheeled to face me and dropped his cutoffs. His eight-inch cock looked monstrous sticking up out of his slender loins.

I pulled off my shirt. Ben reached up, pinched my chin, drew my face down to his, and kissed me smack on the mouth. He fed me his tongue and I sucked it, tasting corn on the cob and butter. I was reaching for his cock as the

door opened behind me. Mike and Tim crowded into the room with us and locked the door.

"What're you doing feeling up our little brother, dude?" said the older boy. "You a dirty old man or somethin'?"

"I bet he's fixin' to corn hole Benjy," said Tim. "All them dirty old men wanna do is corn hole 'im."

"Maybe we oughta show this dirty old man what corn holing feels like," said Mike. "Before he pokes Benjy's hole."

"Good idea," said Tim. "Maybe we oughta poke his mouth too. I can tell he's a cocksucker."

Ben, standing in the corner, slowly fisted his cock, watching as Mike dropped his jeans and kicked off his shoes and as Tim shed his fishnet t-shirt and cutoffs. I didn't wait to be ordered to strip. I pried off my motorcycle boots and shoved down my jeans and stepped out of them. The small restroom reeked of the masculine scents of the armpits, balls, and uncut cocks of the three naked boys and me.

"Bend over, dude." Mike slapped my ass from behind.

As I bent over, Tim grabbed my head and whacked his uncut seven-inch cock back and forth across my face, then forced it into my mouth. "Eat it, cocksucker." He drove his cockhead down my throat.

Behind me, as Mike greased his cock, the smell of fresh butter rose in the air. He'd apparently brought along pats of softened butter from the table to use as a lubricant. His greasy hands gripped my ass and his thick cockhead slipped between my asscheeks. With a smooth thrust, he entered me and buried his cock in me to the hilt.

"Ahhh, tight ass! Hot damn!" Without a pause, Mike began to screw.

My rigid cock stood torpedo-like under my belly and whacked against my abdominals as Mike banged me from behind and Tim, in front of me, humped my face. The two boys moaned and cursed as they fucked me and everybody in the diner would have heard their carrying on if the wailing and throbbing of the jukebox hadn't been even louder. The restroom door rattled as someone tried to get in, but neither of the Cobb brothers slowed their fucking.

"Get the fuck outa here!" Mike yelled at the intruder. "We don't want any!"

"Damned shit heads," Tim complained. "What they want in here anyway? They wanna piss or something? We got better things to do here than piss."

Ben, watching from the corner, continued to slide his foreskin and lubricant dripped from his slowly worked cock. Mike and Tim rammed me from both ends, moaning their pleasure. Their cocks felt as big and hard as Billy clubs inside me.

All at once, Mike started to grunt. His cock started to flex and quiver. Tim grunted with him, and his cock bucked powerfully. The two brothers cried

out in unison and their sperm shot into me from both ends. Hot jets splashed in my bowels and against my tonsils. I gulped Tim's corn-flavored cum to keep from choking. The boys humped and spurted until they'd fucked themselves dry and hauled their dripping cocks out of me.

"Nothing like a piece of tight ass to work up an appetite for dessert," Mike said, pulling on his jeans.

"I'm having me some pie and ice cream," Tim said. He hitched up his cutoffs and pulled on his fishnet T-shirt, which revealed his squared pectorals and abdominal segments teasingly.

As soon as Mike and Tim had left and I'd relocked the door, I pulled Ben into my arms. With a bear hug, I kissed him. He fed me his juicy tongue and I sucked it. He felt so naked and silky-hot in my arms that I could have got off as he squirmed against me, but he broke free before I lost it and slid to his knees in front of me. His freckled nose nuzzled my balls and his fat pink tongue licked them.

He kissed each spunk-swollen nut and sucked on it. My fingers slid in his thick hair, kneading his warm scalp. Holding my foreskin down tight, he licked my knob and the whole upper third of my cock as if it were an ice cream cone. Then he went down on me, sucking like a pro.

"Go easy," I gasped. "Jesus you're good!" The sight of his blue eyes turned up at me and his boyish face stuffed with my huge cock drove me to the brink of ecstasy. At the last possible moment, just as I was about to explode, he let go of my cock and stood up. A few watery drops shot against his belly from my cock. I held my breath, praying I wouldn't come. 'Suck my big one," he said, and he pushed me to my knees. His cock bobbed and wagged, its foreskin peeled back. I grabbed it and swallowed it, enjoying all of its incredible eight inches. Sucking, I bobbed my head and watched Ben's toes clutch with pleasure against the linoleum. I wondered how many times those big toes of his had slipped up the cunt of that sour-faced waitress. I slid my hands up and down his smooth legs, glinting with golden down. My nose rubbed his groin, nuzzling the tuff of pubic silk. I knew I had to pluck a few of those golden gems for my pubic-hair collection.

Ben pressed his hands to my head and rocked his hips. His big cock slid in and out smoothly, thrilling my lips and mouth and throat. I squeezed his egg-sized nuts and felt them contract. I tickled his perineum. His eyes rolled back and he groaned. Humping with quick, short thrusts, he shot a stream of cum down my throat as his cock bucked and shuddered.

"Yeah-h-h!" he moaned.

I sucked rhythmically, swallowing every sweet spurt before he sighed and his body relaxed. Though spent, his cock remained nearly rigid.

He sat down on the toilet and slumped back, panting. The restroom door rattled and Ben shouted, "Get lost, fucker!"

Crouching at his feet, I kissed them. Holding both feet in my lap, I massaged them as he wiggled his toes against my throbbing prong.

"I love your big fucking cock, man," he said, smearing my precum with his big toe.

I lifted both of his feet to my mouth and licked them, then sucked his toes. He grabbed his cock and started jerking off.

"That toe-sucking makes me wanna get corn holed, man."

I let him direct everything. He got up off the toilet and told me to sit on it. He greased my cock with some of the soft pats of butter his brother Mike had discarded on the floor. The butter melted and dribbled down my balls. He rubbed some butter between his asscheeks, then straddled my thighs, facing me, and lowered his ass to my upward-straining cock.

"Corn hole me," he said. Grasping the tops of my shoulders for support, he lowered his rotating ass onto my cock. His asshole opened like a hungry mouth, sucking in my cockhead, then swallowing my shaft to the balls. He moaned, his eyes rolling with pleasure, and he started to slide up and down.

I was in ecstasy. I grasped his middle, my fingers encircling his slender waist, and I helped him ride me. He was a gorgeous little demon. His asshole burned inside, squeezing rhythmically as it fucked up and down my cock. He gazed into my eyes with a look of dazed, unbridled lust.

I sucked and gnawed his nipples and he gasped, his cock flexing with each flick of my tongue against their pointed tips. He rode me faster, bouncing his tight young ass against my balls. I rocked my hips and thrust upward into his seething, sizzling boy-ass, which contracted inside with its first spasms.

"I'm gonna come," he panted. "Yeah!"

"Yeah!" I answered, fucking him with abandon, letting the sensations pulse through my cock with their full, delicious intensity. His eyes rolled back until only the whites showed. His body shook. A stream of white jism shot from his cock and splashed in my face. I rammed into his clutching asshole and exploded inside him before a second spurt escaped his cock. We cried out together, our whimpers and grunts of pleasure blending with the wails and throbs of the jukebox. He grabbed his free-standing, spurting cock and jacked out the remainder of his load as I unloaded inside him.

My cock slipped out of his asshole as he straightened up out of his squat and he shoved his cock in my mouth. I sucked out the last sweet gobs of sperm. I wiped his jism off my chest and belly and licked it from my fingers. Before he unstraddled my thighs, I held him firmly by the cock, grasped several of his golden pubic hairs, and yanked.

"Ouch!" he yelled. "What the fuck!"

"Souvenirs," I said. "I dig your peach fuzz, baby."

"And I dig your big cock," he said. "Maybe I should cut it off with my jackknife?"

After he'd left the restroom, I carefully placed the dozen golden filaments of his pubic silk in an envelope I made of a dollar bill and tucked it safely into the coin pouch in my wallet. I dressed, waited a few minutes, and returned to the dining room, a little apprehensive about what I might find there. To my relief, all the Cobbs had left. But so had Sandy. He was probably back at the wayside by now, getting corn holed by a trucker.

I picked up my bill from the table and went to the cash register where the redneck in the sweaty T-shirt was standing behind it. I showed him the bill. "I think that should be two dollars and sixty-nine cents, not two-hundred and sixty-nine dollars."

"No mistake, punk. That's two hundred and sixty-nine dollars."

I examined the check. He was charging me for four complete dinners, several pots of coffee, three pies, a half-gallon of ice cream, and a glass of ice water. Added to it all were "surcharges." "I bought my friend chicken, fries, and a Coke. I never got my water, but I've never heard of charging for water anyway. I never ordered any of this other stuff, and what are surcharges?"

"The Cobbs said you were paying their bill. Surcharges are for the use of the bathroom and for draggin' that hippie trash in here."

"What?"

"Let me make it simple for you: there's a rental charge for the bathroom and surcharges on all the food."

I stared at him, open-mouthed.

"Look, you take over my bathroom for a half hour, there's a surcharge. The whole town knows what that hippie trash is up to and you bring him in here contaminating my restaurant. The Cobbs say you're paying for their food, and what the Cobbs say goes in this place. That comes to two hundred and sixty-nine dollars. Pay up."

"I'll pay for one greasy chicken dinner and that's it."

The man smirked. "Looks like I gotta call over the sheriff's deputy over there and get this straightened out." He nodded toward a booth in the far corner where a fat deputy was feeling up the teenaged waitress, who squirmed on his lap. The lawman had a hand up her skirt and apparently had a finger inside her.

"You can tell our deputy there all about you and the Cobb boys," said the redneck. "You know, give him all the details. He'll want to know everything. He'll call in the Cobbs and get their story too. The deputy's a buddy of mine, by the way."

The waitress got up and came towards us. In a daze, she walked right past the cash register and down the hallway toward the restrooms. The deputy was right behind her and the redneck called to him.

"Hey, Big Ed, we got us a little problem here. We need you to straighten it out."

"Be right with you, Lyle," said the deputy. "Give me a minute or two." He winked and disappeared down the hallway.

"Stay right here," the redneck said, fixing me with a glare. "Don't move." He disappeared down the hallway. I heard him calling to the deputy.

I'd been in tight spots before and knew that indecision was fatal. I slapped a five onto the counter, on top of my bill, and seconds later was straddling the Harley. The big engine roared to life and I left the diner behind in a cyclone of dust. The Cobb brothers were sitting in front of their tavern, each boy with a pie on his lap. They looked up as I shot past and soon I had disappeared into the forest of corn.

DANGER ON THE LEVEE
Sean Michael O'Day

North Bend Boulevard is an easy place to pick up cheap hustlers for quick sex. Rising above the bend on the Great Miami River through Dayton, the boulevard is a mile-long stretch of trees and grass with no houses and many secluded spots. The area is known as the levee. If no hustlers are in sight, johns stop their cars, set up a rendezvous with another driver, and the two either pull into Kettering Playfield or take off for one of the motels along Keowee Street where rooms rent by the hour. The levee is usually as safe, or as dangerous, as any such place can be. Recently, the levee has been more than dangerous, it's become deadly.

On my first cruise through the park on a sultry night in July, a bumper crop of boys ambled along the boulevard or leaned against trees waiting for drivers to stop. After the briefest of conversations, the boys would crawl in the passenger side and the cars would disappear into Kettering Playfield.

Jumping from behind a tree, one hustler was clad so skimpily that I squinted to see whether he was wearing any pants. He was: tan bikini swimming trunks. But that was all. While I slowly cruised past him, he pulled his trunks down to pee. He gave me a big smile and a wave. I drove on. Good-looking kid, but that kind didn't interest me. Too brazen.

As soon as a police cruiser turned onto North Bend Boulevard, cars and hustlers scattered like roaches in sunlight. Damn! Now I could vanish till that cop got a call to investigate a barroom brawl or a drive-by shooting.

I sped from the boulevard behind five other cars and parked on a side street. Sliding my hand on the floor, my warm fingers made contact with the cold metal of my gun. Then I arranged the twenty tapes scattered on the front seat. To waste time, I piled the tapes in stacks of six, then five, then four. Again I reached on the floor to make certain that I could grab my gun quickly. Fumbling on the dash, trying to turn on the air conditioning, I succeeded only in giving myself a blast of hot air from the heater. That's the trouble with a new car. Takes time to learn how to operate all the gadgets, but the advantage in this situation was that none of the hustlers would recognize my old car as I cruised the park. Recognition would doom me.

After patrolling the boulevard for ten minutes, flashing his spotlight on anything that moved, the cop tore out of the park, red lights flashing and siren blaring. With any luck, he was called to a multiple shooting that would occupy him the rest of the night. I'd never be able to select my dream date with him breathing down my neck all night. Seven cars formed a solemn procession in front of me as we re-entered the boulevard, looking for that perfect, elusive body which we might adore for the night. We drove slowly, examining the figures of hustlers emerging from between trees.

During my next drive through the park I spotted the fellow I wanted. Muscle shirt, tight jeans, enormous basket, broad shoulders, shaved head. As I veered my car to the curb, he gave his crotch a grope. Walking in front of my headlights so that I could give his body a good look, he approached the driver's window.

"Whatcha lookin' for?" he asked, pushing his hand under his shirt so that I could see his washboard belly as he scratched himself.

"Just out for some fun," I said, glancing at his crotch. "You a cop?"

"Did you see what I did when that cop drove in before?" I asked.

"'Took off like a bat outta-hell.'" He gave me a smirk as he rubbed his hand over his basket. "I've had my eye on you all night."

"Want a blow job?" I reached through the window and touched his crotch.

"Yeah, for twenty bucks. But I got some rules. One, I don't suck. Two, I don't play around with your asshole. Three, you keep your motherfuckin' fingers off my shit hole."

"Will you sit in the front seat, or get in back so that people think I'm your chauffeur?"

"I hate smart asses. Twenty bucks with my rules, buddy. Take it or leave it. There are a dozen johns in this park who'd give me fifty."

"Hop in." I smiled to myself as he circled the car to get in, for it was probably the last deal he'd make with a customer. As he opened the door, I felt under the seat to make certain that my gun was there. "You got a special place you want to go?"

"Yeah," he said. "You know where Dryden Road is, behind Carillon Park?"

I eased the car away from the curb.

"We won't be bothered there by traffic or cops," he said. He unzipped his fly and pulled his cock out. Soft, his rod coiled out a good six inches, and without question, it was the fattest dick I had ever seen.

"Nice body," I said.

"Yeah, yeah," he grumbled. "Tell me something I don't know." He shoved his pants a couple of inches lower so that he could tug his balls out.

Roughly grabbing my right hand from the steering wheel, he pressed it onto his soft cock. Even though my warm fingers wrapped round it, his cock remained soft.

"It's so big," he said, "you may have to work at it."

Or, I thought, you're not used to having a man's hand on your dick. He leaned his head forward and let a big gob of spit slide through my fingers onto his limp meat.

"You come here often?" I asked.

"Let's cut the crap, buddy." I could feel his icy stare. "I want twenty bucks and a blow job. Nothing else. No small talk. No nice- to-mee t-a-new - friend chitchat."

As I pulled out of the park, a police cruiser entered. Although I was breaking no traffic laws, the cops flashed their spotlight on my car. I could see the two cops laugh, but they didn't try to stop me. Within seconds my car was out of their sight. After we left the park and drove through the deserted streets, he relaxed. He shoved his pants several inches lower and leaned his head back. As I explored his crotch, my fingers rubbed bristly stubble where he had shaved the hair around his balls. The longer I drove, the harder his cock became. Maybe the guy was used to a man's hand after all.

When I stopped for a red light at the intersection of Monument and Ludlow, I glanced past him toward a newspaper box. The headline read SECOND MAN SHOT NEAR LEVEE--SERIAL KILLER SUSPECTED. I eased the car forward into the crosswalk, but not before my trick spied the headline. A suspicious expression covered his face as his glance darted between me and the newspaper. He shoved my hand off his cock.

"I'll get out here," he said, lunging sideways to open the door. But I had already locked all four. When I pushed my foot on the gas, he fell back in the seat.

"Nothing to worry about," I assured him. "Cool down. That killer's probably long out of this area." I slid my hand across the stacks of tapes. "Here," I said, "pick out your favorite and relax." I spit on my palm and rubbed it over his crown.

He didn't take his eyes off me for several minutes, but then he rummaged through the tapes and selected a recent release by Soul Asylum called "Grave Dancers Union." He pushed it into the deck and stretched back, relaxing to the blend of pop, metal, and punk. It wasn't my choice, but he was the one who needed to relax. I hoped that he would say or do something threatening so that I could reach for my gun, but he gave me no immediate cause to act.

"Awesome sound system," he muttered.

"Should be. It set me back more than two thousand."

He turned the volume higher until we were immersed in music, my heart thumping in rhythm with the beat. Turning the wheel with my left hand, I used my right to massage his rod. It had grown two or three inches but was far from hard. At least he was relaxing.

"Cops give you much static?" he asked, turning sideways to look at me.

"At the levee?"

"Hell, anywhere. At the levee, the porno shops, on the street."

"I'm careful."

"Yeah," he grumbled. "I'm scared shitless that I'll be picked up by that damned maniac, the one who's blowing guys away." He pushed his pants below his knees so that I'd have more room to fist his cock. Spreading his legs wide, he said, "You got a big one?" He touched between my legs.

"See for yourself." I hoisted my ass off the seat so that he could unzip my pants and spread my fly.

He let out a low whistle as he groped my cock and squeezed my balls. Immediately my cock sprang out hard and bumped the steering wheel. "I thought mine was the biggest," he said, "but now I'm not so sure."

My radar detector beeped, and when he pulled his pants up, I felt his cock shrivel under my fingertips. The beeping and flashing red light on the monitor quickened, "There's the damned cop car," he said, pointing in the distance. "It's not bad enough that they're crawling over the levee all day long. Now they're prowling all night."

I put my foot on the brake so the cops wouldn't have the least reason to follow me. The two cops sitting in the car stared directly at me and my trick as we passed through the intersection, proceeding south on Ludlow toward Patterson Boulevard. I glanced in my rearview mirror, but they were not following.

"Did you read anything about that serial killer?" he asked.

"Fact is," I lied, "the first I knew about it was a couple of minutes ago when I saw the headline. What do you know about it?"

"This is what I make out of it." He turned slightly so that I could better rub his cock. "This lunatic goes out cruising for tricks, and then once he lures them inside his car, he gets his jollies by sucking them off or fucking their asses, or whatever other nutty thing he might dream up, and then when they're getting out of his car, he blows their damned brains out."

I pressed my middle finger into the base of his cock, between his balls, and immediately his cock stretched out. At last I had found the magic spot. "Weren't you uneasy getting into my car?"

"A guy driving a Lincoln Town Car isn't likely to be a serial killer."

I smiled to myself and squeezed his cock, now growing thick and long. The longer it grew, the higher it raised until it was thumping against his belly. Since I was more concerned with cornering him than with sex, my own cock had become limp. As soon as I had him in a position where I could place my gun against his head, I'd have time to concentrate on my own pleasure and satisfaction.

"What's the fuzz buster worth?" he asked.

"It was a special order," I said. "About five hundred." "Man, this car's crammed with gadgets."

I had already passed the Stewart Street Bridge and turned onto the boulevard beside the Deeds Carillon where even isolated cars were no longer a

threat. This area was desolate at night. Not even street lights illuminated the road.

"Back in there," he said. Passing a string of small factories, opened only during the day, my car was the only vehicle on the road. Perfect place, I thought.

"Pull into the back of this parking lot," he said. "You can suck me off there. Nobody will disturb us."

Distant noises from the city, sirens from emergency trucks and horns from trucks on the highway, were the only sounds I heard. When I got out of the car, he was already standing, leaning against my car, with his pants pushed to his ankles. He had pulled his muscle shirt up under his armpits so that I could enjoy the sight of his nude body. The full moon cast long shadows on his body. His chest was as well-developed as his shoulders, and his cock stretched out thick and heavy, ready for my mouth.

When I knelt and opened my mouth, he quickly placed his hand over his cock and jerked away. "Hold on, buddy. Twenty bucks up front."

I stood and counted out two tens from my wallet. He reached down and shoved the two bills in his sock.

"Keep your damned teeth off my rod," he ordered, as I again knelt. "Use your tongue and lips. Don't chew it."

I had just opened my mouth and taken his crown inside when the flash of headlights broke the spell. For an instant we were both in the bright glare.

"Dammit to hell," he muttered, turning quickly to avoid the light.

"They're not stopping," I whispered. "They probably didn't even see us." From the corner of my eye, I watched the car disappear down the road.

If in the car I had suppressed passion, I now let emotion engulf me. Grabbing his huge cock with both my fists, I massaged it wildly as I forced it against the back of my throat. The warm taste of his pre-cum filled my mouth. His grunts and groans and thrusts left no doubt that I was satisfying him. He humped his ass forward and rammed his rod in my mouth until I felt that my throat would split. I enjoyed every moment of his mouth-fucking.

"Deeper," he demanded, grabbing the back of my head, forcing me to swallow his monster dong. I did whatever necessary to rocket him to the height of pleasure, for only that would allow me to accomplish my task.

Only after he was lost in sex could I complete my work tonight. He seemed not to object when my hands rested on his thighs. His legs had the same muscular build as his shoulders. My hands slid lower toward his knees.

"Don't take your hands off my cock," he ordered.

Instantly I raised my left hand to his cock, but I allowed myself a moment to touch the folds of cloth below his ankles. I felt the barrel of what I suspected. That would introduce a complication into my plans.

His cock was at least ten inches long, ramming itself into my mouth and down my throat with all the force he had. There was no longer question of using my fingers gently. I clenched my fists round his cock with all my strength.

As soon as his body tensed, he pulled his cock from my mouth and pushed me away. Falling backwards, I watched him wrap both his fists round his rod and rub hard. A stream of cum shot out of his mouth and into the air. I struggled to my feet as he shot another load. While he was lost in his momentary ecstasy, I reached under the driver's seat for my gun and shoved it in my pocket. I had to bide my time, waiting for the instant that he made a threatening move, which until now hadn't happened.

"Satisfied?" I asked, watching him wipe his hands on his pants before pulling them up.

"Yeah," he muttered. He didn't have the least concern whether I had experienced any pleasure. "Let's get back in the car," he ordered.

While he opened the door on the passenger side, I made my way round the back of the car. When I put my hand on the driver's door, he had already slid into the driver's seat and rolled down the window. "Sorry, buddy, but you'll have to regard this evening as your final and fatal mistake."

He pointed a snub-nosed gun at my head. "Tape deck, radar detector, Lincoln Town Car. Man, you'll keep me and my bitch in drugs for a month."

"Only one problem," I said. "The radar detector's also a police radio that's monitored every word we've spoken." The instant he spun in the seat to check out the radar detector, I pulled out my gun. "Go on, pull the trigger," I warned him.

"I've robbed dozens of johns and killed two of them in the past month," he said. "It's not going to keep me awake nights killing a third."

Since the full impact of my warning didn't hit him, I was more explicit. "The other johns weren't cops. I am."

He had fifteen seconds, maybe twenty, when he could have pulled the trigger, but the moment he saw police cars coming both directions on Dryden Road, he froze.

In a matter of minutes the other men and women on the force had the suspect in cuffs and inside a cruiser. I waited for the truck to arrive to tow the Lincoln to the police garage for evidence, and then I headed back to headquarters to complete my paperwork. After that I could knock off work for the night and go home.

Since history repeats itself, the hustlers and johns and just plain adventuresome will soon forget this most recent spree of violence on the levee, but someday, someone who's out for more than a fast buck or quick sex will travel the banks of the Great Miami River, discover the opportunity, and once again provide danger on the levee. I'll be waiting.

RONNIE
Don Valpo

I have some favorite positions to rest in. The best of these is lying close behind Ronnie just after we do it. There have been other kids but Ronnie is best. He's on his side, quiet in that dreamland he inhabits for a while after sex, and I'm on my side behind him, pressed tight. I stroke slowly downward from his shoulder. The delicacy of good skin-texture isn't something a man can take time to enjoy in the heat of action. It can be appreciated better after the fact. And I do.

While he's lying on his side like that, the hollow at his waist – below ribcage and before pelvis – fascinates me. Elsewhere there are bones – he's sort of skinny – but there the skin. texture is particularly fine and the softness is entrancing. Even the insides of his thighs aren't as sweet. His butt is always nice but that's a different matter. Like his mouth, his tail is for action. Not that his butt doesn't have aesthetic value, but you know what I mean. Apples are not oranges.

I've been satisfied and he satisfied himself as I rode him but his flesh continues to hypnotize me. I stroke him and he lies like a cat being petted. I go slowly down his side, into that hollow, down to his thigh, then back. Next time his arm, from shoulder to fingers. Another, his neck and lobes of his ears. He's just a kid and not built very well but I like him as he is. Sometimes we go on like that for quite a while. It's the simplicity and vulnerability of his nakedness that I find most interesting. Particularly the vulnerability. At moments like this I have no words to give him. I'm speechless. He senses that because I'm unusually silent and he doesn't ask why.

We finally get out of bed, clean off, then I stand and hold him for a minute longer, my arms around his skinny body and his face buried in my neck like a child's. The whole process, from throwing off our clothes to that final holding, takes a long time. It's after that he's especially tender and close.

I could go on at some length about his kisses. He's got full lips and uses them, kissing like a sexy angel. Like everywhere else, we just fit. The last kiss doesn't bring my dick up like the first one before we start, but it is sweet. The first one? I can't describe it. Two mouths made for each other, that's all, but his is the wonderful one. He likes the sex well enough, but like any kid, the body contact is most important.

He's not pretty. Barely attractive, I'd say, but we fit. That may not sound like much but it's important to me. We're like positive and negative impressions of one another. Whichever way I lie on or against him, or hold him, he fits: snugly and neatly. I think that's miraculous. He hasn't much experience with anybody but me and seems to take such a rare thing for granted, yet I know it means something special to him as well. Even if we

didn't do anything else together, just lying like that should make him feel secure. I wish it did because he is.

But, being so young, he carries all the burdens of plain adolescent boys: uncertainty, confusion, always ready for a put-down and so reading a remark or circumstance wrongly. I catch him staring in the mirror, obviously wondering what I could possibly find attractive in that reflection of a plain skinny kid. I come up behind, put my arms around him, and tell him to look again at the portrait of the pair of us. I explain what draws me to him and holds us together but he doesn't understand, or what's worse, doesn't believe me. To make certain, he pushes back, tucking his cheeks into the hollows of my groin to offer himself again. He's too young to comprehend that love happens and doesn't have to be paid for. I'd be a fool to refuse him, however, and I don't. Our relationship is not from the modern gay world but from one much older than that: boys are made to be fucked. Men fuck them, care for them, and teach them. Then the boys become men and do the same.

At eighteen and three months out of high school he's overwhelmed, trying to keep afloat in a stormy erotic sea. When you've never had a chance to express passion then it takes some getting used to. He's doing his best, but sometimes I can see him drowning. As I ride him he gets sensitized quickly and can't help but surrender and raise his butt, but its the lying together afterward that's most important. When we start we're man and boy, each seeking what man and boy have always sought – one to give, the other to take. After that the union begins.

Sometimes I think I go to bed with him only so we can be quiet like this when it's over, arms and legs wrapped, snug as spoons. Our fingers curl together and he whispers his love. That's foolish. He knows me well as a lover but he barely comprehends me as a person. He'd deny it, but what he means by that declaration is he loves the intensity of my desire for him. Like any boy his age who has just come out, no one had taken full possession of his body before. Now my desire for it is the greatest thing in his life. He loves yielding and nearly faints when he does. He loves my caresses, my tasting his skin, my breath on the back of his neck. He likes sex but he loves love-making. So do I.

He's not educated but he is quick and has a wry sense of humor: two things which drew me to him at once. I tried to warn him about the usual bumps hit by two males trying to live together, but didn't believe me. He thought it would always be as perfect as it was then.

He wasn't pretty and didn't photograph well.. When I show his picture now, people see he's skinny, plain, and his ears stick out, then they look at me as though I'm crazy.

Two years later he's two years older: almost grown up, no longer a boy but not yet a young man. Boys tend to be passive because that's what boys are like, but young men get demanding as they develop their own proportion and strength. Hormones roar, bodies grow and change,, the bud of masculinity

flowers. It's natural and instinctive. Actually, two years is a long time for man-boy passion to survive.

He became sure of me and aware of himself. He learned to understand passion just enough to play with it, like a toy. He'd prick-tease me, which he had never done before. One time in the car when we were out driving in the country he groped me until I almost came, but when I wanted to pull over and fuck him he just laughed. Being on the bottom was no longer the natural order of things.

Shortly after, he started to hint about sharing. I was sure he'd been talking about us with some bitches and they put questions in his mind he wouldn't have thought of by himself. What they were trying to do was destroy us. They can't stand seeing anyone else happy. What I wouldn't admit to myself was that my boy was growing up. I knew the change was inevitable but
I was trying to hold it off.

What was I supposed to do? By that time I loved him and he was a major part of my life, so I rolled over. I hadn't done that for a while but it wasn't the first time. We all do anything when we're in a mood, but moods have no continuity. He was decently endowed and enjoyed his newly discovered masculinity. I was patient because I thought he wanted to find himself, then once found we'd go back to what we were, man and boy.

I should have known better. He wanted more and was turning me into something I wasn't. When that happens then the fire starts to go out. I kept it going for almost two more years but that was the best I could manage. I'd share my life but sharing ass lay outside my long-term capabilities. Then, before our fourth year had passed, I couldn't get it up and knew it was over.

"You don't rub my body anymore," he complained.

It reminded me of Barbra singing, "...Baby, we're not makin' love anymore..." and I laughed. He didn't understand that I couldn't treat him that way any longer. A man will pet his boy but men don't pet men. Our affair hadn't developed into anything else. That was no one's fault. We'd both tried hard enough but it just hadn't.

In the summer of our fourth year I'd been working at a summer theatre five hundred miles away. As usual, a couple of apprentice boys came on to me. One of those was eighteen year-old Mike. He was five-seven, blazing-eyed and flaming assed. All he had to do was touch me and I snapped up. He wanted me on his cute butt twice a day, three if I could do it. To my own surprise sometimes I did. Usually it was only twice, though, once at lunchtime and then again at night. "Only" twice! I was myself again, held clasped in hot boy-hole.

When I came back I brought Mike with me because I wasn't about to give that up. I went to see Ronnie to explain as best I could. He was badly shocked. Even after four years he didn't realize the kind of man I really was. Neither did he understand that he had grown up and entirely changed, and

trying to change me to match his blossoming masculine urges had been fatal. He wanted us to be men together and fuck each other. Some guys can do that just fine but I can't

Mike didn't have any of Ronnie's qualities nor did I expect him to. His kisses were frequent and demanding but never melting. I never stroked him because for Mike it was fuck or nothing, a constant and desperate sexuality which raised my dick instantly and without fail but dampened my emotions below normal humanity. He had lost his virginity when he was twelve so I never hit bottom with him the way I had so often with Ronnie. That was a real turn-on, but then the tantrums and jealous fits got too bad and I sent him home to his mother. It wasn't easy, because in the nine months we lived together I fucked Mike as much as I had Ronnie in four years!

But it's true enough that sex isn't everything. I have never forgotten Ronnie's sweet hollow, between ribcage and hip, or the clinging of his full lips. From time to time I take out the photograph I have of him at nineteen, shy of looking into the camera. He's intensely aware of me and my wanting to record his presence, but not really aware why – so I can relive that moment and savor it, now, another and later time, now that passion is gone. And Ronnie is gone.

There were many others after Mike but I never recovered what I had given up so it was never the same again. There are moments in life when you want to stop the clock and keep everything just as it is. I felt that way after six months with Ronnie but I'd never felt that with anyone else before and I haven't since.

Later, each of us sailed off into the night in separate directions.

Almost a year later, I saw Ronnie again in a bar with a hot-eyed, nice-looking young man his own age. Ronnie gave me a tight smile as if to say "he gives me what I want."

But there was a brief flash in the back of his eyes that told me he would like to be stroked once more, if only briefly, perhaps to recover what he had lost – his boyhood – so he could give me again what I had loved about him: his innocence.

PURSUED
David Patrick Beavers

Mark stared absently at the orange-red glow pulsing within the car. The half moon only provided enough light to see fully those who came within yards of him along the enclosed concourse. Beyond the low stone walls was a panorama that beckoned highway travelers to stop for a time to snap a photo or two or three of the valley of sequoias and cypress that dumped headlong into the sea. Travelers. Heading to points east or west along Highway 1. Travelers roving in packs. Travelers running solo. The solitary individuals were of paramount interest to him. Specifically, the men. Old. Young. Rough trade. Prep tones. Of various looks and builds. Men all the same. All with the same purpose – stopping along the way to and from places of such disinterest to them that they were compelled to seek out vice. Here. At the rest stop. Here where countless car loads of families and moon-eyed couples would click shutters of cameras in the hopes of forever remembering this special place.

Mark had witnessed many people parading on this brief promenade, blissful and exhilarated by the view, by the stretching of weary backs and cramped legs, by the sheer woodsy, ocean air that purified their lungs and souls. All the while they were unaware of dubious rites of passage, of flagrant acts of passion and lust, being committed only a measure of yards beyond the wall, in a tangle of lush green.

Mark always smiled to himself when Pop, Mom and the kids trucked around, taking in the scenery, chatting and talking and griping all the while. Such a contrast it was. However, the sojourners were most often there in the light of day. His wanton libido led him here night after night in search of someone both specific and general. He'd watched others hop the wall and slither down into the trees and shrubs, following blind trails worn smooth and slick as polished granite, hoping, needing to find concupiscence among the briar patch. A shadowy face might be spied in the darkness. Rough hands always reading flesh like fingers on Braille, adroitly defining the forms of men, allowing for indiscreet selections of cock to service or to be serviced.

Peripheral vision logged all that was around him into his brain, but his eyes were somewhat fixed on the burning ember of the cigarette within the car parked toward the end of the small lot. Smoke rose up from the driver's side, creeping over its shiny, dark roof like ground fog. He'd watched it exit the highway, then slow as it ascended the graded off-ramp, then roll along. He made out the figure of a male driver. The slight illumination from the few lights allowed him to see a glimmer of dirty blond hair framing a face of masculine angles and a strong jaw.

The driver passed, his focus intent on the few empty cars docked randomly before the walkway. The concourse was elevated. Small trees at its

base, between the walk and the wall up high, could camouflage those, like Mark, who didn't want to be immediately spied by those cruising, or by the Highway Patrolmen who sometimes drove through shining their spotlight all around, looking for young, necking lovers to embarrass, or for illegal transactions of drugs, or sex, being performed.

He'd learned of the rest stop from a friend who was a patrolman. This guy was roughly handsome, with a wife and kids and repressed desires. On a quiet night he'd roust through the trees, his body all packed in his tight uniform, in search of two men in anonymous sexual union. He'd shine his flashlight on them, scaring them, threatening them with puritanical phrases from the law, then offer to let them slip away for a small price. The men would service his fat cock and his plump, hard ass with their mouths and tongues, until his jism spewed down some masculine throat and his desire was satisfied.

The patrolman and Mark had known each other for a few years, having met at a bar-b-que given by mutual friends. Mark was fresh from high school. The patrolman was fresh from the Academy, with a pretty little wife and a newborn daughter in tow. Their common interests were few, but Mark had felt the patrolman unduly attentive to him. The bar-b-que progressed with the breeder singles and couples glutting themselves with food and alcohol. The wife felt ignored by her manly spouse. A slight fight ensued between them. The baby fussed endlessly. She chose to leave just as the soiree was winding down. Mark and the patrolman helped the hosts pack it all up. They were the last of the stragglers to leave. As Mark parked in the driveway of his parents' house, the patrolman's car pulled in behind him. Mark's parents were gone for the week, on a vacation to collect more junk to dust and clutter the garage. He invited the patrolman inside. Into the living room, then again into his bedroom, where Mark had a large collection of miniature cars, one of the few interests they shared.

Talk of cars led to talk of other things metallic and masculine. The patrolman produced his handcuffs from his pocket. Demonstrated them. joked about his wife liking to use them as a cock ring on him, clamping both bracelets around his cock and balls, forcing his genitals to swell to dynamic proportions. Mark, being virginal green, comprehended this use but found it unsettling. The patrolman kicked off his boots, then slid down his jeans and boxers as if this were a common action. He massaged his thick meat until it was rigid at attention, then scooped his whole package up in one massive hand and skillfully clamped the bracelets of the cuffs tightly about his groin. Mark felt his own cock swell to capacity. He'd wanted to touch the patrolman's prick. To sense the sensation of a man's dick in his mouth. But, he was afraid. He'd never done this before, save for in masturbatory fantasies. The patrolman flopped back onto Mark's bed, his legs spread, his bobbing cock jutting up between the tails of his shirt. He spoke in detail of the feel of the metal, of the

slight burn and numbing of his flesh as his finger gingerly traced up the length of his veiny shaft to the reddening head of his dick.

Mark's hands found his zipper and he absently pulled his own erection free from his jeans. He stared at the patrolman half naked on his bed. The patrolman asked Mark how old he was. Eighteen was his reply. Eighteen, just out of high school, and very inexperienced. The patrolman propped himself up on bent elbows and smiled. He encouraged Mark to touch him. To feel how thick and hard steel could make a man feel. Mark knelt down between the patrolman's legs, smelling the sweaty ripeness of a man for the first time. Tentative fingers touched the engorged prick before his face. Then his tongue licked the shaft slowly. The patrolman moaned deeply, his labored words encouraging Mark to experience more. Mark's lips slid over the head of this cock. It was hot. Velvety smooth. Musky to taste. Mark almost shot his load then and there, but he clamped down tightly on the base of his shaft, squeezing his orgasm into submission. He'd learned this act for restraint by chance, during a rather vivid fantasy in the dark of night. Now he found its purpose. To keep him from climaxing before he was ready.

He felt the patrolman's hand gently comb through his hair. Mark slid further down on the patrolman's prick, his lips holding fast to the shaft, his tongue savoring the feel of man flesh. The patrolman flopped back again, groaning with pleasure as Mark's mouth watered; as Mark's instincts took over. He sucked the patrolman's cock greedily, occasionally letting it slip from his mouth so that his starving desire could devour the cop's huge round nuts. Mark bit and chewed the hair on the man's balls, his teeth and chin skating across the metal of the cuffs. His tongue connected with the steel, instantly relishing its heady taste.

The patrolman writhed with pleasure as Mark slammed the cock down his throat again and again and again until the patrolman groaned loudly and bucked his hips up, slamming his hairy crotch into Mark's face. Mark felt the delicious burn of salty jism explode in his mouth. The patrolman sat up suddenly and dug his fingers into Mark's hair as he forced his final, choking thrust down Mark's throat.

Mark pulled back abruptly, falling onto his ass. His own cock was throbbing hard and hot. He let the mouthful of hot cum and spit leak from his lips and fall in large globs onto the head of his cock. His hand smeared the patrolman's cum all over his dick, then he pumped his sticky-slick shaft hard until his own load shot recklessly from his piss slit all over his clothes.

They both remained motionless for a time as their bodies relaxed. Then the patrolman got up and gently removed the handcuffs from his crotch. As they dressed, they talked a bit. The patrolman was ten years older than Mark. A bisexual man lacking his male half in the day-to-day world. He told Mark about the rest stop. About the numbers of men who seek out its anonymous pleasures in the quiet of the night. He also cautioned Mark of the

jeopardies involved for those who venture into the woods without awareness. The law presented a danger. But often the bigger risks were taken with strangers.

He'd told Mark to always listen to his gut first, his crotch second.

Mark did listen to the patrolman's advice. His first trips to the rest stop were tainted by suspicion and fear. He went there infrequently the first year or so, always hoping that he'd find someone for himself in the small townships that dotted the area. He did meet a few men like himself. Men wanting men. Needing men. But those he met were pedestrian in his mind. Those near his own age were either quietly coupled, or they were fleeting queens-in-training, more girl than boy. While they all made fine friends for daily wear, they weren't for him. Didn't make him excited or intrigued. Didn't make his prick swell instantly, wanting, needing, to touch and be touched.

So he came back to the rest stop more and more, observing the silent rituals and unspoken rules of those seemingly more experienced than he. With each outing, he became more bold. He graduated from sitting in his car as a quiet observer, to actually walking up the stone steps to the concourse to linger a while to watch and learn. Cigarettes and lighters proved useful props. Men seemed to signal one another of their mutual attraction simply by rustling cellophane wrappers or letting the blaze of a match or lighter linger long after a smoke had been lit. Fiery beacons illuminated faces for a brief time, offering one another a tantalizing sight. Cans or bottles of beverages were sometimes popped open with a fizzing loudness by men just as their hunky prey strolled by. That hissing drew the walker's attention, allowing him a moment to scrutinize the face behind the tongue that probed into the container's opening. Glow in the dark watches that could be covered by the mere tug of a jacket cuff burned like fireflies in the murky abyss of night: lures cast in wait of a catch. And the eyes. Their eyes. Forever intensely scanning to lock sight on another interested pair.

Mark watched them time and again, apprehensive of those men who approached him with their quiet signals, yet wanting many of them to lead him down the garden path into a den of incomprehensible hedonism.

Finally one night, the fog moved in thick and wet, clinging to the earth like a sheet of muslin. Parked on the lip of the wall, with his back to the lot, he adroitly opened a pack of cigarettes, then slipped the noisy wrapping from the pack and discarded it in the trash can. He watched two men down at the other end of the concourse inch slowly toward one another. The better-looking man was older, probably in his forties, with thick, silver hair that intensified his ruddy complexion. The other man was pleasant looking, slightly chunky, yet he looked years younger. The silver-haired man scanned the area quickly, then stepped up on the low stone wall. He remained there for only an instant, then he stepped down to the other side and disappeared into the thick foliage of the shrubs and trees. The chunky man hesitated for a few seconds,

then somewhat clumsily went over the wall and slipped into the thicket as well.

There had been five men on the concourse when he'd arrived. In less than ten minutes, they had all disappeared into the woods below. The three other men had each taken an independent route into the void. The two who just left had trailed off together. Mark was alone. His crotch was straining. He felt more secure under the cloak of fog, so he shoved the pack of cigarettes into his jacket pocket and went in innocuous pursuit of the last two men.

The shrubs were thick. He pushed through the branches slowly, keeping a close eye on the slight path below his feet. His rigid prick snaked up to his left hip, wanting to be touched. He wanted his prick to be touched. By someone other than himself. He'd only had his experience with the patrolman, who had not reciprocated on any level. He'd sucked a cock. He wanted to feel his cock sucked. By a man. He'd had offers from interested guys a few times, but time and place had never worked in his favor. His pleasure had been left to himself to create.

He moved slowly, almost slipping down a steep grade. He grabbed onto a slim tree to balance himself, then side stepped down, all the way down, to a thickly wooded expanse. It was almost surreal to him. The low, dense fog made every tree, every bush, everything seem liquid, as if he was walking on the ocean floor. The sensation excited him even more. His heart beat rapidly. His form flushed with a clammy sweat in the cool night air.

For a brief moment, he felt he was lost in a vacuum tube of time and space. The men he sought had been swallowed whole into another dimension. He scanned the surrounding area. His night vision focused. A rip in the fog allowed a trace of moonlight to catch hold of something nearby. The object glimmered. Mark pressed on carefully, though more quickly. His cock throbbed intensely. His balls were aching. He made his way along, then he froze. He saw them. Not just the two he'd pursued, but all five of the men, crunched together in a tiny clearing among the trees.

Mark inched closer to them, watching the tangle of limbs and torsos ripple unevenly as the men shifted and moved and wound around one another. The chunky man's pants and shorts were in a heap around his ankles. He was bent over, his mouth sucking feverishly on the silver-haired man's cock. A beefy, hairy, bearded man was fucking the chunky maxis ass while he was kissing a slightly balding, tall, blond guy, whose exposed lithe chest was being kneaded by the fifth man, an older, grandfatherly type. This man finally sunk to his knees and started sucking the blond man, then his free hand reached beneath the chunky man, grabbed his chubby little cock and began milking it.

Mark watched this group scene, his first, with rapt attention. He absently fumbled with his belt buckle, loosening it, then he pried open the buttons of the fly of his Levi's and slipped his hand into his underwear to squeeze his cock hard to keep himself from shooting his wad.

The silver-haired man firmly grabbed the chunky man's head and fucked his face with selfish zeal. The slap-slap-slapping of damp flesh slamming against damp flesh seemed to be amplified in that fog-shrouded clearing. The silver-haired man let out an almost inaudible but throaty groan as his hips bucked one final time. In an instant, he was done, packing his fleshy rod into his pants and zipping up. The chunky man was greedy. He pushed the grandfather type aside, twisted his torso, then slammed his face into the crotch of the blond man.

Mark lost sight of the silver-haired man, so he kept watching the others, wanting to walk over with his cock extended before him and join in. His feet would go no farther, though. He couldn't will them to take him in or take him away. He was transfixed.

Suddenly hands wrapped about his waist. Large, open palms slipped beneath his shorts. Mark craned around, but the man grabbed him by his wrists and yanked Mark's arms around his back. Mark felt panic surge through him like a live, unchecked current. Mark tried to pull away, but his assailant held fast, almost breaking Mark's arms. Then Mark felt the slick coolness of the metal as handcuffs clamped down around his wrists. Mark was about to yell when the guy slapped one hand over his mouth, then locked his head in a choke hold. Mark's mind flashed with images of heinous crimes. His attacker pulled him back, away from the fuckfest nearby.

Mark stumbled again and again as he was guided backward, through bushes, under branches, into the cold dark heart of the woods. He was too scared to cry. Too scared to do anything but obey. Just as suddenly, he was yanked back hard against a tree, his head knocking into the rough trunk. His assailant looked him square in the eye. Then he smiled. Mark scowled and howled at the patrolman.

"You fuckin' fuckhead!" Mark shrieked.

The patrolman slapped his hand over Mark's mouth. "Yeah, be fuckin' mad, kid, but don't yell. Not here. You'll have the entire Highway Patrol storm trooping through these woods." Mark relaxed a bit. The patrolman removed his hands.

Mark looked him up and down. "Don't you have to make your arrests while in uniform?"

"I'm off tonight," he said.

"Shouldn't you be home with your wife and kids?" Mark asked flatly.

The patrolman shrugged. "She's got ladies over for a lingerie party, hunting up something hot to slip into that I can tear off." "Would you take these handcuffs off me," Mark said.

The patrolman held a finger up. "One," he said. "I told you that if you were gonna come out here, you had to be diligent at all times. I could've been a real fuckin' psycho with a blade or somethin'."

Mark suddenly felt stupid. He'd violated the rule. Unaware could lead to danger. "You're right."

"Those horny lunkheads back there aren't your type anyhow, kid. Now, I know I've seen you a few times down at the beach with a couple of good lookin' studs your age."

"Yeah, well, they're happy fuckin' each other," Mark said.

"So? There are others, aren't there?"

Mark laughed. "Get real, Cuff Man. Unless you want to spot me with a bogus I.D. so I can get into the clubs up in the city, I don't think I'm gonna find a single guy here who gives me an instant boner."

The patrolman's fingers found the bottom button on the tails of Mark's shirt. He unfastened it. Moved up to the next. Unfastened it. "Some of these bushes are poison oak. You know that?"

"No," Mark said absently as he watched the patrolman's fingers unbutton the rest of his shirt. The patrolman pushed the panels apart, then hiked the yoke up and slid the top of the shirt and jacket back over Mark's shoulders, allowing him better access to Mark's lithe, muscled torso.

"There's ticks, too," said the patrolman. "And fleas, and spiders. Mice. Rats. Lizards. All sorts of shitty critters." His palms pressed into Mark's pecs, kneading them gently. "How many cocks have you sucked out here?" he asked as his hands skated down Mark's chest, then stomach.

"None," Mark's voice cracked. He was suddenly bristling with a static charge.

The patrolman hooked his fingers around the waistbands of Mark's Levi's and his briefs. "None?" He let out a slight laugh. "Right."

"Really," Mark said. "It's taken me this long to get up the guts to come down this far."

The patrolman smiled softly. "So how many cocksuckers have you pumped a steamin' load into?"

Mark flushed crimson. His embarrassment angered him. "Fuckin' lots, okay?"

The patrolman's face went blank. His eyes narrowed a bit. "None," he said to Mark.

Mark's scowl softened. "Well, maybe I'm not pretty enough or ugly enough, or tall enough, or short enough, or got a big enough piece!" he snapped.

The patrolman's fingers slipped around, sliding between the cloth of Mark's clothes and the flesh of his hard hips. The patrolman pushed Mark's pants and shorts down to his knees. Mark's rigid cock slapped the patrolman on the cheek. Mark felt the hot flush of embarrassment red wash over him again. He started to move, but the patrolman pressed him back against the tree.

"I don't want my protégé to be a virgin forever," the patrolman said with a smile.

Mark shivered when his cop's warm, wet tongue flicked across his nipple. The patrolman's lips wrapped around Mark's tit, sucking it gently, teasing the erect point of sensitive flesh with his teeth. The man's strong fingers found Mark's other nibble of sweetmeat, kneading the flesh of his pec slowly, deliberately pinching and tugging the erect nipple. His tongue washed over Mark's chest, back and forth, slathering it with hot, slick spit as his mouth darted back and forth, back and forth, like a hungry pup wanting all the teats to suckle on. Mark's knees buckled under a euphoric wave of pleasure. The patrolman 's broad shoulders braced the youth. Mark wanted to touch this guy, to once again feel the strength of his cock sliding between his lips. He slumped forward, his chest and flat stomach blanketing his cop's face. Mark winced sharply as bristles of whiskers scraped across his stomach, down, down to the soft waves of hair framing his cock. The patrolman's hands pushed Mark up, off of him, back against the tree. Gentle, smooth lips, dripping saliva, sucked the sensitive head of Mark's prick into a hot, active mouth. Mark's entire body twitched with involuntary abandon. The patrolman felt Mark's cock strain and pulse in his mouth. He suddenly opened his throat wide and slammed the entire shaft of Mark's prick deep into his throat. Mark groaned as his cock pumped load after load of cum into the patrolman's gut.

The patrolman sucked hard, drawing every last drop of virgin jism from the youth's tube. Mark's cock remained rigid, though, as if his balls were ready to shoot another round. The patrolman suckled on his young acquaintance's eager dick, lapping at the shaft and head. His long tongue curled around Mark's nuts and drew them into his mouth. Mark was panting heavily. His body trembled as he lost control and began to slowly slide down the tree trunk.

The patrolman's strong hands slapped against Mark's hips, bracing him, then he pushed the youth's thighs up and brought them down, draping them over his shoulders. His hands cupped the cheeks of Mark's ass and he pressed into them, coaxing Mark to shimmy back up on the tree. Mark's cuffed hands caught hold of the bark, steadying him, allowing him to help the patrolman raise him until Mark's cock hovered just above the patrolman's head. Mark was ready for anything, he thought. But nothing can prepare a tender virgin asshole for the electrifying, almost intoxicating sensation of rimming. When the patrolman's whiskered chin pressed through his ass cheeks, his nose inhaling deeply the perfume of his crack, and that hot, long tongue shot up deep into his rectum, Mark lost it. His already cloudy sight fuzzed like static snow on a television screen. Vertigo dizziness made him lickerish. He almost passed out.

The patrolman caught him again, let him come to rest on the bed of needles and leaves. Mark's eyes fluttered open. His pleasure, his appreciation, bled through his eyes, speaking silent volumes to his cop. The patrolman grabbed Mark's still hard prick. He then leaned forward, licking Mark's face,

his lips. Mark could smell himself on the patrolman's face. He craned his head up. His lips wrapped around the patrolman's nose and Mark sucked the shadowy scent of his ass from the cop's flesh. Their lips met. Tongues and teeth strained to fuse their mouths as one starving life form.

Without ever really pulling away, without ever looking down, the patrolman unfastened his pants and slid them down his legs, yanking one foot free, then letting the tangle of cloth remain hooked about an ankle. Mark caught sight of the familiar dick, just as hard and pulsing as he remembered it. He wanted to suck him off, but when he began to sit up the patrolman pushed him back down. Their eyes locked. Mark watched intently as his cop stared at him, then let a wad of spit and residual cum drip down from his mouth into his hand. He reached behind himself. Mark thought for a second, his cop was going to try to fuck him, but instead he succumbed to the immediate pleasure of the patrolman's tight chute encasing his prick. The patrolman just stared into Mark's eyes as he rode slowly up and down on Mark's shaft, pumping it with delicious ease. Within minutes, Mark fell motionless as his entire body bristled with the ecstatic tingle of a slowly milked orgasm. Again he shot a geyser of jism, deep into the patrolman's ass.

They both remained fixed for a time. The patrolman gently traced random trails across Mark's flesh. Then he pulled himself off of Mark, brushed aside some leaves and climbed back into his pants. Mark moved slowly, not wanting the moment to end. The patrolman helped Mark up.

"Shit," Mark said with a grin.

"What?"

"Thank you."

The patrolman pulled the key to the handcuffs from his pocket. He unshackled Mark and rubbed the slight numbness from the youth's wrists. "I should thank you." .'Why?,,

The patrolman cocked a brow and shot Mark a dubious smile. "Don't get to do this much anymore. Especially not with a guy like you."

"What's that supposed to mean?"

"You can read between the lines, Mark."

The patrolman escorted him out of the woods and back to his car. The two sat in Mark's car for a while longer, talking about sex and people. The patrolman clued Mark in on the men he knew frequented the rest stop. Most were harmless dudes just needing some attention from other men. He then made a list of descriptions of cars and their drivers whom he felt Mark should steer clear of. Though he had no tangible proof of the darker aspects of these men, he felt strongly that they were prone to more sadistic sexual bents.

Mark wanted to know if there was any guy who visited the rest stop whom he might connect with. Someone as inexperienced as he. Someone with an intensity and gentility.

"Someone like you," Mark finally said to the patrolman .

The patrolman's face flushed. He didn't like compliments. "I don't know everyone who comes out here," he said. Then he flashed on one young man he'd seen here only a few times. He told Mark about this young man. Described his car in detail.

Mark listened intently, his imagination easily conjuring up the shiny sedan with its customized features of glimmering chrome.

"Think the kid's a car nut," said the patrolman. "I'd come out here now an' then when I got off duty if I'd seen his car parked here late in evening. He'd sit in the car watching. Never did see him get out, though. He'd just sit, sometimes for hours, watching guys come and go."

"And you watched him," Mark said.

The patrolman nodded. He pointed to a tree covered point up on the concourse. "There," he said. "You know the spot. You can watch the guys in their cars throughout most of the lot and they can't really see you."

"You think he's dangerous?"

The patrolman thought about it for a moment. "No," he said. "I think he's just scared. Like you are."

"Was," Mark said.

"Yeah, well, kid, let tonight be a lesson to you. Always, always remain aware of what's around you." Mark nodded. The patrolman gave Mark's crotch a friendly squeeze. "I gotta git, kid."

"Maybe I'll see you out here again?"

"Maybe."

Mark grabbed the patrolman's small note pad and pen. He scrawled his telephone number down and handed it to him. "Call me if you're up for a blow job."

The patrolman took the slip of paper, tugged his wallet from his back pocket, then folded the slip up and tucked it neatly away in one of the many compartments. He smiled at Mark as he opened the car door. "I'd like that. A lot."

"Goodbye," Mark said.

"Later, kid. Remember to keep your wits about you."

The patrolman shut the door, then walked across the lot to his car. Mark felt sad, but excited. Cuff man. His own personal cop. He watched his man drive away, disappearing into the looming wet haze.

Mark's hand slipped down to his lap. He was rigid again. Through the windshield, he made out the thinning pate of the blond man loitering up above on the concourse. He looked around. The lot was empty save for him and the blond one. He thought about venturing out into the woods again, but he was apprehensive. It just seemed safer if there were more men around.

He took his pack of cigarettes from his pocket and patted himself down for his lighter. It was missing, probably lost in his tryst with his cop. He leaned over, popped open the glove compartment and fished around for a book

of matches. As he closed the glove compartment, he spotted the patrolman's handcuffs and a small, worn, leather billfold. He picked up the square of black hide and opened it. It was his cop's badge. The gold shield shined brightly in the dim light. Nimble fingers stroked the leather case. It was damp. With sweat. His sweat. Mark inhaled the faint, musky scent. His cock twitched. He picked up the handcuffs. The key was missing. His fingers dug into the crevice of the seat, furrowing around. like a mole, scooping the assorted debris up and out onto the seat. Pure happenstance. In the ball of crumbs, dust, gum wrappers and coins was the key.

Mark locked and unlocked the cuffs a couple of times, testing them. The faint light gleamed on the metal. The oily silvery blue hue fascinated him. His finger tips stroked the smooth surface methodically. His cock strained and twitched, involuntarily expelling another sticky load in his briefs. His hand snaked down into his underwear. The warm, thick jism was puddled in his pubic hair. He withdrew his hand. White cum jelly stuck to his fingers. He wiped his fluid. on one of the steel bracelets. Rubbed it in. The brilliance of the metal went matte dull.

Another car pulled into the lot. Mark glanced over at the newcomer, then back up at the blond one still lingering on the concourse, then back to the coupe. A pleasant looking man, maybe in his late twenties, climbed out of the car and charged along the walk, up onto the concourse. The blond man immediately moved off, out of view. He'd scented his prey and was moving in for the kill.

Mark laughed to himself. Lit a cigarette. Pocketed the badge, the cuffs and the key. He climbed out of the car, quietly closing the door. He popped open the trunk and dug around for a flashlight. An industrial flashlight. His father's.. He tested it, making sure the batteries were still charged. Satisfied, he gently closed the trunk, then made his way up the steps, onto the concourse, then over the wall. Once he was deep into the thicket, he paused to listen, to discern the various low sounds of the night. The dead quiet was noisy, he learned. Wildlife moved about. The plant life rustled now and then as a weak breeze picked up, tearing away the blanket of fog. Distant cars hurried along. Even the faint sound of far off waves lapping at the beach could be heard. A rustling. An abrupt rustling of spidery branches and trembling leaves. Just to his right. Then he heard them. Barely breathing. Smacking slurps. The slight jangle of a belt buckle.

Mark stepped slowly, softly along, toward the men. He slid the badge from his pocket. Readied his flashlight. He spotted their shadowy forms nested between two trees. The blond man was on his knees, his face buried in the young man's crotch. He held up the flashlight. Click!

The men fell apart, stumbling into the trees and shrubs, their eyes blinded by the intensity of the light. Mark thrust the badge out into the light for them to see.

"Highway Patrol!" he barked.

The blond man shot off, blindly crashing through the whipping branches, fleeing into black obscurity. The young man scrambled to pull his pants up as Mark moved in on him. The young man stumbled again and crashed bare-assed on the ground. He shielded his eyes.

"Please!" he said.

"Get up," Mark said in a low, throaty growl.

The young man climbed to his feet, trying to avoid the blinding beam of the flashlight. But he couldn't. Mark made sure it was always in the guy's face. The young man fumbled with his pants, pulling them up. Mark's prick raged instantly at the sight of the guy's long, uncut cock. He'd seen pictures of uncircumcised men, but he'd only seen two in real life. Both were guys in his high school who were exchange students. One was from Brazil. The other was from Denmark. The fleshy log was quickly tucked into the guy's pants.

"That guy," the young man started, "he just grabbed me when I went to take a leak."

"Turn around," Mark barked. The young man did so, putting his hands up in the process. "Hands behind your back, please."

"You're arresting me?" The young man was about ready to cry.

"Hands behind your back, sir!" Mark ordered.

The young man slipped his trembling arms behind his back. Mark tucked the flashlight under his arm, snagged the handcuffs, then clamped them down on the guy's wrists. The guy started sobbing. Mark spotted a handkerchief poking out of the young man's back pocket. He plucked it out. A long one. Adult size for big snot, Mark thought. Interesting. He set the flashlight in the crook of a nearby branch, then slipped the handkerchief around the young man's eyes, blindfolding him.

"What're you doing?!" the guy wailed.

Mark grabbed the guy's shoulders. His foot pressed into the back of the young man's knee, forcing him to kneel. "On your knees, sir," Mark said.

"I'm sorry...! I'm really sorry...!" the guy sobbed.

Mark grabbed the flashlight and trained it on the guy's face. He looked young. Like him. 'Take a few deep breaths and get hold of yourself," Mark said flatly.

The guy strained to breathe. To quit sobbing. He finally succeeded. "Why... Why am I blindfolded?"

"Because I'm not going to haul you in. Yet." Mark purposely paced in front of the guy. "How old are you?"

"Twenty," he said hoarsely.

"Your name?"

"Gus," he said.

"Look, Gus, I don't want to bust you, but you have to know that this isn't the place for this sort of behavior."

"I know, sir," Gus said. "I was stupid."

"Maybe I could call your folks to come get you..."

"No! Please!" Gus cried.

Mark suddenly felt sorry for this guy. "Okay. Where you from, Gus?"

"South Bay, sir. We... We just moved here."

"From where?"

"Florida, sir. Orlando."

"Your folks from there originally?"

"My mom. My dad was born in Cuba."

"Cuba?"

"Yeah! His family fled when Castro moved into power." "And you don't want me to call them to come collect you. "No!" Gus shrieked. "Please! They'd kill me!"

Mark realized Gus was genuinely panicked. "All right, all right, Gus." Mark crouched down in front of his prisoner. "Gus? Gustav?"

"Gustavo," he said.

"Gustavo. Handsome name," Mark said. "Look, Gus, answer me a question." Gus nodded meekly. "You like to suck dick?"

Gus stammered, his brain searching for some correct answer. "I've done it," he finally said.

"That isn't what I asked."

Gus hung his head low. "I like men. Yeah."

"I'll do you a favor, Gus, if you do me a favor."

"What?"

"Suck me off, I let you go."

"How... How do I know you'll..."

"Stick to my word?" Mark asked. "Well, that's a crap shoot, isn't it?" Gus had no response. "Look, Gus, you will be surprised." Mark loosened his Levi's, then shimmied them down a bit. His prick sprang free, as hard and needy as ever. He inched his cock toward Gus' mouth, then traced his lips with a cockhead brush. Gus' lips parted slowly. His moist, pink tongue slid out, blindly flicking Mark's piss slit. Mark tucked the flashlight under his arm, then gently pressed his palms against Gus' temples, coaxing him on.

"Suck on the head, man," Mark said.

Gus' full lips wrapped around the plump helmet, his expert tongue twitched rapidly along its underside, then suddenly jabbed the piss hole. Mark's legs trembled, almost giving out from under him. Gus' tongue slid out over his lower lip, snaking down the underside of the shaft. Drool dribbled, bathing Mark's stiff prick like thinned honey. Mark's fingers dug into Gus' hair, into his scalp, slowly clawing and pulling it all into a twisted knot. Gus groaned. He slammed his face into Mark's crotch, shoving the entire length of the silky erection down deep into his throat, letting his throat and raspy, slick tongue close about the tasty cockhead.

Mark's whole body convulsed with a strange rush of euphoria. It felt like the tip of his prick was caught in a pump of oiled velvet rapidly milking rush after rush of a tingling, static, bristling current of energy from him. His whole cock strained, as if it wanted to stretch beyond the confines of human flesh. Gus started pumping himself up and down the still swelling rod of meat, twisting and tugging, faster and faster. Every connective nerve in Mark's body surged to overload. Just as his quivering body almost gave way to complete collapse, he grabbed Gus by the back of his head and held him fast, fucking his prisoner's face with brutal abandon until he slammed a geyser of sticky, hot sperm down Gus' throat.

Gus guzzled Mark's jism greedily, his drool cascading down Mark's crotch and thighs. Mark started to ease himself out of Gus' mouth, but Gus clamped his lips down and smashed his face into Mark's crotch, sucking until the last drop was drained. Mark pulled himself away. Gus turned his head and calmly spat the cum and spit from his mouth. He took a few deep breaths.

"Shit..." Mark groaned. "You're fuckin' intense, Gus." "Yes, sir..."

Mark hitched his pants up onto his waist, leaving his now spent cock dangling in a slow deflate. He hooked. a hand under Gus' arm and pulled him to his feet. "Now, I was gonna let you go..."

"Please, sir!" Gus panicked again.

"Gus, Gus, Gus! Shhhh... Calm down." He gently guided Gus back to the tree, pressing him against it. "I said you'd be surprised." Mark's fingers unfastened Gus' pants.

"What? What're you doing?" Gus said fearfully.

Mark reached into Gus' shorts and pulled out the long, fleshy prick, milking it slowly. "You've shown me I need some practice." Mark gingerly slid back Gus' long foreskin, mesmerized by the fine, baby smooth skin of the head of his protected penis. It still glistened with the dampness of the blond man's spit. Mark's mouth suddenly flushed with heat as saliva flowed freely. The instant his smooth lips slipped over the succulent head, Gus' entire prick swelled like a fresh soaked sponge, pushing itself deeper into Mark's mouth. Mark gagged, then relaxed his tongue and throat, allowing the donkey dick complete access into him. He braced himself on Gus' hips, pressing the young man's ass hard against the tree trunk. He then slowly took the full length of this fleshy cock down into his throat, pressing his face, his nose, into the shaggy patch of sweaty pubic hair. Mark savored Gus' smell. Musky. Faintly acrid with residual traces of urine. As his nostrils strained to inhale this smell like some sort of poppers, his throat relaxed even more and he felt the cramped dick almost slip all the way down into his gut.

The back of his tongue arced up, pressing against the shaft. His throat constricted a bit, almost undulated, as if trying to dislodge this hunk of meat. Gus' whole body shook fiercely as a choked groan crept from his mouth.

John Patrick

Mark pumped Gus' erect piece, relishing the thickness, the length, the sheer silkiness of it all. Finally, he let the stiff prick slip from his mouth and bounce against his face. He wrapped his fingers around the base of the shaft and the balls, pushing them up, watching the swollen equipment strain. He suckled on Gus' nuts while he squeezed the shaft and pushed the flesh up, forcing the prepuce to ride up over the cockhead. Gus gurgled a throaty growl of pleasure.

Mark's lips found the pinch of stretched foreskin. The tip of his tongue pried under the fold and skidded around the head again and again, sometimes flicking at the sensitive underside. He then peeled it back, exposing the knob. Precum oozed from the slit. Mark wiped it down his chin, down his neck, wanting the sticky fluid all over his skin. He then opened his mouth and swallowed the prick whole again, this time twisting and tonguing as he rode it up and down with an almost violent intensity. Gus began to lose his balance as he approached climax. He stifled an almost pained groan as his abdomen contracted sharply and he involuntarily crunched over.

Mark pulled back quickly. His hand pumped the shaft vigorously. Heavy globs of steamy jism shot out, spraying Mark's face and chest. Mark continued pumping the prick, fascinated by the gushing cum, spraying, dripping, coating his face, his hand, Gus' cock. He continued milking the young man, massaging the globby, runny goo into Gus' fleshy tube like it was lotion.

Gus panted heavily as his penis went flaccid. Mark burrowed his face into Gus' crotch, loving the feel of so much male flesh grinding into him. He finally pulled back, admiring Gus' manhood. Gave it a gentle pet, then stood up and wiped the cum from his face. His shirt was splattered. It would wash, he thought.

Gus let out a deep felt sigh. "Shit..."

"Quite a fuckin' piece you got," Mark said as he fumbled for the key. He guided Gus away from the tree and turned him around, then retrieved his flashlight and turned it off. He felt for the keyhole then unlocked the cuffs and stowed them away in his pocket. "Keep the blindfold on."

"But..."

"Final condition," Mark said. "Count to thirty, then remove it. Take it off before thirty and I'll have your ass hauled in."

Gus nodded and began to count. Mark slipped off into the dense, liquidy darkness of the trees. He hid himself, though he was able to keep an eye on Gus. Gus did count to thirty. At least he seemed to. He removed the blindfold, squinted into the night, then hastened from the spot.

The fog had lifted a bit. Moonlight allowed Mark a solid look at Gus' face. Handsome. Handsome and young. He'd keep an eye out for him as he floated around the county, but he knew he'd probably only ever see the young man here again. Mark sighed. The rest stop was becoming an addiction.

He used the cuffs and badge a few more times, then gave them back to his patrolman during an ensuing encounter. The Cuff Man liked Mark's ballsiness. Still, he cautioned Mark to take care and to be diligently aware.

Mark did. He eventually became bored with the guys who regularly frequented the rest stop. He was forever seeking new faces. New meat. New bodies. Most specifically, he kept a watchful eye peeled on the parking lot, hoping to find the young man with the customized car that the patrolman had told him about.

The time came. Months of waiting, of staking out, paid off. The guy was still sitting in his car. The highly polished chrome was a brilliant blue in the night light. The pulsing glow of his cigarette ceased with a billowing cloud of smoke that seemed to Mark to fog the entire interior of the automobile. A mini-supernova flared up behind the windshield. Smoke and reflected glare masked the man behind the wheel. Another orange-red glow pulsed. More nicotine fog wafted out and over the gleaming metal roof.

Mark took note of the men finally emerging from the woods, hurrying along the concourse and down the steps to dump themselves into their cars. The game had been disbanded. Their minds and cocks and been expanded. Had exploded. Their needs met, they all drove home.

Mark's car was at the opposite end of the lot. The man in the customized car had few choices now. To seek out the only one still there, to wait for more to come, or to simply drive off as all the others had done.

Mark scooted over on the wall, positioning himself to be somewhat seen. He lit a cigarette. Inhaled deeply. Allowed the expulsion of smoky residue to sail out through the branches of trees like a beacon. Minutes ticked by silently. Forty-five. No one else showed up. Mark was about to give up when he heard the strained creak of hinges, followed by the thunk of the car door slamming. He was out of the car. Mark could see him. Tank top glued to his torso like cling wrap. Faded wool plaid in blue and gray as a jacket. Baggy khaki trousers breaking atop worn boots. Blunt cut, dirty blond-brown hair. Clean shaven. The patrolman said he had cropped hair and a van dyke. Time had passed, Mark thought. Quite a few months since the last sighting of this bent gem. The patrolman had almost busted him once, over a year ago, down in the woods, but he got caught up watching some other guy completely service the young stud. The kid had gotten so worked up, he shucked all his clothes, letting the man worship his entire lean body, the guy's tongue bathing every molecule of flesh. Cuff Man said he'd pumped two loads from his stiff prick while watching them. He had the kid's car plates run at work. Found out his name. His address. His age. Mark's age. Cuff Man told Mark he'd spotted the kid there two more times, but on both occasions, the youth remained locked in his car, just watching the men cruising. He sat and watched and then went on his way.

Mark watched the stud slowly climb the steps, then stroll onto the concourse. He stopped directly opposite Mark. Turned away. Stared into the indigo shadows of the trees beyond the low wall, his hands thrust deep into his pockets.

Mark always hesitated making a move on someone, especially some dude this good-looking. He just sat there, chewing on his cigarette butt, taking slow drags. The kid suddenly turned around and looked him up and down.

"You a cop?" he flatly asked Mark.

"Not tonight," Mark answered.

The kid shifted a bit, still staring at him. He nodded. "Got another smoke?"

"Maybe." Mark said. "You out?"

"In my car," the kid said.

Mark proffered his pack. "Yeah."

The kid moved toward him slowly, cautiously. He slid one of the cigarettes from the pack. Mark flared his lighter. The kid leaned in. Lit the butt. Plumes of gray smoke streamed from his nostrils as he stepped back again. "Thanks."

Mark liked what he saw in the fire light. The kid had almost navy blue eyes. Icy cold. Whites whiter than bleached cotton. Large eyes. "Sure," Mark said absently.

"Anyone else here?" he asked. Mark shrugged. The kid looked around, then turned back to Mark. "Pull out your cock."

Mark was a bit taken aback by the command. He froze for a second, staring into the eyes of his new friend. He flicked his cigarette butt aside, then slowly unfastened his belt, undid his fly, then reached into this shorts and massaged his meat. It responded quickly. He pulled out his swelling dick and loose, fleshy balls. The kid flipped his cigarette aside and stepped right up to Mark. His smoky fingers gripped Mark's meat, squeezed it hard. He tugged it slowly, watching it rise up rigid. He bent over, then took the entire length of Mark's erection down his throat with ease. Mark caught sight of the kid's other hand, still sunk in his pocket, moving around. The kid let Mark's prick fall from his mouth as he stood up again. Mark saw the movement in the pocket again, only now he could see the huge, hard lump straining to rip through the left side of the kid's loose pants. Change jangled as he played his game of pocket pool.

"Pull yours out," Mark said.

The kid stared blankly at him for a moment, then he grinned. Full, wet lips framed straight, hauntingly white teeth. "Later," he said.

Mark stroked his meat. "You got a name?"

"Dino."

"Mark."

Dino grabbed Mark's cock again. Stroked it. Almost studied it. He bent over again and took it down his throat. His mouth rode up and down Mark's prick over and over, all the while pumping his own dick through a fistful of pocket cotton. Spit ran freely, coating Mark's cock, streaming over his balls, soaking his shorts. The kid's right hand gripped the base of Mark's erection and slapped the stiff pole against his face and outstretched tongue. He then slipped down to Mark's ball sac, sucked his nuts into his mouth, almost cracking them with his teeth. Mark flinched. Dino let Mark's testicles go free. His tongue snaked down, trying to probe Mark's ass.

Mark instinctively shoved his pants and shorts down to his knees. Dino's hands shoved them down to his ankles, then forced Mark's knees to spread. Mark shifted his body, almost lying flat on his back. The hard, cool stone of the wall grated his ass cheeks..

Dino's left hand found its way back into the pocket, as his right hand jerked Mark's meat. Then Dino suddenly slammed his face into Mark's ass. His tongue found Mark's asshole. Forced itself into him. Mark shuddered. His eyes fogged from the light-headed intensity of the pleasure. His focus shifted from Dino to his own desires as Dino tongue-fucked him hole while pumped his numbing prick.

Mark heard the click. Felt the icy cool of the steel pressing flat under his balls. He snapped back to reality. Dino held a switchblade at Mark's crotch. He pressed the flat of the blade against Mark, the sharp side just a scant shadow away from slicing into his testicles. Dino's cold eyes stared at him. He smiled smugly, then gingerly dragged the tip of the blade up, between Mark's nuts, following the natural seam of his ball sac, then up the length of the underside of Mark's shaft.

Mark's heart raced like he was pumped full of speed. Dino pressed the entire knife against Mark's cock. The handle and blade were just an inch shorter than Mark's dick. Dino wrapped his hands around both cock and knife, gripping them hard, almost as if he were trying to fuse them together.

He started to carefully pump Mark. Mark just stared in disbelief, with almost abject terror, as he watched. He could feel the tip of the blade snag on his cock, though it didn't feel like it stabbed through his flesh. The sensation. His fright. The feel of the metal. It all suddenly excited him.

Dino masturbated him harder. Faster. With deliberate and expert precision. Mark couldn't move. Wouldn't move. Even the slightest twitch might cause the tip of the blade to dig in under the head of his dick, slicing through it. He felt a surge ripple through him. His hips wanted to buck, to speed on his quickly approaching climax. He remained fixed, though. His cock and balls throbbed. His breathing became rapid and shallow. Then hot, thick cum spewed up from his piss slit like lava, shooting high up into the air, splattering all over him, on Dino, all around.

Dino let Mark's cock go. He wiped the jism stained blade across Mark's thigh, then pressed the sharp edge against the base of Mark's deflating dick as he unfastened his own pants and loosened his thick, thick prick. Mark's mouth ran wet with a sudden hunger. Dino's cock was pretty long, but it was the fattest prick Mark had ever seen.

Dino slid the blade up and over Mark's torso, close to his throat, then he pressed the huge, swollen head of his cock against Mark's shit hole. He pressed forward and in, just barely getting the hammerhead of his dick to nest inside Mark's rectum.

Mark's hole strained with pain. He'd never been fucked. Dino's knife prevented his protest. Dino's face hovered over Mark. Stared into his eyes. He suddenly grinned again as his dick slid out of Mark. He then jabbed his beefy log into the juncture between Mark's cock and balls. His hand pumped his prick fast and furiously, until watery jism exploded all over his genitals.

Dino sighed a euphoric sigh. His right hand clamped down on Mark's throat as his left hand adroitly manipulated the switchblade. He pressed the narrow flat of the blade against his thigh and closed it up. Mark felt a slight bit of relief.

"Tight fuckin' pussy you got, guy," Dino growled. He then slid the handle of the knife into his wet mouth, coating it with spit. He then pressed the cool, wet handle against Mark's sphincter, pushing it up into his chute. Mark shuddered. Dino fucked him with the short, metal and enamel handle until Mark's cock rode up again and shot another wet load out, onto Dino's pants.

Dino then drew away from Mark. Pocketed his knife. Mark sat up cautiously, pulling his pants back up. Dino wiped the cum from his clothes with a handkerchief.

"Fuckin' weird fuck..." Mark said.

"Fuckin' hot, man," Dino said.

"You're too fuckin' pretty to be so bent."

Dino shrugged. "Wouldn't have cut you, dude."

"Yeah, right."

Dino turned his body around, though he kept his head and eyes trained on Mark. The waist of his pants went loose again. He lowered them for Mark, revealing his tight, boyish ass. "Wanna get even?" He bent over, his hands gripping each firm cheek, and spread his crack wide, offering his puckered hole. "It's a tight fuckin' fit, dude."

Mark took the bait, wetting his index finger as he approached Dino's hole. He jabbed his digit up into Dino abruptly. Dino writhed and moaned. "Fuck your boy cunt right here..." Mark said.

"Do it."

Mark pulled out his prick. Slickened it with gobs of spit, then stabbed Dino's asshole and jammed himself up into his burning hot guts. His hips slammed into Dino's ass violently, pounding the boy's butt with all the brutal

force pent up in him. He fucked and bucked so furiously, Dino was almost knocked to the ground from the force.

Just as Mark was about to shoot again, he pulled out. He watched himself spray thin, watery cum all over this blond boy's pretty ass. Dino's hands wrapped around and ground the silky jism into his skin. Mark packed himself back into his pants. Dino hiked his britches up and tucked himself in. Mark could see his residual wetness seep through the fabric of Dino's pants.

Dino turned around and snagged the pack of smokes from Mark's pocket. He took one. Mark lit it for him, then lit one for himself.

"Fuckin' hot," Dino said through a cloud of rising smoke. "There's hotter," Mark said.

"Wanna raise the stakes sometime?" Dino asked.

"I'm game."

Dino pulled out a hand scrawled card from the pocket of his shirt and handed it to Mark. "My number. I'm home all day tomorrow."

Mark glanced at the card, then pocketed it. "I've got nothing else planned."

Dino nodded to him. "Call. Come by. Maybe we'll do it downright nasty."

Mark nodded. Dino grabbed Mark's crotch one last time. Gave it a hard squeeze, then grinned again and meandered off. Mark lingered for a while longer up on the concourse. He watched Dino speed off. He smiled to himself. The patrolman had given him back the biting handcuffs. "Downright nasty," he said to himself. Then he started laughing.

CLOSERS
Keith Banner

The KFC parking lot is clear of cars, the sky above it glowing black with a smear of jet smoke. Ray picks up straws, napkins and cigarette butts, sometimes pulling weeds, while Andy's inside, cleaning off the back shelves methodically. Ray had to get out of there. This is a time he won't remember, a time spent just picking up other people's crap, but he does remember what happened last night, remembers it now as he stoops to pull up a thick gray weed growing from a crack in the sidewalk. Remembers Andy's face in the back of the van, Andy saying, "Get the fuck away from me."

Inside, Todd the manager taps things into a calculator on a table out front, fucking with his inventories. He has long curly hair, like Robert Plant, and wears a tie, white dress-shirt, blue polyester pants and scruffy Nikes. He looks up. "You get the lot?"

Ray just nods his head. "Can I go ahead and do the big fryer? It's 8:40 now, and nobody's here. I cooked enough Original for the rest of the night."

"It's dead, sure." Todd goes back to his work.

Ray walks down the hall to the kitchen-door. Andy is pulling all the cardboard boxes filled with straws and wetnaps down to clean behind them. He is completely quiet, and Ray, confronted with his quiet once again, feels fevered. Shame makes him say, "What the hell is your problem?" Even though he knows the answer.

Andy just keeps on being Andy, fuming silently as he rinses out his dishrag. Skinny with black straight hair, his paper KFC cap dangling back to his neck, he stands on the stainless steel table, wiping off the rusty shelves as if it were the most important task in the world.

Ray gives up, goes to the big fryer the size of a baby's casket, shuts the simmering tub down, drains the grease, starts scrubbing the fucker out.

Andy and Ray had first tried it together at the lake in early June. It was almost as if they had planned it without planning it. The rain was a warm relief, the lake boggy. Droopy trees surrounded the van, and Andy and he smoked pot. They were friends, sharing a very fat joint. The silence out here was broken up by the van's stereo: Rush's "Permanent Waves."

Andy was shirtless, in the back. His dad had given him the van when he got the new one, right after the divorce. It was metallic brown on the outside, with a painting of a desert and Arabs on camels beneath a starry sky. Inside were a luxurious but worn out cream-colored shag carpeting, vinyl seats, a cushiony foam mattress on one side, with black speakers lining the walls. "A pussymobile" is what Andy's dad called it, giving him the keys.

The joint made the world seem closer to Ray. The lake gleamed in yellow moonlight, with weepy trees like sleeping nerves. This was where he belonged, he suddenly knew, the back of Andy's van, still tasting the hickory flecks of pot, a seed rolling on his tongue. Andy always ate the roach. Andy the daredevil. Once Andy had played a trick on his mom, putting red food-color all over his wrists and smearing it on the bathroom sink, screaming bloody murder, his mom getting ready to call the ambulance, and then he burst out laughing. The red dye still clung to the grout on the sink, like a scab, and Andy kept saying his mom had never forgiven him, even though he did that little stunt when he was in eighth grade.

Now, though, there was peace, and Andy shirtless. All the queasy lonely feelings Ray had ever felt took shape around Andy, a halo. People in Middletown, Ohio don't feel things like this, he knew, but veiled in marijuana people could do a lot of things. That was the trick, to have something to blame it on. Andy yawned, then went outside in the dark, pulled his dick out, and pissed. Ray watched with his stomach clenching. Fie could feel himself getting hard just by that. He could die in that swoon, he knew, turn curly and effeminate like the queers at school in choir and drama, faggy boys people pushed into water fountains and down stairs. He imagined busted lips and swollen eyes turning black.

Andy came back in saying, "Come here."

"What?"

"Just come here."

Ray followed Andy through the wet grass that lined the small lake. "Wait," Andy said, and he ran back to the van and got his small bottle of vodka. He drank it straight, then handed the vodka to him. Above the lake, in the distance, were the tiny lights of an interstate, floating molecules.

"What?" Ray said, taking a drink. "It's a lake."

Andy took a lighter out of his cut-offs pockets, bending down. At first Ray didn't know what the hell was going on, but eventually in the flimsy light of the lighter he saw five or six bloody animal carcasses, dead coons stripped of their pelts. Ray noticed eyes in the gnarled orange flesh in the lake.

"Fucking poachers," Andy said. "They just kill coons, then like rip their skins off right there on the spot."

"Jesus," Ray said.

"Makes you sick," Andy said, flicking the light off. "Let's go back."

Andy switched the music to old Pink Floyd. In the quiet, the gnarled bodies turned into ghosts in Ray's mind. He pictured them walking around, clumsy as babies. Andy lay on the foam mattress as if he were posing, his cutoffs unbuttoned. It didn't mean anything. Sometimes Ray wondered if Andy were truly insane. Maybe they both were: geeks clinging to each other. Both of them had gotten jobs at Kentucky Fried at the same time, just rode down in Andy's van and marched right in, filled the application out in the

dining room. Like that, they had summer jobs as closers. Andy and he were trying to save up to go to Florida, but the money, when they got their checks, just evaporated, turning into bags of pot, tapes and fast-food.

"Man," Andy said, no reason.

Ray moved in closer then, no reason. There was the freedom of having seen the dead bodies together, as if they were witnesses to the same crime. They sat like that for a while: Andy on the foam mattress, Ray beside him.

"My dad poaches," Andy said. "Kills deer out of season. Deer meat sucks. You ever eat squirrel?" Andy was whispering now near Ray's ear.

"No."

Andy started it. They did it so quietly that Ray was afraid he had lost the ability to speak when it was over. Andy wanted him, it seemed; his hands groped and found Ray's dick, and felt around his balls, up near his asshole, then entering him with his finger, pulling in and out while they both jerked off. They came almost in sync, splattering their stomachs, then pulling away from each other and wiping it off with a Kleenex Andy pulled out of nowhere. Outside it started to rain harder.

Todd says, "Original down!"

Ray looks up from cleaning the inside of the fryer with a green Scotch pad. Andy is up front, running the cash register. A line of people with disgruntled faces are staring back.

"We're out of fucking Original," Todd says, holding a pair of greasy tongs.

While cleaning the fryer, his head submerged in greasy steam, Ray had forgotten about the rest of his job. Looking up at Todd's pissed-off face, he just stands there sweating and says, "What?"

"We're out of motherfucking original man," Todd whispers desperately.

"You said I could shut down," Ray says.

Andy comes back, shaking his head. "People are pissed." Todd glares at Ray. "What am I supposed to do?"

"You said I could shut down the fryer." Ray wipes sweat from his forehead.

Todd says, "This won't just be my ass, it'll be yours too buddy." He stomps off, goes up to the front and says, "Sorry, we're out of chicken. Our fryer's on the fritz."

The people up front moan like it's the end of the fucking world.

Andy and Ray stand by the big boiler, where Ray had been cleaning. Under his breath, Andy says something.

"What?" Ray feels hopeful now, that maybe Andy is siding with him about the issue, and they both will be able to laugh behind Todd's back.

"I said, your ass is going to be fired I bet."

Andy smiles. The smile hurts Ray. He can feel it eating into his feelings like a piranha.

"Thanks a lot," Ray says.

Andy scoffs. "Hey whatever. You're the one that fucked up." He walks back up to the steam table area.

Todd comes back, still panicky, "Can you drop some extra-crispy? Did you keep that fryer on?"

Ray nods his head.

"Good. Some of them will take extra-crispy. Get your ass in gear. I'm gonna have complaints coming out of my fucking ass-hole."

"Hey man you were the one--"

Todd glares "Just do it and shut up!"

Ray goes into the coolers, gets a box of chicken, cussing. The cooler inside smells musty and bloody, and when he opens the box, inside are pink and purplish chicken bodies, like the bellies of old ladies, he thinks: plump with their legs and wings flying outward, nestled in crushed ice. He takes the pieces out and pulls some of the yellow fat off of the thighs, then dunks them into the milky mixture before breading them at a rickety stainless steel table. The bodies remind him of the coons at the lake, and then he looks up and Andy is standing beside him helping put the breaded pieces of chicken on the tray.

"Todd told me to give you a hand."

"Thanks," Ray says sarcastically. He thinks of last night in the van, how Andy just turned on him, just like that. "Get the fuck away from me." They were parked at the back of Andy's housing addition, near a soybean field. "Get the fuck away from me." It was sudden and terrible. Ray knew why it had happened: because he had worn the jock-strap, one article of clothing, kinky and strange but familiar too, a beige one from gym he'd slipped on before going to work. Something he had done for Andy, and it made Andy sick, as if that one gesture had made Andy see the whole picture, made him see exactly what they were doing together. Who they were. Ray remembered putting it on before going into work, feeling sexy all night knowing he was wearing it, waiting to reveal it to Andy, even hinting at it sometimes as they worked. Feeling beautiful, secretive, queer.

Andy looks up at Ray. "Quit fucking staring. How are you getting home tonight?"

Ray doesn't say anything. He picks up the breaded chicken and drops each piece into the dank grease. Andy walks back up to the front, where people are waiting. Todd is running around, almost pulling his hair out. "This is going to be my ass man!"

Ray walks over to Andy while Andy runs dishwater. "What is your problem?"

Andy smiled condescendingly. "No problem."

"You gave me a fucking ride here tonight. You picked me up like usual."

Andy laughs. "I'll take you home tonight, but you better be thinking about the rest of the summer."

"I can't believe you," Ray says.

Andy turns his back to him, and Ray tries to turn him back around. Andy pushes Ray back into the stainless steel fridge. The breath out of him, Ray wants to hit Andy back, but Andy seems too ready.

Andy whispers, "You got your fucking panties on tonight?" The timer goes off. Ray backs up and pulls the chicken out of the boiling foam, lets it drain on a tray, then shoves it into the warmer.

Todd says, "Great man, great. Maybe they won't be so pissed, huh?" He shoves the cooked pieces into boxes and serves everyone what they ordered.

In the van, Ray says, "What is wrong with you?" again, although he is nervous. Andy is driving on the interstate toward Dayton. Strangely lit buildings, like space stations, float past the windshield. Andy won't speak, until they are out in the middle of nowhere, on a country road off the main highway, surrounded by blank woods and cornstalks. Andy pulls off at the side of the road. He jumps out and leans against the front of the van. Ray gets out.

"Where the hell are we?"

Andy says, "I don't know."

"Fucking, it's like midnight, isn't it?"

"Yeah."

"So why are we here?"

1 don't know. I didn't want to go home."

"Oh."

"My dad and his buddies come up here to hunt," Andy says.

"Hunt what?"

"Animals." Andy laughs condescendingly.

Ray looks out at the corn, at the surrounding raw black trees. The smell of skunk and humidity mix in with the stink of KFC on his clothes. Then Andy is right on top of him, in front of his face suddenly.

"Why did you do that last night?"

"What did I do?"

"That fucking jockstrap. Man, that's total fag. Total fag. I couldn't believe it."

Ray laughs. "We are fags."

Andy punches him in the gut. Ray leans down, embarrassed and in pain at the same time. After a while he stands up, and Andy is walking out toward the cornfield. Ray gets totally pissed, his breathing going back to regular. He wants to run after Andy and beat the holy shit out of him, only he doesn't want to at the same time. He starts walking down the road, not

knowing how he will get home. He could find a gas station, call a cab, but he doesn't have any money. Saying that they are fags had been like telling the truth for once, but now in the wet darkness smelling skunky he wonders if it's true: maybe he's the fag, and Andy is the mixed-up straight guy. Actually Ray doesn't even know what a fag is. His love for Andy comes from all kinds of sources, not just Andy, from the way he felt all along, seeing guys, feeling them in his head. Then he remembers the punch in the gut. Ray's love for Andy comes from hating him too, from realizing Andy's a fucking flake, violent and dopey and probably will end up like his dad working at a car plant, shooting deer and flaying them, getting married and having two or three bratty, good-for-nothing kids.

Andy honks the van's horn. Ray turns around. Andy stops and gets out and runs to him.

"I'm sorry," Andy says. "Listen, just forget what I did, okay? God. I lose my head sometimes. Come on."

Ray stands in the white lights of the van. He looks into Andy's face, but then his glance darts away. He gets into the passenger side, and Andy peels out.

In Andy's basement a small antler-less deer head hangs above the television on a wood plaque. The eyes look like drops of black oil frozen in time.

"My dad's here," Andy says. "Since they got a divorce, he comes home more. It's so stupid."

Andy has changed out of his KFC uniform. Shirtless, in a pair of cutoffs, he turns on the air conditioner full-force, giving the musty atmosphere a sweaty chill. On MTV, Beavis and Butt-head are spray painting Metallica on an old man's house and setting it on fire. One time, Todd at work called Andy and Ray Beavis and Butt-head, and now everybody there does. Once he and Andy even imitated them at a crew meeting getting their pay-checks. Now he feels sad looking at the cartoon characters, thinking that people see Andy and him that way. They're so fucking stupid, but then he remembers they're just cartoons, and wonders what it would look like if the two of them started kissing out of nowhere. Andy lies on the brown couch, begins smoking a cigarette. Ray is on the black vinyl lounger.

Andy's dad comes down the stairs, in a pair of work pants and a t-shirt. His shoes are on the other side of the couch. Andy's dad has long brown hair which is thin on top and pulled into a ponytail.

"Your mom's still at work," he tells Andy. He kicks at Andy. "Quit wallowing on the couch. Sit up."

Andy sits up. "I thought you guys were divorced," he says.

His dad laughs. "We are. Don't worry. I just needed a place to crash because they sprayed for bugs at the complex. Your mom said I could sleep here until tonight. She was working a 16-hour at the nursing home anyway."

"I know that," Andy says.

Andy's dad smiles at Ray after tying his shoes. "How you doing, bud?"

"Pretty good," Ray says.

Andy's dad stands up and laughs. "You guys still working at Kentucky Fried?"

"Yeah," Andy says.

"I was gonna ask Andy if you two wanted to go hunting this weekend." His dad yawns.

"I don't know. I think we have to work."

Andy's dad looks at Ray. "This guy hates to hunt." Andy sits up, angry, but doesn't say anything.

Andy's dad looks disgusted for a minute, and it seems as if the two of them hate each other completely, a change in the air. For a second it's like they can't pretend anymore.

"Yeah you're a big man going out killing fucking Bambis," Andy says, putting his cigarette out on a plate on the end table.

Andy's dad's eyes go soft and hurt, then tighten up with sarcasm. "Whatever. I'm outta here. Quit telling your room I don't wanna take you places. I offered, buddy. Later, Ray."

Andy is still pissed, "I never told her anything about you."

Andy's dad is gone. Andy goes silent. They watch the rest of Beavis and Butt-head, then a few videos. Ray gets tired, but still keeps his eyes open as he sits on the sofa, wishing he could go home suddenly. Andy stands up then and goes over to the TV, flicks it off, then turns around.

"I bet Todd's gonna fire you," he says.

"Thanks a lot," Ray says.

Andy smiles. "Oh you're welcome. You'll be out of work, Butt-head. Hey, you get fired, I'll fucking quit. We can try Burger King. Or Famous Recipe, huh? Keep our careers more in the direction of the chicken industry?"

The two of them laugh. Andy's smart mouth pleases Ray. He feels a rush of love. Andy's chest looks weak and small, the nipples pink and tender. Andy walks over to the deer head hanging on the wall and slams into it. It falls and bounces on the carpeted floor. Andy picks it up.

"Let's go outside," he says, opening the door at the back of the basement, holding onto the deer head.

Andy's backyard is small, surrounded by bent fence and soybean fields, and beyond that railroad tracks going into and out of the car plant. The plant glows like a mosque. There's a big maple tree above an old fire filled with sand. Andy runs underneath the tree and throws the deer head up into the limbs a bunch of times. The head disappears into the thick green leaves. Andy laughs his head off. Ray stands on the tire, looking up into the leaves. The deer

head has gotten caught in the limbs, and the limbs crack together, as if they have become real arms holding onto the head, maybe crushing it.

They get the sleeping bags. The TV is on low-sound, Stone Temple Pilots singing "Plush." Ray watches, but then Andy comes back into the room in his underwear, with an electric fan. He plugs it in, turns the TV up, and reveals the joint. He lights it and they smoke it, the fan blowing the smoke out an open window.

Sometimes, like at work, Ray doesn't even feel alive, but now he knows he is, and that's one thing to remember. That he is alive, that he can feel this way in private, and not tell anybody--not care if he's fired or if he'll be able to get out of this shitty town or if he'll end up like Todd the manager, so screwed in the head that he almost loses it because they run out of Original. Then Andy is naked, pale in the TV light like someone he doesn't know but desperately wants to. Ray takes his shirt off, and Andy sits Indian-style on one of the sleeping bags, toking, with the fan whirring. Ray falls to the floor, onto the bag near Andy. They stay like that for a while.

"This doesn't mean anything," Andy whispers when they start.

Ray doesn't say anything. They kiss, roll around, a feeling of floating in space. Tomorrow they'll wake up, and Andy will be sorry or at least pissed, and he'll climb the tree and get the deer head and put it back on the wall. But now they are here in the middle of it, Ray kissing Andy's nipple. Ray moves down Andy's body to kiss around his cock, licking the hair there, smelling the raw heat. Ray's hard-on makes Andy feel safe, not scared anymore. He sucks on it, tasting the salt of sweat and pre-cum. On the floor, they twist around so Andy can suck Ray too, and for a while they do that, the sound of sucking and moaning filling the basement.

Ray stops, out of breath, but Andy continues. Andy can't help feeling this is the way it should be, every night, and at points he looks up and sees Ray's face close in on itself, as if Ray believes this too when he isn't thinking.

Before he's about to come, Andy pulls Ray off, and silently makes Ray lie on his stomach. It's all silent, every move. Andy's spit-slicked cock fits into Ray's ass without even hurting, Ray relaxing into the mildewed flannel of the sleeping bag. Ray can feel Andy's breath on his neck, feel his asshole tighten around Andy's cock, and he jerks himself off awkwardly while Andy fucks him. It doesn't take long. Soon Ray feels Andy's cum spurt inside him, and for that moment too he feels that safety of flux, of being one person together, like a married couple or Siamese twins.

When it's over, Andy runs to the bathroom. When he comes back, he is silent, lost in thought. Ray knows he should wash off too, but he lingers on his sleeping bag, while Andy rolls over on his side. TV-light explodes softly on Andy's back, and Ray watches, thinking it's okay that what they do together doesn't mean anything, because Ray knows it means everything. It has to.

TERROR
Dirk Hannam

Often when I was a boy I heard the grownup men talking among themselves and one would say: "I was scared shitless." I thought it was just a saying. Later, after I had been out in the world for a while, I learned that guys, overwhelmed in war or catastrophe can indeed be so struck with terror their belly muscles clamp tight in a sudden spasm so that they involuntarily empty their bowels in whatever clothes they are wearing. It is probably part of some escape mechanism carried forward from before the time of Neanderthal Man when the earth was a dangerous and fearful place and death waited around every turn. A shitless man could probably run faster and so escape from a stampeding mammoth or a raging bear.

I don't know about this from personal experience but I do know that the pit of a guy's stomach can react to fright so violently he becomes "scared pissless." Believe me, it can happen and the guy ends up both shaken and helplessly ashamed of himself, with the crotch of his pants sopping wet.

One time we were humping ore at the Aurifodina Mine, out in the desert up near the head of Cowbones Canyon. A lot of people think that the Western Desert is all rolling sand dunes like pictures of the Sahara but that's not so. There are all kinds of desert out there, a lot of it mountainous. And it's not all naked rock and dirt. There's scattered grass and bushes like greasewood and sage, and wildflowers in spring, in even the most desolate places. Lots of native creatures live there: coyotes, foxes, lizards, rabbits, mice. It is hot, almost suffocatingly hot, especially in the canyons and draws and, of course, extremely dry. Surprisingly enough, however, there are occasional springs here and there. Fortunately there was a good one near the mine – a pool of good, sweet water under a rock overhang.

Cowbones Canyon is a narrow, twisting cleft which cuts back for maybe a mile into the mountains East of the Sierras. It is a deep blind gully with blood-red rock walls overlaid up above with black lava from some ancient flow. In certain lights it looks dark and scary. At other times it is blindingly bright and blazing hot.

The mine was about halfway along this canyon, the entrance quite high on the cliff to the right. From below it looked like merely a black hole driven into a massive rock outcrop. There was no scaffolding or other superstructure, just the scree of broken rock – the tailings from the tunnel – scattered over the cliff below. A dangerously thin trail led from the canyon floor to the opening. And that's about all a person would have seen if he came wandering up that way.

The working was owned by old man Crowley who was driving the tunnel off and on whenever he had a little money to buy grub and explosives

and, sometimes, pay for help. Crowley may not have been as old as he looked, or he might easily be a lot older. He was short and stooped, always dressed in the same old, stained coveralls, frazzled flannel shirt and leather boots. You couldn't see much of his face because his hair and beard were so long and scraggly. Never cut either one, he said, because that would lose him his strength. Never washed, because soap and water were bad. for the skin. Unkempt, unsavory, often unfed, he was a cantankerous old bastard but persistent as hell. He insisted against all the evidence that there was gold back there in the mountain and he was determined to find it and strike it rich.

He had a canvas fly stretched over near the spring and a ring of rocks where he built his fire. Supporting one side of the fly was a pile of wooden boxes he'd packed in over the years to store his food and some of his tools and other possessions. The explosives he kept safely away in a cache near the foot of the trail.

This time I'm telling you about there were the two of us helping the old man: Lou Bailey and me. Lou and I were working during the fall and winter to save enough cash to get back on our feet. We'd bummed around and tried this and that and we both finally woke up to the fact we were no longer children and we still had no trade, no profession, no special skill by which we could earn a decent living. We made no more per hour, the minimum, than when we dropped out of school. So here we were, two teens, he from Oregon, me from California, humping ore. Working like galley slaves as a point of fact, and none too sure that old man Crowley would actually have the dough to pay us when it got too hot and we had to go back to the city.

The way we worked was kind of primitive. Crowley didn't have the money for fancy equipment. About all we had were hand tools: shovels and pickaxes, rock drills and hammers. There was a narrow-gauge track into the end of the tunnel with an old iron mine-cart riding on it to haul out the ore.

Crowley had complete charge of the explosives. Lou and I and the old man took turns hammering in holes in the rock at the end of the tunnel. When they were deep enough Crowley would fill them with dynamite sticks or black powder, depending on whether he had enough money to buy a case of dynamite. He'd lay a fuse and we'd all get out and away. He'd light it and in a little while there would come a hell of a deep W-H-U-M-P in the mountain. Then, after the gases had cleared out, Lou and I would go in, dump the pieces of shattered rock into the iron cart and push it out along the track to the entrance. The old man wouldn't let us dump it. He examined each piece carefully first, looking for traces of gold before throwing it over the side onto the tailings.

It was slow, hot, exhausting work. We never found a single hint of gold all the time we worked there. I said old Crowley was persistent. It was amazing how deep he had burrowed into the mountain. That mine tunnel was a monument to sheer bull-headedness and hard labor. I don't know exactly how

far it went back into the rock. It seemed to me like it must have been at least a quarter of a mile. About a hundred feet from the entrance it bent away to the right so that in a short space you lost the daylight and the hole was pitch black. It just seemed to go on and on into the darkness.

In this kind of rock you don't need mine timbers to brace the sides and top. Anyway there are no trees for a hundred miles or more which could supply timbers; this is desert country. So inside the tunnel the bare rock, broken and uneven, forms walls on either side and hangs overhead. You can expect no comfort in such a place; everything is hard and sharp, pitiless, without any smooth edges. It could be frightening, I suppose, to think about all those thousands of tons of stone pressing down in the mountain above the tunnel. Lou and I and the old man never gave it a thought. All we were concerned with was driving that hole deeper and deeper, blowing out the tunnel-end, clearing the rubble and getting on with it.

Of course the tunnel didn't go forward at an even height all the way. Sometimes the blast was stronger or maybe the rock fractured differently so that the roof overhead dropped a bigger than usual load. This would produce almost a cavern instead of just a tunnel.

We didn't work in the black dark, of course. We had hard hats with flashlights on the front. You could always see what you were doing but out on the edge of the flashlight beam and overhead in the caverns the blackness pushed against the light. We were mostly so busy lifting rock or hammering drills and often so dog-tired we never paid attention to what lay beyond the light.

We labored in that damned tunnel six days a week. The only reason we didn't work on Sunday was because old Crowley was some kind of a religious nut. Every Sunday he spent all day reading his tattered Bible, praying out loud and delivering sermons, like St. Francis, to the bushes and any animals within the sound of his voice. The whole day he kept at it, on and on and on. Lou and I couldn't stand it.

The two of us had a sort of stand-up bath with water from the pool on Saturday nights, standing naked under the stars while we soaped up and rinsed each other off. On Sundays we'd go off on long hikes down to the flats and up other canyons. In the afternoons when it got too hot we'd go back to Cowbones, climb up the trail to the mine and slip inside. We'd stand at the entrance for a time listening to old Crowley haranguing the Lord and the sagebrush down below then get back in where he couldn't see us and make out. We had a pile of gunnysacks and an old blanket on the floor that we kept especially for the occasion.

Lou is one of those boys you like and believe in at first sight. He stands just under six feet, stronger than hell for his size; the muscles on his arms and back are like steel from all the hard work he's done. His face is square and deeply tanned, firm nose and chin, sparkling clear blue eyes,

honesty written all over it. He's had a rough life but he hasn't soured on it. He laughs and jokes in a man-to-man kind of way which makes a young guy like me feel like he's an equal partner in everything. I know he is very popular with the men who live and work in and around the desert. With me he is absolutely tops. Was then, is now. I wasn't a child, of course, I was fully grown – and I sure as hell was no virgin – but I looked up to Lou as a guy who had a lot more experience in everything than I had, a guy who I could trust absolutely.

Because of all this Lou and I had no hang-ups. He was a sexual guy and so was I. We frankly needed and enjoyed each other. So we'd stand hugging and kissing in the semi-gloom of the tunnel back from the entrance until we felt each other getting aroused. I'd start unbuttoning Lou's shirt . He'd loosen my belt buckle, unzip my fly and grasp my balls. I'd pull his pants down over his ass and lay hold of his buns, feeling for his asshole. We'd waltz around this way, half undressed until his cock and mine were hard and urgent. Then we'd get down on our makeshift bed and forget the whole world in a kissing, licking, sucking, fucking, wrestling match, a regular tornado of sex. There were no fancy considerations of Greek active or passive, top-man or bottom-man. We were both hard-muscled and strong, loaded with juices from a week of abstinence, healthy, vigorous, full of fire. I'd get into Lou's ass in a rapid-fire thrusting that built up to a crashing climax. He'd enter me and fuck the living Dejesus out of me. We'd rest awhile on the sacks then he'd come back at me, stroking my cock and fondling my balls, and I'd grab his and work him over. We'd both get hard and uptight again and get back to fucking each other over and over until we were both drained dry and our energies were spent. Sometimes, of course, we'd vary the routine by sucking each other off but mostly it was hard fucking, one to the other. Finally, by the time evening came on, we'd end up on the blanket and gunnysacks stark naked, covered with sweat and streaked with mud from the rock dust, two exhausted but satisfied buddies. It was the only thing that made our isolated life in the canyon livable.

We worked and played and worked and played like this for quite a few weeks. Then there was a day in January when we were working away at the deep end of the tunnel, Lou and I, filling the mine cart. It was hot as blazes at the shattered face and the air still smelled of explosion gas. We were both wearing jeans and heavy boots but no shirts, covered with dust and smudge marks, a real pair of young, hard-rock miners. Crowley was outside checking on hand drills or something. Suddenly there came a rumbling deep in the mountain and the mine cart started to roll back. I felt a tremor underfoot and pieces of rock fell from the roof.

Lou yelled: "EARTHQUAKE!" and we both made a dash for the entrance.

But Lou caught his shoe in the iron cart-track and went sprawling on his face on the broken rock underfoot. I stopped to help him up. As we started

to run again there was a roar and the whole mountain swayed under and around us. There were sounds of breaking and smashing and the scream of stone grinding against stone. Ahead of us the roof gave way, crashing to the ground, tons and tons of rock. The tunnel was jammed with huge chunks of broken granite and the air was cloudy with dust. Our escape was blocked.

We had our lights, of course. We could see each other and the wall of broken stone plugging up the exit ahead of us. We were both stunned, but more surprised than frightened at that point.

"Jeez," said Lou, "if I hadn't fallen we'd both be buried under that pile. Come on, let's clear those chunks out of the way and get out of here."

We tackled the pile in a fury, desperate to get out of the place before another shake collapsed the whole tunnel over our heads. It didn't take long to get the smaller pieces out of the way but we discovered that at the center of the fall there were blocks far too big to move. We tried and tried to find a way around or over. They were just too massive for us.

"Jamey," Lou said, "we can't do it. Stop struggling so hard. Save your energy. Rest for a minute and let's try to think our way out of this."

I tried to move a huge rock out of the way by main strength and failed. "All right," I said, "I'll quit. Start thinking."

"Well, first of all, I think we should turn off one of our lights to save batteries, said Lou, "We don't know how long we're going to be stuck in here. I'd hate like hell to be in here in total darkness. I'll put out mine; you keep yours on. I also think we should try to conserve our strength. Let's just sit here on the floor for awhile and rest. I hope to god old Crowley is okay. He can tackle that rock fall from the other side and maybe clear a way out for us. If he's careful he can use dynamite to break up those big hunks.

We sat down, Lou on the right, me on the left with our backs against the side of the tunnel. For a long time neither of us spoke. The horror of our situation, trapped in the bowels of the mountain with the threat of more quakes ever-present, stared us in the face. We were both frightened. I started to shake uncontrollably. I could feel Lou next to me. He put an arm over my shoulders and sort of hugged me to still my shaking -- and, perhaps, to keep himself from doing the same. There was nothing to see, just the two of us and the rough rock walls on either side, the hanging rock overhead and the pile of heavy rubble blocking our way out.

Finally I could stand it no longer. I had to do something, anything, to help us get out of there.

"I'm going for the tools," I told Lou. "Maybe we can bust up some of those rocks or lever them out of the way."

"Just be damned careful you don't disturb anything," said Lou as I stood up and started for the end of the tunnel, "Don't let's trigger another fall."

Feeling a little more confident because I was taking some action, I picked my way through the broken chunks on the tunnel floor until I got to the

far end. Our shovels and pickaxes were lying scattered about. I gathered them up and hauled them back to where Lou was sitting waiting in the dark.

I put them down at the foot of the rock fall and turned to Lou when, suddenly, without warning, the roof at the far end of the tunnel dropped crashing to the floor. The whole back half of the tunnel, thousands of tons of stone, had collapsed. I had just come from there! I was so terrified I lost control. I couldn't help myself. My belly clamped shut in total spasm and I felt the piss rushing out of me into my pants, a wet, warm, relentless flow that poured out of my pecker and down my legs. I was helpless to stop it and too appalled at our danger to try.

The rock fall went on and on while I stood there in terror. I was about to be crushed alive. I knew it, It was going to be NOW! Everything stood still for me, my heart stopped, my mind was paralyzed, while I pissed my fear into my jeans.

But nothing more happened; the air was fogged with dust and individual smaller chunks fell or rolled off the massive rock fall but the tunnel roof directly over us still held.

My heart started pounding and again I was overpowered by the shakes.

"God, that was another close one," said Lou, "you were the lucky one this time, to be back out from under before that fell. Come over here and sit by me, Jamey."

"I can't, Lou," I said, suddenly aware of my sopping wet crotch and deeply ashamed. My face burned with embarrassment. "I'll sit over here," I told him.

"What's the matter, fella, you shit your pants?" he asked. 'No, not that, I'm wet down there, I think I've pissed myself.

"Well that's nothing to be ashamed of. You've had a bad shock is all. It isn't the first time it's happened when a guy gets frightened. It's happened to me. Come on over here, sit down where I can hold you. If wetting your pants is the worst thing that happens to us we've got it made."

Reluctantly I went over, uncomfortable and stinking, and sat down beside Lou.

"God, I'm sorry, Lou," I said, "I don't know what got into me."

"Forget it," he said, "But if I was you I'd get out of those wet jeans. If we're here very long you'll get a damned uncomfortable rash between your legs and around your balls from that urine. Take them off. You can fold them so the dry part is up and then use them as a cushion to sit on.

So I took them off. I wasn't wearing any underpants so after folding them up for a cushion I had to sit bare-ass-bare-balls beside Lou. Again he put an arm across my shoulders and we just rested there for what seemed like several hours saying nothing, each deep in his own thoughts, worried and

frightened, breathing the dust-laden air, and fearing what might be coming next.

My battery started to give out and my hat-light began to fade away. At Lou's suggestion I turned it off and he lit his. With the brighter light things seemed more bearable and I became more aware of my nakedness.

"Lou," I said, "if I have to sit here bare-ass, why don't you slip off those jeans and sit bare-ass beside me?

"Sure," he replied. He unbuckled his belt, unzipped his fly and shucked his pants down and off. He folded them into a cushion and sat down again beside me.

"Well, this is kind of cozy," he said in his old, joking way, "Come here, you fucker, I'll give you something fresh to think about."

With one arm he pulled my shoulders firmly over to his and kissed me full on the lips. With the other hand he grasped my shriveled cock and balls and started to play with them, gently squeezing and caressing.

I was in no mood for sex in such a terrifying situation and I would have pulled away but he kept me firmly within his grasp and in spite of myself I began to feel tension build up between my legs and ease off in my mind.

"Jamey, we may never get out of here," said Lou as he fondled me, "You know that. I don't hear any sounds from the other side of the rock-fall. Maybe old man Crowley is hurt or dead and we're going to have to stay in here forever. If that's so, Jamey, I want you to know I really like you. Love you, I guess. Always have since we first met. I sure as hell don't want to die in this black hole but if I have to, I have to, and you with me. So, Jamey, before we get too weak from hunger or lack of air I want to make love to you one last time. Really fuck the living Dejesus out of you. Okay?"

It came as a shock to me to have Lou coming on so strong in the middle of disaster but he kept on caressing me and kissing me, hard hat to hard hat. I was resistant, then confused, then hesitant, and finally willing to make love for one last time. Actually I came to understand we really were going to die together, starving or choking in the darkness, so, in despair, I turned to this boy I admired so much to give him what he wanted. I started to caress him, hugging and kissing and stroking his warm skin. In no time we were breathing heavily and the two of us had raging hard-ons.

Lou took his hard hat and placed it on a rock so that the light was turned on the two of us. He took mine off and laid it to one side. We had had no shirts on so we were both naked except for our heavy boots.

I looked at Lou in the dusty light, at his splendidly muscled arms and chest, his flat belly with its forest of curly hair, his surging cock and heavy ballsac, his powerful thighs and tight buns. All at once I felt such a wave of affection and, yes, hunger for him, come over me I was struck dumb.

He was looking at me, staring at me. I could see his eyes roving up and down over my bare body. "God, you're beautiful, Jamey," he said, 1 never

realized it before, you're downright fucking beautiful, fella. Come to me, I want to hold you.

Eagerly I went to him, and we stood and hugged, lips to lips, belly to belly, cock to cock.

We couldn't lie down, there was nothing to lie on; our sacks and blanket were under the rock fall.

So I bent over, hands against the rock wall while Lou caressed my neck, my back, my armpits, my waist and finally my buns. He took his time. There was no rush; we obviously weren't going anywhere. Finally, in the dim light, he spread my cheeks and placed his fingers on my sphincter. He brought saliva to it and gently massaged across and into it, one finger, two, until I quivered in anticipation. At last I felt it, his bulbous cockhead, thrusting in till his balls were pressing against my buttocks. Then, lovingly and firmly he started to withdraw then thrust forward, back and forth, back and forth. It was done so kindly I felt consumed by pleasure. Gradually he increased the tempo while I held steadily to the rock until, in a final mighty thrust, he shot his juices into my belly.

We just stood there, me bent over and with my hands pushing against the rock wall, Lou tight up behind me, his thighs against mine, until his cock softened and shriveled back and out.

It had been a siege of such intense feeling we could only gasp and in the end go back to our cushions to sit down and rest.

Perhaps another hour went by without either of us saying a word. But I was still on the verge of arousal. I finally spoke: "I want to make out with you. I need to fuck you, man."

He went over to the wall and bent over, hands outstretched against the stone. I caressed his neck and back and buns just as he had done to me.

"Come on, Jamey," he cried, "Stick it into me. Let me feel that big old cock of yours one last time. Fuck me, man, fuck me."

I did as he asked and forced my stiff tool into him deeper and deeper, but gently, as far as I could go. Just I reached the end of that first thrust and my thighs pressed against his, there was a dull THUMP in the rock fall. I yanked myself out and immediately went soft.

"Lou! Lou!" I cried, "did you hear that? Old man Crowley is blasting the rocks out there! We're going to get out of here! Let's get our pants back on."

"Jamey, I sure did. God, it's not a moment too soon. I'm with you. Get ready to scramble over that pile of rocks as soon as you see light from the other side."

Then we waited. It seemed forever. From time to time we could hear the thump of an explosion as the old man worked his way toward us. He obviously wasn't taking time to use the rock drill to make holes. He was

probably just burrowing in under the biggest boulders and trying to shatter them from below.

As he got closer, we could feel the jar of the explosions in the floor and pieces of stone fell from the ceiling.

Lou and I started yelling: "Hey, Crowley, take it easy."

Of course he couldn't hear us so he just went right on trying to force a way through the pile.

Naturally our spirits were buoyed. Lou put an arm over my shoulder and hugged me to him. "Jamey, you still have a fuck coming to you. When we get out of here you get first turn."

"When we get out of here, Lou, I won't give a shit whose turn it is. I've discovered I love you, man. We're going to fuck each other forever, regardless of turns."

Just then we could hear a far rumbling deep within the mountain.

"Oh my God, Jamey," he cried, "it's too late! It's too late! The roof is going to come down on us. Jamey, JAMEY! I love you. I love you. I love you!"

We stood holding each other in terror as the rumbling grew louder and closer. With a crash and a roar the quake shook the tunnel. The floor heaved and a huge crack opened up over the entrance rock fall. Suddenly the floor under the fall gave way.

The huge chunks of rock dropped down and away off the side of the canyon and sunlight streamed into the tunnel. We found ourselves standing on the very edge of the cliff. A cloud of dust billowed up from below.

Without a word we both dashed out of the hole and scrambled head over heels down the still rolling scree to the floor of the canyon.

"Angels in heaven!" cried Lou, "that was close. Where's old Crowley?"

We looked back up toward the tunnel. There was still a black hole up there but the entire face of the massive rock outcropping had fallen away from the canyon wall. It now lay scattered down the cliff and over the canyon floor. There was no sign of the old man.

We searched and at last we found him where he had been thrown by the collapsing outcrop. He was dead. We took him back up to the remains of the tunnel and buried him under the broken stones on the floor. It seemed the right thing for the old man to rest forever in the ruin of his life's work. He will be undisturbed. The pool under the overhang where he had his camp went dry overnight, sucked down into some subterranean cavern. So no one goes up that way any more.

And as for Lou and me, we're still buddies, partners and bedmates. Will be forever, I hope.

TAKE IT LIKE A MAN
John Patrick

Steve showed up on my last trip to New Orleans in November. He looked so young; I guessed not even of legal age, and green as far as river barges went, but at least he knew port from starboard. He claimed to have spent two years in the Navy, but I doubted it. There was something not quite real about him that I could never put my finger on. He made me think of a handsome actor form one of those TV comedies, playing the part of a barge worker.

That month we were shipping taconite ore from the mines up north, to be loaded on some Japanese freighter and then hauled back to Louisiana in a year as a boatload of Toyotas. The Daisy May was not the largest barge I'd ever worked, but I knew her skipper, Earl, and had actually saved his life. Well, maybe not saved his life, but pretty close. I'd walked out of the Torchlight Bar in Memphis one night and seen Earl passed out beside a dumpster and a couple of really young guys rolling him. The kids ran off as soon as they saw me coming, and I'd heaved Earl over my shoulder and carried him to his hotel room to let him sleep it off. I hadn't known who Earl was then, but since everyone who went to the Torchlight worked the barges I knew he had to be a river man. The next morning, Earl hired me on.

I had kept pretty much to himself until Steve arrived on the scene. Why he became so chummy with me I could never figure. Why with 26 men on the Daisy May, had Steve chosen me? I asked him that once, after we'd spent a night drinking and we were walking back to the barge at 5:00 a.m., guided by the rank, flat smell of the river. Steve just laughed and threw a couple of phantom punches to my ribs, and said it must have been the twinkle in my baby blue eyes.

Bullshit, I thought. It was more than that. I began watching him more closely. When the other guys went to town, he'd split and say he had something he had to take care of. By the time we were in the next port, I discovered what he was taking care of was his cock – and not in the way most river men do either.

I'd always wondered about gay guys, but that was about it.

I was never highly sexed, I just did what was expected of me. When I was very young, my shipmates would invite me along and I'd watch them fuck their whores and then turn 'em over to me. When they saw the size of my cock when it was hard, they always wanted me to go last. "After you've been in there, they'd be stretched for days," one of them kidded me. Some whores didn't even want me to do it. "You ain't stickin' that in me, honey," they'd say. In a few towns, guys had regular girlfriends who would put 'em up for as

long as they were on leave, but I met few girls that weren't whores and when I did most of 'em didn't want anything to do with me after they saw my dick.

I began to develop a complex about my horse dick. I began to think of myself as a freak, that my prick was downright ugly. But Steve was the one who set me straight. It began by his talking about my hands. We were a couple days out of Rock Island. My shift was over, and I was sitting in the aft lounge, the "ass lounge" the crew called it, watching some porno flick on the VCR and smoking Camels with the chief cook and a couple older bargemen. Steve walked in, sprawled over the chair beside me. There was something almost too perfect in his features, his jeans were too perfectly worn and faded, his T-shirt dirty in just the right places, and I found myself strangely attracted to him.

Much to my surprise, he asked for advice. Steve always wore gloves topside, he said, but he'd heard your hands would toughen quicker, and so be less likely to get injured, if you went barehanded. "You've got the biggest, toughest damn hands I've ever seen," he said with a quick grin. "So what d'ya think?"

I shrugged, embarrassed, and glanced over at the other guys, but they were engrossed in the movie. I looked at my hands. I hardly thought of them as part of my body. They were huge and the palms were covered with thick yellow ridges of callous from years of fighting ropes the size of a man's wrist. All my fingers had been broken at least once and jutted out at strange angles. Even my fingernails were deeply creased and hard as horn. Between the calluses and the fractured bones, I had little feeling left in my hands. Now I felt like I was in high school and one of the popular kids had just said something nice to me.

I wasn't sure whether this was a compliment or perhaps he was setting me up for a joke. "I dunno," he said. "I had gloves when I first started on the barges, but I left 'em on deck one day when I went down for lunch, and they were gone when I came back. Didn't have money for a new pair." I held my hands up and laughed. "Yeah, they're pretty fucked up."

Steve took one of my hands in his and squeezed it. "But they sure are meaty." Then he laughed, "I bet you're meaty everywhere."

I pulled my hand away and stood up. "That's what the whores all tell me – too damn meaty!"

The next night, a thunderstorm had blown down from the Dakotas and the river was running high, rocking the Daisy May and sending deep clangs and hollow booms through the length of her. We were heading into Des Moines and had a game of five card stud going in the ass lounge. I was playing more recklessly than usual. Steve just sat in back of me with his chair tipped against the wall, but I could feel his eyes on me all night. In the end, I had lost nearly my entire paycheck. Steve told me not to worry: "Your luck will improve." It was such a stupid comment I ignored it.

The next evening, as we were heading down to mess, Steve stopped me in the stairwell. "Hey, Meaty, let's do the pizza thing tonight, my treat."

I shook my head. "Nah, I hate bummin' off people." Something about Steve made me jumpy, reminded me of the sensation I got driving over really high bridges, when the guard rails pulled at me so hard he sometimes felt I had to fight the steering wheel to keep the car between the lines.

"Come on," Steve urged. "You can owe me. Besides, I got somethin' I wanna show you."

In the end, Steve convinced me, and we shared a couple of thin, greasy pizzas and two pitchers of draft beer at a windowless Italian place on the pier. As we left, Steve whispered, "Check this out," and beckoned me around back. We stood near a loading dock, next to a dumpster overflowing with crushed pizza boxes and empty beer bottles. A half-dead florescent lamp shot a cold blue light over everything, and I had to force myself not to blink in time with its flickering. Steve opened his coat and flashed a dog-eared phone book.

"What?" I said blankly. "This is what you wanted to show me? That you could rip off a phone book from a pizza joint?"

Steve chuckled. His eyes, framed by long girlish lashes, looked flat and wet in the jittery light. "I have a plan, my man, if you're up to it. It's something that'll take care of your financial problems."

Shit, I thought, I could see where this was headed. Over the years I had collected a half dozen misdemeanor counts for public drunkenness and disturbing the peace. The last thing I needed was serious trouble with the cops. The smell of rotting pizza and sour beer floated up from a pile of garbage at my feet. Steve watched me and grinned, his sleek black hair looking blue in the weird light. I knew what he was thinking; I dare ya old man ....

"What the fuck," I said. "Let's do it."

"Yeah, all right."

Steve ripped the blue government section and the city map from the front of the book and threw the rest behind the dumpster. He studied the pages for a moment, then took off down the alley.

We walked for half an hour through a quiet residential area of square white houses with bicycles in the front yards. From somewhere to the south, I could hear the clanking of boxcars being unloaded. The sound was faint but incredibly clear in the crisp night air. I even thought I could hear voices sometimes. In truth, I hated trains. That was why I'd ended up on the river instead of in the freight yards like my old man.

We had to move a lot when I was a kid because my old man was always getting fired. The winter I turned thirteen, we moved to Rockwall, Texas. Like always, I pumped myself up to go out and face whichever gang of boys ruled that neighborhood. After three or four fistfights in a vacant lot, they decided to accept me. I'd be initiated, along with another new kid, from

Austin, at midnight along the train tracks. I had no trouble slipping away; Dad didn't care and Mom was passed out by 6:00 every night. Our initiation was to stand on the tracks with a freight coming at us until Chuck, the leader, said jump. If we moved a muscle before then, we'd be out of the gang and probably get the shit beat out of us on top of it.

A train was due at 12:20, and the kid from Austin went first.

He stood on the tracks, arms stiff at this sides and stared straight ahead. His breath came out in cottony puffs. Me and the six other guys stood with our fists stuffed in our pockets, shuffling our feet in the frost-blackened weeds lining the tracks. The gang passed around a pack of Luckys, but deliberately skipped me.

When we heard the train, everyone stopped moving and peered intently down the tracks. Soon I could see the big headlight barreling towards us. It was an express, moving fast, making no stops in Rockwall. I glanced at Chuck then back at the kid from Austin, who was breathing faster. He had carroty hair and a pinched freckled face. His bottom lip was swollen from a recent battle in the empty lot.

When the train was still a couple hundred yards away, I could feel the rumbling through the soles of my shoes. The other kid hadn't twitched. His eyes glittered but he didn't blink. I knew somehow that he wouldn't move, no matter what. Panic rolled through my guts. I glared at Chuck, planning to yell at him, "Say jump!", or even shout it myself. Chuck's face stopped me, though. Chuck also knew the kid wouldn't move. The look on his face was hungry, ravenous, the expression of a starving man about to get a feast. The boy's curly orange hair was blowing wildly as the freight bore down. I thought I saw the same look on the kid's face, the same determination, the same hypnotic hunger, just before the train hit.

At the last instant, the engineer saw him and slammed on his brakes. The steel wheels threw a high-pitched shriek into the air along with arcing lines of blue sparks. I felt the sound like an ache in my groin, like finally pissing after holding it for hours. The kid exploded into a cloud of red mist.

We all stood transfixed, until the last car had blown by. I kept thinking, "I'm next, I'm next", and I felt a weird sensation, half dread and half anticipation surging through my body. I realized dimly I had an erection. One of the gang was puking in the weeds, the rest were ready to follow at any minute, except Chuck. He chortled under his breath, "Well, look at that!" and he patted the bulge in my jeans.

I wouldn't have to stand on the tracks. No, Chuck saw to that. We left the others to their puking in the weeds and we went into the woods nearby. Chuck made me take my cock out.

He held it in his hand, stroked it. "God, that's the biggest one I've ever seen," he said. "You'd kill a girl with that."

"Nah," I said, so embarrassed I couldn't look at him. "Yeah," he said, continuing to stroke it. I came almost instantly.

Walking back to join the others, he swore me to secrecy. "Damn Tight," I said.

I was in the gang after that, but I found myself avoiding them, especially Chuck, as much as possible. Then my old man got fired again and we moved to Waco. Two years later, I left home for good.

Me and Steve entered the school through an unlocked classroom window. Schools were perfect, Steve said. No alarms, no safes, and all that lunch money, a couple bucks per kid, six maybe seven hundred kids, all of it just waiting in the principal's office.

"Betcha ten bucks," Steve said, "it's in the top right hand drawer."

But he hadn't counted on a security guard. The guy must have been about seventy, thank god. No gun. Steve acted on instinct when the old man turned a corner, cold-cocking him, then slamming his head against a locker. I stood for a moment, stunned and breathing hard, more from shock and excitement than effort, and glanced at Steve, who winked and said, "Hurry up, Meaty."

We counted the money in an alley near the river. I leaned against the cold bricks, ruffling the bills, wondering if the old watchman was O.K. I felt super-charged with energy, then realized I had an erection. Steve noticed it too. Just like Chuck, he just put his hand over the bulge and squeezed it.

"God, meaty is right." Unlike Chuck, Steve couldn't wait for me; he unzipped my jeans and took my cock out. Like Chuck, he'd never seen anything like it either. Stroking it, he said, "I'd love to see this goin' into one of them whores."

"Most of 'em say it's too big."

I know some that'd love it. Sure enough do." He continued massaging it, stopping every once in awhile to admire it. He fondled my balls as he jerked it until I came. As the cum slid down his fingers he laughed, "Big load, too. Yeah, I know some whores that'd really love this. C'mon."

We walked a few blocks and stopped in front of a club that Steve said was "not for the faint of heart." The bar was off the main strip of the downtown red-light district, set between an abandoned warehouse and an old flour mill, at least three miles from the docks. It was hardly a river man's hangout. I paused at the door, my hand going to my back pocket where I always kept a knife and a set of brass knuckles, but Steve grabbed my arm and pulled me inside.

We ended up at a pay-by-the-hour motel with a slim boy in a red satin dress named Kitty Kane. If not for his too-large Adam's apple and the fact that the bar was full of drag queens, I would never have guessed he was a man. In the room, I slumped against the wall, holding a bottle of tequila, and watched

Steve fuck the guy's ass on the creaking little bed. "I'll warm her up for you," he said, going at it energetically.

"I'm used to that. Go ahead. Fuck your little heart out."

I felt light-headed and a little sick at the sight, like the first time I saw a bull mount a cow, or spied on my parents through a crack in their bedroom wall. But just like those times, I was mesmerized. I could already feel a hard-on fighting the effects of the booze. The sound of their breathing and the squeaking of the bed springs seemed too faint for the cramped space. I knew I shouldn't have taken the second bottle of tequila. Steve, I recalled fuzzily, hardly had anything to drink the whole night.

Suddenly, Steve's face was right in front of mine. "Come on," he said, taking the bottle from my hand and grinning, "it's your turn now."

I moved a little unsteadily towards the bed and looked down at the damp, wrinkled red dress and a hard angular hip. Steve came up behind me and unzipped my jeans. Slowly, he drew my cock out and told Kitty to roll over. Kitty grinned when he saw my pecker, now stiff and coated with pre-cum.

"Didn't I say this was somethin'?" Steve said.

Kitty nodded but didn't say a word, just took the whole thing in his mouth, all the way down to the pubic hairs. Nobody'd ever done that before; most of the time, whores just licked and sucked a little on the head. I held his head while he continued. Then I realized Steve had gotten on the bed next to Kitty and the two of them were taking turns. I could scarcely believe my eyes: the kid who'd been working alongside me for weeks had jacked me off and now was giving my cock a bath. I ran my fingers through his hair and groaned as he began nibbling on my balls while Kitty deep-throated my cock once again. Kitty could hardly wait to get my cock up his ass. Even though Steve had been in there, it was still tight, tighter than any whore I'd had. While I fucked him, Steve jacked off beside the bed, but tight as Kitty was, I just couldn't come. I'd had too much tequila. Steve finished inside Kitty, but it was to me Kitty gave his card. "You're welcome anytime, honey," he said, patting my crotch as we left the room.

When we got off the Daisy May in St. Paul, Steve said he wanted to go to Minneapolis, across the river. Winking at me, he said he knew a place I'd like. The Pussykat Lounge had black cinder block walls painted with naked pink bodies. Cheap vodka, straight up. Steve didn't find anybody to his liking, but as we were leaving around two, he found a guy passed out beside a dumpster near the bar. "Come on," Steve whispered. "Let's have some fun." Steve kicked the man in the stomach and he rolled over, groaning. I realized he looked a lot like Earl laying there by the dumpster; same beer belly, same thinning brown hair. Steve kicked the guy again and he staggered to his feet, clutching his stomach. "Don't kill me," the man begged.

I began gulping air like water. I felt like I was going to faint, but I could tell I was getting the biggest hard-on I'd had for weeks. Steve waved me over. "He doesn't want us to kill him. What should we do with him?" he panted.

Steve forced the guy to his hands and knees beside the dumpster. "My buddy's not going to kill you, but it'll seem like it at first." Steve came up behind me and undid my pants. The man's eyes bulged and he began begging, "No, no, not that!"

"You'll love it, shithead," Steve snarled as he guided my cock into the guy's ass, then stood over us, jacking off. By the time I got my cock deep in him, I went crazy with it, fucking the hell out of him, but only for a couple of minutes. The guy in the red dress was one thing, but this fat old man was something else. I stood up, swaying a little. The vodka burned in my stomach. I felt like I was going to puke. "Are you done?" Steve demanded, his voice tight. "Is that all?"

"Yeah. I feel sick. Why don't you fuck 'im?"

"Okay, I will." Steve grabbed the guy by the hair on his head and shoved his cock in him. The man was now hysterical. I went behind the dumpster and heaved.

I woke the next day to find Steve and a short Mexican-looking guy standing in our hotel room staring down at me. Only a dim, grayish light came through the bars on the window, but my eyes ached and I was momentarily blinded.

"This is my friend, Lupe," Steve told me. "Lupe, meet Jake."

Lupe snorted and said, "Yeah, right. Big Jake."

I swung my feet, still in my work boots, to the floor and sat up groaning, trying to get my mind in gear.

"Got a surprise for you," Steve said. "Lupe drives limos. He's got one outside right now. Thought you'd like to take a little ride."

About a half an hour later, I was pulling my forehead back from the window and looking at the faint smear of grease left on the glass. Then I stared at my hands laying motionless on the creamy leather seat of the limo. Rubbing the back of my hand across my eyes, I realized my hand was covered with dried, flaking vomit. I wondered briefly if it was mine, then the memory of the previous night hit me and I thought it might be from the guy in the alley. He had really looked a lot like Earl. I stared down at my blood-stained jeans and the rips in my work shirt. Hell, it could just as easily have been me passed out next to that dumpster. The thought sent a ripple of nausea through my stomach.

I glanced over at Steve, and was suddenly sick of the sight of him, ready to tell him to fuck off, when he buried his head between my legs.

Soon the limo rolled smoothly through a tight right-hand turn and my body followed it, pressing against the armrest. We were leaving the suburbs

now and heading into the countryside. It was a bright, very warm day for May and our Mexican driver switched on the air conditioning.

I looked down at Steve's head, now bobbing up and down, my cock between his lips. I leaned back and closed my eyes. God, I thought, the guy sure loves to suck dick.

Before long, Lupe had parked the car in what looked like a forest. In all the years I'd shipped out of St. Paul on the river barges, I'd never seen the countryside. In fact, I'd never seen the countryside anywhere. Somehow, no matter where I lived, I always ended up on some dusty street that reminded me of towns he'd known as a kid in west Texas. In town, my hotel on Payne Avenue was flanked by bars, strip-joints, gas stations and beauty parlors. Their windows were filmy with dust, the signs cracked and faded as though they'd been exposed to the blazing sun of the desert instead of the mild pale light of the north. I always half-expected to see a tumbleweed skittering along the crooked sidewalks.

But here we were awash in lush, cool green. "Let's have a picnic," Steve said, letting my cock plop from his mouth and thud against my belly.

Lupe lead the way, carrying a basket, a blanket, and some towels. "But first we go swimming," Steve said. It didn't take much encouragement. The pristine pond shimmered in the bright sun, reminding me a picture I'd seen in a book once. Besides, I thought a swim in the chilly water might cure my hangover.

While Steve and I undressed, Lupe began laying out a banquet on the blanket.

I dove into the pond and Steve was right behind me. We played in the water for awhile and my head was beginning to clear. Steve reached down and stroked my cock occasionally. "Lupe loves to get fucked," he said, giving me that lewd wink of his. "I told him all about you, so I hope you can stay on him for more than a couple of minutes." The memory of the man next to the dumpster came back to me. And the boy in the red dress. I dove under the water and swam away from Steve.

After a few minutes, I came up for air and looked back toward the shoreline. Lupe was getting undressed. I saw the poor man on his knees. "It coulda been me," I said under my breath. I watched Steve emerge from the water, really noticing his tight little ass for the first time. "How'd he like it?" I wondered, and my cock stirred to nearly full attention.

As I walked toward the two of them, Lupe was now naked, reclining on the blanket, sipping some wine from one of the plastic cups he'd had in his basket. He looked up at my erection and blinked. Steve, wrapped in a towel, grinned and began pouring me a cup of wine, then one for himself. Lupe took a few preliminary licks on my cock and then we sat there quietly eating the fried chicken, French bread and drinking the wine.

When we were finished eating, Lupe returned his mouth to my cock, sucking hard, showing almost as much talent for it as Steve. Satisfied that he had me as hard as I could get, he rolled over. Steve ran a hand up and down the back of the young Mexican's hairless thighs. "I'll warm him up," Steve said, stroking his hard-on with his other hand.

"Go right ahead," I said. "Enjoy yourself."

While he was fucking Lupe, I stood over them, jerking my dick, dropping spit on it, getting it ready. When Steve was close, his body trembling, I got behind him and took his asscheeks in my hands. "Hey!" he said. Spreading them, I shoved the head of my cock into the incredibly tight hole. He screamed, "What the fuck – But it was too late; he was having his orgasm.

I showed no mercy. I was in him in a flash. He was hanging on to Lupe, coming down from his high, crying hysterically.

I laid across him and brought my hands to his neck. "Quiet, asshole. Take it like a man."

"No, no," he cried, fighting me. "You bastard! You fuckin' bastard!"

He wouldn't stop shouting, calling me every bad name he could think of.

I couldn't stop fucking his tight ass. And squeezing his neck. I just kept squeezing, choking him. "It coulda been me," I kept saying, unable to let go.

When I finally came, I realized his screams had stopped.

A KISS IS JUST A KISS
John Patrick

"My first gay video experience was watching Ryan Idol fuck Joey Stefano in 'Idol Eyes' and I liked it because of all the kissing. Now when it comes time to come, I fast forward to the kissing shots. It does it every time for me."

– Porn Star, Callboy and College Student Erik Houston

I hadn't been in Hollywood more than an hour before I saw the kid, talking on a pay phone in front of Spokes 'N' Stuff bike shop on the corner of Santa Monica and Spaulding.

I drove past him, then turned around, turned onto Spaulding, stopped, and waited. He hung up the phone and walked past me, then turned around. He bent over to see inside my rented white Mustang and gestured with his thumb. I nodded. He was quickly sitting next to me and I was admiring his startling smile, good teeth, and mop of blondish-brown hair that hung enticingly down his forehead and into his soft blue eyes. It was the weekend "The Flintstones" opened in theaters and he was right up-to-date with a commemorative T-shirt two sizes too big for him. "Yuba Dabba Doo," I said under my breath.

"What?" he asked.

"Nothing. You come down here often?"

"No, I'm from San Diego. I come up here every once and a while. Name's Jim."

He extended his hand, I shook it lightly.

"I'm John."

"That wouldn't be cop John, would it?"

I chuckled. "Hell, no. Do I look like a cop?"

"What does a cop look like?"

"I wish I knew."

"There you go."

Where we did go was to my hotel, "I've been here a lot," Jim said. "No problems here."

"No," I said as I turned into the parking lot, looking at his pleasant young face. "No problems at all." He certainly had no problem; it was I who had always let hustlers intimidate me as they filled me with desire. They don't live by conventional rules yet they survive and thrive; they just make up their own.

On the way we had discussed price. I said I knew nothing of what things were going for in Hollywood these days. He said when he goes to Numbers he gets $200. "But I have to get dressed up," he added with a sheepish grin.

"Well, you don't have to dress up for me. Un-dress is more like it."

He chuckled and we agreed on $75, provided I was satisfied. Two hundred really wouldn't have been too much for this boy, I thought. Hell, it's only money.

In the parking lot, as he was getting out of the car, the wind blew his T-shirt, which hung down almost to his knees, hiding his best asset, an incredible basket.. I knew immediately I would be quite satisfied.

Alone in the elevator, I hugged him to me; he was the perfect height for me, the top of his head neatly tucking under my chin, but he pulled free, nervous about the door being opened.

In the room, I sat on the bed and he stood before me. He didn't touch me. I wasted no time getting that damned T-shirt off of him and those jeans unzipped. His pees were nicely developed and he had just a brush of hair on his chest. I reached into his jeans and pulled out an astonishingly beautiful cock; about eight inches and extraordinarily thick, way out of proportion with the rest of him. "Wow!" was the only way I could express it, and I dove right in, sucking it adoringly.

It seems when I am with a hustler, I am embarrassed about my body, anxious about my performance, fearful of even the hustler's rejection, but in this case I stripped off my clothes between sucks and, after a few minutes of feasting on the big prick, I lay on the bed on my back and he finished undressing. I asked him to straddle me and face-fuck me. His cock and light brown pubic hairs smelled of soap, I decided I was his first trick of the day and he must have been horny because he didn't fuck for very long before he was asking, "Do you want me to come?"

"Yes, but not quite yet," I said, kissing the shaft.

"Kiss my balls," he ordered, taking his erection in his own hand.

I jacked off while I sucked his balls and when I came he sensed he could go ahead. I held his thighs while he spewed cum all over my face, slashing my cheeks with his mighty cock. I was charmed. So often the working boy doesn't come – he has many in a day and needs to conserve – but Jim was coming at noon, with a hefty load at that. He was a real find. Well worth the money.

"Stay there," he said with a polite smile, "I'll clean you up.'

Yes, a real find.

After gently cleaning my cock and balls and scrubbing my chest, he went back to the bathroom and took a shower. Clean kid, I thoughts A real find.

As he was dressing, he asked if I could take him back to his motel and on the way he gave me his beeper number, saying if I needed some more company while I was in town, call. I'd had all the company I needed, at least for now, but I told him I would keep it in mind. He also said he was traveling with a girlfriend. "Does she know what you do?" I asked.

"Sure."

"And she doesn't mind as long as you don't fuck other girls, right?"

He nodded. I had been down that road many a time. He was gay for pay but he sure got off on it.

Jim had told me that Numbers was packed between nine and eleven every evening. I decided to get there around eight. I had to see the ones who were going for $200. I asked Jim, "Are they worth it?"

"They don't think of themselves as hustlers," he said, evading my question with a grin.

Now I had the afternoon to kill, which wasn't too difficult considering weak high pressure had developed over Southern California, coupled with a decreasing marine layer, which meant mostly sunny skies with temperatures in the 80s inland. With no smog in Los Angeles for once, I headed for the hotel pool. I had to rest up for the night to come.

Numbers reminded me of Rounds in New York, both being restaurants coupled with bars, heavily mirrored and catering to the expense-account set looking for deductions. As Jim had said, the crowd was thin at eight but there was one young entrepreneur two stools away drinking Perrier and smoking Marlboros. He was handsome, with a shock of light brown hair stylishly cut. He looked a bit like Erik Houston, the porn star/UCLA student I had really wanted to see but who was in New York for the weekend. The boy sitting at the bar was dressed in neat jeans and a button-down shirt. No Flintstones T-shirt for him. I moved over two stools and bought him a Perrier along with another glass of wine for myself. The prices, I saw, were not as inflated as those in New York. Maybe the boys could be had more cheaply as well. I introduced myself. The lad's name was Denny and he too was from San Diego. Must be nice, I thought, to have Hollywood so close; you can live in San Diego and no one is the wiser, then spend the weekends "working" in L.A. Nice deal. "Nice boys in San Diego," I said.

"Some," said Denny.

One of the "nice boys" he knew was his roommate, the former porn star Kevin Williams.

"I thought he was dead," I said.

"That's Chris Williams. No, Kevin's very much alive. He makes a good living traveling, meeting men."

I had always been fond of Williams, especially when he was taking all the late Chad Douglas had to offer. I remembered Kevin's first appearance, in a William Higgins' "Screen Test." When the blond bombshell couldn't get it up, a guy had to be brought in to fuck him Now there was a bottom! Just imagining Kevin and Denny together down in old San Diego got my juices flowing rapidly. I cut directly to the price.

"One fifty," Denny said with a smile, "but it's negotiable"

He said he never went with anyone he didn't like. Now I understood what Jim meant about these guys not thinking they were hustlers. It's all in knowing what to say and Will Rogers said it best: "I never met a man I didn't like"

Awaiting us in the parking lot, amid Rolls-Royces and

Mercedes, was Denny's shiny new Jeep, with the canvas top pulled back. I offered to pay the attendant but Denny said, "No, I park for free here." I had managed to avoid the $5 parking fee (plus tip) by finding a free spot on the street and told Denny to follow my Mustang.

Our ride up in the elevator was more interesting than the one earlier in the day with Jim. Denny, I discovered to my joy, was a kisser. He had covered his tobacco breath with a mint and my body was soon flooding with excitement as his intense mouth worked on mine. What a kisser! In the elevator, down the hall, on top of the bed. I hadn't been kissed like that in years. Even if this was all there was, it was plenty. If he carried on like this with everybody, no wonder he could charge "one fifty."

After about a half an hour of smooching that took my breath away, my lips began to tire. I asked what he did in bed, "besides kissing."

"I'm very oral."

"Well, oral it is," I said, shoving his head into my lap. My erection needed servicing and for that high tariff, I figured Denny could handle it.

He unzipped me and revealed my erection. He nibbled on it, licked it and finally put as much of it as he could in his mouth. He was not the most proficient cocksucker I had known and so, after a few minutes, I brought him back up and began kissing him again. He was just so darn kissable.

Foolishly, I said that I could do this forever. Then came the bomb: "For $500," he said, squeezing my erection, "I can stay all night."

"Oh, goodness, no," I said. "I've got appointments in the morning. Early."

But I decided to get my money's worth while I had him in the room. If I wasn't going to come from his oral expertise, or lack thereof, perhaps he'd be willing to bend over for his "one fifty."

"Do you have a rubber?" he asked, slipping his briefs away. "Dozens," I said, running to the bathroom.

I stood over the bed sliding the Maxx onto my dick.

He swallowed hard and stared at my erection. "God, I don't know. That's awfully big. Do you come quickly? I don't think I can take that for long."

"I don't know how long it'll take tonight. I guess if you kiss me like you have been, it won't take long at all."

That was all the boy needed. He turned the passion back on His mouth was wet and a little saliva dripped out as he opened it to lick my face as

I entered him. He put his hands on my shoulders and pulled me hard against him, forcing my cock all the way in. He moaned and pulled harder on my shoulders as if to pull my whole body inside his asshole. I lost my balance for a moment and slipped out, but then he put his feet on my shoulders and set his knees apart. I ran my hands up and down his milky thighs and found his lips slightly parted and shining with moisture. I leaned over slowly and, as my cock sunk in all the way again, he lifted his feet from my shoulders and kissed me, so softly that his lips barely brushed mine. As I kissed him, I whimpered and he grabbed my hair and pulled it. I dived at him, no longer gentle with him. My tongue slid up and down across his open lips, lapping at his wetness, trying to swallow him. I stuck my tongue inside him, wanting to go as deep as I could, with my cock lodged deep within him down below.. My nose was pressed hard against his and my head rocked back and forth, inhaling the boy. He was still pulling at my hair. I kissed him again, harder now, my tongue flicking in and out, darting around. As his pelvis rose to meet every thrust, he placed his hands on my waist and then slid them down to hold my ass, to push me even deeper as I climaxed.

When I pulled out, I realized he never got an erection, much less come. But at that point, I couldn't have cared less. Earlier in the day, I had sucked one of the nicest cocks I'd seen in years, and undoubtedly one of the nicest available on the boulevard so whatever he could have done would have paled by comparison. Yet I did find it odd he was so completely uninvolved. Or maybe I just wasn't trying. After all, I hadn't even touched his cock and if there's one thing a hustler is proud of it's his merchandise. Still, for "one fifty" I was going to do what I wanted to do – and I did.

But before sending him on his way with two C-notes pressed in his palm (he deserved a tip), I wanted to feel his lips upon mine one last time. It was a lingering, passionate kiss. Then he kissed my neck and nibbled on my ear, his hands caressing my cock. I moaned in dismay. God, in his own special way he was good: money be damned, I'll keep him overnight.

He continued to kiss my neck some more, sucking, nibbling, licking as his hands moved up to my pees and he twisted my tight nipples. He stepped back a bit and ran his nails lightly over my back, tracing, tickling, teasing me. I could feel my loins stirring again.

But then I groped him; he was still soft. I came to my senses: A kiss is just a kiss.

A few months later, I was on my way to New York City and again called Erik Houston in Hollywood. He had just been in New York, and was on his way to San Francisco. "Sorry," he said. Maybe someday.

After taking a cab into the city from LaGuardia, I got settled into my suite at the Regency on Park Avenue and turned to the classifieds in the New York Native and some other local rags. Soon all the ads became a blur. Faced with so many choices and so little time, I decided a massage would be just the

ticket on this trip. But even then, which one should I call? The "Magic Touch" of Tony, who promised to soothe all of my aches, or the "Erotic Body Rub" proposed by Joseph, who described himself as a "hairy bodybuilder?" Or even Ivan, the "clean, friendly Jewish guy" who was "sensitive to the needs of married men?" Well, I had been married, but no more. Confused, I decided to do something I never do at home: consult my horoscope. One read: "Currently your career path is less important than your spiritual path. Hey, it's only money. Ask yourself, 'Did I have a good time?'" Another read: "If an opportunity, or a great dark man presents itself: chest out, shoulders up, stomach in...go for it!" That settled it. I returned to the classifieds to find "a great dark man who would promise a good time."

I dialed the number of the guy who had advertised himself as a "muscular black actor" eager to perform "professional stress reduction and muscle techniques. Deep work where indicated. Available for matinee and evening performances."

My "matinee" with Steve was set for three o'clock. I was to go to his apartment, on 42nd Street near Tenth Avenue, a pleasant area of theaters and townhouses and restaurants. I identified myself to the man in the lobby of the high-rise and he called Steve. I was told to go "right on up."

Steve seemed to be everything I could have wished for in a great dark man: he was tall, muscular and reasonably good-looking. His hair was cut short and he wore gray sweats. We shook hands and, handing me a towel, he told me to disrobe and lie face down on the table. He discreetly left the room while I made myself comfortable on a table covered with a fresh white sheet.

In his deep baritone voice, Steve began by quietly explaining he had incorporated Chinese practices from 5,000 years ago into his techniques. He told me I was to listen to the relaxing music, breathe in the lavender aroma and, as my muscles were worked, experience a sense of renewal and rejuvenation.

"Living is not only breathing and sleeping and working and eating," he said, "it's feeling good. You just allow the tension to escape while you feel blood flow more freely and nerve endings tingle.

"Circulation is life, it's like the sap in the tree, the fluid that carries all the nutrients," he said as the calming music continued.

From the head, down the neck, torso and arms to the feet, legs and back, his huge hands caressed and kneaded so his clients could, as he said, "go off into another world."

Of course, escapism has always been a part of massage. The ability to float away while muscles are manipulated is a benefit for taking a massage, but it was hard at that moment to forget who was doing this to me, and the implications of "deep work where indicated."

As he leaned over me, it seemed his groin was pressing into my hand and I squeezed it. He let me do this several times and I had ample opportunity

to feel the heft of the balls, the great length and width of the shaft of his penis. Then he lifted my hand away and gently placed it back where it belonged.

Having sampled the enormousness of what the sweats had concealed, I was even more intrigued by the promised "deep work where indicated," and when he rolled me over onto my back, my erection throbbed against my belly. He quickly covered it with a towel and continued his massage. Finally, he stood with his groin at the top of my head and said, "I can see you are still tense. You need to totally relax."

I opened my eyes to see at some point he had removed his sweats. I reached up and brought his long, cut penis over my forehead. As I began kissing acid stroking the cock, it hardened and he moved a bit to the side. It was obvious I wasn't the only one who needed to "totally relax." I rolled onto my side so that he could fuck my face with it while his hands slipped away the towel and he began stroking me "Oh, yeah, suck that big dick, baby," he ordered.

As I touched and honored this gigantic presence, I started massaging the insides of his thighs.

I could have gone on just letting him use my mouth but, after all, this was an hour session and fie had other appointments. Soon he stepped away and returned carrying a bottle of lotion. He had also sheathed his cock in latex. After lifting my legs up and mounting the table, he applied the lotion to my cock and asshole.

His touch was driving me crazy. I wanted his fingers on me, in me I couldn't get enough of him. As he took one greased finger and moved it back and forth to spread my anal lips, I was hardly able to contain my grunts and groans. He took one finger and pushed it deep into my ass. Two fingers followed, then three. I was close to coming when he removed them. He let me catch my breath, then lined up his cock and leaned forward. I was delirious as he slowly inserted it.

Then, as he began plunging his cock in and out of me, I soon started the early contractions of orgasm. I moaned and moved my hips in rhythm with his thrusts. He bent all the way over me and I began flicking his nipples with my tongue. Sucking noises escaped my mouth when I lost contact with his tit, but I just sucked more frantically and I got it again.

He was becoming heavy in his ecstasy and a shiver of pleasure ran through me and my hand gently stroked his back. I looked up and saw his face gazing down at me, eyes intense, mouth open and wet. I sensed he was close and I pushed my thighs apart and inhaled deeply, intoxicating myself with his scent. I put my arms around him and held on for the wild, lust-driven ride ahead of us both.

I closed my eyes and my face was again buried in his chest. My own cum flowed unchecked, Low growls told me how much pleasure he was feeling and I began to groan too. My vibrations affected him deeply and I

wanted him to come hard. Again I contracted my ass muscles around his penis and this sent him into his last frenzy. His pulsations continued for several moments and I stayed with him in an incredibly heightened state of enjoyment. Even when I was sure he was finished, he was still plunging in and out of me. I could feel another orgasm coming on the heels of the one he just had and I tightened my ass again so he can fuck me as hard as he could and come again without losing the sensation of the one before. When I heard him grunt out his pleasure, his body was in perfect synchronization with mine.

"Just be still," he said, climbing off the table and placing the sheet over me. Just as he was about the lower the end of the sheet over my face, he kissed my forehead. I had on many a massage table, but no masseur had ever fucked me as well nor ended it quite so nicely.

When I was dressed and leaving, it seemed as if he wanted to engage in conversation. He asked how long I would be in the city, what I planned to do, and so forth. I asked him how he got started and he said, "I was doing it for dancer friends of mine and discovered I enjoyed it. And the extra income helps, of course."

After I paid him, adding a generous tip, he took me in his arms and hugged me tightly, whispering, "Come again."

On my way to the elevators, I knew I would indeed be coming again, thanks to the memory of Steve and his "deep work where indicated." I began playing the scene over in my mind, remembering his two orgasms and the kiss on the forehead and, most all, the bear hug. I smiled with the new realization that, yes, a kiss is just a kiss, but a hug from a whore is quite another thing.,

I'LL DO ANYTHING
James Wilton

Joey owed me, the asshole. A while back he'd sold me two cords of fire wood. He cashed the check I had been stupid enough to give him and never delivered the wood. Sure, he had plenty of reasons but that is what he was so good at; he was a con artist through and through. Before long Joey had some trouble with the law so he went to jail. Then I heard from my friends that he was periodically showing up in town when things were tough, trading sex for a warm bed, food, and, he hoped, some pocket money. At least he had the sense to keep away from here – until one cold, rainy afternoon I heard a knock on my door and there was Joey, soaked to the skin. He'd hitched into town to find that Len, his most reliable benefactor, was not home. For some reason he thought that he might be able to wait at my house until Len returned. I slammed the door in his face.

He knocked again. And kept knocking. I opened the door and took good look at him. The cold had gotten to him and he sniveled about the rain. Once he was one hot little kid with a hairless, well-defined body, but the years of mischief had taken their toll. He still looked hot but with a little more flesh and some deep age lines. Still, the sight of him made my crotch stir.

Joey again begged to come in. I asked him why I should do him any favors when he still owed me $250. He struck a cutesy pose and said he'd make me happy if I did. I told him I could take care of making myself happy. This brought on the line I was waiting for: "Please, I'll do anything. It's so cold out and I'm freezin'."

"Anything?"

"Anything."

He stood hunched and shivering inside my door. I sent him down to the basement to put his clothes in the dryer. He asked what he should wear and I told him that we'd worry about that later. He came up blue with the cold. I smiled to myself as I looked at him and planned my revenge. His hair was plastered down with rain water. He was bent over and hugging himself but I could see that his cock and balls were shriveled up like raisins. Not being a monster, I handed him a towel and had him get into the shower he both wanted and needed.

Meanwhile, I changed into a jockstrap and bathrobe and dug out my old paddleball racket.

Joey came back into the living room wrapped in the towel and I checked him out from head to foot. He was clearly warmed up and his basket bulged out under the terry cloth. His chest and arms still showed some definition and his square jaw was held up high. He had sprouted some hairs on his chest. He was not altogether bad looking.

But having been with so many men in the past, he seemed to sense my thoughts and gave a smug look as if to say that he was doing me a favor by being there. Not right! Looking him right in the eye, I said, "You were a shit once and you're still a shit."

Immediately his eyes dropped and he apologized. He didn't know what for but the bullshitter in him told him that was the part to play.

"I can never forgive you for what you did, you little bastard!" I reached out and pulled his towel off.

He looked at me and then down at his crotch. Both of us watched his cock stir and begin to rise. I was tempted to grab it but decided against giving him any kind of thrill.

I had him bend over my lap for the spanking he deserved. I ran my hand over his firm, hairy ass. It was like two velvet-covered melons. I raised up the paddle and let him have a sharp thwack on both cheeks. He stiffened and moaned in pain and surprise. I came down again and again, letting my anger get control. After about ten good ones I stopped and rubbed my hand over his red buns. They were nicely warmed. As I rubbed his buttocks, I felt a slight humping motion from Joey's hips. I rearranged my position and spread my legs a little further apart. Suddenly a hard cock slipped off my left thigh and into the space between my legs..

I was spurred on to a renewed attack. As I raised the paddle for another several whacks, I closed my legs together around his hard dick. Every time the wood slapped on Joey's ass he humped his tool between my thighs. Every time he humped me I mocked him for liking the spanking. "Why you little pervert, you're getting off on this abuse. You deserve to be whipped!"

After this round was over I again rubbed his beet-red buns and this time ran my hand down his thigh so that my fingers slid down his crack and onto the root of his cock. It was swollen and hard. As I manipulated the base of his balls Joey moaned with pleasure and humped my legs. By this time he was dripping precum and my legs were welt lubricated.

Enough! This was not supposed to be a turn-on for Joey. Besides, I had a throbbing erection of my own and was afraid that I might pop if we kept this up. I kicked him off my lap.

"What the fuck you doin', boy?"

He stood there with an enormous hard-on.

"Are you a masochist? Is that what you are?

Fie blushed. "No."

"Then why do you have an erection if you aren't into abuse?"

"I don't know. It just happened."

"Well, would you like it more if I hurt you some more? I can get a belt and really lace your behind."

"Oh, no! Please! The paddle was bad enough. I don't think I'll be able to sit down for a week."

As he said this, his eyes became riveted on my cock. I was so hard the elastic tented out in front of me. "Do you see anything that interests you, you little pervert?"

He nodded.

"Okay, drop to your knees and lick my balls inside the jock and don't use your hands."

He worked his tongue into the "tent" and did an admirable job of keeping me excited. Then I had him work the balls out of the pouch and take them both into his mouth. He did so well I thought my cock would rip through the fabric.

"Pull this jock down with your teeth and work on my cock, asshole. And, keep your hands away from your own cock, too. You're here to service me, not have a good time." I pushed his hand off his hard-on with my foot and gave him a kick in the balls. He howled with surprise and pain and hunched over but didn't miss a beat on my tool.

It didn't take long before I was ready to shoot. I pulled out of his sucking mouth and gave my dick a few jerks. The cum shot out with surprising force. He tried to back away but I grabbed the hair on the back of his head and held him there. "Oh, no, you little shit. Your pretty face is gonna be my cum rag." My cum splattered all over his face and dripped off his chin and nose. I grabbed a fistful of hair and dragged him into the bathroom and had him kneel down in front of me. I moistened a face cloth and ordered him, "Wash your filthy spit off my cock."

As my dick softened, I began to feel the urge to piss. I hadn't planned it but this was a perfect chance to continue my humiliation. When he held my dick up to wipe my balls, I let out a stream of piss that hit him in the face. Again, I grabbed the back of his head and held him there to suffer this new indignity. My urine washed the cum off his face and rinsed it on down his chest and crotch. I looked down to see he had another erection.

"So, you like to be pissed on, do yah? Is there no end to your degeneracy?"

He had no answer.

As my stream slowed, I pulled back on his hair, opening his mouth so the last few spurts flowed down his tongue. "I thought you'd like something to drink."

His face screwed up into a look of disgust at what he had just swallowed. But in spite of his revulsion at the thought of swallowing piss, the whole scene obviously excited him. I stepped back to view the kid as he knelt before me with my piss running down his body and dripping off his throbbing dick into a puddle on the floor.

"Well, well. What a sight. I had no idea you were so depraved. Look at you. Now I'll have to wash you off before you're fit to leave this room."

With that I dragged him into the shower with me. I soaped him down, front and back, enjoying the feel of his body as I went. He still had an erection. He'd been up for so long I figured that he was getting pretty uncomfortable. That was fine with me. As I soaped his crotch he tried to hump my hand for relief but I wouldn't let him. Every time he reached for his cock I pulled his hand away and gave him a hard slap. As I washed his crack I worked a finger into his hole. He bolted upright. Once he was used to the feeling he groaned with pleasure and backed down onto my finger to get more into his ass.

"So, we like something hard up our asshole, do we?" This time he wasn't too embarrassed to answer and whimpered a yes.

Since the one finger was clearly not filling him I worked in a second, a third, and, finally, a fourth. He was writhing and sobbing. I was afraid he would slide away from me and fall in the tub, but he kept pressing down onto my hand, trying to get more.

I'd never fisted anyone but this looked like the way we were headed. Sure enough, with the soap for a lubricant I massaged that tightly stretched ring until it relaxed enough to ease the tip of my thumb in. Joey shrieked as he was widened even more. But he quickly settled down to his chants of "Oh yeah! More! Oh yeah, man."

With one arm around Joey's heaving chest I worked the other up the chute bit by bit. My crock was hard again and I humped his thigh as I worked on his ass. Suddenly I had passed the wide part of my fist and his anal ring closed down toward my wrist pushing my hand all the way in.

Joey sucked in a long hiss of air as I fully entered his rectum, I could feel his pulse all around my fist. My hand was in a tight, warm, moist sack. Slowly I pulled back until the ball of my fist was against the ring again, then I eased back up the canal until I hit the top. Joey was panting and hanging on my other arm.

As I gave him another plunging, he straightened up and began to shoot without even touching his cock. Amid his gasps of ecstasy my arm felt what only my cock had felt before: a climax from the inside. His whole rectum contracted with the ejaculations. Against the side of my hand I felt his prostate pulsing and the muscles at the base of his cock contracting. It was such a turn-on that my humping dick shot out its own jism on his side.

Joey was so exhausted, I had to hold him up as I eased my hand out of his ass. He was gasping and shuddering as I leaned him against the side of the stall, then I washed off my arm and left him to clean himself as I dried off.

While Joey was in the basement getting his clothes out of the dryer, I called Len. The phone rang several times until he finally answered. After telling him Joey had showed up on my porch, I said, "Please, come get him before I do anything to him I'll regret later."

While we were waiting for Len to arrive, true to form, Joey tried to hit me up for some cash.

"You little shit!"

"Hey, don't you think I earned at least something for all the abuse I took? You couldn't get a hustler to do that for less than a hundred bucks,"

"Maybe, but you obviously enjoyed yourself so I figure you owe me something for your pleasure. Let's say you knock fifty bucks off what you already owe me?"

"Fifty?"

"Yeah, that leaves four more sessions just like that and then we'll be even."

"Four more like that?"

I was firm.. "Four."

He looked down at the floor, shook his head and softly asked, "When do we start?"

BROTHERS OF THE NIGHT
P. K. Warren

When my father returned home from work he was always late and usually drunk. Just the sight of his car entering the drive would induce a cold sweat; I knew he'd be looking for his personal whipping post the moment he entered the house. I ran.

On the streets I felt safe from my father's wrath but they were hardly a sanctuary; they could become a deadly place in the blink of an eye. Early on, I began hustling. As a teenager, with my slim build, brown curly hair, and cute ass stuffed into tight jeans, I seldom had any trouble finding tricks. Soon I was following in the path of my street brothers, turning several tricks in a night.

One of the brothers, Conner, I'd known since fifth grade. During those years, before we both dropped out of school, I'd watched him develop into a five-foot-two, blond, blue-eyed Adonis. Everybody wanted him, including me. But, like most of the other hustlers, he said he was straight, just doing it for the money so he could get drugs. Worse yet, when the gang hung out at the pizza parlor, their girls were always with them. It became torture to see Conner necking with his girl Cathy; I desperately wanted to be in her place. And, naturally, since I didn't have a girl, the others would accuse me of really being gay. I'd shrug it off, saying that I wasn't ready for any relationship. But, surprisingly, when the teasing went too far, it was always Conner who brought it to an end.

One warm weekend in the middle of May, the guys decided to take the girls to the lake. They wanted to fix me up with a blind date but I refused. - Somebody has to work the streets," I joked, but what was really bothering me was I knew they would go skinny-dipping and just seeing Conner nude would give me a hard-on.

After that weekend, Cathy was crying on my shoulder. She wanted me to talk to Conner about his smoking pot and drinking; the Adonis was having problems keeping it up. I promised I would talk to him.

That night, I found Conner on the usual corner and asked him how the weekend went. He said it was great and then told me that before they left they had to scout the woods for another of our brothers, stocky tittle Neal, and his girl. "He's always horny," Conner said.

"Yeah, he never has any trouble gettin' it up."

"What's that supposed to mean?"

"Nothin'. He's always sayin' he'll fuck anything."

"Don't you wish? " Conner spat, walking away from me. The following night I found Conner sitting alone at the pizza parlor.

"So where's everybody?" I asked him.

"Neal's gone to pick up a dime," he said glumly.

"Where's Cathy?"

He just stared at me, saying nothing.

"All right, all right, I'm sorry I asked. I was just curious." "We had another fight," he said. "She caught me smokin'." "Conner, listen. If you'd cut back a little ® "

"I told you before, mind your own fuckin' business," just then, Neal finally showed up with a six-pack and the dime bag. I was invited to join them at their hangout, a storage room on the fifth floor of an abandoned building right in the center of town.

On the way up the stairs, Conner was fast behind me, and grabbed my ass. I stopped and turned.

"What do you want?" I asked.

"Anything I can get."

"Yeah, sure," I said, running up the rest of the way.

The three of us finished the beer and most of the pot. Neal decided he would get more. "You do that," Conner said, still in an ugly mood.

After Neal left, Conner said, "He's gonna get some pussy, that's what he's gonna do."

"He's always horny," I nodded.

"What the fuck would you know about it?" he said, lifting himself from the old mattress we had moved into the room.. He began to walk to the door. He steadied himself on the wall, then flung open the door. I could hear his footsteps as he went down the hall. Then I could hear him taking a piss.

I lay down on my side, facing the wall.

When he returned I could hear him taking off his clothes. "Hot in here," he said, getting on the mattress. With the Adonis so close to me, nude, the room felt as if it were a hundred degrees; I began to sweat.

He lit another joint and asked if I wanted a shotgun before the roach went out. When I rolled over, I saw he had a hard-on. As he was blowing into my mouth, my hand dropped to it. He didn't push it away..

Next my mouth went to his cock, which was not long but it was Conner's and that made it special. I went at it as if I had never sucked a dick before. Before long, he was lifting himself off the mattress, trying to shove every inch of it down my throat.

"Damn, that's good," he said.

I could sense he was almost ready to come so I plopped it out of my mouth and said, "I know what would be even better."

Before he could get a moment to think about it, off came my jeans and I was on my back with my legs spread wide. Without hesitation, he got into position and I guided his hard-on, wet with my spit, into my ass. The pain was worth it.

All my fantasies came true when he held my ankles and slowly, gently entered me to the balls.

"Oh, yeah," I cried when he gave one final thrust, bottoming out. When I relaxed, he started humping me slowly. Enjoying every stroke, I sucked, kissed, and licked his naked shoulders. Suddenly the door opened and Neal walked in.

"Oh, shit," Conner said

"Oh shit is right," Neal chuckled, stepping into the room and closing the door. " I thought I was the only one who'd fuck anything."

Conner slowed his pace, softened a bit, but he wasn't about to stop now. Tuckin" sissy's been askin' for it!"

"Looks like he's gettin' it," Neal said, stepping closer. He removed his shirt; he had a tight, muscular chest with hard, brown nipples.

Conner kept on, as if Neal wasn't even there.

Neal hurriedly removed jeans and his bikini briefs, exposing his thick, uncut cock. He shook it at me as he stepped over to the mattress. Conner raised up on his knees so that Neal could kneel next to us. I took hold of Neal's thick, hooded meat and drew it to my mouth..

Conner, holding onto my legs, was now hard again and slammed into me with renewed vigor. Neal's cock stiffened as I sucked and he held my head as he thrust into my mouth.

When it was fully erect, Neal's cock was a good three inches longer than Conner's and the head was very large. It was, I decided, the perfect cock. No wonder he was always horny, I thought, as I took it all the way down to his pubic hair.

Before long, Conner couldn't help it; he cried out as he blasted his cum into my ass.

"Oh, yeah, fuck that fairy ass!" Neal cried. And when Conner pulled out, that's exactly what Neal decided to do. Never in my wildest fantasy had I imagined I would have both of these guys one after the other, but that's what I was getting. This time, I jacked off while I was being fucked and the rush was so intense I trembled as I came. The intensity of my orgasm urged Neal on and he pushed himself over the brink quickly. Conner was standing near the bed and chuckled delightedly as Neal finished, He stroked his cock, which was now hard again, and I grinned happily when he said, "Hey, man, get outta there now. I'm ready for seconds."

Was he ever. Neal returned his cock to my mouth as Conner invaded me once again. I was delirious with joy as Conner came again and laid back down next to me. I rolled over and Neal took me from behind. "Yeah, fuck that fairy ass," Conner said, his eyes riveted on Neal's pistoning prick,

After Neal came, he rolled away and lay quietly next to me, spent. I reached down and took each of their sopping cocks in my hand, sighed deeply, and closed my eyes.

I was awakened by an elderly Italian poking my shoulder with his cane. "Wakeupa, you sonamabich!" he yelled and poked harder with his cane.

"Ya getta outta ma place wit yo friends! I calla de policia, ya done getta out now!"

After what seemed like hours of sexual bliss, the three of us had fallen asleep. We jumped up and scrambled to get dressed without knocking each other over.. I was the first one out of the room, with Conner close behind and Neal bringing up the rear. Four blocks away we finally stopped running and looked around to see if the cops were coming -- the old guy hadn't called them.

"He scared the piss outta me!" Neal said

"No, shit!" I said, trying to catch my breath.

"I think he got a bigger surprise than we did," Conner said. "Lucky he didn't have a heart attack finding us like that!" We laughed so hard our stomachs hurt.

The following week I got a job as a lifeguard and couldn't hang out with the guys as much as I had been. When I did see them, they both acted as if nothing had happened. I began to wonder if it did happen or if I'd imagined it. Then one night Conner and I were alone at the pizza parlor and he said he had made up with Cathy. He said he had agreed to stay off the drugs and get a GED if she'd marry him.

"If that's what you want ..."

He shrugged.

By summer's end, I was hanging out with a new crowd and that finally ripped the door off my closet. Conner dropped out of sight for five years and when we met again he was married with two kids. He told me Neal had moved upstate to live with his father and eventually married his steady girl.

TURNING ON THE JOHNS
Tony Stephenson

"You want to see a kid really gone to the bad? Look for one whose daddy's a preacher. Preacher's brats are the worst. At least that's what they used to say in my hometown.... up near North Bay.... I wasn't a preacher's brat like they meant, though. I mean, my daddy wasn't a preacher. No, he worked for the township._ on the garbage trucks. But what happened was I got took up by the Reverend Joyhill. He kinda treated me like I was his son – did nice things for me – bought me clothes asked me to go with him to the church conference in Winnipeg. That's when I really got to be the preacher's brat. We shared this motel room... only one bed... Know what I mean?"

Wesley looks as if he has been strongly influenced by a strict non-Conformist upbringing. Unlike many of his peers on the street, he makes no attempt to appear sexy or trendy. His tarnished copper hair is cut short at back and sides and slathered with a greenish brilliantine in the manner of small barber shops in remote provincial towns. This has the effect of making his rosy and relatively well-formed ears appear to stick out from the sides of his head like the handles on a loving-cup. He has rather fine, though worried-looking, eyes, a delicately molded nose, and a small inviting mouth with lips like faded rose-petals. Unfortunately the overall impression is almost spoiled by a scattering of acne blemishes on cheeks and chin, and when he smiles the results of second-rate dental care can be seen in the irregularity and general dinginess of his teeth.

His body is wiry rather than willowy, yet he seems at odds with it, as though he doesn't quite trust it to do what he wants- In any case, he looks uncomfortable, which perhaps isn't surprising, given what he's wearing. They are very much the kind of clothes that a not-too-particular Methodist or Presbyterian teenager would wear to Sunday school; a white nylon shirt through which a sleeveless undershirt can be seen, a drab, limp tie knotted tight at the neck, a dark single-breasted suit of some cheap fabric gone shiny at the seat and elbows, a pair of grey woolen socks concertinaed at the ankles, and scuffed black loafers with brass buckles. The sleeves of the jacket are too short and his hands, red and big-knuckled, protrude nakedly. The pants are hitched too high in the crotch, which gives him endless problems of adjustment, both at the front where he has to wriggle and squirm to shake things back in place, and at the back where the tight seat has crammed his jockey-shorts into the cleft of his buttocks, giving rise to the occasional furtive attempt to dislodge them.

In spite of all this, his effect on me is powerfully sexual. "Tell me about the Reverend Joyboy," I say. "Did he bring you to Toronto?"

It's three am on a summer's night in the mid-'60s, and we are sitting in a booth in an all-night diner in downtown Toronto, not far from the YMCA where Wesley is temporarily living. There's a plate of French fries and a glass of soda on the table in front of him, and before he answers me, he picks up a French fry in his fingers, dips it in ketchup and inserts it between his lips. A blob of ketchup lands on his chin.

"Joy-hill, not Joyboy," he says after he's finished chewing and licked the ketchup off, "I come here with him a year ago. He got transferred down here to work in a poor parish, be a minister to delinquent kids, unmarried mothers, that kinda thing. He said I could help him – and my folks were glad to have me out of the way. One less mouth to feed; a lot more beer for them. There was no point in staying, anyways; there was nothing for me to do up there. So I came and, like, helped lick envelopes and answer the telephone. I stayed in the church house, of course, but we didn't share a bed in case the housekeeper caught on.

"But, still, he came to my room every night. He'd make me kneel down with him and we'd say a bedtime prayer together."

I can't believe this. "You'd what?" I say.

"Say a bedtime prayer! 'Gentle Jesus'."

"You mean: 'Gentle Jesus, meek and mild?'"

"You know it too, huh?"

"Yes, I know it. It hardly seems appropriate for a middle-aged minister and his teenage boyfriend."

Wesley blushes. "Well, he used to say we all had to become as little children."

"So he was into infantilism, too – Sorry, bad joke... But do you mean to say that you and the minister knelt down side by side, said your bedtime prayers together and then he got into bed with you and screwed you?"

Wesley wriggles, and this time I don't think it's because of his jockey shorts.

"You don't have to talk nasty," he complains.

He is looking hurt and embarrassed so I apologize. I certainly don't want to turn him off me at this point; after all, at three a.m. where would I find another trick? I reach under the table and squeeze his knee. It feels bony and virginal.

"Come on, smile for me," I plead, and reluctantly he shows his imperfect teeth in a crooked grin.

"All right... But you should consider people's feelings."

"I do. All the time. Anyway, tell me some more about the Reverend Joyh ill."

"I don't know what to tell you," he begins, and then adds defiantly, "but he was a good man, whatever you think. He helped a lot of people and he cared about me."

"Helped? Cared?" I say. "Why the past tense? Is he dead?" Wesley lowers his eyes. "No, he's not dead."

"Did he kick you out?"

"Kinda."

I decide that this is not the time to press it, so I suggest that he might care to come home with me.

"I already got somewhere to sleep," he says surlily.

"It wasn't so much sleep that I had in mind," I tell him. "I need some company. I get lonely all by myself in my apartment."

"You mean you want to stick it up me."

"Now, who's talking nasty? I would just like someone to snuggle up to."

"How far away d'you live?"

I can tell his resolve is crumbling. He's been yawning for the last fifteen minutes and his eyelids are slowly closing.

"Just around the corner," I answer. "We can walk there in five minutes. Come on, the fresh air will do you good."

After I've paid the bill, we go out into the city night. A late streetcar is clanking past us towards the university campus. A cop in a cruiser frowns at us as he crawls by. The moon is high over the hockey stadium, and a cool breeze blows up off the lake. We turn the corner northward onto Yonge Street, Toronto's main drag, which Torontonians boast is the longest street in the world. The neons still flash their messages in the unpeopled dusk and the store-windows stare blankly at each other across the empty sidewalks.

Wesley shivers and I put my arm around him for warmth, but he pulls away. Clearly, public demonstrations of affection make him nervous, so I don't make a big deal of it; I just walk silently at his side, occasionally letting my knuckles graze his. One block up, we cross over towards the Westbury Hotel and turn into Alexander Street where the big concrete apartment blocks rise above us.

I've lived in one of these buildings for three years. It has a reputation as a gay apartment complex, and there's some truth in that. Certainly, there are a number of us who make our homes here, partly because the apartments are quite spacious considering the moderate rents, and partly because there are gay bars and discos close by. Anyway, Wesley seems quite impressed when I take him up in the elevator and show him into my one-bedroom pad on the top floor where from the wide windows you can see the lights of the city skyline glittering.

Fie sits tidily on my op-art couch, which is covered in an eye-jolting black and white fabric that might have been designed by Bridget Riley.

"You've got a nice place, here," he says, keeping his knees together, his feet flat on the floor, and turning his head stiffly on his neck to look around.

"Relax," I say, "Take your jacket off. Have a beer." "I don't drink."
"Have another soda, then."

He accepts the soda and after a little persuasion removes his jacket. His tie looks as though it's choking him so I suggest he loosen it or take it off. He gives me an old-fashioned look but he eases the knot down and unbuttons his collar.

"So why did the reverend gentleman kick you out?"

An abashed look comes over his face. "I cheated on him." "Cheated? Like went to bed with somebody else?"

"There was this kid he was helping. A j.d. – you know, juvenile delinquent. The Reverend was trying to make sure that he didn't go back into the reformatory. Anyways, I was doing some filing in the church office when he come in about something. The reverend wasn't there, and the kid started to put the make on me."

"And the reverend caught you at it. What were you doing?"

Wesley avoids my eye. "I'm not telling. But the Reverend Joyhill was very disappointed in me. He said it wasn't so much that he was hurt for himself but that I was hurting the kid's chances of getting straightened out... It was something he couldn't forgive, and things could never be the same. He gave me some money to get a room at the Y and said he'd buy me a bus-ticket home. But I said I couldn't go home – I'd rather find a job in Toronto."

I give a sigh. "And I guess you found that wasn't so easy." "The places I tried, they kept telling me I didn't have enough education, and the kind of office work I'd been doing well, they hired girls for that."

They hire girls for the kind of work he's doing now, too, I think, but then I reprove myself. The mere fact that I picked him up on St. Joseph Street doesn't mean he's a hustler. Not all the boys who hang out there are trade.

"So how long have you been looking for work?"
"Ages. Three weeks."
"And the reverend's still paying your tab at the Y?"

"No, not exactly," he admits. "I met this other guy at the Y – his name's Dean – and he told me he knew a way I could make some quick bucks. He said he knew this rich middle-aged guy who would pay for company. I really thought he meant that it was just that – just company, you know?"

"No kidding," I say

"Well, it wasn't. He was staying at the Lord Simcoe and I went up to his room... kind of a nice room with a TV and a coffee-maker and everything. He had room service bring up some hamburgers and stuff."

"So he fed you. Then what?"

"Oh, you know we chatted for a bit. What was a nice country boy like me doing in this big wicked city? That kinda junk."

"And then?"

"And then he went into the washroom. I thought he was just going to take a leak, but when he came out a few minutes later, he had changed into a pair of, like, little-kid-type shorts, and a tee shirt and a baseball cap. He said, 'I've been a bad boy and you've got to spank me. I'll give you twenty dollars, if you do.'"

Wesley gives a half-shame-faced giggle as he contemplates this picture in his mind's eye. "Then he handed me a belt and bent over. Well, holy Moses! I didn't know whether to spit or swallow a dime..."

If the picture that comes into my head is anything like the one in his, I can't blame him: a porky, fat-assed businessman bent over with little-boy shorts stretched tight across his flabby buttocks. There couldn't have been much of Eros in the spectacle.

"So what did you do?"

'I gave him a little bit of a swat, but I couldn't go on. It felt like spanking my dad. So I dropped the belt. He was moaning 'Go on, go on,' but I told him it was no good. I thought he'd get mad, but he just straightened up, went back into the washroom and came out a bit later in his regular clothes. He never said anything more about it. We just sat and chatted for a bit about hockey and stuff. And when I got up to go, he handed me a twenty dollar bill'"

"Easiest twenty bucks you ever made, I bet."

Wesley and I talk a while longer and it soon becomes clear to me that whatever has happened to him so far in Toronto, he hasn't quite sacrificed his amateur status. Dean, it appears, gave up on trying to pimp for him after one or two fiascos similar to the Lord Simcoe episode, and shortly after that he met another displaced provincial like himself, who felt sorry for him and helped him out in various small ways. So he's been able to hang onto his room at the Y, and eat once in a while. But it's a situation that can't persist for long. With no likelihood of a job, he'll eventually lose his room, and might end up having to go back to his family, an outcome neither he nor they will rejoice over

By now, Wesley is yawning more and more, and slumping further and further down on the couch. I come to a decision and move closer to him, easing my hand onto his leg.

"I've got an idea," I say. "Why don't you move in with me? I'm out all day and I hate doing housework. You could keep the place tidy. Have some dinner ready for me when I get back. You can cook, can't you?"

He nods dubiously.

"There you are then. I'll even pay you a weekly wage. Not much, mind you. I do all right at the agency, but I'm not rich. How about twenty-five dollars plus room and meals in exchange for light household duties?"

"What about...?" He jerks his head towards the bedroom. "We'll see what develops," F say. "No-one's going to force anything on you – or up you."

"Nasty talk again!" He shakes his head reprovingly, but his crooked smile cancels the reproof, "Well, if you really mean it...?"

"Good, we'll go and pick up your things at the Y later. Now I think it's time to turn in."

His eyes wander nervously to the bedroom door again.

"Do you have some pajamas I can borrow?" he mutters self-consciously.

In fact, I don't wear pajamas. I like to sleep naked whether I'm sharing my bed or not, but if the kid wants to wear pajamas, I don't mind. In fact, it might be quite a turn-on taking them off him. So I go to a drawer in the armoire and take out a set of cotton and polyester pajamas, still in their original wrapping a Christmas present from my Aunt Iris. They are the old-fashioned kind- a buttoned jacket and pants with draw-string, all in a fetchingly striped material of green, maroon and white. Wesley takes them with a mumbled thanks, and disappears into the bathroom.

"You'll find a new toothbrush in the medicine cabinet," I yell after him, hoping he'll take the hint to brush his teeth. "And help yourself to a shower, if you like."

When he comes out of the bathroom, half-an-hour later, he looks like a kid off the cover of the old Saturday Evening Post: freshly-washed, hair all spiky from the shower, eyes sleepy, and looking half his age in pajamas that are a couple of sizes too big for him. I'm already lying in bed with the covers pulled up to my waist. He blinks rapidly a few times when he sees my bare, hairy chest. I turn back the covers on his side and wave him over.

"Come on, climb in."

"I've got to do something first."

And what do you know? – he kneels right down at the side of the bed and says his Gentle Jesus prayer. He says it quietly with great concentration, and I can't help thinking of A.A. Milne's poem about Christopher Robin, especially the lines:

"Hush, hush, whisper who dares;
Christopher Robin is saying his prayers."

When he climbs into bed finally, I put my arms around his thin body and hold him close. He stiffens and then relaxes; his head drops wearily onto my chest; he closes his eyes. My heart is stunned, shocked, incredulous; I can't believe what I'm feeling or put a name to it. All I know is it makes my throat feel tight and sore as if I was holding back a sob. As I lie there, holding him carefully, his body gives off a scent like new-mown hay mingled with the faintest hint of civet. And, for whatever reason, the idea of taking his pajamas off, of stripping him, now seems like a violation. I close my eyes, giving myself up to the sensation of a warm body beside me, and soon I am asleep, having the best rest I've had in months.

Four weeks later we celebrate our one-month anniversary. (I suppose that should be "mensiversary," but I don't like the word's connotations). Anyway, so far things are working out just fine. I get up in the morning to go to work, and Wesley has breakfast ready. I come home at six and the apartment is clean and he has dinner in the oven. We eat, listen to records, play Scrabble (at which Wesley always loses), we have a few drinks (non-alcoholic for him) and we go to bed. He's in his pajamas (he has more than one pair now) and I'm naked. He says his bedtime prayer, we hug and that's it.

For me, it's a bewildering relationship. I mean, it's not that I don't get horny, but if I do, I ease carefully out of bed so as not to wake him up, and I go to the bathroom, and I give myself a hand-job. I do kiss him occasionally and he doesn't seem to mind that, but I'm somehow inhibited from doing the things I have done in the past so many times and with so many boys. I even worry sometimes about whether Wesley himself gets horny and what he does about it. Maybe he takes care of it during the day when I'm at work. And that raises another possibility: maybe he's doing it with someone else. Until you've had the viper of sexual jealousy writhing inside you and filling you with its poison, you can't possibly grasp the kind of pain I would feel at those moments.

And yet, Wesley seems loving and frank. I can't believe there is any deceit in him. On the other hand, there is all that time, Mondays to Fridays from about 8.30 a.m. to something like 6 or 6.30 p.m., when I'm away from the apartment and he's out of my sight. I know there isn't enough housework to keep him occupied all day, and I know he doesn't like to watch television in the afternoon. So he probably strolls out on nice days, takes a walk down Toronto's equivalent of 42nd Street (the stretch of Yonge Street that forms the downtown core), maybe buys himself a soda at Lindy's and plays the jukebox, checks out the latest rock 45s at the teens' favorite record shop, or wanders into a department store to look at shirts. (Oh, yes, that's a change: he's become more clothes-conscious).

Anyway, all I'm saying is: he goes out alone. Which is fine. I don't want him to stay in the apartment, locked up like Rapunzel or the Lady of Shalott. I just wish I could be there with him, idly walking the streets, instead of being stuck in this miserable advertising office, drinking too much coffee, and trying to figure out how to write an original corporate ad for a company that makes steam boilers. Of course, we do go out together at weekends – and that's great. In fact from Friday night to Sunday afternoon is our magic time; then comes Sunday evening and I start worrying about steam boilers and liniments and canned peas again. Still, those forty-eight hours or so keep me living through the rest of the week.

After work on Friday, I usually meet him at the St. Charles, the city's oldest- established gay bar, just across the street from my apartment building. I have a couple of beers and he has a soda and then we go and have dinner at

one of the more upscale restaurants in the city's core. About seven-thirty or eight,, we go home and get washed and dressed for an evening on the town.

As I said, Wesley's taste in clothes has, well, if not improved, at least advanced. His typical outfit for a night at the gay discos is an Everly Brothers-style dark blue and gold striped shirt with the collar turned up at the back, a medallion of some sort round his neck, a pair of low-rise, hip-hugging black chinos with flares, and Beatle boots. He also now sports around his wrist a gold-plated identity bracelet which I bought him at People's Jewelers. All in all, he doesn't look too different from thousands of other teenagers, straight or gay, who have succumbed to the "rebel youth" image. If it's a cool night, he finishes off the effect with a fringed black suede jacket.

Where did he get all this stuff? Some he saved up for; some I bought for him (I guess I like to spoil him); some he borrows from my closet. Anyway, I like to see him looking good, and now that I've introduced him to Clearasil, his skin has improved too. Even the yokel haircut is growing out, and he's trying to cultivate a James Dean style. Beatle mop-tops haven't quite become the rage yet, and it's a long while before the boys will start growing their hair down to their butts.

And what do I wear to complement his image? Well, I'm only twenty-eight after all – and I have a sneaking conviction that I look no less than six years younger – so what do you think I wear? I'm right in there with the rest of the kids, even if they can get into pants with a size twenty-eight waist and I have to settle for a thirty. Anyway, all you have to know is that I cut a pleasing figure and get my share of cruisy once-overs in the street.

The night begins back at the St. Charles, where we greet various friends and acquaintances. Then around eleven we move over to the gay discos on Yonge Street; one is over a shop and the other is in a basement, and at weekends they're both jammed with guys from the ages of about seventeen to upwards of fifty. Neither place has a liquor license, so all you can get to drink is coffee, orange juice or soda, and the floor gets quite sticky with spilled sugary drinks. Everybody smokes too, so the place is full of swirling grey fog. Half the crowd is standing wedged shoulder to shoulder watching the rest of the crowd, mostly its younger members, leaping and gyrating to the music, grinding groin to groin, and working themselves up generally into a sexual frenzy. Their straight teenage contemporaries would never dare be so openly carnal with their female partners.

The gyrating and the closeness of body to body generate quite a bit of heat, and soon the air is heavy with the pungency of sweat mixed with the cloying scent of popular colognes like Canoe and Hi Karate.

One such evening, when the crowd is particularly dense, I suddenly hear a voice in my ear.

"Bloody zoo," it says. "I don't know why I come here."

Naturally, I recognize it right away. It's the voice of Adam Lukes, one of the guys who live in my building. He's a freelance TV and film director and makes a steady income shooting commercials for various ad agencies in town. We once worked together on a commercial for a breath freshener.

"Hi, Adam," I say. "Of course you know why you come here. To check out the fresh talent."

Adam is always on the prowl. He's one of those who, once he gets into a boy's pants, loses interest rapidly. So he needs a constant supply of new tricks and, being a well-preserved thirty-four, he gets them. He wears his pale blond hair in a Caesar cut and has a kind of Belmondo face, ugly but compelling. His customary cruising uniform is a leather jacket, boot-cut jeans, and a few chains hanging here and there. He likes his boys to be soft and pretty and submissive. He can never understand why I pick up the kind of boys I do. Wesley is just about the last straw,

"Beats me what you see in that kid," he says over and over again. "He looks like Alfred E. Neumann."

Alfred E., of course, is the mascot of Mad Magazine, a freckled, jug-eared, snaggle-toothed oaf with an idiot grin. I take offence at this comparison, but Adam is not the most sensitive guy in the world. Next time I see him he'll say it again, though never, to be fair, when Wesley is within earshot. However, Adam soon has something else to be incredulous about.

"I hope he's at least good in the sack," he says on this particular evening in the basement club.

"I don't know," I blurt out. "We just cuddle."

Adam looks at me as if I had just admitted to being Oral Roberts' illegitimate son, As for me, I can't believe what I just said. I mean, why am I telling this to Adam Lukes of all people?

"You do what? You're putting me on, aren't you? I mean the kid lives with you, right?"

"Right."

"And you guys sleep in the same bed, right?"

"Right."

"And you don't fuck or suck or anything?"

"Right."

Adam makes a sound like a balloon deflating.

"You must've fried your brains," he says. "Man, that kid has the best gig in town. Lives off the fat of the land, has his clothes bought for him, and doesn't even get fucked!"

"You wouldn't understand," I tell him. "This is something different. I can't explain it, except that fucking him would be like fucking myself when I was an innocent kid. I'd feel I was desecrating something."

"Fucking yourself? Well, I'm sure lots of people have told you to do that, but come on, this kid is no virgin!"

"I hope that's not something you know from personal experience."

"Well, no – he's not my type, but I've certainly heard stories about him."

I guess he sees how stricken I look because he adds hastily: "I mean, stories about before you met him. That kid Dean told me some."

"Yeah, well, Dean is a pimp and he knows bugger all about what Wesley did. He might have set Wesley up with some dates but he doesn't know exactly what went on at them."

"O.K., O.K., don't blow your cool, man. Jeer, you're really hung up on this Wesley guy."

Adam sounds perplexed and I see him turn and scan the dancing crowd till he has Wesley in focus. Wesley is performing rather circumspectly compared to the wild turnings and twirlings of his fellow-dancers. He takes precise, distinct steps and moves his arms and hands in a very contained way. But you can tell he's enjoying himself. Adam watches him thoughtfully for several minutes before turning back to me and saying; "I don't get it, man."

This time, though, there is a hint of uncertainty in his tone, suggesting that he is beginning to question his own view of Wesley, Can it be (he perhaps wonders) that he is missing something? In any case, he drops the whole subject for that night, and eventually lopes off in indolent pursuit of a dark, curly-haired waif with interesting buns.

I'm not saying that Adam Lukes is the only one who is critical of my relationship with Wesley. Bob Westerberg, commonly known as "Your Mother," a generously built fiftyish tax lawyer, also expresses his doubts about it, "Listen to your mother," he urges, "...you can do better than that. You have done better than that! Pull yourself together, girl, and give him the heave-ho." Of course, Bob is suspicious of anyone under forty, but anyone over forty is too old to attract him, so he spends a lot of his time brooding about not having anyone to go to bed with, while trying to discourage those who do.

And the list could go on – Kenny Parsons, Wolf Hauptmann, Lester Chan, Fabrizio Gozzi – all the regulars, in fact, frown at the Wesley thing. The only one who is even a little bit on my side is Eddie Glen, who has had a similar relationship with a young airman from Camp Borden squelched by the group. They are hard taskmasters, the members of this group, all experienced judges of youthful male potential, quick to identify the users, the self-centered, the fickle, the flighty, the callous, the cruel, the boring and the brainless. Not many pass their collective scrutiny without some shortcoming being noted. And, of course, those scrutinized, being young, could hardly be without shortcomings. The result is that none of the group dare be seen to favor any particular young man for fear the rest of them will hold the boy to a strict accounting and generally find him wanting.

Most of them, in fact, have secret liaisons that they keep carefully hidden from the others. Lester Chan, a second generation Chinese-Canadian

who teaches math at a local high school, has an eighteen-year-old lover of Polish descent who sells vegetables at the St. Lawrence Market. Kenny Parsons, a junior executive with an oil company, is having a sub rosa affair with one of his office boys. I'm not sure about Wolf and Fabrizio but I suspect that they're up to the same roguery,.. And don't ask me how I penetrated the secret lives of Lester and Kenny because I never divulge my sources.

None of them are quite as insulting about Wesley as Adam is, but they all make it clear that he is (a) too provincial, (b) insufficiently sparkling, and (c) physically substandard. Moreover, they find my persistence in the affair, after their criticisms have been voiced, totally unintelligible. Of course, when Adam begins to spread the word that I'm not even getting any sex out of it, they are merciless.

"This must stop!"

"You can't go on like this!"

"You're being taken advantage of!"

"No sex! It's unheard of!"

These and similar remonstrance are the daily bread of their discourse as long as Wesley and I are together. So I'm surprised when Eddie Glen, the only one who hasn't joined in the chorus, tells me that all four of them have tried to put the make on Wesley. I'm sure they told themselves that they were doing it for my own good, that they had to test Wesley's constancy, that they needed to subject him to closer inspection, but in any case I am furious with them.

When I tackle Wesley about it, he admits that they had all shown some interest but he swears he didn't reciprocate. From what I could gather it was pretty clumsy stuff: an invitation to go for a ride in Kenny's Thunderbird convertible, a suggestion by Lester that they might go to the movies together – that kind of thing.

"You weren't tempted?" I ask.

"Not after what happened with the reverend," he says.

I find that I'm in two minds about this response: grateful that he thinks well enough of me not to be lured away, but suspicious that the lesson he learned with the juvenile delinquent is 'Cheat on your boyfriend and you might end up back on the streets.' Anyway this episode is soon behind us and we resume our comfortable domestic routine.

One night when Wesley is kneeling there by the bed, with his head bent in his hands, mumbling away about: gentle Jesus, I ask him if he believes in God. He looks at me with total dismay.

"Why? Don't you?"

"I'm not sure..."

"You're an atheist?"

"No, an agnostic – that's what 'not sure' means."

Wesley wrinkles his nose and makes a dismissive sound with his lips.

"Aaaah, you're just trying to be different. You'd soon go crying to God if something bad happened."

I take some time to think about this, then I tell him that I think that's called opportunism, calling for help from someone you've ignored up till that time.

"Well, you may have been ignoring him, but he hasn't been ignoring you," says Wesley in a matter-of-fact way that carries a great deal of conviction.

That ends our theological discussion, but long after Wesley is gently snoring beside me, I lie awake wondering whether he's right.

Things slowly began to go amiss between us. There wasn't much to notice at first: a slightly sharpened tone occasionally in conversation; an absence of mind and perhaps spirit now and then; less meticulousness in the ordinary conduct of day-to-day living. My suspicions about his activities when I'm at work increase and eventually reach a point where I feel I must satisfy myself about them. So, one day, I feign illness after lunch and leave the office. All the way home, I am reassuring myself that I will find all as it should be. I think of Wesley kneeling beside the bed with his head resting on his hands and I tell myself that he is a genuine innocent, incapable of guile, and straightforward in his conduct. Then I think of Wesley in the Reverend Joyhill 's office fondling and being fondled by a juvenile delinquent. I think of him going out on dates that Dean the pimp set up. I'm so stirred up by the time I get to my apartment building that I actually collide with them in the lobby before I realize who they are.

"Whoa! Steady on."

Its Adam Lukes" voice. I clear my mind and focus on my surroundings, only then to realize that Wesley, looking conscience-stricken, is standing next to Adam.

"Hi. You're home early."

"I felt ill," I tell him.

Adam butts in at this point to smooth away the difficulty, blathering something about having run into Wesley in the elevator and inviting him for a cup of coffee, but I can tell from Wesley's eyes that more than coffee is involved here. I head for the elevators and Wesley, voicing a concern for my health, comes with me, leaving Adam standing bereft in the lobby.

"It's okay," I say to Wesley. "I'm not really ill. I just wanted an afternoon off. Go ahead and have your coffee."

We stand waiting by the bank of elevators, while the indicators move slowly up and down.

"Go on; don't let me spoil your plans,"

The concern in Wesley's eyes begins to change to relief and perhaps elation, or at any rate hopefulness.

"Well, if you're sure you're all right,.."

"I'm sure."

"I won't be long."

"Take your time."

While this is going on Adam has begun to move towards the main doors. He looks surprised and then gratified as Wesley hurries across the lobby to join him. Neither of them took at me as they leave. The elevator arrives.

So now I'm left with an empty afternoon to fill. What to do? Shall I make date squares? Listen to Fidelio? Play patience? Write a letter to my sister in Santa Fe? Read some Norman Mailer? Throw myself off the balcony? I reject all these possibilities and turn on the TV. There's an old Astaire-Rogers movie playing. Ginger is wearing a riding outfit and for some reason, they're dancing around a bandstand in the pouring rain. Fred sings something to the effect that it doesn't matter if the rain's coming down because when he's with Ginger, it's always a nice day. Lucky him, I think. I switch to another channel and it's a repeat of a Perry Como special. Perry, of course, is singing too. He sings that girls were made to kiss but Nina never knew. This seems irrelevant to my situation, so I switch again. This time it's a masters' golf tournament from somewhere in Florida. I give up and turn off the TV

The black glooms close in around me and stay there. I lie on the couch staring out of the window at the sky but seeing only a pointless future and wondering why every attempt I make at intimacy ends in ruin. I'm still there when Wesley returns two hours later"

"Feeling better?" he says as he comes through the door.

"I told you, I'm fine," I say. "I just got fed up sitting in that bastard office trying to think up things to say about furniture polish. I thought it would be nice instead to go for a walk in the sunshine – with you!"

"Why didn't you say? We could have done that!"

"You obviously had plans already."

"Yes, but..."

"Oh, never mind. What's for dinner?"

Wesley looks penitent. "Oh, jeez, I forgot. Look, I'll run out and get a pizza."

"No, to hell with it, we'll go to Lindy's. I fancy a nice thick steak and some Boston cream pie."

So that's what we do. We sit in one of the little booths that have their own jukebox selectors and I feed it quarters and we listen to Bobby Curtola, Gerry and the Pacemakers, and, inevitably, the Everly Brothers. The steak is a little tough, but the fries are good, and the Boston cream pie is to die for. Wesley has a cheeseburger and some Black Forest cake,

After we finish eating and are lingering over coffee and cigarettes, the conversation lags. I look around the restaurant at the other diners. They cover a pretty broad spectrum. There are hetero teen couples sharing root-beer floats with two straws, middle-aged solitary men who have stopped in on their way

to one of the XXX-rated movie houses further downtown, women clerks from one of the department stores celebrating a birthday or engagement.

The only ones I relate to are the solitary middle-aged men, since I can't help feeling I'll be joining their ranks sooner rather than later.

"Guess what," says Wesley after a while,

"What?" I answer unhelpfully.

"Adam's come into a bit of money,"

"Oh."

"Well, more than a bit, really. It's like an inheritance, It means he'll never have to make another commercial."

"TV viewers will be forever grateful, So what's he going to do?"

"He's going to Europe., To make a film."

"A film? When did you ever call them 'films'? Isn't " movie' good enough for you any more?"

Wesley's eyes are getting brighter and his cheeks bloom with the rosiness of enthusiasm.

"Adam explained all that to me. Movies are, well, like for entertainment, and films are more serious, more artistic. Kinda."

I have never heard Wesley talk this way before. Next thing I know he'll be reading Cahiers du Cinema and whittering on about 'auteurs.' But what he says next really floors me.

"He wants me to go with him."

"To Europe?"

"Yeah, isn't that great? I've never been out of Ontario before."

I am speechless. I feel as if all the air has been sucked out of my lungs, and to my horror there is a prickling feeling around my eyes, a signal that my tear ducts are going into action.

Finally I manage to gasp out: "What about me?"

"Oh, for gosh sake! You'll be okay."

"And that's the gratitude I get. I take you in off the streets, feed you, clothe you, love you...and it's goodbye without so much as a ' thank you, Mr. Shit'!"

I never expected to hear myself saying these time-honored lines, but I guess we all become more of a cliché as we get older.

Wesley winces. "You didn't love me, hon. I was like a little housedog... something to jump up and lick your face when you got home, something to pat and cuddle up to... There's lots of boys out there on the street who'd do the same thing for you."

"No, there aren't," I moan, as the tears begin to slide down the side of my nose. "You're special... You're like a son to me."

"But I wasn't looking for a daddy," he says patiently. "Do you really think I wanted to be sonny-boy?"

"Well, why didn't you say something? Why didn't you do something?"

"Because you didn't really want anything else. I was your charity kid...your bit of social work. You'd rather keep me on a pedestal, and then sneak into the bathroom and jerk off while you imagined fucking me rather than actually just doing it."

It's the first time I'd heard him say the 'f' word, and it sends me over the edge.

"This is bloody Lukes' doing. He's taught you to have a filthy mouth and a filthy mind. I'll kill the rotten bastard!"

The tears are flowing quite prodigally now, and interfering with my speech. I snuffle and snort and choke to the point that everybody else in the restaurant is staring at our table. Wesley reaches out and puts a consoling hand on my arm.

"Don't, hon. It's not worth it. Didn't I warn you that preacher's brats are the worst?"

But I'm too angry to be consoled and I shake off his hand. "Leave me alone. Go and get fucked by Adam Lukes. I'm through. Go on, get out, you little hustler."

He stares into my tear-blurred eyes for a long moment and then he does go. Very pale suddenly and with an unsmiling face. I see him open the door and walk through it and continue on up the crowded sidewalk without looking back. I sit motionless, hearing with half an ear the voice of Dionne Warwick singing "Walk on By" on the jukebox. The rest of the people in the restaurant have turned their backs and are studiously not looking my way; their heads dip together as they whisper. The waiter comes by with the check, smirking as if saying to himself: "These faggots are always so fucking melodramatic."

For the next few days I live in a stupor in which no kind of action seems possible. I don't try to kill Adam Lukes. In fact I never see him again. Wesley packs up his few bits and pieces from my apartment and moves them downstairs to Adam's, completely unresponsive to all my pleadings that we forget what I said and begin again. Very soon after that they are both gone. They do make it to Europe apparently, and Lukes directs a film in Britain which is a modest success on the art-house circuit, enough of a success anyway to bring him more offers. I hear from various contacts in the gay community that he and Wesley are traveling the world: Venice, Rome, Athens, Istanbul, Tangier, Paris, Rio, the Cayman Islands, Bangkok, Manila, Shanghai. Some of the guys get postcards, but not me. Not one line of apology or concern.

Gradually the pain dies away, though I keep feeling the odd twinge when I see the striped pajamas, or when I come home at night, hoping to smell cooking, and smell only stale air and dust. I miss his crooked, ruined smile,

and his funny ears, and the smell of new-mown hay and civet. I miss his bedtime prayer.

But life goes on. The quotidian smothers the transcendental, minute by minute, ads for detergent on top of ads for pantyhose, followed by ads for hemorrhoid treatment and ads for non-stick pans. I still go out at weekends of course, still troll through the St. Charles and the Yonge Street discos, still exchange bitcheries with Kenny Parsons, and Wolf Hauptmann, and Lester Chan, and Fabrizzio Gozzi. The only difference in that crowd is that Bob Westerberg ("your mother") has died of a heart-attack.

A year goes by. I leave the agency I'm with and get a job at a better one, paying more money. I have a sort of half-assed affair with a guy I meet at one of Eddie Glen's dinner parties. But he's almost my age. Too old. The affair is over in three months, and I find myself thinking about God again. I begin to go back to church, trying a different one every Sunday, and in Toronto, even in the mid-sixties, there are plenty to choose from. I try Catholic, High Anglican, United Church, Quaker, even the Church of Christ Scientist. I try to talk to some of the clergymen, but they seem more interested in getting me to contribute to their church's restoration fund than in answering my questions about God. In fact, they seem outraged at the suggestion that God could actually be snubbing one. Their line is that he sees all and forgives all. But after several months of this, I still can't decide whether God is ignoring me or not.

Two years later, I see Wesley again. The gay grapevine has reported nothing in about six months, but now here he is on this summer evening, back on St. Joseph Street where I first met him. From the dark interior of my Ford Falcon parked across the street, I watch as he slouches along the pavement and leans up against a tree. The pattern of leaves cast by the lamplight creates a kind of camouflage that hides the details, but I can see he has changed; has broadened out; is no longer the skinned rabbit I held in my arms all that time ago. The Sunday-go-to-meeting clothes he wore then have been replaced by skin-tight white jeans and a day-glo lime-green T-shirt that celebrates a currently popular rock group. I drive off down the block, turn around and come back up the other side, parking right by the tree where he's leaning. He peers suspiciously into the car, then smiles in recognition. His teeth have been straightened and capped to a dazzling evenness and whiteness.

"Jeez, it's you!" he says. "Want me to get in?"

I nod and he opens the car door and slides into the passenger seat, letting his leg contact mine,

"Seems like old times," he smiles, squeezing my knee.

But it isn't at all like old times. Wesley hasn't just broadened. He has plumped up – and there's a powdery pinkness to his flesh as if it's been dusted with confectioner's sugar. His hair has grown much longer and is now in an

elaborate coif like swirled caramel. He looks like one of those baroque putty made of pink and gold icing, a sugary Viennese cherub. And the smell of new-mown hay is gone, replaced by the overpowering reek of the catamite's favorite cologne – Jade East.

Wesley looks at me intently, then says: "You've changed." "For the better I hope."

He thinks about this. "No," he says, "not for the better, or for the worse. You're just different. You've got more of a junior exec look – not so laid back. But I like it. I really dig getting it on with the businessman-type: unfastening his tie, unbuckling his belt, kneeling down and licking his oxfords, sniffing his socks."

There's no doubt about it: Wesley is getting aroused. He moves his hand up from my knee to my crotch. But I, sadly, am limp. I can't respond to what Wesley has become, but neither can I insult him by letting him know that his reinvented self turns me off, so I change the subject.

"How was your round-the-world trip with Adam?" I ask. "Groovy. We stayed at great hotels: the Danieli, the Georges Cinq, the Savoy, the Rio Palace,"

"It certainly looks as if you ate well too."

"Does it show that much? Yes, I guess we did... all the best restaurants. Oh, hon, it was a blast."

"And where's Adam now?"

Wesley turns his head away for a moment and then turns back to me with a face on which the icing sugar seems to have hardened. "Oh, you know – all good things come to an end. He met up with this actor who was doing a small part in one of his movies."

"Movies? I thought they were 'films.'"

Wesley snorts. "The first one, maybe, but believe me, hon, after that they were movies. Anyway, he paid me off in London. Got me a plane ticket back to Toronto... and here I am... back on the scene. Shall we go to your place?"

I shake my head. "It's not your fault, Wes," I sigh. "It's just that I'm really hung up on somebody right now." I don't tell him that it's God.

He brushes my forehead with his lips and gets out of the car. "It's O.K. Be cool," he says, and moves back to the tree.

As I begin to drive off, something occurs to me and I stop for a minute and roll down my window again.

"Wesley," I call to him. "Do you still say your bedtime prayer?"

He winks back at me. "Sure, hon," he says. "You know what? It really turns the johns on!"

POSING
John Patrick

Jack, who ran the only escort service in town, let me have the new boy, Ronnie, first, before any of his other customers. It was a routine to which I had grown accustomed. Jack needed photos of the boys to send to clients in other cities and had no patience with F-stops or lighting. Photography had been my hobby since I was a kid so I gladly agreed to provide the service. No money changed hands but if the boy was turning me on, a tip was always tendered.

Ronnie, Jack said, was just my type; he appeared much younger than his years, was blond and slim, good-looking in a not-too-pretty kind of way, and was generously endowed.

"You'll want to take a couple of hours with him," Jack told me. Then, after clearing his throat, he added with a chuckle, "to photograph him properly, that is."

How right he was. From the moment I saw Ronnie, standing at my front door, I was smitten. Dressed in skimpy red shorts and a tight white tank top to show off his golden tan, he was the very picture of my idealized beach boy.

"Is photography your business?" he asked, after making us vodka-tonics. We sat next to each other on the sofa in the living room listening to the new Diana Ross album, 'The Boss."

"No. Just a hobby."

"These won't show up anywhere – I mean in a magazine or anything?"

The boys were always worried about that. "Oh, no. These are strictly for Jack's customers. You'll get a lot of work from out-of-state through Jack."

He stared at his drink. "I'm just starting to do this," "It's not for everybody."

He moved closer to me, his soft blue eyes taking me in fully. "1 don't know why I'm doing it, just to see if I can... I guess, Besides, I just lost my job and I have car payments."

I had noticed his shiny white Toyota coupe parked in the driveway. "A car like that could keep you in the poor ouse,"

His thigh pressed against mine. I squeezed it.

"I love it though.'

Squeezing his thigh once again, I said, "What 1 love is taking pictures of guys like you. Shall we?"

He finished his drink and followed me to the pool. He remarked how nice my place was. "What do you do?" he asked. .

"I have many investments I have to keep track of. Keeps me busy," It was my standard line to cover the fact that I had retired at fifty and really did nothing except live off the trust fund my father had set up. It was hard to spend it all but every year I somehow managed.

"Oh," Ronnie said, dipping a toe in the water. "Where do you want me?"

"Uh ..." I paused, wanting to answer truthfully – in the bedroom – but I said, "Right where you are."

Click! Click! Click! I always started out with Polaroid's, to give the boys an idea of what I was after. As they developed before our eyes, I knew Ronnie, if he chose to, would make a terrific model. He was one of those unique kids who miraculously looks better on film than in person. Pleased so far, he stripped off his tank top and stood by the edge of the pool. The sun was slowly sinking into the western sky so there was a reddish glow behind him as he bent over, skimming the water with his hand, then splashing it, all the while smiling for the camera.

Even though it was nearly six, it was still very warm and the sweat was glistening on his back. I suggested he cool off by taking a dip. He gladly slipped off his shorts and jockstrap and dove in. When he emerged from the water, his cock was already semi-hard. I snapped away and he playfully jiggled it from side to side, then stroked it. I could stand it no longer. I set my camera on a table and dropped to my knees before him.

When Jack said Ronnie was "generously endowed," he was, for once, understating the facts. Ronnie's cock was more than generous, it was downright extravagant. It was cut, beautifully shaped, and was very wide at the base. Sucking it was such a pleasure, I didn't want to stop and Ronnie didn't want me to, either. But duty called. I told him he'd get more business if the customers knew about his endowment. I snapped several more photos of him proudly displaying his dick-of-death at full strength, then went back down on it. I worked on him with my mouth, bit and kissed the insides of his lightly-furred thighs, sucked his balls, then returned to his cock. I kept my hand around the base as I sucked, and my fingers played in his pubic hair.

He groaned as I licked the head while my fingers traced the line of blond hair up to his navel and beyond to his nipples. I twisted his nipples as I continued to work on the head of his cock. He was close and begged for me to stop, to take him to bed.

In the bedroom, I took his lovely cock in my mouth again and sucked slowly while I fucked his ass with my greased fingers, slowly, carefully, so I wouldn't hurt him. His hands clenched, unclenched. His mouth was open. My tongue traced the tender ridge of his cockhead as a third finger slid in without a struggle. He loved it.

I stopped sucking him and, with my fingers still inside him, I bit his nipples softly. He yelped.

I got between his thighs and parted them, making him incredibly vulnerable. I rubbed the head of my erection between the lips of his now wet, open asshole, teasing myself as much as I enjoyed teasing him. "Do you really want this?"

"Oh, yes," he moaned, thrusting his hips up, attempting to grab my ass and push me into him. I moved just out of range and pinned his wrists over his head. He was stunned.

"Hey!"

"Don't move," I ordered as my cock slid into him.

Soon he was babbling incoherently. I pulled out a bit, with just the head in, enough to torture him. His muscles were tense, clenched, waiting, ready to come.

"Fuck me," he begged. "Stick it in all the way. All the way."

I obliged and he squirmed.

"God," he sighed, "you feel good. Fuck my ass."

I kissed him, stuck my tongue catlike into his mouth. "Okay, "
I said.

We moved in slow motion, drawing it out. I didn't want to come; it was too good. Fucking Ronnie, his arms around me, his hands on my ass, his hot breath in my ear, I lost all concept of time; we seemed to drift in a state of ecstasy. Eventually, my stomach tight to his cock, he came. But I was in no hurry; I stayed in him, but lifting myself up so that I could watch as my cock impaled him. Finally, I came. "Oh, yeah," he said, pleased with himself, taking my ass in his hands again, pushing. His eagerness to keep me inside him kept me hard for a few more thrusts.

Slowly we disengaged and I lay next to him catching my breath.

He pulled away and went to the bathroom. When he returned, he got on his knees, elbows and chin deep in the pillows and I got behind him. With one hand on his back, I eased my cock to his hungry hole. He rocked back, swallowing all of me. I held his hips and fucked him, first slowly, then hard, my belly slapping his ass. His rough breathing soon turned into a continuous groan and, supporting his weight on one elbow smashed into the pillow, he reached down to jack himself off.

"Yeah, come again. Come again, Ron."

Soon he was yelling, slamming back onto me as hard as he could, his muscles tightening as he was soaring. I pushed his ass up to better take my cock. After awhile, I came as well, my fingers digging into either side of his ass, before I collapsed, still inside him, across his back.

It was several moments before we could move. Finally, I rolled off of him and lay beside him.

"You'll do well," I said, but his only response was to kiss me.

I called Jack right after Ronnie left the house, saying the boy was eager and malleable, and after the customers found out he had a beautiful cock

and loved to get fucked besides, jack would be getting a lot of calls for him. I contrived to make Ronnie part of my routine. Jack was willing; we agreed on Monday night, the slowest night of the week for the service

By the time Monday rolled around, Ronnie had been out on four "dates," as Jack preferred to call them. The customers seemed to be happy but Ronnie was not; "the business" was playing havoc with his social calendar. He had decided to seek another nine-to-five job so that he could continue to party with his friends and, I presumed, lovers. I asked about Monday night. Jack said Ronnie refused to take any more tricks but he told him, "This one has been booked for a week. You've got to go."

"No." Ronnie was adamant.

And then Jack told him who the trick was.

According to Jack, Ronnie said, "Why didn't you say so?" which made me smile.

Ronnie was twenty minutes late. He gave no excuses and I didn't expect any. It was just good to see him, this time dressed in a plain white T-shirt and blue jeans. He welcomed a drink and we sat at a table near the pool talking. He seemed to be in no hurry and for that I was glad; nothing worse than entertaining a prostitute on a tight schedule. I acted as if I knew nothing of his plans to "retire" from the business so quickly. He asked for copies of the photos, and then, as he perused them, said, "Jack won't be sending these out."

"No?"

"No. I just can't do it."

He went on to tell me he didn't know what he had been thinking; the hours were so irregular and he was afraid of being summoned to someone's home whom he would later see at the bar when he was there with his friends.

"I've never seen you at the Club," he said, finishing his drink.

"No, bars really aren't my thing."

What was my thing was obvious: just watching him had given me an erection, I stroked the bulge at my crotch and he smiled.

"God," he said, lifting himself from the chair, "you're a horny one."

It's not that I was horny, it was that I was horny for Ronnie, to feel again the warmth of his ass surrounding my prick. But that would have to wait, because tonight Ronnie wanted to suck.

He stood over me unzipping my shorts and pulling out my erection, then he bent over at the waist and began sucking it. After a minute or two, he got on his knees between my thighs and went to work on my balls while his hand jerked my cock. I lifted up so that he could remove my shorts completely and then he went back to sucking. It was as if he couldn't get enough of my cock. This was not in my game plan. I had jerked off all week to visions of sucking Ronnie and fucking him. That he would be such a willing, accomplished cocksucker was a surprise, a not entirely unpleasant one either.

Neither did I anticipate that he would begin kissing me the moment I stood up, and that his passion would continue as he led me into the bedroom. He shed his clothes, got in bed and raised his legs so I could prepare his ass and kiss him at the same time. After I greased him up, I entered him slowly, allowing him to adjust. As before, his hand went to his own erection and he began moaning between kisses. As I came in him he gasped and shot onto his stomach. My cock still in him, I took him in my arms and kissed him hard.

Breathing heavily, we lay still for a moment before pulling apart. After he wiped himself with a towel, he cleaned my cock as well, then proceeded to again suck it to hardness.

The second entry was easier than the first and I couldn't imagine wanting anyone else again.

And I didn't have anyone else again for a long time. Ronnie never again worked for Jack, but he did come around every Monday night for months. I never asked him about his other lovers but occasionally he would tell me about them. It was the last boyfriend who caused the problem, following Ronnie to my house and then confronting him about his so-called "part-time job."

It was this "part-time job" that covered his car payment each month and he didn't want to give it up, but his young lover insisted. Eventually the two of them moved away and I never saw Ronnie again. Still, I have the photos and the memories of the sweet youth who had posed for me at twilight.

ALL YOU CAN GET
David Patrick Beavers

Vincent draped a lazy forearm over his eyes, shielding them from the morning sun. The tall, sharp-edged blades of the bear grass scissored all around him in response to the mild breeze. Their fragrance was dull but sweet. Pollen tickled his nostrils. He stifled a sneeze.

With a groan, his arm fell from his face. He squinted as he pushed himself up off the sleeping bag and stretched. Knots in his muscles popped like kernels dropped in sizzling lard.

He kneeled down and dug through his gear, finally fishing out the hand mirror he'd pilfered from... Someone; he couldn't remember. It was a rather large, square mirror, he kind hair stylists use to show their clients their skills of transforming the most normal head of hair into the most ridiculous-looking, trendy coif. He stared into the minor.

His shoulder-length brown hair was bleaching dirty wheat from his time in the sun. His skin was now ripening to a deep olive brown. Only his eyes looked familiar to him. Fawn eyes, his sister used to say; large, wide-set and heavy-lidded, with dense, long black lashes that women coveted. The brilliant brown irises flecked with a ruddy-hued gold that now seemed to set off the bleachy-blond streaks in his hair.

He ran an open palm across his cheek, under his chin, feeling the sharp whiskers that needed to be cut. He ran a brush through his hair haphazardly, ripping through oily tangles, then clumped it together at the nape of his neck and tied off the ponytail with a rawhide strip.

He stowed away the mirror and brush, then shook out the sleeping bag and rolled it up neatly, binding it with two old lengths of canvas belts. He hooked the end of a bungee cord to the one of the belts, threaded it through the loops of the shoulder straps of his pack, then hooked the end of the cord to the other belt tie wrap, effectively securing his bed to his gear. Simple enough: Make-shift. Vincent always knew how to rig something he needed, He hoisted the pack onto his back, then studied the scratched crystal of his watch. He figured he could hike to the beach by noon at the latest. Pierce would be at work by then. He could grab a shower, a bite to eat, a nap, then go raid his post office box. If he hiked by way of the old frontage road abutting the highway, he might snag a ride.

Car after car passed him as he walked, the whoosh-whiz of their formidable speed caressing his ear, causing it to plug up. He tried shifting his jaw back and forth to pop it. Nothing. He shucked his pack, then crouched down to dig through one of its side pockets for a pack of gum.

He no sooner stuffed two sticks of sugarless bubble-gum into his mouth when an archaic, pale green Valiant squealed to a halt just yards ahead

of him. Vincent stood casually, hiking the pack back on. The driver stepped out of the car, leaning on the opened door. The shaggy brunet with the bronzed complexion grinned at him.

"Dude!" he howled.

Vincent let out a lusty laugh. "Shit! You shouldn't be let behind the wheel!"

"You wanna fuckin' cruise, or not?"

"In that?"

"Shit, man, Manny's Mobile Monster's gonna see me all the way to the thirty," he said with pride. "Maybe even thirty-one."

Vincent trudged up to the passenger door, smiling. "You'll be lucky to see twenty one."

"In!" Manny barked as he dropped back into the driver's seat and slammed the door.

"Man, you're motor vehicular challenged, you know?" Vincent said as he opened the door, chucked his gear into the back, then climbed in.

"Got a license. Got no tickets," Manny said as he ground the gears and let the clutch and gas fly.

They bucked into second, then into third, then sailed along the pavement. Vincent's hand held tightly to the taped-up vinyl arm rest. Manny fumbled through the many partially empty packs of cigarettes littered about. He had almost every brand Vincent had ever heard of.. He finally pulled a smoke free from a pack, then dipped into the pocket of the unbuttoned flannel shirt for his lighter.

"Wanna butt, man?" he asked Vincent as he expelled a cloud of lung exhaust.

"Quit," Vincent said.

"No fuckin' way," Manny said.

"They got too expensive to buy while I was out on the road."

"Yeah!" Manny said as his brain kicked from first to fifth gear. "What the fuck was that all about? You bailed in, what, January?"

Vincent shrugged. "Yeah. Now I'm back."

"Fuck, you missed a great fuckin' dig at graduation." Manny suddenly cocked a curious brow at Vincent. "You got out, right?"

"Finished the required units and course work at the end of the fall semester," Vincent said. "They mailed my diploma to my grandma's house."

"No more fuckin' school," Manny said with a smile. "You gonna go to the J.C.T'

Manny's burst of laughter was so hard, it set him coughing. Vincent grabbed the dashboard as the old Valiant weaved along in the traffic lane. The green monster finally steered a straight course once Manny quelled his cough-laugh jag.

"Yer too fuckin' much, dude," Manny grinned. "Got a job makin' boards for Oberland."

Vincent remembered Oberland. Terry Oberland custom-made surfboards for the locals, for some of the semi-pro surfers and for tourists who hadn't a clue how to ride one. The guy found the beach back in "65 and never ever left. Any local who knew how to surf had learned from Terry – except: Vincent. He'd learned to surf on his own, as he'd learned to do most other things. Surfing was fun, but he never became passionate about it.

"You gonna do that for the rest of your life?" he asked Manny.

Manny shrugged. "Why not?"

Vincent shrugged. "Why not?" he said in agreement. "Where the fuck did you go?" Manny asked,

"North," Vincent said.

"Lotsa North," Manny said as he flicked the now-dead butt of his cigarette out the window. "All the way to Alaska." "Just bummed around," Vincent said,

Manny let the issue drop. "Where you wanna be dumped?" "Pierce's, if you're going that way," Vincent said.

"Why not? What's that street he's on?"

"Portola Avenue," Vincent said. "Down at the esplanade."

"Yeah!" Manny said abruptly. "I remember. The Igloo."

Vincent smiled to himself. Yeah, he thought. Pierce's place was an igloo. A sort of geo-dome home built in the sixties by some avant garde architect. It was one of three in the entire county.

Vincent leaned back in the seat. His grip on the arm rest relaxed as he listened to Manny prattle on and on, relaying all sorts of uninteresting gossip about their former classmates from Holy Cross High School.

The green machine's tires grazed the concrete curb. Manny scrawled his telephone number on an empty cigarette pack and handed it to Vincent as he climbed from the car.. Manny wanted to go party some time. Vincent politely accepted both the number and Manny's invitation, then he sent him on his way.

As soon as Manny was out of sight, Vincent's smile dropped. He spat the wad of gum from his mouth into the gutter. He studied the cigarette pack, then tore it open, revealing a bent butt. He crumpled the pack and let it join the discarded gum, then stuck the smoke between his lips and fumbled through the junk in his pockets for matches. The lung steam was harsh. The tobacco was old. He took another drag, then dropped it onto the sidewalk and crushed it out beneath the heel of his shoe.

He slung the pack over a shoulder then walked up the boxwood-lined, flagstone walkway to the porch. The Igloo was rather large. Hundreds, maybe

thousands, of pentagon-shaped panels of some white synthetic material were pieced together to form the shell. He'd never liked this house.

He knelt down at the edge of the porch and pried up a loose hunk of flagstone. Pierce's spare key was hidden beneath. He haphazardly replaced the stone, then unlocked the door and went inside.

Pierce checked the shop's front door one more time. It was securely locked. He walked down the aisle, noting the items that needed to be restocked in the morning. He never realized just how much work owning a business could be. But The Sport Shop was his.. All his. It was the only real sporting goods store in two counties and he carried everything save for surfboards and wetsuits; Oberland had that market cornered,

He killed the lights, set the alarm, then slipped out the back door, locking it carefully. As he climbed into his car, he felt the rush of exhaustion that often accompanies twelve hour work days. Still, feeling tired felt good to him.. His focus was work. Security. Success. Success earned him the new car he was driving, paid the mortgage on the Igloo, allowed him the luxury of having free time in the evenings to work on himself. He could now afford his personal trainer who helped him pull his thirty-eight year old body together. He wasn't going to hit forty without looking at least five years younger. His focus was on himself now and not some firm young man, as had often been the case with him. Pretty boys. Local boys. Always cruising down at the esplanade. He always drove down the strip flanking the esplanade on his way home. This was more out of habit than anything else these days.

The beach area was deserted, though, save for a few gulls foraging for food in the sand. Mid-week doldrums. He accelerated, pressing on, past the bungalows, the small shops, the restaurant, on up the slight incline of his street, then turned a hard right into his driveway.

Key in hand, he fumbled with the knob and stepped into the living room. He froze in his tracks. Something indefinable kept him locked in intangible immobility. Something... He listened carefully, hoping for, yet fearing some hint of sound to validate his suspicions. He heard nothing. He slowly closed the door and made his way through the house, cautiously peering into each room, around each blind spot, waiting for someone to leap on him.

But there was no boogey man. Just the pack leaning against the dresser in the bedroom. Vincent's pack. Months had come and gone with no word from the young man. He'd slipped out unnoticed one day, and that was that. Pierce had been both extremely upset and extremely relieved to know the youth was gone. Now, with the noticeable presence of Vincent in direct sight, Pierce felt an odd sensation of panic well up within him. The slight slam of the front door sent him into an immediate tailspin as his feet and legs involuntarily scissored a hasty path to the living room.

Vincent leaned against the front door, sorting through a fistful of mail. "Hey," he said with a slight smile.

"'Hey'?" Pierce parroted. "That's it?"

"Just had to go, man," Vincent said as walked past Pierce and fell onto the couch. "Same as you did when you were my age."

Pierce could only stare at Vincent. At the now long hair that had turned blondish. At the tanned face. His seductive eyes. Full lips, slightly chapped. Rounded nose of perfect proportion. Pierce's crotch stirred immediately. From flaccid to raging erect in a nanosecond. Pierce threw himself down in the nearby chair, trying to conceal his arousal.

"Yeah, well, maybe you should've kept going," Pierce said.

Vincent's eyes locked on Pierce's crotch. He smiled smugly, then went back to his mail, opening envelopes. "Maybe," he said. "But, I didn't."

Pierce studied Vincent as the young man scanned letters, looked at photos enclosed in the letters, smiling at some and sneering at others. The latter were crumpled up and pitched aside.

I thought you'd given up the box at the post office." Vincent shrugged. "I'd paid for a year's rent."

"So, you lied about that, too."

Vincent set the letters aside and leaned forward. "No. I said I'd given up placing any more ads." He kicked off his shoes and pulled off his socks, letting them fall where they may. "Can't help it if guys still wanna respond to the old ads," he said as he stood and stretched, then shucked his shirt.

Pierce squirmed slightly. Vincent's torso was leaner. The slight bit of youthful softness had melted away like butter on toast. Toasty. His long trunk was a honey-hued brown, basted by days in the sun. The dusting of downy soft hair that blanketed his pecs, square and wide, was almost as golden as the long locks that framed his face and accentuated his eyes. Vincent's eyes bore through Pierce, seeming see into the deepest recessions of his imagination. The flat of his right palm pressed hard into the meat of the his pec, plowing through the hard tissue and muscle and hair, coming to rest on the left. Long, rough fingers caught his nipple in a slight: scissor-pinch.

His left hand slid down the flat of his stomach, down past the deep depression of his navel, down just into his jeans, His wrist arced, the pressure of its rise pressing against the top button, loosening it easily.

Pierce was paralyzed. His cock strained to rise up, but got caught up trapped beneath the snugness of combed cotton briefs, twitching involuntarily. He wanted to tell Vincent to leave, to get the fuck out of his house and out of his life. Again. He was too old for this shit, he thought. There was twenty years between them, next to nothing in common. Speak up, he thought.

Vincent ran his hands up his torso again, then dug the heels of his palms into his flesh and skidded down to the waist band. With a jerk of his hands, the button fly separated. His hands snaked beneath the cover of faded

denim. Slowly, deliberately, the dirty jeans rode down his thighs, then calves. He stepped out of them, then snapped the cheek straps of his jock. Lean, firm legs stepped over the coffee table, stepped toward Pierce,

Pierce felt a wave of static charge ripple up his spine. His jaw trembled slightly as Vincent straddled his legs, then let his hands come to rest on the back of the chair, boxing Pierce in.

Pierce stared at Vincent's crotch. The mesh weave of the pouch of the jockstrap strained with full, fleshy, soft proportions of youthful cock and balls. He wanted to slam his face into Vincent's crotch, to chew with shark like force through the cloth to the beautiful snake beneath.

"You look good, Pierce," Vincent said coyly.

Pierce tried not to look up, but he couldn't help himself. A halo of blond fringe hung down from the ceiling of Vincent's face. Shadowy whiskers magnified the strong square jaw. The boy had left. A man loomed over him now.

"Why did you leave?" Pierce heard himself say.

Vincent smiled, beguiling with innocent charm.. Pierce had found a naif, he'd thought, last Thanksgiving season, at the university library, reading books by Burroughs and Fitzgerald. Vincent had said he was a freshman, majoring in English. He added that it was a worthy degree which could give him entry into the world of advertising. Pierce had been there to review the books of architectural design. He'd wanted to add some sort of flair to the aesthetic of the store he'd purchased. They found they shared a common interest in some lesser known sports, such as fencing, lacrosse, even skeet shooting.

By Christmas, they were driving north to Santa Clara two evenings a week to challenge each other in classes for rapier and sword. By early January, Vincent was ensconced in the Igloo with Pierce. Though he never invaded Vincent's private world beyond their relationship, he inadvertently stumbled upon Vincent's driver's license loose in a pocket of some jeans being readied for the wash. His young man was, he learned, just six days shy of turning eighteen on February 3. When he confronted Vincent in a panic, Vincent grew steely and cold. That was January 29th. The next day, Vincent was gone.

Pierce had sweated out for weeks, even months, waiting for the that knock at his door from law enforcement officials, baiting him with questions, wanting to haul him in as a criminal. He'd done nothing really wrong, for he'd been lied to by the youth. But the morality police never came.

By spring, he'd relaxed a bit. His focus went toward his store, toward men his own age. Still, rarely a night had passed without his mind wandering to thoughts of Vincent. Months passed. The lingering heat was staving off fall now.

Now, here was Vincent, transformed, his arcing form the curve of the wall before his eyes. Hesitant, anxious fingers reached out, brushing lightly

over the concave tautness of Vincent's abdomen, down to the feathery wisps of brown hair that trailed from his navel down beneath the waistband of the jockstrap.

Vincent giggled slightly and pulled away abruptly, stepping over the coffee table again. His squared buttocks were full, with a fire trail of silky brown threads separating them. Pierce could almost feel his face nuzzling that slightly hairy crack, as he'd done so many times before,

He flopped down on the couch, a hand slapping down on his crotch. Fingers kneaded the stiffening rod beneath the cloth of the pouch. He looked over at Pierce, smiling dubiously. Slowly, flattened palms pressed into the elastic waistband, rolling it down, exposing hair, then flesh. He pulled his swelling prick out, his fingers pinching the fleshy foreskin closed, concealing the plump head of his dick. His other hand scooped up his loose, large ball sac, pulled it out, let it catch on the taut elastic to shove his nuts up high and round. He pulled on them, and twisted them slightly. He let his foreskin go free and the shaft shot up stiff onto his stomach. His fingers found his mouth, His long, spit-soaked tongue licked his palm. The drool-coated hand wrapped tightly around the thick shaft and he began to slowly pump his meat.

Pierce felt his mouth filling with wetness. Like a hound near the dinner table, he was hungry. He swallowed hard as he rose abruptly from the chair and hurried from the room.

Vincent smiled to himself as he heard the bedroom door slam shut. He tucked himself somewhat haphazardly back into his jockstrap, then sat up and fingered through the letters and photos he was interested in. He picked up one, then leaned back into the couch and reached for the phone on the end table. He scanned the telephone number in the letter, then dialed.

As he stripped, Pierce stood before the dresser mirror. There were a few lines in his boyish face. A little gray wove through short, chestnut hair. Though his regular visits to the gym had increased his strength and thickened his chest, shoulders and arms, he could never quite get rid of the slight softness around his stomach. He still looked quite a bit like a power lifter, and all this beefiness made him think he looked shorter than five eleven. When he was leaner, he thought, he looked taller. He lay back on his bed. His fist gripped his hard prick and he began to pump it hard. His eyes closed. In response, images of Vincent then, of Vincent now, flashed through his mind. His fist pumped faster, harder, and his body tensed sharply. Cum rained down on his stomach and chest. He held fast to his dick until it fell flaccid, then, letting out an annoyed huff, he sprang off the bed and hurried into the bathroom to clean himself. When he returned to his room, he dressed quickly, all the while silently cursing himself for not having changed the locks; for not having removed the hidden spare key. He wouldn't let Vincent lead him about again like an eager stray pup.

He fastened the belt on his jeans, stepped barefoot into the old topsiders, then walked out of the room, down the hall toward the living room. He heard Vincent's voice, low, sensual. Pierce paused, listening.

"Yeah, man..." Vincent almost groaned. "Sniff all around my fuckin' jock. Yeah... Lick it... Yeah, man. I wanna feel you fuckin' soak it good with wet spit. Fuckin' faggot, yeah, chew on it. Tryn chew through with your teeth... Lookin' for my fuckin' meat, man. Feel it gettin' hard? Yeah..."

Pierce stepped into the living room. Vincent was sprawled on the couch, with the phone cradled under his chin. He held a photo high before him, scrutinizing it as if he were far sighted. "What the fuck're you doing?" Pierce said flatly.

Vincent grinned at him as he continued on with his telephone partner. "Fuckin' shit, man. Yeah... Got a fuckin' hot mouth... Yeah, go on... Scoot that nose of yours down. Let it zipper through my crack. Tight fuckin' hole..." He covered the mouth piece of the receiver. "This dude's a live one," he said to Pierce. He went back to his caller. "Yeah, dude, fuckin' lick that tight boy cunt hole. Sniff it good..." He covered the receiver again. "Guy's fuckin' retarded," he said to Pierce.

Pierce stepped around and pushed down the button in the receiver cradle. "Enough is enough."

Vincent sat up and handed Pierce both the receiver and the photo. "Get a load of the pic."

Pierce hung up the phone and studied the photo. "So? He looks hot."

"Hot?!" Vincent laughed loudly. "He fuckin' took a Polaroid of a greeting card!"

Pierce turned on a lamp and studied the photograph. Indeed, upon close examination, he could see that it was just that, a photograph of a card. A sexy card, but a card nonetheless. He flipped the pic back to Vincent.

"So, he's got good taste," Pierce said.

"But does he taste good?" Vincent reclined on the sofa again. His hand reached out. His fingers hooked the waist band of Pierce's jeans.

Pierce's cock responded, swelling quickly, automatically. He took hold of Vincent's hand. Lightning to the rod, he felt that churn in his gut, that tingling, almost nauseous ache of wanting. Vincent's fingers let loose of the cloth and wrapped around Pierce's hand. Vincent's gentle clasp grew firmer, then harder, until he was almost crushing Pierce's hand. He suddenly sat up. His other hand slammed against Pierce's chest. Fingers dug beneath the placket of the shirt. Buttons shot off ripping fabric as he yanked Pierce down onto him.

Pierce stumbled headlong into the boy's wet, biting, licking mouth. His fingers wove roughly through Vincent's hair as their teeth chewed each other's tongues. Pierce pulled his head up abruptly, panting. Vincent's fingers hooked the shredding shirt again, his nails digging into the smooth flesh of

John Patrick

Pierce's chest, and violently ripped the cloth away. Human claws raked skin, leaving a wake of swelling furrows. His face slammed into Pierce's pec, his teeth clamping down on the sweetmeat nipple.

Pierce straddled Vincent. His arms wrapped around the youth's torso and pulled him upright. He gripped fingerfuls of blondish hair and pressed Vincent's face, his eager mouth, firmly into his chest. Vincent's teeth chomped down painfully on Pierce's tit. Pierce dug his nails into the youth's scalp and yanked his head back, off of him.

Shimmering brown eyes narrowed with hateful coldness as the jaw clenched tightly, pulling lips into a malicious sneer. Pierce felt a sudden panic, felt a surge of excitement rip through him. His grip on Vincent's hair tightened, keeping his head almost immobile. A low, almost inaudible growl slipped through Vincent's lips.

Vincent's arms slipped up between Pierce's, between the arm's length span of space between them, then quickly snaked around Pierce's neck, up, until his fingers viciously gripped a fistful of hair atop Pierce's head. He pulled Pierce's hair firmly, strongly, until Pierce felt strands ripping from their follicles. Pierce suddenly released his hold on Vincent. Vincent let loose his hold, then the butts of his palms slammed into Pierce's shoulders, sending him flying onto his back.

Before Pierce could react, Vincent's weight dropped on him, pinning him down. He caught Pierce's wrists and pushed them back up and behind his head. Vincent grinned. He sniffed Pierce's neck, then slipped down a bit, inhaling slowly the scent beneath his arm. Pierce's torso arched reflexively, Vincent's tongue washed through the hairy pit, then he dragged razor sharp whiskers down Pierce's triceps, through the hair, down his side.

Pierce groaned his pleasure. Vincent grinned knowingly as he drew back a bit to better study Pierce's face. He brought his pelvis up, then pressed his swollen crotch into Pierce's abdomen. His hips automatically rotated, grinding the straining pouch into the man's flesh.

Pierce could feel Vincent's heavy meat through the cotton mesh. The heat of it felt like it was searing his skin, branding him. His hips bucked sharply, trying to pitch Vincent further up on him_ His flesh was sweetly heady, earthy like tanned hide and redwood. His cock was straining hard beneath denim. The slightest motion made his erect organ tingle.

Vincent shimmied up Pierce's trunk, draping himself over the edge of the couch, letting his bulging pouch come to rest on the man's face. He involuntarily moaned as Pierce's mouth began to chew his cloth covered glans. Pierce tried to pull his arms free. Vincent quickly tightened his grip, keeping wrists locked together. His hips arched up, then he slammed his crotch into Pierce's face. Pierce sunk his teeth into the top of pouch and tugged. Vincent flinched as he felt the pinch of his pubic hair being jerked out. His movement allowed Pierce the chance to force himself to roll over, and roll he did, sending

- 207 -

the both of them crashing down between the couch and coffee table onto the floor. Limbs hit hard wood as skin scraped textured fabric. Bruises and slight abrasions were ignored as Pierce pinned Vincent down.

Vincent smiled at him. "You want it? Take it," he said as he let his body go limp.

Pierce shifted quickly. His face came down gently on Vincent's crotch, inhaling its addictive scent. His fingers gripped the waistband. He slowly pulled the jockstrap down, relishing the prize revealed. Vincent's stiff rod sprang up, slapping Pierce's face. Pierce peeled the jock down his legs, then offs He pressed the dirty jockstrap into his face and inhaled deeply.. He then set it aside and loosened his belt and the fly of his jeans. Vincent lazily drew a leg up, letting the sole of his foot press against Pierce's chest.

Pierce stood up slowly, letting Vincent's foot ski down his body as he pushed his jeans and shorts down and stepped out of them, losing his shoes in the process. Vincent planted both his feet on Pierce's crotch, pressing his hard cock against his belly. Pierce's hands took hold of the young man's feet, holding them fast.

"Why'd you come back?" he asked.

Vincent drew his hands up under his head. "Why not?"

"Where'd you go?"

"North."

"Was he worth the trip?"

Vincent let a laugh escape. "Different."

"How so?"

"What can I say? He was just one of the ads, man." "Young?"

"Not young. Not old." He shrugged. "Others Others were older, though."

Vincent slipped his feet out from beneath Pierce's hands. His legs outstretched wide. Pierce grabbed each foot, keeping Vincent's legs spread open. Long, lean limbs covered with silky fuzz led his hands down, brought him down to his knees, then down even more. His arms looped like ivy around Vincent's thighs as his fingers gripped the base of the youth's thick, rigid cock. Pierce slowly, gently, pulled the drape of foreskin back, exposing the slick, pink, swollen head of man-boy dick. His tongue traced a trail just beneath the edge of the head. Vincent shuddered. Pierce smiled to himself. The tip of his tongue flicked rapidly over the tip of the cock head. The shaft twitched slightly in response.

Vincent's hands made their way down his body, his finger-tips blindly tracing a path up Pierce's cheeks to the crown of his head. He gently pressed down, coaxing, encouraging Pierce to taste his member completely.

Pierce buried his face between cock and balls, savoring the sweaty smell, then his tongue ran up the underside of erect flesh to the prized crown. Wet lips split apart as he took the glans into his mouth, sucking it, swabbing it

all around. Down further he went on the shaft, his tongue and lips working in tandem to draw foreskin up to feel the fold of flesh loll in his mouth. He felt the pressure of Vincent's hands, pushing him down. All the way down. He swallowed it whole, gagging slightly as he relaxed his throat, as pubic hair spiked his nostrils. He heard Vincent's pleasurable moan. He slid up and down on the youth's meat vigorously, wanting his reward.

Vincent's feet slammed into Pierce's shoulders abruptly, knocking him back. His head hit the coffee table hard, stunning him, In a blurry moment, he saw Vincent bound to his feet, scoop up his jockstrap and gear, then disappear down the hall.

Pierce pushed himself up and went after him. "You little prick!" he yelled. Vincent's laughter unhinged him. The bedroom door slammed in Pierce's face just as he lunged for it. He heard the lock click. "You fuckin' little shit!"

"Got me too excited, man," Vincent said. "I'm not ready to shoot yet, ya know?"

"Then go fuckin' crash with one of your ads!"

"You got any fresh blades?!" Vincent asked loudly.

"What?!" Pierce pounded on the door. "Open this fucking door, Vincent!"

"Chill, man!" Vincent's voice had a hint of laughter. "I just wanna shave this shit off my face."

"You want to shower?" Pierce asked. He didn't want him to. "You gonna de-stress?"

"What?"

"Relax, man." Vincent's voice was just beyond the barrier of the door. "Didn't mean to crack your cranium like that." The lock clicked again. Vincent opened the door. "You just got my nuts boilin' over too fast. We used to take it slow, you know?"

He was back in his jockstrap, holding a can of shaving cream in one hand and the razor in the other. Pierce was instantly hard again. Vincent glanced at Pierce's stiff cock. With razor in hand, he gripped the man's rod, pressing the handle of the razor into the shaft as he squeezed it hard.

'Watch it," Pierce said.

Vincent let go of Pierce and held up the razor. "No blade." He was right. He'd removed the old cartridge. "You just want to shave..." Pierce said.

Vincent shrugged. "And maybe brush my teeth."

"Then what?"

"We could go night surfing."

Pierce let a loud, nervous laugh unhitch. "You crazy?!" "Why not?" Vincent said. "It's been done before."

"I got rid of my board about ten years ago," Pierce said. "Oberland always keeps some old boards out around his shop. "

"Junked boards."

"We can look'em over."

"As I recall, you'd said that you didn't like surfing."

Vincent shrugged again as he padded off toward the bathroom. "That was then. This is now."

Pierce trailed after him, pausing in the doorway of the bathroom, watching Vincent rifle through drawers and cabinets. "They're in the medicine chest," Pierce said.

Vincent opened the cabinet and found the razor blades. He slipped a cartridge on the handle, then ran a basin full of hot water and wetted his face with a washcloth. He lathered up, then carefully began shaving.

Pierce watched the youth methodically strip away whiskers. Vincent was slow, each stroke deliberate. As he adjusted his stance before the mirror, his full pouch nested on the lip of the counter. Pierce began to slowly stroke his hard prick, Vincent seemed to ignore him, but Pierce knew that the boy got off on being watched. Sure enough, the bulge beneath the jockstrap soon inflated.

Pierce pumped his cock steadily with a firm grip, teasing himself until his prick felt numb. He let his member go as Vincent rinsed first his face, then the basin. He snagged a hand towel and blotted himself dry, then turned to Pierce and stepped right up to him.

He hung the towel on Pierce's hard rod, then slid his hands across the man's chest, the tips of his fingers tracing the scratches he'd made earlier. Eyes looked up from a downcast head, locking on Pierce's eyes. Sad eyes, Vincent thought. Round, sad, translucent green eyes.

Pierce fixated on the young man's deep brown irises, trying to see beyond to read the thoughts he knew were tangled in his mind. Their hard edge softened as Vincent lifted his face, as his arms snaked up and around Pierce's neck. Soon their lips once again fused, silently admitting the veracity of their mutual attraction. They kissed hard until Vincent once again reeled back abruptly.

"Gotta take a leak," he said, "so?"

Vincent cocked a curious brow, stifled a smile, then went to the commode and raised the lid and the seat. He pushed down the jockstrap, letting it catch beneath his balls, then tugged his semi-erect penis. Nothing. He cast a glance at Pierce. "I'm sort of pee-shy," he said.

Pierce didn't leave. Instead he came up behind Vincent, wrapped his arms around the young man's waist, then took hold of Vincent's cock and balls with his hands as he nuzzled and tongued the youth's neck,

"Close your eyes," he whispered.

Vincent let his hands fall to his side, leaned his head back on Pierce's shoulder and closed his eyes. As Pierce manipulated his prick and balls, Vincent felt his bladder suddenly relax and release.

Pierce intently watched the pale yellow stream of urine jet out from the fleshy opening of the prepuce. He pulled Vincent's skin back a bit with one hand, exposing a portion of his cock head. The commode water churned and bubbled as piss blasted it. Pierce let his hand slip down, into the jetting arc of hot, yellow wetness, making it splash back on Vincent's cock, on his crotch and thighs. The steady stream dwindled. Stopped. Another couple short bursts came jetting out. Then the trickling drip. Drip. Drip. Pierce's hand felt slick to him. He grabbed hold of Vincent's cock and massaged the wetness into flesh.

Vincent sighed his relief. His pleasure. Pierce guided the young man around to face him as he sunk to his knees and pressed his face into Vincent's damp crotch, drying it off with his own face.

Vincent's fingers raked gently through Pierce's hair, holding him fast. Pierce's tongue probed into the sheath of loose, damp skin, tasting his first golden drop of human water, something he'd always recoiled from. His lips wrapped around the budding head, sucked it, then sucked the fleshy overhang back into his mouth. He felt Vincent grip his head tightly. Pierce suddenly felt the unexpected. A slight spurt of hot, salty piss shot down his throat. He didn't cough. Didn't gag. Didn't jerk away. He found himself sucking the last residual drop from within Vincent's dick.

It was Vincent who pulled away, gently cupping Pierce's cheeks as he stepped back. Pierce grabbed hold of Vincent's hips and pushed him back. His hand reached out and flipped the seat down. The dull, hollow thud of plastic on porcelain echoed. Pierce forced Vincent down onto the seat of the commode, then lifted the young man's long legs and draped them over his shoulders. Vincent repositioned himself a bit so that he was slung low on the seat. Pierce pulled the youth's ass cheeks apart, exposing his fuzzy hole. The instant his tongue hit the puckered mark, Vincent hiked his pelvis back, onto the seat, and sat up completely,

"Too fast, man," he said as he stroked Pierce's cheek. "I let you eat it, you're gonna wanna fuck it."

Pierce let his head rest on Vincent's thigh" "You're making me crazed. Making me do things, want to do things, I've never wanted to do."

Vincent slowly rose up. Pierce leaned back, sitting on his heels, "Gotta hit the beach, man," Vincent said as he tucked himself back into his jockstrap.

"Why?"

"Just gotta."

Pierce pushed himself up off the floor. "What the fuck did you come back for?"

"You wanted me to come back""

"Bullshit!"

Vincent walked away, into the bedroom, Pierce saw him squat down and dig through his pack. After a moment, he stood up again, holding up the

credit card he'd stolen from Pierce when he left months before, "You didn't cancel this," he said.

Pierce moved into the bedroom. Stared blankly at it. "You didn't spend much."

"Wait'll you get your next bill."

"So? I would've cancelled it, eventually," Pierce said" "When?"

"Okay," Pierce said, sitting on the bed. "I'll kill it tomorrow."

"No, you won't." Vincent dropped the card back into his pack. "I left here a greenhorn""

"Yeah," Pierce said. "I admit you've changed,"

"Yeah, I've gotten a real education"

"You said you wanted to go to the University,"

Vincent laughed. "Yeah, I told you I was a frosh at the University,"

"The fall semester starts in a few weeks,' Pierce said. "I know a few people who could get you in.'

"But, into what?" Vincent flopped back, making the bed jiggle. "I'm a student of the world. Besides, hop into school mode and I might latch onto some hot stud. Then what?" Pierce's hand came to rest on the youth's crotch. "Just stay," he said.

Vincent stared at Pierce, at the hand kneading his cock to rigid attention. He pulled his legs up and pulled off the jockstrap. He tossed it onto Pierce's erection. "Put it on, man."

Pierce complied. As he pulled the jockstrap up over his thighs, up into place, his cock strained, the shaft and head strapped to his abdomen by the wide elastic band. He massaged his balls, his length, wiping Vincent's scent into his skin. Vincent guided him further up on the bed, bringing his head to nest between his lean thighs. The fullness of the youth's genitals rested on Pierce's forehead. Vincent slowly arced over Pierce's trunk, his penis and scrotum dragging slowly over the man's face. Pierce inhaled deeply as his head rose up to burrow into Vincent.

At the same time, the boy pressed his hips down and he felt Pierce's hot breath, his salivating mouth boiling his cock. He slumped down, pressing his chest into Pierce's stomach, pressing his face down into Pierce's crotch, pumping his meat deep into Pierce's mouth. Pierce's hands slapped down on his ass cheeks, gripping them hard, urging them to pump harder, faster.

Vincent's mouth ran wet as he inhaled himself, then Pierce's perfect cock beneath the pouch. His arms burrowed beneath the beefy legs as his teeth chewed up mouthfuls of cotton-clad nuts, soaking it all with spit. He pushed down the waistband, exposing fully the silky rod. His tongue stabbed the piss slit again and again. Finally he let loose of the man's cock and pushed himself up. His body tensed. His hips bucked rapidly, hammering his burning prick deep down Pierce's throat until he came., yanking his swollen, throbbing cock from between Pierce's lips.

Pierce cried out for Vincent's cock, but the youth's firm ass landed on his face. Pierce accepted this pacifier eagerly, greedily. He licked the puckered orifice, coating it slick with spit, then he drilled his tongue deep, into Vincent's rectum. Trembling, Vincent gasped and his pelvis began to gyrate slowly, helping Pierce's tongue bore in him.

But suddenly he sprang up, landing flatfooted with a hollow thud. He grabbed his pack.

"What is it?" Pierce cried.

"The beach, man," Vincent said.

"Fuck the beach!" Pierce yelled as he rolled off the bed,

Vincent bolted from the room. By the time Pierce reached the living room, Vincent was in his pants and pulling another T-shirt on. After shoving his feet into his shoes, he pulled a windbreaker from his pack.

"Sorry, man," Vincent said.

"Vincent, please.,."

"Gotta." he said.

"Got to what?" Pierce barked. "You know how fuckin' crazy you made me when you ran out before?! I'd just gotten you out of my mind when, wham!, you're back!"

Vincent stared into his eyes. "I really like you," he said to Pierce. I do. But – He pressed his lips against Pierces, then pulled away sharply. Stroking Pierce's cheeks, he said, "I'll be at the pier."

"Down at the esplanade..."

"New Brighton pier, down by Oberland's. Said I gotta take one of his old boards out, man."

"I'll go with you," Pierce said.

Vincent laughed. "You know, I've had fantasies about given it up down at the seashore."

"Giving it up?"

"My cherry."

His eyes wide, Pierce blushed.

Vincent pulled on his pack. "Yeah, some dudes I hooked up with made the attempt."

"Oh?"

Now Vincent was blushing. "Kinda hokey, but I wanted... I thought, maybe you ..."

"I want to go with you tonight. Let me get dressed."

"Sweats," Vincent said, hooking his finger between Pierce's stomach and the waistband of the jockstrap. He snapped the elastic. "And my strap."

Pierce smiled. "Wait here..."

As Pierce rushed back to the bedroom, Vincent scooped up Pierce's previously discarded pants. He pulled the key chain from the pocket and

slipped a key off, then shoved the keys back into the pocket and let the pants drop to the floor. He opened the front door.

"I'll meet ya there!" he called as he rushed out of the Igloo.

"What?" Pierce called back.. He listened for Vincent's response. None came. He raced back into the living room. Finding it empty, he ran to the door. "Vincent!"

There was no response.

Pierce combed over the entire length of New Brighton Beach, walking in circles between the pier and Oberland's shop. A couple of hours passed. Maybe more. Vincent was nowhere to be found. Suddenly the shrill bleats of his beeper startled him. He unzipped his pack and quickly dug it out, silencing it. He squinted to read the illuminated display. It was the alarm company,

Manny's Mobile Monster chugged to a stop in front of Taco Bell. He stuck his head out the window. "Dude!" he yelled. "Call to party!"

Vincent chucked the bag full of tacos and burritos though the window, into Manny's lap, then hurried around the rear of the car and climbed in. The green machine bucked from first to second gear as they sped away.

Manny dug a paper wrapped burrito out of the sack. "There's a kegger over at Lisa Clancy's place."

"A kegger?"

"Yeah! Then m "

Vincent cut him off. "Quit thinkin' small, Manny. Let's head into the city."

"San Fran?"

Vincent nodded. "You think this old beer can's clutch can hold out?"

"Shit, yeah!" Manny said. He then looked at his gas gauge, "Fuck. Got enough fuel to get there, but not back. I only got a couple of bucks."

Vincent slid his hand into his pack and pulled out a plastic shopping bag. From it, he withdrew a wad of fifties, twenties and tens. "We got enough."

"Shit. Where'd you score?"

"A loan from a friend. Then there's this – He flashed Pierce's credit card.

"Well, fuck me naked. That'll get us through the night." "And then some," Vincent said as he stuffed it all back into his pack. His fingers latched onto an envelope. He pulled it out, then leaned back in his seat and removed the letter and photo. "What's that?" Manny asked.

"Just a letter from a friend."

"What else you got?"

Vincent dug through the pack again. He found one of the small boxes he'd taken from Pierce's store when he'd removed the bank deposit bag from the floor safe that Pierce never locked.

He flipped the box into Manny's lap.

Manny studied the box for a second, then burst out laughing. "You gotta be kiddin'!"

"Hey, take all you can get."

"A jockstrap?"

"Why not?"

Manny chuckled and pitched the box into the back seat. Vincent settled back in his seat and studied the picture of the handsome young man with the Marin address who'd answered his old ad. All you can get, he thought

"So," Manny said as he lit a cigarette, "what's Pierce been up to?"

"Tryin' to get all that he can get."

Manny nodded his understanding as they ascended the on-ramp onto the highway.

A HUSTLER'S CONFESSION
Michael C. Botkin

At the end of 1981 I had come to a crossroads of sorts. I'd lost a cushy work-study job doing environmental research – an early casualty of Reagan's election – and I'd dropped out of college after my third year as a junior. For six months I coasted on unemployment and food stamps, but eventually even that scanty gravy train reached the end of its tracks. Soon, I knew, I would have to join "the real world."

I had few occupational skills, incipient bad attitude and a distinctly non-professional appearance. A hacked resume and a meek demeanor failed to get me a position as a bank clerk or any other of the "situations" listed in the classifieds. Finally, just two weeks before rent was due, I responded to ads in the local gay rag recruiting "escorts and models," i.e. hustlers.

The "manager" of the service I called, Richard, lived only a few blocks away. After a complicated procedure involving calling in from a phone on a nearby corner so he could look me over in safety, he approached me and invited me up for a "performance interview." This consisted of stripping down to my jock and sucking on the pimp's dick and balls while he jerked himself off, with scarcely a glance in my direction. The dick was impressively large (though no challenge to my native skills). All this, combined with the numerous pictures scattered about of a slightly younger and far more attractive Richard, made me suspect that he'd started out as a working boy himself.

The ground rules were simple. The standard rate started at $60 an hour, of which I got to keep half. Longer periods yielded a small discount on the hourly rate, so a two-hour gig was $100, three hours $135, and an overnighter cost $300. Virtually all johns made do with the standard hour, although most of them tried to go over without paying extra. (If only I had my trusty beeping pillbox back in those days!)

Richard would call me when he had a gig and give me the address, most often a downtown hotel. I was to deliver Richard's share to him immediately afterwards and await my next call. Sometimes I would get them daily, especially at first; other times I would go a couple of weeks without work. The activity embraced the current standard lexicon of gay sex: fucking and sucking. Interest in anything "kinky" gave you license to extort an extra "tip," but in practice I rarely encountered "kink," and most customers were monumentally unimaginative.

Even so, I managed to fuck up my first assignment. It was a professor at Northwestern University who had a standing order for "new" boys. I was to loiter on a designated corner in Evanston until approached by the john, and then I was to pretend to be a poor lost NU student in search of a lift. A slushy

day was resolving into a bitter cold night when I reached my rendezvous. My sneakers were caked with ice as I climbed into his car.

But the small talk went wrong almost immediately. I actually had been an NU student, briefly, many years before, and played my role far too well. He panicked. Flustered, he suddenly dropped me off. Later I learned that he thought he'd accidentally picked up a real NU student instead of his hustler! Looking back, I can see that what he expected – and perhaps desired – was an illiterate hunk ineptly faking a preppy style. I would have better fulfilled my brief if I'd simply kept my mouth completely shut, and limited my replies to simple grunts and monosyllables. I had a lot to learn about hustling.

My second gig, a less elaborate house call on a different NU professor (whose wife was out of town), went off without a hitch. Towards the end, the professor flopped onto his belly and demanded to be fucked. At this time I was pretty exclusively a bottom and fucking anyone would have been a challenge, let alone this 300-pound troll. But I'd now figured out that strict veracity wasn't required. I stuck some fingers up his butt, pretending to hump him, with a vivid verbal description of my dick plowing his butt hole, finally faking an orgasm. If he suspected the deception he was tactful enough not to mention it. When I warned him that our session ended in three minutes, he worked himself up to a quick climax. I was beginning to get the hang of the profession.

Like most services, Richard's was a scam in many ways. He listed it under several different ads, all supposedly catering to a different clientele and offering a different type of boy: preppies or butch types or pseudo-athletes. He also ran a number of individual ads, each purporting to be from an independent escort. All these diverse calls ended up being routed to Richard's switchboard, and whatever the ad promised, he always sent out the first boy to answer his phone. I went out successfully on calls as a six-foot tall stud (I'm actually about 5'8") and as an eighteen- year-old (I was 24 at the time). The clients didn't seem to notice or mind: standards were low,

The customers were a fairly pathetic crew, mostly out-of-town businessmen engaging in some covert kicks a safe distance from home. I never felt threatened or abused by them. The sex ranged from bad to mediocre, but I'd had worse encounters on my own time. A hustler who could get and maintain an erection with a john was apparently something of a rarity, and it wasn't routinely expected,

Some johns tried to be friendly, but most were indifferent, only concerned to squeeze as much value out of their session as possible. I can only remember a single gig that ended earlier than the designated hour (later, as a psychotherapist, when I worked an "hour," it only lasted 50 minutes; hustlers don't get that ten minutes' grace).

One john, an older guy with a completely shaved body, fucked me almost nonstop for the full 60 minutes with a grinning but grim determination, as though he were trying to prove something. I finally had to ask him to stop as his stubble was giving me "beard burn" all over my body.

Only one john hired me for an overnighter. I thought it would be an easy gig; he'd come once or twice, and then we'd sleep, right? Wrong. Looking back, I suspect that he enhanced his performance with powerful pharmaceuticals, but maybe he was just a natural maniac. We fooled around all night and he came five or six times. His erotic energy was contagious: I eventually got into it, to my surprise, and towards the end I was sucking him off with enthusiasm. Afterward I felt thoroughly used and somewhat used up, but a bath restored my spirits. Ah, youth!

The only john who ever ripped me off was, ironically, also my only celebrity client: the late, great, infamous Divine, the 350-pound drag queen who starred in "Pink Flamingos." Divine was in town for a movie promotion, and Richard was thrilled to offer him a boy at half price ® he'd waived his share of the fee in return for an autographed photo of the diva. Even I was excited as I made my way to his room in what turned out to be a surprisingly seedy residential hotel.

He wasn't in drag of course, just a muu muu that hid his rotund bulk as much as anything could. He rolled a joint and, after we smoked it, he leaned back so I could suck his dick. I did this for a very long time, although it never got very hard. Finally, getting worried at his lack of response I paused and he had a seizure. He looked like he was having a heart attack; wheezing, heaving, clutching his chest. Then he passed out and seemed to drift into a normal sleep, while I debated whether to slip out, to call for help, or to do nothing. This must be every hustler's secret fear; what do you do if the john dies on you?

He soon came to and appeared unaware of what had transpired. When I presented him with the bill for three hours work (I saw no point in deducting the time he'd spent unconscious), he claimed not to have the full amount. Flustered by all that had occurred and anxious to flee before he had a relapse and croaked on me, I accepted part of what was due on the promise of full payment the next day plus an invitation to a party, a transparent ruse I would have immediately rejected from any non-celebrity. In retrospect I should have insisted on collateral, like his watch. It would have made a suitable souvenir. Of course, I never got my balance due or even the party invite. And of course, from that day on I could never watch a Divine movie without recalling our close encounter.

But most of the johns were nice guys; none of them was ever impolite (unless you consider trying to go overtime without paying rude), and overall, their standard of behavior ranked favorably compared to the way I see most

yuppies and "respectable businessmen" acting in other settings, like department stores and restaurants.

Richard's complicated multiple referral system had a second advantage, aside from casting a wide net. Whenever the vice squad wanted to bust hustlers, they did it on the cheap by hiring a hotel room and then ordering boys from several services at once, planning to bust a bevy of us, one after the other, as we showed up. Naturally, they almost always called more than one of Richard's "services" and, since a legitimate customer looking for multiple partners would obviously get them from a single source, he could recognize their trap in advance. He didn't stand them up – that would show he'd figured them out and reveal the links between his fronts – but rather sent them boys he was ready to retire from his employment to take the hit. He routinely promised to bail us out if busted but never actually did so. At least I didn't get turned in. Male hustlers faced much less legal and general persecution in Chicago at that time than did our female counterparts. You could work the street without risk, if you had any savvy, and many independents were in operation as streetwalkers or phone-ordered escorts. Women prostitutes, by contrast, had to have a pimp for "protection" from other pimps and the cops. If they tried to work the street or even a phone service independently the pimps would seek them out and assault them or turn them over to the police (whom they paid off regularly).

The laws that supposedly "protect" female whores from "exploitation" thus served to keep them vulnerable to crooked cops (the vast majority, of course) and pimps; anyone who claims otherwise probably knows little about the realities of prostitution. From what I can see, the situation continues pretty much the same today in most of the United States.

Richard didn't fit the media image of a pimp, but he was not a nice person. He was probably a Mafia vassal. He avoided daylight like a vampire (perhaps distressed by his faded looks, much deteriorated from those photos taken of him in his youth), and openly delighted in exploiting his workers. Once, as I was dropping off his share after a gig, I saw him screen a job applicant on the building's intercom. "I remember him from when he worked for me three years ago," he confided as the aspirant was on his way up. "I'm not going to hire him this time – too old – but I'm going to 'interview' him before I tell him that," he giggled.

I don't know why he told me stuff like that, or the other stuff which few of my co-workers were aware of; it could be my persona inspires such confidences, or that he needed someone to boast to and was gratified by my innocent responses to his slimy revelations. A year later I was to have an ostensibly New Age ecofeminist lesbian boss, Eileen, who, while driving us mercilessly in the office, espoused great concern with her peons' spiritual and general well-being. Her mind-fucking ploys turned out to be a much greater hassle than Richard's simple and open weirdness. Sure he was strange and

crooked, but he made no pretense of being anything else. Naturally no serious hustler would put up with such a quirky boss for long. Career boys (as opposed to chippers like myself) would naturally split off and create their own "service," ideally taking a few of Richard's clients with them to give them a starting base. He protected himself against this as best he could by promising customers a free trick if they could fool a boy into giving them their home number, but even so suffered constant attrition. This was why most of his clientele were out-of-towners and one-timers rather than local repeaters.

My friends reacted variously and interestingly to my new job. Joe, my boyfriend, was a self-proclaimed "sex radical" (back when this label still suggested "political incorrectness") and Social Revolutionary; furthermore he had a "thing" for hustlers when he met them in bars. Despite this, he was horrified when I became a hustler. In many ways it was difficult to differentiate his anguished Trotskyite "lumpenization of the proletariat" spiel from the Catholic moralism of his youth. Our chaotic relationship had been on the rocks when I began hustling; oddly, this seemed to patch it up for a while. Other acquaintances were titillated. Al and Stu, a pissy rich gay couple I knew through a close friend (who was sleeping with them) had "cut me cold" a few months earlier when they learned I was getting food stamps ® this labeled me as a "welfare cheat," and they could not risk being polite to me in public. This attitude reversed when they learned of my new profession. Now they were fascinated by me, apologized profusely for their past behavior and tried their best (unsuccessfully) to lure me into their bed (for free of course: they would never sink so low as to PAY A WHORE!, though it wouldn't surprise me if they'd hired working boys since then). Men I met in bars were invariably turned on when he learned how I supported myself. And I was a little impressed myself. In my two years since "coming out," I'd been painfully aware that I lacked most of the standard attributes of fagdom: I was indifferent to Judy Garland, hated the opera, found promiscuity uncomfortable and could never get the hang of gay fashion. As a hustler, my gay credentials were suddenly impeccable. And my doubts about my "market value" were swept away by my explicit price tag and the warm reception I got in the bars when my peers learned my occupational status. It was a major boost to my self-esteem.

Aside from that, I found it an acceptable job. I knew that, according to the mainstream it was illegal, immoral, dangerous, distasteful and oppressive, but in fact it required less routine abasement than being a bank clerk (or, as I was later to learn, junior management or a psychotherapist). The hours were short and flexible. I had virtually all my time to myself. It was cash under the table, so I paid no pesky payroll taxes. Within the gay ghetto it was, as mentioned, actually a prestigious career. Even so, after a couple of months my gigs began to taper off, and it was clearly time to either set up as an

independent or move on to something else. As it happened, another opportunity presented itself around this time.

This was a job at "Brooms Hilda," a storefront outfit that provided housecleaning to neurotic yuppies at about $10 per hour. About $4.50 went to us, the housecleaners; the rest went for "overhead." Please note that in this case the pimp's cut was roughly 55% instead of 50%; I assume that this difference was due to Broom's being a legal exploiter instead of a clandestine one.

As with hustling, most of our clients were nebbishes of one sort or another. Any serious employer of housecleaners would seek out an independent worker and avoid paying 55% overhead to a pimp. Our customers were mostly guilty yuppies and nervous nellies who liked coming home to a clean apartment but wished to avoid any personal contact with scum low enough to scrub their toilets, and they incorrectly assumed that our agency was bonded in some way that protected them against petty theft. They paid the premium in inflated prices, lousy services and incessant pilfering. It was a crude facsimile of true cleaning they were getting, the mere outward appearance of hygiene; it was as poor a substitute for the real thing as the "fucking" I provided as a working boy.

We weren't exactly model workers. Any serious housecleaner would stay with Brooms just long enough to develop some regular customers and then steal them away (easy to do; by cutting out Brooms, you could cut prices by 30% and still net nearly twice the agency pay) – not unlike the more savvy hustlers working for Richard. Some combined a little discrete hustling with the housecleaning, providing the clients with sexual services in addition to (or instead of) maid work. Those of us who hung around were slackers, though the term wouldn't be coined for another decade.

Thus, bosses, customers, and workers all shared a cynical and apathetic attitude about the business, just as in sex work. It was supposed to be a humiliating job, and everyone I encountered looked down on it. This was something that no one who could avoid it would do, even in their own home, let alone a stranger's. Nor did it have the paradoxical prestige of hustling. Al and Stu, the priss queens, lost all interest in me again (though this time they did consider hiring my services). Only Joe was relieved at my return to proletarian purity.

The pay was low, but the work was easy and often solitary. Oddly, doing housekeeping professionally was much less objectionable than doing it for oneself. I suppose that's because cleaning your own place comes out of your "free" time, while this was slow paced squandering of someone else's time. Despite the lack of status, I actually didn't have to take much shit from anyone. Virtually all other jobs I've had required significantly more routine kowtowing and ass-kissing. We didn't care, our bosses didn't care, our clients didn't know any better, and the net result was a very low-pressure situation. In

this regard it was like hustling; The dominance games were mostly a sort of (debased) courtly ritual that had none of the soul-crushing sting of "office politics."

The similarities between the two jobs were interesting. Both were essentially scams run by pimps, perpetrated upon ignorant clients and employing impaired workers (in the sense that we couldn't figure out more profitable scams on our own). Both, in a way, provided "wifing," supplying the basic but highly personal services which most heterosexual men would get free from their spouses, Viewed in that light, it was actually probably a better deal financially than marriage. Neither job paid well or provided any benefits, and neither really required any skills beyond "getting by" with providing as little as possible in return for our wages.

Are such jobs demeaning, oppressive and exploitive like the mainstreamers say? Perhaps, but compared to what? Operating the deep fryer at McDonald's? Kissing butt in an office? Selling overpriced commodities to foolish consumers? Being "all that you can be" in the military? I found hustling better than most employment options offered before or since" This may say more about the nature of work in our society than it does about either of those two jobs (and I suppose it speaks volumes about me), but I ask you; Who are the whores, really?

MY FIRST HUSTLER
Jesse Monteagudo

"Is this your first time here?"

I looked up. A young man who was close to my age, about my height, handsome instead of pretty, with bright blue eyes and wide, kissable lips was smiling at me. His gymnast's body was encased in a tight white T-shirt and dark chinos that accentuated the curves in the front and back. But what struck me the most about the guy was his long hair, which was dirty blond and poured over his shoulders and down his back almost to the waist. His smile was bright, completely disarming me and putting me at ease.

"Yes, it's my first time," I said, wondering what he saw in me. Though I thought I was rather good-looking myself, I figured a guy that hot could have his pick of the place. There must be a catch. "Is it obvious?"

"Uh-uh," he said, downing his beer while assessing me from top to bottom. "You look like you don't belong here Or maybe it's that you belong here but don't know why you're here."

Looking deep into his eyes, I nodded in silent agreement. How right he was. It was 1973, I was twenty years old, and it was my first time in a gay bar. After months trying to convince myself that it was the right thing to do, that I must be true to myself, I finally found the strength to walk into the Nook, an out-of-the-way dive in a nondescript part of town. I took several deep breaths before I walked through the door, headed to the bar, and ordered a beer. Now, an hour later, 1 was still sitting on the barstool, staring into my second beer, when this boy roused me from my reverie.

He took another long swallow of his beer, then put the bottle down, leaving a trace of foam on the wisps of blond hair that barely passed for a mustache. My own mustache, which I had recently cultivated, was like my head of hair: short, dark and curly, falling over lips that registered a perpetual pout.

"Hey, relax! No one's gonna to eat you!" he laughed. "Of course, unless you want 'em too," he added, giving me a lascivious wink.

I smiled.

"Name's Rocky," he went on, holding out his hand.

"And I'm Jesse," I said, shaking his hand firmly. "I guess I'm sort of nervous, this being my first time and all. See, I'm only twenty."

"Hell, I'm only nineteen, and I've been hangin' around here for almost three years now."

I blinked.

"Hey, don't look so surprised. You can do anything with a fake ID!"

"I'll bet -

"And I'll bet you're a college kid, right?"

"Yes," I said, wondering how he knew that. I was enrolled in a local college at the time, working on a degree in a major that seemed to keep changing every few months. Every morning I took the bus to class and every afternoon I took the bus to a part-time job in a shoe store. Living with my parents, I had little opportunity for sex.

"I bet you cruise those tearooms on campus every day!"

I blinked again. The look on my face registered my surprise, and guilty admission.

"Hell, no, I didn't catch you in the act. Every closeted college kid I've met first tries the toilets. How did you do?"

"Not well," I said. In fact, after a few brief, sadly aborted quickies, I was still, for all intents and purposes, a virgin "I'm afraid tearooms aren't my scene."

"Mine neither."

Shit, I thought, with his looks, he doesn't have to cruise toilets. "What I want is to meet a nice guy." Like you, I added, silently.

"Hey, that comes later, much later. Right now, you need somebody to show you a good time. He paused, smiled, then continued: "Somebody like me."

"Are you coming on to me?"

He laughed. "In a way. But. I only do it for the money. Even with cute college boys like you."

I was devastated. I thought he liked me, and all he wanted was to make a buck. My self-esteem, low enough as it was, sank to the floor,

"Hey, cheer up. You're a good-lookin' dude. I'll bet you're gonna have a lot of guys goin' for you, but I'm workin', That's just the way it is." He reached forward and touched my arm. I pulled away, instinctively.

He leaned into me. "From the looks of it, I think you need a teacher. You're not going to meet 'a nice guy,' or anyone else for that matter, if you don't know what you want when you get him."

I didn't move. I rather liked having him so close to me. "What do you mean?"

"What I'm talkin' about is that I can teach you how to have a good time with another guy. And it'll cost you less than you think!"

"Oh?"

" How much money do you have?"

"Twenty-five bucks."

"That's exactly what it'll cost you. In fact, I like you so much that I'll charge you just twenty bucks. You'll have money left to buy a drink, take a cab home, or whatever."

For all I knew, Rocky, or whatever his name was, was taking me for a sucker. But he was hot, I was horny, and twenty dollars for a "lesson" in sex was a pretty good deal. What did I have to lose? I looked around and noticed

that the bar was empty, except for the bartender and a couple of obvious drunks. Rocky was obviously the only game in town.

I finished my beer, then asked, "Where can we go?"

"There's an alley behind the bar."

"An alley?"

"Hey, don't sweat it! Nobody ever goes back there.'

What was I getting myself into? I could be robbed, beaten, left for dead. But I was young. I was foolish. And I was horny. So I went along, hoping that, if anything goes wrong, I would be able to take care of myself. "Show me the way."

"Now you're talkin'," he said, beaming. "Follow me."

The "alley" was a small passageway that separated the bar from a warehouse behind it. Except for the full moon, the only light we had came from a small bulb that shone from the bar's back door. But the place was clean – except for some garbage – and, even better, it was private. It was obvious that Rocky, and perhaps others, had used this place before.

My hands shoved in my pockets, I anxiously paced back and forth. Rocky nonchalantly leaned against the wall.

"First give me my twenty bucks." Without a word, I stopped in front of him and took a bill out of my pocket and handed it to Rocky. Without a word, he put it in his pocket. Having done that, Rocky pulled me to his side, surrounding me with a fierce bear hug. His lips passionately kissed mine as he drew me closer to him, grasping my buns with his firm hands. Our aroused cocks groaned against our pants, begging to be released. I instinctively reached out for Rocky's cock and my own.

"Hey, not so fast." Rocky said as he unbuttoned my shirt and began playing with my tits. I moaned with pleasure as this young hustler brought my nipples into a state of arousal, sending a volt of electricity throughout my body. Just when I thought Rocky did all that could be done to my tits, he took a nipple in his mouth, licking and biting it into a greater degree of ecstasy. Rocky continued to work on my young man-tits for what seemed to be an eternity, using his experienced hands and mouth on one nipple and then the other.

Having worked on my tits for a while, Rocky let go of them, leaving a sting that would remind me of his work for some time to come. Without a pause, he turned me around and dropped me against a nearby garbage can. He rapidly pulled down my pants, exposing my thick cock, heavy balls and round ass to the night air. My dick stood in attention as Rocky grabbed it from between my legs, stroking it with one hand while pulling my testicles with the other. I surrendered myself to my merciless young teacher, and held on to the garbage pail for dear life while Rocky continued to milk my tool and squeeze my man-eggs. I was about to reach the point of no return when Rocky stopped.

'Ready to come, uh? We'll, you're gonna have to wait for a while, 'cause I got something in store for you!" Grasping my buns with his firm hands, Rocky spread my cheeks, revealing the virgin hole within. Rocky then spit into my asshole, which allowed him to slip an experienced finger past the entrance, giving me a sensation I never felt before.

Rocky taught his lessons well. After teaching me the ways that a man's tits could give him pleasure, he went on to show me all the joy I could get when another man works on my ass. Rocky's finger went deeper and deeper into my man-hole, working its way up to my prostate. As my young lover massaged my gland with one hand, he worked on my cock and balls with the other. I could feel Rocky's breath behind me as he pulled his finger out of my ass and reached over to whisper in my ear.

"You like that, don't you? Well, there's more in store." Dropping to his knees behind me, Rocky began to work my ass with his expert tongue. With the skill of an experienced hustler (which he was), Rocky rimmed his way around my bunghole. He then worked his tongue around my swollen testicles and down to my restless cock. Rocky's quick tongue and hands did their work on my dick and ass, keeping both on an intense level of excitement.

"Oh, man, I can't take it anymore", I moaned. "I need to let go, man. I need to!"

"What you need is my cock up your ass!"", Rocky whispered in my ear, as he pulled back his long, luxurious hair. "Tell me what you really want, Jesse. Tell me!"

"I want you to fuck me, Rocky. I need you to fuck me!" Like a captive young animal, I begged to be possessed by my long-haired, blond trainer. The world seemed to disappear, leaving nothing but myself, Rocky, and my own burning need. "Please fuck me, Rocky, Please fuck me!" I sobbed. My legs spread out even further as I begged to be taken.

"You got it!" cried Rocky, as he opened his zipper and pulled out his cock and balls. Looking behind me, I saw Rocky's dick was the way I expected it to be, long, thick and cleanly circumcised. His balls, which I only got a glimpse of, were round and full, like two golden plums. I wanted to reach back and touch them but was held back by Rocky's hand on my back. "You want my cock, don't you, Jesse?"

I moaned.

"Don't you?"

"Yes, yes."

"Well, you're gonna get it – now!"

After lubricating my hole with his spit, Rocky positioned his seasoned hustler dick against my virgin ass. With the skill of a master, he slowly inserted his cock up my young rectum.

Though Rocky had opened and relaxed me with his finger and tongue, I was not ready for the sharp pain that shot through me. Part of me

wanted to be spared this feeling but part of me wanted it to go on. In any case, it was too late to change my mind.

Having placed his cock deep inside my ass, Rocky began to drive it in, slowly at first but with increasing determination. Like a young lion, his mane flowing in the wind, Rocky rode hard over me, driving us both to greater degrees of ecstasy. As Rocky continued to fuck me, his hands reached over and grabbed my nipples, giving them the same intense workout he was giving my ass. My own hand tried to keep in stride, pumping my own restless cock.

"Stroke yourself, dude," whispered Rocky, as he pulled me towards him. "I want to see you come. I want to see you come while my cock's in your ass and my hands are on your tits!" Rocky didn't have to say another word. With an incredible force, a geyser of cum shot through my prick and onto the ground. At the same time, Rocky made a final, vigorous thrust inside me, shooting his own man-milk into my receptive ass. Like two exhausted young warriors, we fell on top of the garbage can.

"Oh, yeah," he mumbled. "You've learned your lesson well, Jesse. From now on, you'll know what you want from a man and you're gonna get it. There are a lot of guys out there who would love to fuck your ass and work your tits!" As Rocky took his cock out of my ass, I felt him put something there in its place. As I lay there, still recovering, it was suddenly very quiet. I turned around, only to discover that Rocky was gone. That is when I realized he had left something up my ass. There, crumpled and coated with cum, was the $20 bill I had given him.

THE FIFTY-DOLLAR TRICK
William Barber

The moment I first clapped eyes on him in the Anthracite Bookstore, in downtown Allentown, Pennsylvania, knew that I would have to have him. It all happened so quickly. I had been browsing in the back of the store, looking through the latest skin magazines, getting myself in a mood. Leaving the store, I stopped to purchase cigarettes, and it was just at that moment, as I was about to leave, that he entered. Our eyes locked for that extra second and, as our shoulders brushed in passing, I realized somewhere I'd seen that face before – I could never forget that long, crooked smile and those devilish eyes. But who was he?

I lingered outside the store at a newsstand, pretending to scan the covers of tabloids, as if I really gave a damn about Roseanne Arnold's newest tattoo. I tried glancing back into the store without being obvious. A chorus of words ran through my head: "You want that, say something, get a line together, be cool!" My heart raced. What was happening to me?

I began to search the file cabinets of my mind. An "All Points Bulletin" had been issued and, at last, the photographic image arrived, a clear recall of his face. I had first seen him at the local gay bar, weeks, perhaps months before. He was ordering a drink beside me. As I studied the background of that image it became clear, That night he was with "Fat Albert," the town's richest john and collector, of cute boys. I had looked at him that night, taken that mental photograph, and then dismissed him as out of my price range. This file photo had remained buried all this time in the far back reaches of my memory,

The next time I saw him was at a restaurant with another wealthy john This time we recognized each other, and he smiled, I took a chance when his escort was in the men's room to slip him my phone number. He smiled wickedly. I remained calm. I knew what I wanted, I knew where to find it, and I knew how to get it. That settled, I let the time pass easily. He came to me in my dreams. In my fantasies I had already begun to disrobe him and have sex with him.

And then one Sunday afternoon, I got my chance. He was walking down a deserted Main Street, glancing into windows. He wore his thick, expensive leather jacket. Our eyes connected. I crossed the street. The rest was easy. My luck was holding. I had fifty dollars in my wallet. No more wimpy excuses.

We walked to my house and I asked him what his going rate was. After the usual tales of enormous sums, we settled on fifty dollars. A bargain, considering that, close up, he was even more handsome, more exotic, more friendly than I'd imagined. His name, I learned, was James. I kept the pace

slow, under my control, although there was a voice inside me dying to get out and scream.

Other information he shared: he had an "old lady" and two small kids by her. He needed the money for them. He also had a girlfriend; he worked days in a sheet metal factory. He was twenty. He did a stint in the Navy. He viewed sex as a "high," a release from his frustrations.

He promised me that he was "pretty versatile," but his list of "no-no's" included no kissing, no getting fucked (don't they all say that?) and keeping this "our little secret." His smile was broad and easy and very inviting.

I fixed us each a very strong vodka and we went upstairs. I let him go ahead of me so I could watch the churning strength of his ass muscles beneath the tight-fitting denim. His ass was so inviting I kept asking, Is this really happening?

He asked to shower and stripped for me, glancing at his reflection in the full-length mirror. I watched as he revealed his body to me, tight, strong, the arms decorated with tattoos. When he was naked, we hugged and I let my hands roam freely over the strong curves of his ass.

I watched through the steamy glass door as he showered. He showed off for me, almost like a child. Naked on my bed, he asked if he could use my phone. He called his girlfriend and made a date for later that night, all the while accommodating me, He rolled over for me, lifted his leg, rolled back around, lay sideways, played with my hair. This fascinated me, filled me with a sense of mild depravity. After he hung up the phone, he opened my pants and began sucking my dick. He was an eager lover, which surprised me. I was expecting trade.

In my frenetic state, I suggested that we play a game. He loved this idea. I would be a Doctor, my bed would be the examination table, and James would be the innocent patient. I got a pair of Triflex Sterile Latex Surgeon's Gloves, 7 1/2s, which I keep around for purposes of safe sex. I clucked and worried about the importance of a proctologic examination. James spread himself face down and lifted his strong ass. I poured mineral oil all over his cheeks and began to massage them firmly. I spanked him, softly at first, and then a little harder. Using a horrible German accent, I called him "naughty boy," and he agreed that he had been "very bad."

I asked him "how bad?" and he laughed heartily. I urged him for details. He revealed that last week he had "sucked off a priest in a confessional." I called him a "bad, bad boy" and spanked him harder. He started to give me the details but he stopped. He was enjoying the spanking too much.

All the while James watched this whole process in the large mirror beside my bed. My eyes remained transfixed upon the mounds of his ass, the

brown cheeks, my bright pink hand prints, the tight crack and, then, within the crack. My fingers began a gentle probing.

His little puckered asshole was in excellent condition: no hemorrhoids, no fissures, no warts. It had a winking eye, and shone from all the oil. Although he professed to never having been fucked, he seemed to welcome this attention to his hole. He looked right over his shoulder to watch the "operation." I asked him how it felt.

"It feels real good, Doc, real good."

One at a time I inserted my rubber fingers, reaming them around slowly, carefully, keeping up a steady banter in my phony German accent. I told him to shove a pillow under his hips to hold his ass up higher while I continued my examination. I found his prostate and massaged it. After that, the rest was easy. He reached back willingly to spread his cheeks. I gave him a nice, long, three-finger fuck.

"Oh, yeah, that feels great!" he moaned from time-to-time. Then, as he got closer to the edge, came. Yeah, give it to me, Doc. Puck me hard."

This drove me to a frenzy. My own rubber-covered dick was banging around in the air from side-to-side. I moved toward his side-turned face and he sucked me wildly. I watched his bouncing head in pure amazement.

"Let's try the real thing," I whispered harshly.

Without waiting for permission, I mounted his body. I pressed my slobbered rubber in the crack of his ass and humped him. With my right hand, I lined my cock up against the hole. The penetration was instant and complete. I pinned his muscled shoulders to the bed and fucked his ass off. His whimpered protests only made me fuck harder. There was no stopping this and he knew it. Beyond control, I exploded prematurely,

Sweat dripped from my body, making his smooth back glisten. He moaned a bit and closed his pretty eyes. We stayed like this awhile, both breathing deeply. I stared down at him, wondering what his dreams were, his ambitions, his fears.

Now I endured the clumsiness that comes right after sex, the getting up and off the body, one's legs trembling slightly, the uncomfortable laugh, and the sticky messes that must be attended to, the anxious towel, the broken little pieces of intimacy that must be quickly replaced with motion and ego. I wanted him to feel as good about this as I'd felt, but his mood seemed to darken.

"You won't tell anybody about this, will you?" he mumbled.

"Oh, no, of course not!" I lied. I could hardly wait to call my best friend Jack and tell him all about my good fortune. I wondered for a moment what his world must be, what illusions, delusions was he selling and for what price and at what cost? I quickly got my wallet and laid out the fifty, then went and got three more tens from a bureau drawer. He was worth it. I laid the bills on the bed.

After we'd both showered and gotten dressed, we went downstairs and I fixed another drink. James browsed around my desk, picking up magazines, articles, a book I'd written that had my picture on the back cover.

"You wrote this?" he asked, as if I had achieved the impossible,, I confirmed that it was true. He stared at it strangely, as if holding a map to a buried treasure. He looked at me, then looked back at the book. "So you're a writer?" he asked, as if this was beyond his ken.

I nodded but I thought, "Oh, God, no..."

James made a little nudge with his chin. "I want to be a writer some day," he said, more to himself than me.

"Good for you," I said with a cheery resignation, but I thought to myself, "Don't you realize what a curse it is to be a writer?" So many writers, so little pay.

"Would you write a book about me?" he asked.

What could I say? "Maybe" was the best I could come up with.

"Boy, my life could make a book," he continued. "You wouldn't believe some of the things I've seen and done."

I did not doubt that for a moment." You should write your own story," I suggested.

"No, I want you to write it. Would you do that? Would you write my story?"

"What do you want me to say?"

"Oh, everything. Things like today, when we were playing doctor and I let you fuck me. Could you write about that?"

"But you don't want me to tell anybody," I reminded him.

"That's different. If you write a book about me, you could make me famous." Talk shows, I think, are ruining our nation's youth.

"Do you really think so? Do you want to be famous?" I was running out of cards. This really hadn't figured in my plan.

"Gimme your number and I'll call you," he said, and I knew he meant it. "I'll tell you my whole life story, You won't believe it.

"I'm sure I would," I said, and I was willing to be open-minded enough to be sure I would.

I drove him downtown to the bus station so he could catch a bus to meet his "girt." We shook hands in parting.

James did call about a week later. He wanted me to meet him at a stripper bar. I was broke and made excuses.

"Did you start that book about me yet?" he asked.

"No, not yet."

"Or was that bullshit? I hear a lot of bullshit in this business.." I heard the tinseled disco of the strip club in the background. The clink of glasses and the static of men's voices.

"No, it wasn't bullshit," I offered, running out of things to say.

"Good. I'll call you next week," he finished. "We'll get together and play doctor, okay?"

"Okay."

As I hung up the phone, I pictured him at the bar, having no trouble finding other customers. And later, perhaps walking the downtown square, cars pulling up to the curb, offers being made and accepted. How many others will he know before I find him again? What other stories will he have to tell me?

And now I have started it, as James requested, and I am still waiting patiently for his call.

DIRTY BOOKSTORE HUSTLERS
William Cozad

The dirty bookstore was just that; it needed to be cleaned up. In the arcade, cum and soggy tissues littered the floors of the booths, but it's my favorite place to go for fast-food sex, you might say. And besides the horny guys like me, who come in all sizes, shapes and ages, there are the pros, the hustlers, available for free to youngsters like themselves but for others at prices that start out at twenty but can be haggled down to ten or less, depending on the hour and the desperation of either party.

Usually there are an abundance of hot men after the same thing I am, and not interested in financial gain, but I had always been curious about the pros and one night decided to see what I could get for thirty bucks.

I'd hung around the arcade, done the shuffle to avoid the security cameras and sweeps by hot dog clerks who got off on harassing the clientele. Maybe they were on a power trip, or were just company men who wanted to make as much money as possible off the video machines by telling customers that they needed to find a booth or leave the arcade.

I spotted one obvious hustler. He was black with a short Afro and looked like chicken, yet he was in the place so who was I to question. I saw that his manner of snagging tricks was to roost in a booth with the door ajar, If a trick was interested, they'd just go inside. More than once that night I'd seen the door fly open when a cruiser thought he might have happened on a hot number, only to discover there was a price tag attached. Knowing the score, I decided to make the kid my first arcade hustler. I peeked into the booth.

"Want some black dick?" he asked.

"Yeah, I'm an equal opportunity cocksucker, a rainbow rider."

"Come on in."

Entering the booth, which reeked of stale poppers and dried cum, I stood beside the hustler.

"It's twenty bucks – up front."

Looking into his dark eyes and blubbery lips, my cock tingled, but I decided to haggle, like I like to do at the flea market.

"Can't spent that much, sorry,"

"Okay, man. Fifteen. I've never, gone for less."

"I wanna be sucked off till I blow my wad." Just saying that made my cock lurch.

"Oh man, I don't suck dicks. I ain't no queer."

"But you want money."

"Only to let you blow me."

Well, I wanted to be satisfied, not just service him. "All I can give you is ten bucks."

"Okay. Just don't tell anybody that I went for ten."

"My lips are sealed." Around your fat black dick, I thought, if that basket wasn't lying.

"Money first. I don't wanna get burned."

He unzipped his tan chinos and flashed his soft cock. I gave him the Alexander Hamilton.

"Got any tokens for the machine?"

I took eight tokens out of my pocket. "That should do it," I said.

He dumped the tokens into the slot and switched the channel to a hetero sex vid.

Squatting down, because I didn't want to get any crud from the floor on my pants, I fondled the kid's dick. I could see it was a beauty, even in the flickering light from the monitor. Sticking out my tongue, I lapped at the black snake. Even limp it was a monster – easily eight inches and fat.

I laved it with spit while he watched the video. 'Try as I might, I couldn't get him hard. He was either not in the mood or, more likely, petered out from earlier action.

I tried everything I knew to get him hard but his dick wouldn't stiffen. I licked his nuts while I jacked it but nothing happened.

The machine dipped to black.

"Okay, man, I gotta go," he said.

I was pissed, feeling what it was like to be hustled. Not so much as a drop of jizz oozed out of his piss hole. Doubt that he could have cum no matter how much money he got.

With my tenspot in his chinos he left the arcade. I knew from previous observation that he'd be back in an hour or so to hustle another john.

Still, I was determined. This was indeed my night to check out the pros, When I saw a twentyish freelancer I hadn't seen before come in off the street with a middle-aged john in a suit, I decided to take a look-see.

I got in the next booth, bending over and staring through the peephole, and they weren't aware that I was watching. I watched the man sit on the plastic chair and fondle the tall, swarthy stud's basket. If I were a porno movie director, I couldn't have choreographed it better, although the lighting wasn't good.

I had a bird's-eye view of the boy's crotch. His dick got hard, I could see the outline. The john kissed his faded blue denim crotch bulge. Anxious, the young man unzipped his fly and showed the guy a hot, cut rod, not so thick but amply long.

The cocksucker slurped it down in one fell swoop. Then he just bobbed his head up and down. The hustler was at such an angle that I could see his dick sawing in and out of the man's mouth.

Watching the blowjob gave me a boner. I freed my prick and jacked it, joining in, incredibly hot from watching. The hustler was slamming his prick down the john's throat and moaning.

"Ready? It's gonna cum!"

He buried his cock down the man's throat and blew his load. When he pulled his cock and wiped it with the handkerchief the john gave him, the john was licking his chops.

I didn't see the exchange of cash but that had probably been done before they entered the arcade. They left the video booth together, the hustler's eyes darting about, the john grinning with cum caked on his lips.

Suddenly I realized that I wasn't the only watcher. I remembered that there was a peephole on the other side of the booth as well. Another guy left that booth and went into the one just vacated. I heard the door button lock. I imagined he'd be in there sniffing musky aroma of fresh sex or looking for fallen cum drops.

Coming around the corner, I saw a kid named Kevin in his usual spot, out of range of the security camera. I knew his name from listening to other guys talk to him.

He was blond and blue-eyed, nerdy-looking with his eyeglasses, "Hi," he said with a smile. Vanna real good blowjob?"

"How much?"

"Ten."

"Just spent ten."

"Five?"

Five? Kevin was a bargain cocksucker, with that look of a schoolboy about him, as if he should be home studying his lessons, not sucking dick for five bucks.

He put his hand on the bulge in my jeans. I was still hard from watching the couple in the booth.

"Okay," I said.

I stepped into the booth with him and sat down on the skinny bench.

Kevin didn't bother with the videos. He knelt on the cruddy floor and quickly took my dick out. He took a few preliminary licks, then he deep-throated my dick. I was amazed that he tried to stuff my nuts into his mouth as well, but couldn't manage. What he did manage was to suck my dick like a champ, and with the visual image of the hustler/john blowjob still in my mind, I popped my load in no time.

Kevin took his mouth off my dick just before I came and it rained cum drops all over the floor.

Panting, I gave him the fiver. And in a rare burst of generosity, from the exhilaration of a blowjob well-done, I gave him a fiver bonus.

He thanked me profusely, telling me how much he could use the money. I chuckled seeing how steamed up his glasses were.

I found an isolated spot at the back of the arcade and leaned against the wall to recoup. My knees were kind of wobbly from the shattering orgasm.

Not Kevin. He wasted no time. On to the next john. I watched him take a silver-haired gent into a booth. At five bucks a blowjob he dealt in quantity, although the quality level was high too.

Down twenty bucks on my bankroll, I decided I'd had enough action for one night. I was checking out the hustlers for kicks, not going for broke.

Just as I was about to exit the arcade, a hunk came into the arcade. I turned on my heels and followed him. He could compete with the expensive boys on the meat rack. He had a muscular bod despite the loose-fitting homeboy drag he wore, with his baseball cap turned around on his head. Maybe he found live ones who sprang for more then twenty. Maybe he had a small dick. Whatever, I decided to check him out.

I roamed around the arcade before finally stationing myself across from a wall of booths.

Catching my eye, he stepped into the booth right opposite me and left the door ajar.

I walked up to the booth and stopped.

"Get in here," he barked.

Don't know why, but I obeyed, wondering what his trip was. "Lock the door."

I locked the door.

He dropped his black jeans and briefs, showing me his hot bubble butt.

"Like that ass?"

"Gorgeous," I said, truthfully. I hadn't seen buns like that in years.

"Wanna fuck 'em enough to pay?"

"I'm sorry, I'm kind of short on cash."

I was telling the truth; buns like that could cost hundreds and be well worth it. For a fleeting moment, looking at those luscious mounds of ripe boy flesh, I was tempted to go to the automatic teller machine and withdraw whatever it cost. I was surprised he was a bottom because he appeared so macho.

"You got twenty?"

"Only ten. Maybe some other time_" I started to unlock the door.

"Wait. Okay. I need the money."

I'd heard that line before. But I forked over the sawbuck.

The hunk didn't bother with even starting the videos; he just reached in his pocket and pulled out a condom out, tearing it open with his teeth.

Unzipping my fly, he covered my cock in latex, spreading the circle over my crown, holding the tip and peeling the rubber down my stalk.

I sat on the bench, thinking he would sit on my dick. I'd like that, him riding the peg. He turned around and I realized it had been months since I'd

had an ass like this to play with. Spreading his mounds, I saw the pink pucker. Crazed with lust, I just dove in with my tongue. I lapped at his asshole.

"Oh, yeah, eat my ass, dude,"

He bucked back and I darted my tongue up his ass. "Tongue-fuck me. Do it!"

While I slurped and slobbered with my face buried in his buns, he moved his butt around. He even clenched my tongue with his butt muscles. I lapped away and he practically jumped through the wire-mesh screen at the top of the booth.

Reaching underneath him, I felt his cock. It was hard and huge. I mean, it felt like nine inches to the touch. His cockhead was leaking pre-cum. I stroked his prick.

"Got my ass on fire with that rim job. Do it, dude. Shove that big prick up my butt hole."

Standing up, I gripped his narrow waist. He reached back and grabbed my boner and positioned it right on the target of his butt hole.

My cock slid smoothly into him. As I fucked, it seemed I was feeling every nook and cranny of that hot ass. Only with great effort did I keep from cumming off right away.

"Fuck me, dude. Fuck me!"

It was at that moment that I noticed the peephole in the wall and realized that we were being watched. But I didn't care. Let the guy get his jollies. I still had a diamond-cutter hard-on from watching that hustler get blown and then getting blown myself.

I pumped my rod up the hunk's butt. He wiggled his ass around and humped back. His canal worked my cock, squeezing it, bringing it to the bursting point.

"Fuck me harder! Faster! Oh yeah, that's it, dude. Your cock's so fuckin' big, man,.. God, it's so hard. Oh yeah, it's gonna shoot... Do it, dude, Get your rocks off. Shoot your fucking scum up my ass!"

By now I was sweating heavily, huffing and puffing as I gave it everything I had, throwing the roughest fuck I could remember up the hunk's hot asshole.

"Do it, dude. Cum in me! Oh-yeah, that's it. Can feel it shootin'. Oh shit, yeah."

I could feel my jizz squirt into the rubber, deep in his fiery ass: As my cock plopped out of him he turned around. My knees buckled and I sat down in the bench. His cock was stiff, throbbing.

"Do me, dude. You can have your stinkin' money back if you suck my dick. I'm so horny I gotta get off or bust a gut." "Gimme the money."

I said it as a joke, but he fished the tenspot out of his trousers.

Well, if I could get hustled, I could hustle back. Although I intended to give him back the money, since he'd earned it and he said that he needed it. Besides, he was just a kid to me.

But he had a man's cock that was demanding action. It was a natural, uncut beauty. Perfectly shaped. His big balls heaved in their sac.

For starters, Todd painted my lips with his dick gloss, the clear pre-cum that oozed out of his slit.

Holding the head of his cock, I flicked my tongue over the shaft. Then, holding the shaft, I darted my tongue into his piss hole and tasted his sweet lube.

"C'mon, dude, suck my dick."

Getting his flared purplish dickhead in a lip lock, I tongued the crown.

He rubbed my hair, then pulled it. "Suck it. Oh, suck that big meat."

I gobbled up his cock and gave it everything I had. I deep-throated it till his pubes tickled my nose. I tugged on his low-hangers.

"Oh yeah, dude, I'm ready! Gonna shoot. Gonna cum in your mouth!"

He slammed his balls in my face and rammed his prick all the way down my throat.

My cock was semi-hard in the condom and I peeled off the rubber. Remembering the watcher in the next booth, I tossed it against the wall, still keeping up the pressure on the hunk's dick. I heard a grunt, then a slurping sound. I even saw a tongue in the hole, This voyeur was even more of a pervert than me.

Soon the hunk was ready and he pulled his cock from my mouth and jacked himself to an intense orgasm, His cum splattered on the floor and he moaned, "That was good, dude, really good." Quickly he hiked up his black jeans.

I thought maybe he wasn't really a hustler at heart, only doing it because he'd lost his job or something. Maybe I could take him home with me, help him out. In return, I could fuck that hot ass of his and suck his big dick a few more times. It would be worth it. I started to say something when he stopped with his hand on the lock and said, "Uh, I hate to ask, dude, but could you let me have the money back? 1 mean, I got my old lady back in my hotel room and the rent's due ..."

"Sure, baby, you earned it."

My romantic bubble burst but it was okay; no way did I want to get involved with anyone, having recently been dumped by a boyfriend. Yup, I'd done my time. I was free now, and liked it that way.

I gave the hunk back his ten bucks, then watched his fantastic butt undulate in the black jeans as he sauntered out of the arcade.

By now the place was deserted. I'd gotten my rocks off twice and had spent only thirty bucks, a better bargain than the bars, where I usually spent more and just ended up with a hangover. Yeah, I guess it's like they say, you give it away when you're young, then you sell it, and when you're older you buy it back.

WORTH EVERY PENNY
John C. Douglas

His lips, warm and wet, gripped my cock, his teeth barely touching the shaft just below the flared rim of the swollen glans. That sensitive knob he held captive, laving it with saliva and caressing it with delightful lapping. His beardless cheeks hollowed as he sucked, long hungry tugs that sent powerful thrills down the strutted column of my dick.

The hand cupping my balls jiggled and squeezed just enough to make my ass jerk in response, and I pushed my hips forward, my cock sliding deeper inside the greedy young mouth.

I wanted to grab his blond hair and ram all nine inches down his throat, but I also wanted the boy to yield himself completely and instinct told me that he was sucking the largest cock he had ever encountered. Later, after we had done other things, I would fuck that mouth any way I chose.

The mere thought brought another surge of pre-cum up through my dick, and Chris murmured his excitement as he savored the tartness, swallowing and sucking a little harder.

I began easing the cock in and out between those plump lips, being careful not to force the head down his throat, but letting the boy claim it when he was ready. He had relaxed a little, and was taking more and more of my prick as his head bobbed back and forth, creating a storm of pleasure in my loaded balls.

I looked down at his blond head, past my inserted cock, and focused on the boy's rearing dick, its head already shiny with seeping jism. My mouth watered with lust, and I pulled my prick out of his mouth with a wet, slurping sound.

"Did I not do it good?" he protested, his hands gripping my hips and attempting to pull me back.

"You were excellent," I assured him, urging him to his feet. "Let's get on the bed, Chris, I want some of your dick."

I let him precede me into the bedroom, feasting my eyes on that delightfully curved bottom, the cheeks swaying with every step. His prick waggled as he placed one knee on the bed, turning toward me with a questioning look,

"How do you want me?"

"On your side," I instructed, lowering myself to the yielding bed, with my head toward his feet. He realized my intent, and swung his body into position.

His fingers found my cock, guiding it back into his mouth, and he gave a little snort when my own lips fitted themselves over the head of his prick. I felt the delicious hardness jerk against my exploring tongue, and tasted

the youthful tartness of his seminal fluid when a little spurt oozed from the slit. We sucked each other with noisy tugs, slurping and gulping when our mouths filled with the jism-laced saliva. Fingers toyed with balls, and teased assholes, while we moaned our pleasure at the taste and feel of each other's thrusting prick.

Our hips gyrated, pushing and pulling the swollen cocks in and out, quivering with the intensity of mounting passion and ever increasing goodness.

The boy's forefinger found my anus, gently flicking the tender circle, reminding me of how wonderful it would feel when the dick I was sucking invaded my asshole.

Chris had managed to relax his throat, and my balls were spreading against his nose as I fucked that nursing mouth, the head of my prick driving deep. He was taking all nine inches, and loving every inch.

He moved willingly when I urged him onto his back, straddling his blond head while continuing to feast on that rearing prick, my own stabbing his hungry mouth as I fucked it with long, delightful strokes.

His hips worked faster, as did mine, our cocks sliding in and out between greedy lips, and our hands rubbing and toying as we sucked each other.

I held back as long as I could, enjoying the twin pleasures of the boy's oral talent and my own delight at the thrill of sucking that delicious young prick that filled my throat again and again.

The lad was earning every penny of the money I had given him, bringing me the most intense joy with that willing and hungry mouth, and I was savoring every drop of seminal juice that seeped from his throbbing dick. But, all too quickly, I felt the threatening spasms of my orgasm, and the boy sensed its nearness, sucking harder and faster, his tongue lashing the head of my prick each time my hips retreated.

I nursed his driving prick with hungry tugs, feeling his warm, yielding balls press my nose and forehead, and his pubic hair tickle my chin with each thrust. His cock jerked and swelled, indicating that his own release was imminent.

Our hips and mouths worked with savage hunger, seeking both a release and an offering. Until that moment, we had blended the sounds of our suction with our soft moans and grunts of delight. Now, there was only the liquid sound of wet lips and sliding cocks.

His legs were spread wide, and each time my head descended, I got a close look at that tight pink asshole, its striated lips puckering in rhythm with my oral assault. Anticipation heightened my pleasure as 1 imagined how it would feel when I slid my cock into that tight embrace.

Then I felt the youngster's dick swell and jerk inside my mouth, and my own balls tightened responsively as the first spasm of ecstasy tore through my balls and erupted from the head of my cock.

Only a few times in my life have I experienced the almost painful thrill of mutual and simultaneous orgasm, and it felt as if my entire being was being expelled through my prick and into the boy's greedy mouth. While, almost spurt for spurt, the wads of cum were being replaced by the ropy, sperm-laced semen he was spilling against my tongue and palate.

At the apex of our pleasure, our hips surged, and we buried our cocks in each other's throat, each gulping the last delicious drop of cum and hoping for more.

Moments later, still panting, we were locked in a torrid embrace, mouths fused and tongues probing, each tasting his own ejaculate in a fevered kiss. The boy's lips were soft, warm and moist, as kissable as they were fuckable, Our hips pressed prick against prick, both still hard and ready for further use.

"That was the best I ever had!" he gushed, his lips moving against mine.

"You give damn good head," I said. "I don't think any of the other boys could do better."

"I hope I can please you in other ways," he said softly, his green eyes searching mine for reassurance. "We need the money so badly."

Even in the aftermath of a gut-wrenching orgasm, the boy sought to insure the immediate future.

"Does Adano like to suck a dick?" I asked, my fingers playing over his smooth ass cheeks, At the bar where I had picked him up he had pointed Adano out as his "roommate." I would have taken both of them but Adano was already involved with another john.

"He has sucked only mine," was the reply. "But he loves to do that. Most of all, he likes to be fucked."

"Do you like to be fucked, Chris?" I let my index finger slip into the crack of his ass and tease the puckered anus.

He hesitated. "I have never had one so big," he admitted. "But I will let you fuck me. You have paid me much money, Michael. I must earn it."

I am quite accustomed to paying for sex. The circles in which I move in Atlanta are such that I have to disguise my sexual preferences. I know a few successful authors who have emerged from the closet, but the "coming out" has not always been painless.

The easiest way to ensure my continued privacy was to buy a body for an hour or a night, never letting the hustler know my identity. More than a few of them would have demanded far more money had they known it was Michael Locke, well-known writer, sucking their dicks.

Chris may have heard of me, but on Pythos, the tiny island where I had retreated to finish my book, it made no differences I was a big dick with a lot of bread, and he was willing to do almost anything for money.

I leaned across the bed, opening the drawer of the nights stand to extract a tube of lubricant. I handed it to the boy. "Get your ass ready, Chris," I told him. "Let's see if you can fuck as well as you give head."

His cheeks reddened when he took the tube from my hand. He flipped the top back and squeezed a glob of the clear jelly onto his fingers.

"Adano and I just use spit," he murmured, arching his hips and thrusting his hand under his balls to reach his anus.

"I'd like it that way," I admitted. "But I doubt that Adano's dick is as big as mine. You'd better get that hole pretty slick."

His fingers worked, and the expression on his pretty face told me that he was inserting the jelly deep in that tender channel.

My cock stiffened with lust. He recapped the tube and wiped his fingers on a towel I had tossed onto the bed a little earlier. He settled back, those shapely legs spread, his own dick erect and throbbing.

"How do you want me, Michael?" he asked, his eyes half closed, the lashes long and quivering.

"Just like that, kid," I answered, climbing to my knees and looking down at his naked body. "Pull your knees up, and spread them apart."

Evidently he had been screwed like that before, for he knew exactly how to position himself for my entrance. He gripped his own ankles as his hips lifted, and I mounted him, steering my cock until the tip felt the heat of that well-greased anus.

I added weight, and suppressed a grunt of pleasure when the tiny circle yielded and the warm, wet membranes slipped over the head of my cock, almost painfully tight.

The youngster's eyes squeezed shut, and his lips drew back against his clenched teeth. A muffled groan escaped him as I forced my prick deeper into his reluctant ass, feeling the muscles contract about it.

"Does it hurt?" I demanded, staring down at his contorted features, my hips motionless as I let his asshole adjust to the unprecedented filling.

"A little!" he managed to gasp, his eyes still closed. "Your cock is so big!"

"And your ass is tight!" I countered. "Just the way I like it. Hot and tight!"

"Don't stop, Michael!" I had no intention of stopping before I unloaded in that young tail. "I can take it!"

He gasped aloud when I added another inch of penetration, and his rectal muscles flexed in helpless reaction. His hips moved in a little grinding circle, moving his asshole about my cock and producing little pulsations of goodness in that wrist-thick organ.

"Why did you stop, Michael?" he gasped. "It is so good!"

I flopped onto my back, and pulled him down on top of me, his open mouth covering mine and his tongue dancing a warm wet welcome as my tongue invaded it, tasting anew the deliciousness of youth in his saliva.

Against his parted lips, I whispered, "Straddle me, Chris, and sit on that big dick."

There was no need for hands. The boy worked his knees forward until he was astride my waist, his hips lifted. Then, slowly and carefully, he lowered them and I felt that hot, wet circle press the tip of my cock.

"Take it, Chris!" I groaned, my ass pushing upward.

"UHHHH!" I sighed when the sultry embrace claimed my stiff prick, sliding down the shaft until I was buried once again in the boy's tight asshole. "Fuck it, Chris!" I panted, my hands gripping his slender waist as he began a steady posting that sent his rectum riding up and down my cock.

"It is so good, Michael!" he panted, riding me with furious writhing of those lithe hips. "You are making me cum again!"

My own cock jerked as I felt his rectal spasms, his prostate pulsated and his prick spurted his ropy semen over my belly and onto my heaving chest. My orgasm trailed his by microseconds, and my cum jetted deep in the youngster's belly even as his own showered my nakedness. It was beyond ecstasy, and beyond description. On this remote island, I had found my best piece of ass ever.

The lad bent forward, keeping the head of my cock in his still contracting ass, to press those soft moist lips to mine in a kiss that spelled more than mere passion.

I had paid for the sex, but something told me I might have received something far greater. I cradled him in my arms as we kissed, my hips stirring the head of my prick in that cum-filled orifice. His weight, naked and warm, was somehow comforting.

It was more than an hour and two drinks later that I had him lie face down and spread his legs so 1 could fuck him again.

HOTEL DANCING
Bert McKenzie

It was my first trip to Las Vegas. I was attending a convention and looking forward to spending some of my off-hours enjoying the fabled "Sin City." How wrong I was! In the past couple of years, the fathers have made a concerted effort to upgrade the city's image by featuring fun for the whole family. Well, I'm not exactly into their kind of "family" entertainment, but there's still a bit of Sin City around if you search for it.

I was particularly interested in the shows at the big casinos and went to see several. One in particular featured a cast of incredibly good looking young men and women who sang and danced through an energetic revue. Half way through the show the women appeared topless, and with each succeeding number they seemed to wear less and less, until only small strands of rhinestones covered the essentials. I was told this is a tradition in Las Vegas shows. But what I found most entertaining was that in this production the men did the same thing.

I was sitting right by the stage and at the finale I had an excellent view up under a rhinestone loincloth worn by a disco Tarzan. He had only the thinnest g-string supporting his obviously hefty family jewels. How I longed to meet him, invite him back to my room and...

Of course, how was I to arrange that? But back at my hotel room alone, I couldn't get the image of the hot dancer out of my mind.

Earlier, in my search for the true pleasures of Vegas, I had walked down the strip in front of my hotel and bought some of the adult entertainment newspapers in the vending machines. Now, as I stretched out on my king-size bed, I picked up one of the guides. Inside was page after page of ads featuring naked women, saying they would come visit you in your own hotel. They called themselves escorts or models or nude dancers. On page five was an ad featuring a number of really attractive naked men. Their dicks were shadowed so it was impossible to really tell what they had, but they too promised to dance in your room. On a whim I decided to make a call, After all, it was a local number. What did I have to lose?

The first number I dialed, "Entertainments Unlimited," had a young woman answering the phone. I panicked and quickly hung up. But I was still curious so I picked out another number. This time a young man's voice answered. "Specialty Performers. May I help you?"

"I'd like to order a..." I hesitated.

"A T'

"Dancer." I knew I sounded stupid and naive. One never did this sort of thing back in Springfield.

"Did you want a gentleman or a lady?"

"A gentleman." Then I asked him what the dancer would do.

"Well, he'll come to your hotel room and dance for you. "In the nude?"

"Yes, he can dance totally naked but I can't say anything more over the telephone. Shall I send someone?"

"How much does this cost?"

"Only $125 for one hour of nude dancing. We accept all major credit cards."

I hung up. I was not about to pay $125 just to have some naked man dance and not even touch me! I decided I might as well masturbate while looking at the photos in the guide. At least it was better than nothing. But I was suddenly interrupted by the phone ringing. "Is this the gentleman who just phoned about dancers?" the voice asked. They must have some sort of caller ID to know the number.

"I'm the manager of our firm, sir. I understand your reluctance, but we can't really discuss everything our dancers will do over the telephone. How about I send over one of our boys and he chat with you in person and give you the full description of what he can do for you? If you don't like what you hear, you send him away."

"And I get charged $125? No thanks."

"Oh, no, sir. You only pay if you are satisfied and decide you want him to stay and entertain you. Now what sort of man do you like? Do you like muscle builders, the big brawny sort?"

"No...I..."

"How about a college preppy sort of man? I can send Tim right over. He's young and blond and has a great body." "Well..."

"He can be there in about twenty minutes."

"Okay." I hung up the phone. What had I gotten myself into? I had never hired a hustler before. This closet case from Springfield was now sitting in a hotel in Las Vegas, waiting for a nude dancer who would charge all that money to do god knows-what.

I got up and put on my dressing gown. I wasn't going to answer the door naked, no matter how anxious I was. In precisely twenty minutes there was a tap at the door. I opened it and saw a boy who introduced himself as Tim. He was about 20, had short, curly blond hair and a dazzling smile. He was dressed in very preppy designer clothes. He was cute, I had to admit, and I let him in. He sat on the chair while I sat on the bed opposite him.

"Well, let me tell you a little about our service," he said. "Frank, my manager, said you were new to this and I should go easy on you." He smiled as he opened the thin valise he carried and took out some forms and a clipboard.

"The $125 charge on your credit card is for the agency fee. That covers my coming over here. What I do beyond that is entirely up to you."

"What do you do?" I asked.

"I can do just about whatever you want, and then I charge my tip when we're finished. My tip charge depends on what we do."

"And what kind of prices are we looking at?" This was really getting to me. It sounded so technical, so business-like that I had completely lost my erection.

"Well, for example, I was just over at the next hotel with a businessman who wanted me to blow him. I did and then we kissed and I danced for him. He liked it so much he tipped me six hundred dollars."

I blinked in astonishment. Six hundred dollars! I knew this was the capital of the high rollers, but back in Springfield we have to work very hard to make six hundred dollars. "So shall we do it?" he asked.

I figured this was my once in a lifetime chance to experience sex with a professional. "Okay, but I don't think I want to spend an awful lot."

"No problem," he said, taking my VISA and writing down the number on the forms on his clipboard. He handed it to me to sign. There were two forms, one blank for his tip and one made out for $125. "This covers the agency charge," he explained and then he dialed the phone to get approval on my charge.

After the paperwork was out of the way, he asked what I would like to do. "What do you recommend?" I asked, scooting up on the bed.

"Well, I don't do anything risky," he replied, pulling a condom from the valise. "We could put this on and I could fuck you. That costs the most. Or you could suck my dick or I could suck on your dick if you don't cum in my mouth."

"Okay," I said, spreading my legs apart and parting the robe to give him access to my still-limp cock.

Tim climbed onto the bed and bent down to take me in his mouth. He was good, but I have had better, and for free. But soon my dick was hard and I was moaning with pleasure.

"Can I see you naked?" I asked. He was still dressed. This seemed to surprise him, but he stood and obediently removed his jacket, shirt and pants then climbed back on the bed in his under shorts. "What about those?" I asked, pointing to the briefs.

He smiled. "Well, I'm kind of small and I don't want to be embarrassed. Can we turn out the light?"

I reached over and flipped off the bedside lamp. There was plenty of light streaming in from the bathroom so I could see what Tim had to offer. He stood and slipped off his briefs. Seeing him in the nude was not the experience I expected. He had a nice body, firm and lean, and I supposed it would stand up to any of the nude models in the porn magazines, but I guess I just expected something more. What, I don't know.

His cock was flaccid, but it was not as small as he implied. I stroked it and it grew to a full six inches and was surrounded by a mat of dark, curly hair. I realized that his blond curls came from a bottle.

He climbed back onto the bed and began to suck me again. It felt good but I still wanted something more. I pulled him back. "You want to fuck me?" he asked.

"No," I said. "I want to suck you."

"Okay," he said and rolled over onto his back. I reached down between his legs and began to lick his balls. He had gone limp again and I wasn't getting much reaction. I then took his cock into my mouth and applied my best cocksucking techniques. Soon it began to grow again and fill my oral cavity. At the same time, Tim rolled over and took me as well. He became harder and harder as I felt myself getting closer to the edge. At the last possible moment I pulled out of him and shot my load all over my own stomach.

Tim started to sit up, as if the show was over. "No," I commanded. I want to see you come."

"But..." he began to protest.

"I want to see you do it."

"There'll be a charge ..."

"That's okay."

He dropped back on the bed and presented his wilting cock to me. I continued to suck, bringing him back to full hardness once again.. But no matter what I did, he never really got close to orgasm. I figured maybe he was just too overworked from his previous encounter that evening.

"Let me beat it for a while," he said and took his penis in his hand. He started to jack it like mad, pumping up and down and breathing hard. I thought he was about to unload several times, but he just kept working at it. Finally he asked, "Do you have any lube. Man, my dick's really starting to get sore."

"No," I said, and he spit in his hand and continued to work on it. After a while I began to grow bored and said, "You might as well go."

Tim quickly took this as a reprieve, immediately jumping up from the bed and grabbing his clothes. He darted into the bathroom to wash up and came out dressed as when I had first seen him.

"Thanks a lot," he said. "I've got to get back to the club. I left my girl friend there and she's probably wondering where I've gone, You got any gum? I wouldn't want her to smell cock on my breath." His girlfriend obviously had no idea what he was doing for a living. This astounded me. What did she think when his beeper went off and he disappeared for an hour or so? Well, I reasoned, perhaps she was hopelessly in love, never guessing her boyfriend was out making it with tourists, "How long will you be in town?" he asked.

I told him I had been there a week and was leaving tomorrow afternoon.

He handed me his card. "If you get back to Vegas again, please call me direct. That way you'll avoid the $125 agency charge."

After he had left the room, I rumpled up the card and tossed it in the wastebasket. I was disappointed. I guess I expected my first experience with a professional to be the fuck of my life. I expected him to make me feel wonderful, both physically and psychologically. I wanted to be praised and flattered. I wanted to be made to feel like I was a stud. "Well," I said to myself, "You get what you pay for." Only later did I discover my account had been charged $600 for his tip. Maybe I didn't get the fuck of my life, but I certainly did get screwed.

And on top of everything else, he never did dance for me.

BOBBY'S TAPES
Lawrence Benjamin

TAPE ONE

...Testing. Testing. Testing. One. Two. Three ....Hello? ...Is this thing working?

I'm not very comfortable talking to a machine, but this – it's a micro-cassette recorder – is a gift from my friend... Actually, it's a birthday present. And, actually, he's not my friend, he's my lover. I've never had a lover before, and he's never had a lover before who was also a hustler. So, I guess that makes us about even...

'What am I supposed to do with this?' I asked him. 'Just talk to it,' he said. 'Tell it your story.'

'Loverman,' I said, 'Like Scheherazade, I could tell you a thousand and one stories...'

'Good, then get on with it.'

Loverman is a writer, and he says the most important thing in telling a story is making the reader SEE what you're talking about, so I suppose I ought to give you an idea what I look like. I have a face that someone once said had to have been chiseled by God with high cheekbones that make me look more Indian than Puerto Rican – which is what I am, a big mouth and night eyes full of mystery beneath high, arching brows. I have broad shoulders and what Loverman calls 'a muscled blue-collar body' with a big cock you can see snaking down the leg of my pants.

Now, I suppose you want to know who I am. I could start with my name, but my given name, along with the person I was born, got left on the curb when my mother, threw me out, at age sixteen, for the last time... Since then, I think of myself as Q-Dog. Dog, for the dog that all men essentially are. I think, if I ever have a son, the first thing I will tell him is, 'Son, all men are dogs; sooner or later they all begin to bark. The only man a boy can trust is his dad' – and in my particular case, at least, Loverman.

....The Q stands for queer. So, there you have it. That's who I am: a queer dog. Although, mostly, I get called Pitch_ ...I have to get dressed now – I'm telling you this so if my voice fades in and out you'll know why. Even though it's my birthday, I have to go out because it's Thursday and, well, I'm a working boy.

I've already taken a shower, so now all I have to do is dress. "There's a secret to hustling – well, actually there's several – but this in particular has to do with cleanliness. You should always be clean, but not too clean, 'cuz guys like you to smell ...I don't mean stink, but to smell, like yourself so you leave

behind your own particular scent on their sheets or on their person. I never, EVER wear cologne for that reason.

Also, I almost never wear underwear, especially since I'm partial to sweat pants. You know what they say, 'It pays to advertise.' Of course, if I know beforehand that a trick LIKES underwear, then I'll wear it., Take my first trick for today; He's a standing order, every Tuesday and Thursday. He works in City Hall. He sits behind a big oak desk. His office has these weird glass windows that you can't really see out of; all you can see is different colored shapes moving around. His secretary sits on the other side of the glass wall and even though the door is always locked, I'm sure she knows what I'm doing there. Whenever I go there, she always touches this big old beehive hairdo that she has that's spray painted lemon yellow and says primly, 'You may go right in. You're expected,' Damn right, I'm expected! She does this this morning and as soon as I'm behind that weird glass wall, my trick is on his knees, pulling down my pants. He likes to see my cock get hard through my underwear. I don't know why, but it just about drives him wild. Within seconds, he's gnawing at my underwear, slobbering on my dick. Fortunately, he's also considerate. He always keeps extra underwear in his file cabinet so I can leave in DRY drawers, I don't know what he does with all my worn underwear, Sometimes I picture him sniffing it and beating off when I'm not around. Or maybe he sells it., Like I said, some dudes get off on guy smells.

I'm going to have to fake an orgasm. For one thing, I have several tricks lined up for today, so I can't afford to shoot a load this early in the day. Also, I'm seeing Loverman tonight, and I try to save my cum for him whenever I can. Besides, this guy gives terrible head – too many teeth!

He's slobbering all over my shorts, chewing on my cock, licking my balls, dribbling spittle down his chin. I discreetly clear my throat, coughing up some phlegm. Casually, I bring my hand to my mouth and spit into it. Holding his head by the hair, I pull out of his mouth and pass my hand over my cock, then I shove it back into his mouth. I shudder, cry out, pull out of his mouth. He swallows, wipes his mouth, never knowing what he has swallowed... trick of the trade.

Feeling slightly guilty at the deception, I place my soft cock back in his mouth and let loose a stream of piss. He drinks greedily while pumping his cock furiously. A geyser of jism arcs into the air as my stream of piss slows to a trickle against his writhing tongue. His jism's slightly yellow in color and lies on the floor like spilled custard. Still feeling guilty, I lean down and tenderly kiss his pissy mouth. He looks up and smiles. ANOTHER SATISFIED CUSTOMER!

Afterwards, his money in my pocket, I sit in the park and smoke a J. I start thinking about Loverman and that makes my dick hard. On impulse, I call him. I know he's home writing and won't answer the phone. When the

machine comes on, I say, 'Loverman, I love you.' He picks up, says, 'I love you, too.'

You can't see me, but I'm smiling, happy, even though, having told me he loves me, he's hung up.

TAPE 2

...I stood so long with that phone pressed to my ear I was almost late for my next appointment. Fortunately, he only lives across the square. He lives in this big building that has a fountain out front. Sitting in the middle is this ferocious looking stone lion whose mouth is open like he's gonna roar, only he doesn't, he just sorta vomits this green water. You should see it. It's really disgusting. I would never live in a place that had such a disgusting fountain in front of it...

Anyway, I'm getting sidetracked, 'babbling,' as Loverman would say. I don't mean to...

....It's kinda hard remembering everything as it happened even though it was only a short time ago. My memory's not too good. Loverman says it's because I don't much use my head. He says your brain is like any other muscle in your body--you have to use it regularly if you want to keep it in good shape. I guess, at least I won't ever have to worry about my dick going to pot.

...Someone asked me once if my dick had a name. Why would I name my dick? That seems pretty stupid. I mean, it would be like naming an arm or a leg. It would be too alienating, like it didn't really belong to me at all, like having a dog and naming it Rover, then one day he could run away, Or get run over – SPLAT! – chasing a car or the neighbor's cat. I don't want my dick getting run over and going SPLAT!

...Anyway, like I said, I was late so when I finally got there John was already naked. He was laying on these black sheets kinda strokin' his dick which was only half-hard. I got undressed right away and got into bed next to him. He doesn't like to kiss or anything, so we got right to it. I straddled him with my back to him and leaned on my elbows, my ass in the air so that he got a clear view of my tanned bubble-butt. His dick was wobbling around in the air just below my face, so I swatted it with my open hand like it was a fly or something, It suddenly got hard and swung into the air, bumping my chin. I slapped it again. It got harder, the head flushing red. Behind me John groaned and grabbing the inside of my thighs he pulled me towards him until my ass plopped squarely on his face. I could feel his tongue tracing my asscrack, circling the rim of my hole. His tongue felt really good there, and I pushed back against his face and felt his tongue dart up my hole. I was holding his balls in my fist and could feel them tightening. I reached out and slapped his dick with my free hand: one... twice... again. He was moaning, his mouth tight against my manhole, sucking.

I used to have a trick who liked me to punch him in the balls. I used to giggle every time I did it – it just seemed so ridiculous, but that used to piss him off, so I finally had to stop it and control myself. Now I reached out and flicked his imprisoned balls with my finger. He started really groaning and thrashing around on the bed. I pushed my ass harder against his face to get more of his tongue and I wondered if maybe he wouldn't suffocate with my big ass on his face like that.

....He was saying something, but of course the words just got swallowed up by my asshole, like his tongue. I was really hitting him hard now, slapping the mess out of his dick, squeezing his balls, occasionally biting the head of his dick. He really started thrashing around now, like he was having a seizure or something. I was still biting the head of his dick when he fired a load of jism against my teeth. I pulled my head back and he shot another wad this time hitting me in the face so that huge gobs of semen were running down my face, falling from my chin onto his stomach. I thought that was really hot and now my dick was really hard and I had to fight hard to keep from cumming myself: Finally I got control of myself and rolled off him. He lay on his back, his face looking red and tender from where my ass had sat on it. He was gulping air, his mouth sucking as if my asshole was still there. He looked like a fish out of water does, kissing nothing, trying to breathe...

He must have really enjoyed himself, because when he paid me, he tipped me an extra twenty and asked me to call him later in the week.

I have a few hours to kill before my next trick, so I go by the block, figuring to hang out for awhile and maybe I'll get picked up and make a few extra bucks. Kinda like overtime. I know most people don't think of hustling as a job, but it is. Hey, if I don't work, I don't get paid, same as anybody else, except maybe city workers.

...Sometimes, when I have extra money, I take my mom flowers, especially on her birthday and Mother's Day. On Sundays, I take my dad a six-pack of beer. Sometimes when he hasn't seen me in a while he'll call me up and say, 'How ya doin', son? Still hustlin' them faggots?' And we'll both laugh, because Dad, well, when he was a lot younger, he used to do the same thing. So, I guess you can say I'm following in my father's footsteps, sorta going into the family business...

Sometimes, though, I think about quitting, even though I make pretty good money. I have some clothes – and not just work clothes either, which are mostly tight jeans and T-shirts and sweats, which is what I mostly wear, like I said. I have a coupla suits and some nice shoes. Most hustlers I know, for some reason, only wear sneakers...

And I have a place to live. Most hustlers don't, they all sorta hang out on the street or crash with a trick until he gets tired of them and then it's back to the street. Not me. I have a room. It's not much, but it's mine_ And I have a

stereo and TAI and Nintendo. So, I can always go home and kick back and listen to some music and smoke a joint or drink a beer.

I realize I'm daydreaming and should be working, so I go back to posing and acting interested in every man who walks by when all I really want is to be with Loverman...

The other working boys notice me and start acting competitive. Loverman calls them 'angels,' 'A confederacy of Angels,' he says.

.,.I've seen this one angel who I think is really hot. He's really cute and I start thinking about how great it would be to fuck him, but then I thought about Loverman, and suddenly it doesn't seem so great anymore...

I start thinking about quitting again. I guess I first started thinking about quitting after I met Loverman" Once, in bed with him, it occurred to me that we weren't having sex, which is what I have all the time. It was something else. I mean, the moves were the same, but there was all this FEELING. I remember thinking that maybe what we were doing was MAKING LOVE...When I first met him, I had sold him my body, which hadn't surprised him. What I did that night was make him a present of my heart. That had surprised us both.

– Like I said, what I really wanted to do was see Loverman, so that's just what I did, picked up my big cock and went home.

TAPE 3

The first thing I do when I walk in the door is go to the kitchen and get two beers out of the fridge, then I go upstairs and Loverman's standing in front of the mirror in a sky-blue baseball cap, naked as the day he was born, He turns around. 'You're home early.' I could only nod and stare at him, he's so beautiful. The hair on his chest starts at the edges of his shoulders and spreads over his chest and down his belly where it narrows to a V. His nipples are big and very pink, For some reason, the hair on his chest reminds me of a wolfs head, his outrageous nipples, the wolf's red eyes. There's a spot on each of his hips by his pelvis, where there's no hair. The skin there is so white and soft, I could cry, Instead I kneel and kiss him on each hip. The bottles of B fall from my hands and I hold the half-moons of his ass, feeling the hairs there. I sometimes tell him that one day I'm going to braid it, there's so much hair there. I lay him gently on the floor and go to the basin and fill a glass with warm water. Then I get a dildo and drop it into the glass to warm it. I lay down next to him and take his cock in my mouth. It stiffens and I slowly draw it between my lips. He mumbles my name. His hands are tangled in my hair. I start licking his body, moving towards his chest. I suck on his nipples. His hands are still tangled in my hair. I bite a nipple until his blood fills my mouth. I slide down his body and lifting his legs in the air, I slide the warm dildo into his waiting hole. I pull it out, then push it back in, feeling him open up to

accept my gift. His hands fall to his side, clutching the carpet. His head rolls from side to side. I work him over with the dildo using a slow steady rhythm like I know he likes. The lube starts to melt and runs down the crack of his ass over my hand. My dick is so hard it feels like its gonna bust. I really wanna fuck him, but I force myself to wait. He's so excited his dick is standing straight up in the air and is dripping pre-cum like a leaky faucet...

When I finally slip inside him, it's a feeling like you get when you go home after you've been away a long time...

Inside he is warm and slippery, I guess from the K-Y, and I don't want to come – EVER. I just want to stay here moving slowly in and out of him, so I try to hold back, I practice my exercises. When I finally come, it's like the fireworks I saw once, on the Fourth of July. Only it wasn't all dark and scary afterwards..

I've been lying here with my head on his chest for a long time, the hairs tickling my ear. 'I'm thinking about retiring,' I say, 'from hustling, I mean. Whaddaya think?'

'I think that would be swell,' he says.

'I could learn to do something else – to earn money I mean, like get a real job.'

' I think you could, Pitch,' he says.

'Bobby,' I say. 'My name is Bobby.'

' I love you, Bobby,' he says.

I just smile, smile so hard my face hurts...

MATTHEW:
ONE OF LENNY'S BOYS
A Complete Novel
By Michael Taylor

PREFACE

It was the giddy, glorious Seventies, when everyone did everything to everyone, in every imaginable combination, and it seemed as if the whole planet was in heat.

We were in Manhattan, global capital of carefree copulation, and we were young and beautiful – and going to stay that way forever.

Oh yes, the stock market went to hell, the government was a mess, inflation was fifteen per cent, and sometimes people had to wait in line for an hour and a half to buy gasoline for their cars, but none of that touched us: We were Lenny's boys.

ONE

"There ain't enough cots," Lenny shouted, "let him sleep with you, Michael." The Master had spoken and retreated behind the locked door of his room.

I took the new boy, dressed only in his underpants, into my bed, a double-size cot with a thin mattress on its curled-wire web. He was reed-thin and didn't take up much space as I covered us with the dingy white sheet. He lay his blond head down carefully and I looked into his large, Windex-blue eyes, seeing fear and confusion. "He kept you in there longer than anybody so far, but you're safe now," I said, gently patting him on the top of the head. I'd caught a brief glimpse of him the week before when Lenny brought him to the large, open space we called home, a one-time sweat shop on the second floor of an otherwise-abandoned warehouse building in downtown Manhattan. We were all sitting in the front of the room watching "The Brady Bunch" on TV when Lenny brought him in the front door and, with his arm draped over the kid's shoulder, steered him into his private chamber. There the boy stayed, undergoing the initiation we had all somehow survived: the hours of brainwashing, the degradation of being enslaved, doing whatever Lenny wanted, all so that we would be the best callboys in the city.

"What's your name?" I asked. My new bedmate was staring at the ceiling.

"Matthew," he said meekly.

"You can relax, man," I told him, rolling over, my naked back to him "I won't bother you."

A few moments later he was whispering in my ear, "Michael, will you hold me?" I looked over my shoulder. He was trembling. I took him in my arms.

"It's okay, kid. It'll get better."

"I know," he said, and slipped his thumb into his mouth and sucked like a newborn child as he stared out into space, holding me tightly.

Lenny had already given us our shots and the five other boys were now asleep. I lay my head on top of Matthew's and closed my eyes, The drug was finally taking its effect.

The next day, we stood before Lenny in his room as he sat sideways in his armchair beside the unmade double bed. Wearing just his boxer shorts, he was attractive in a brutish sort of way – over six feet tall, with broad shoulders, a massive, hairy chest, and a trim waist. He wore his black hair cut short and his nose was hawk-like. "You'll listen to Michael," he instructed Matthew, his dark eyes dancing. "You'll stay with him and do what he says. Understand?"

Matthew nodded, staring at the floor, but that was not satisfactory to Lenny. He stood abruptly, causing Matthew to tense and pull back in fear.

"Well, do you understand?"

Matthew focused is moist eyes on him and nodded.

"That's better." Lenny smiled at me. "You've got your work cut out for you," he said, "but you'll enjoy it."

"Yes, sir."

Chuckling, he went to his desk, tore a piece of paper from a pad, and handed it to me. "And just two hours, not a minute more, understand? I may have another one for you later."

Nodding, I looked at the paper. He always wrote the address down for us, along with the time we were to be there and leave. With a nod of his head, Lenny dismissed us, and as we left the room, the phone was ringing again.

It was early October and there was a chill in the air. As I zipped my sweatshirt jacket shut, I asked Matthew, "So how'd you come to meet Lenny?"

"He kinda found me. I was hangin' out around Grand Central and he was watchin' me."

"And he took you for a nice meal," I said.

Matthew looked at me in astonishment. "Yeah."

I smiled. "And he treated you real nice, huh? Told you he'd get you some nice clothes and give you a job, right?" "Yeah."

"Why you out?"

"'I wasn't gettin' along with my mother's boyfriend. He started up another fight with me.., this time he threw me out." "Your mother knew?"

"She was standin' right there. She saw him beatin' on me. She didn't do nothin', man. She just stood there watchin'. She don't give a shit" Another devoted mother, I thought. "I was just in their way all the time anyhow."

"You try to go back?"

"I stayed out two weeks" He grimaced and hung his head sadly. "When I went back, they were gone."

'Tough," I said, remembering the terrible moment six months after my mother delivered me to him that Lenny told me she wouldn't be back for me.

Matthew wiped his nose with a finger. "Some strange lady answered the door where we lived. She said she didn't know my mother. She said she lived there now. So I went to the super, and he was surprised to see me. He thought they took me with them, down south he said. So I hitched here. Then Lenny found me."

I knew the rest. I pointed down Hudson Street. "We gotta go down here."

"What're they gonna do to us?"

"You never know."

I matched the address on the paper with the number on the door and tucked it back into the front pocket of my bellbottoms. "This is the place."

We climbed the creaking stairs to the top, then a door opened and we went inside. Matthew was close behind me. We followed the man – in his forties, balding, pudgy – down a long, narrow hallway and he smiled over his shoulder at us, "Want something to drink?"

"Yeah," I answered. Not all of them were so nice. Some liked to socialize first, treating you like a guest, offering chips and beer or wine, playing music. Others thought of you simply as a service they'd paid good money for, and they needed no warm-up, they got right down to business.

He held the door open for us. Camera equipment and lights were set up around a large bed. "Relax," the man said, "make yourselves comfortable." He extended an arm toward the wicker chair with a high, round back in a corner next to a fichus tree. "You can put your things over there. I'll get the drinks." Before leaving the room, he paused to look us over. "I told Lenny young and innocent and he came through for me this time."

"We're the youngest," I said, unzipping my sweatshirt.

Matthew was trembling again, watching me. "And he's the newest."

The man looked at Matthew closely. "Is he gonna be all right?"

I nodded and took Matthew's hand. "This is his first time." "Oh, how nice," the man beamed. "Okay. I'll get the drinks."

I started unbuttoning Matthew's shirt for him. "Hey, come on, man, this is gonna be an easy one. We lucked out! He just wants to take our pictures." After I helped him pull his jacket off, he managed to get down to just his jeans but made no attempt to remove them,, I reached for the snap and

he stopped me. "Shit, this guy's not gonna hurt us. You got through Lenny, his guy's gonna be a cinch compared to that."

Lenny spent two days with me in the locked room before he actually put his dick in my mouth. The sex was secondary with Lenny. Getting you hooked on the drugs was the important part; once he'd done that, the rest followed.

Matthew still refused to give up his jeans. "You either do what this guy says or you get beaten when you get back to Lenny's. You don't have much of a choice."

"He looks strange to me."

"They're all strange, one way or another. I'm sure he'll be fine."

just then the man returned to the room carrying a jug of red wine and three glasses. He smiled when he saw me naked but looked puzzled that Matthew still had his jeans on.

"He's just a bit nervous."

"Yeah, you said it was his first."

"Yeah.

"Okay,' he said, "just sit down."

Matthew sat next to me on the bed. The man put a glass in Matthew's hand, another in mine and poured.

"This'll warm you up," he said.

Matthew gulped the wine and the man, who now introduced himself as Shaw, poured him another.

Shaw sipped his wine as he set about adjusting the lights. It was soon very warm in the room and Matthew was sweating. "Hey, take your jeans off, man," I whispered, finishing my glass of wine.

Getting more relaxed by the moment, Matthew nodded and stood up, unsnapped his jeans and stepped out of them. He still had his underpants on.

Shaw posed Matthew first, snapping the shutter of the big camera on a tripod as he ordered Matthew to stretch, turn around, sit back down on the bed, lean back, smile, pout, rub his hairless chest.

As Shaw fussed over Matthew, I sat in the wicker chair and watched them. It didn't look as if Matthew minded his seduction one bit.

"You're a natural born model," Shaw said as he fixed the straight blond hair lying on Matthew's brow. The boy's face was angelic: round and soft, with his lovely eyes giving him a wistfully sad appearance.

Shaw eventually managed to get Matthew's underpants off of him and sucked on the rather small but thick, uncut cock for several minutes until it was hard. I poured another glass of wine for myself and sat back down in the chair stroking my swelling penis.

Shaw looked up and saw I was hard. He lifted himself off Matthew and came over to me, dropping down on the floor between my outstretched thighs. He blew me for a few moments while I finished my glass of wine, then

ordered Matthew to suck my cock. I stood up and went over to the bed. Matthew scrambled over to me and as soon as he took my cock in his mouth I realized Lenny had trained him well. Or maybe he was just a natural born cocksucker as well as a model.

Shaw was beaming as he watched Matthew feverishly give me head and he switched to a handheld camera and began snapping away once more, zooming in for many close-ups.

Finally Shaw stopped to reload his cameras and instructed me to get on the bed with Matthew and fuck him. Here again, Lenny had done a great job in training his youthful charge. Smiling, Matthew got into position on his stomach and lifted the firm, luscious mounds of his ass. Shaw moved the tripod closer to the bed in order to capture the entry from a high angle. And what an entry it was – I hadn't had anything that tight in months. My cock, which is a more than respectable seven inches, cut, with a fairly large head, quickly found a home deep inside Matthew. He surprised me by reaching back and spreading his asscheeks wider apart so as to take all of me down to the pubic hairs.

Shaw kept sighing, "Oh yeah," over and over as I plunged in and out of Matthew. Matthew only whimpered a couple of times when I slipped out and roughly slammed back in.

"When you're ready," Shaw pleaded, "pull out so I can get it on film."

I nodded and did just that, my load shooting all over Matthew's back. Shaw was right on top of me, getting it all in close-ups.

"You can get dressed now," Shaw said, stepping away from us. When Matthew climbed off the bed, I saw that he had come without even touching himself.

When we got home, Lenny called me into his room and shut the door. "So how was the new kid?"

"He's good," I said quite nonchalantly.

"Ain't he though," Lenny sneered.

"Yeah," I muttered.

"I told you you'd enjoy it. But don't worry," he said, snaking an arm over my shoulders, "he's got a long way to go before he catches up to you."

After he gave me my shot, he told me to bring Matthew in. I found Matthew dozing on the mattress, sleepy from all the wine he'd drunk. Grinning, Lenny came out, took up his arm, found a vein, injected the drug, then disappeared back into his room.

The next afternoon, I woke to a hand gently sliding up my back to my neck. I opened my eyes and turned my head to find Matthew's face in mine, smiling. I didn't smile back. I didn't smile very much, or very easily, in general. I closed my eyes and turned onto my back so he'd have to stop rubbing it, but this only served to start him rubbing my stomach, playing with

the hairs that had just begun to sprout on my nipples, and working his way down to the crotch.

"Stop," I said, and he did, while continuing to smile at me with his head tilted slightly.

"Leave me alone," I snapped, rolling over. He got up and went to sit on the couch in the front of the room, next to two of the boys who were watching a re-run of "Hawaii Five-O."

I didn't want Matthew thinking he could get close to me now that we'd had sex together. I sat up, shaking myself awake, and noticed that he was watching me rather than the 'TV. He giggled when I got up and, with my piss-hard-on poking out of my boxer shorts, went to the bathroom. I was standing at the toilet pissing when the door opened slowly. I turned my head to see Matthew grinning at me.

"Can't anybody have any privacy around here?" I screamed, pushing him out and slamming the door.

A few minutes later, Lenny came home and dropped one bag of hamburgers on the coffee table and took another to his room where he'd eat while returning the calls that had come in his absence. With the number of times the phone had rung, I knew it would be a busy night.

Dinner from McDonald's was a treat. Normally, Lenny would have the deli down the street deliver. He had an account and, once a month, a couple of us would go to the home of the deli's owner, Bernie, and settle up. Sometimes it would take several of us a couple of days to work off the debt but it was always paid in full.

In the area just outside Lenny's office, two couches and two overstuffed armchairs were placed in front of the television and we called it our theater. Sitting in the armchair, I glanced to my left to see Matthew on one of the couches nibbling on his cheeseburger and occasionally dipping into the bag of French fries tucked between his hairless thighs. I thought he looked like a child, maybe ten years old at best, sitting between two other boys who could easily have been his school buddies, happy and content.

On Matthew's right was Danny, a slight, quiet kid who, like me, pretty much kept to himself. With his open face and thick, wavy blond hair and brown eyes, he looked like the kind of wholesome boy you could picture playing baseball in front of a nice little house with a picket fence, with a little dog running about his feet.

On Matthew's left was Jeff, the oldest; he'd been with Lenny the longest and was Lenny's trump card when it came to paying off the deli. Lenny would deliberately stall on sending Jeff until Bernie couldn't take it any more and then Jeff would go over and settle the account. Jeff was tall, with a swimmer's build and long black hair cut into wild, full layers, making him look like he belonged in a rock band. He always wore boots and black or leather jeans, skin-tight on his long, thin legs. His eyes were still smeared with

black eyeliner from the night before. He stared quietly at the TV while munching an onion ring which dangled off of his index finger. Every now and then he'd glance at Matthew, looking at him as if he was planning on giving him some advanced training of his own.

On the other couch were the other three boys which completed Lenny's current group: the two Jimmys and Ralph, Ralph was Any Boy, just another pleasant but plain face in the crowd at the schoolyard or in an assembly, pledging allegiance to the flag. Everything about him was Medium: his brown hair, his brown eyes, his weight, his height, and, I knew from first-hand experience, his ass and his cock. Medium Ralph.

One Jimmy had shiny copper-color hair with eyes to match. The other Jimmy had dark brown hair and light blue eyes, a stocky build and adorable dimples in each cheek when he smiled. They were inseparable. Only when Lenny sent them out on different calls were they alone, and when they returned they would go to the bathroom and fuck.

Finally Lenny came out to give us our assignments. "You gotta be there by seven," Lenny told Danny, "seven o'clock sharp. Understand?"

Danny nodded, folding the paper into his shirt pocket.

Lenny moved past Matthew to Jeff, who just kept watching the tube. "You gotta meet a guy at Washington Square at ten thirty. Stand under the arch." Lenny handed Jeff his piece of paper. "It's all written down." Jeff took it from him without a word spoken.. "And fix that eyeliner."

He turned to the two Jimmys and handed each a piece of paper, then took each piece back, looked them over, switched them, and handed them back. "That's yours and that's yours."

I was next and as he handed me the address, he snickered, "You'll have fun again tonight Michael. This guy wants both you babies." Matthew turned his attention away from the TV to smile at me.

On his way back to his room, Lenny paused to look at Danny, who was still eating "You gotta move your ass, kid.

Seven sharp! It's all the way up town. By the time you get back, I'll have another call for you. Get going."

Danny shoved the rest of his burger into his mouth and headed for the bathroom. As Lenny slammed the door to his room behind him, I glanced at Matthew; he was staring at me, with a big grin on his face.

Danny was the first to leave; grabbing his denim jacket, he dashed out the door.

At one point, with a moan, Jeff stretched on the couch beside Matthew. Matthew stared at the huge bulge at his crotch. "What the fuck you lookin' at?"

"L.." Matthew's eyes went to Jeff's ear. "I like your earring." Jeff laughed. "My earring?"

Matthew nodded.

"Yeah, you'll get yours," he said, standing up and adjusting his basket. As he went to the bathroom, Matthew looked at me, puzzled. I ignored him and ate my hamburger. When the Two Jimmys left together, Matthew came to sit next to me on the other couch.

"I'm gonna get an earring?" he asked.

I nodded without looking at him as I chewed my last French fry.

He examined my earlobe, searching for a hole. "You got one?"

I nodded and he continued to search.

"Other ear," I said. He hopped up and swung around to my right side, pushed my hair up gently and, looking closely, found the pierce hole

"Where 's the earring?"

"Pocket."

"Why don't you wear it?"

"Don't like it. I only wear it when Lenny notices I don't have it on and tells me to."

"Why don't you like it?"

"It's stupid," I said.

Jeff came back in the room with his face scrubbed and his eyeliner neatly re-applied, His hair was brushed, fluffed out like a lion's mane, framing his square face. He pulled on his black leather jacket while looking down at Matthew, who was again staring at Jeff's crotch,.

"You're hot for me, ain't ya?" Jeff asked, groping himself, Matthew lowered his eyes and shook his head.

"I'll baby-sit ya, kid," Jeff said, taking Matthew's head in his hand and pushing it into his crotch. "Hey, Michael, give him to me, I'll show him what's what."

"Go to work, Jeff," I said. "Lenny told me to watch him."

"Babies watchin' babies. I'd break him in real good,` Jeff laughed, letting go of Matthew's head and ruffling his tousled hair.

I gathered up the hamburger wrappers strewn about and stuffed them into the white paper bag. "Fuckin' slobs," I mumbled, feeling Matthew's eyes on me. "Got enough damned roaches around this place ..." I took the trash to the kitchen and pushed it into the pail, which was in need of emptying but I didn't feel like doing it.

"Where do we have to go tonight?" Matthew said, following me.

"Lenny wants you to get some decent clothes." Lenny seemed to know somebody in every business who was willing to barter. Jacob's office was in the garment district and he was always willing to outfit a new boy in exchange for a blowjob. Jacob was delighted to see Matthew and they disappeared behind a closed door for fifteen minutes. When Matthew came out, he had four new outfits in a bag m and a big grin on his face. Jacob remembered me and asked if I needed anything. "Not now," I said. "Thanks. We're on our way to see somebody."

"Of course. Well, you know where to find me, Michael." He patted my ass as I left the office.

"Easy, right?" I asked Matthew as we walked along. He was still smiling, clutching the bag to his chest.

"Yeah, real easy."

"You didn't come for him, did you?"

"No."

"Good. It might be a long night."

I was silent for several minutes, which seemed to bother Matthew.. "You don't like bein' stuck with me, do you?" he asked finally.

"It's just that I'd rather work alone."

"Didn't you like last night?"

I gave him a sidelong glance.

He smiled. "We make a good team."

"I'm not on any team," I said. "I got no one."

He frowned. "We could be friends."

"I got no friends. Friends are just people who tell you one

thing and then fuck you over when you turn your back." "It's okay, nothing new," he whispered under his breath. "Look, I don't dislike you. I just don't know you is all." "Well, we got it on pretty good last night, didn't we? That's gotta say something 'bout us ..."

"What happened doesn't mean anything, okay?" I snapped, "That wasn't my choice. Last night happened 'cause it was our job. It was just business."

"You didn't like it?" he asked.

"No, not really. "

He fell silent and I wished I hadn't said it with such finality. Of course I liked it – I loved it, in fact. Who wouldn't have loved it, but I just couldn't let him know that.

We took a bus uptown, getting off in a neighborhood of neat brownstones. I still found it amazing that so-called respectable people who lived in such expensive places would call on a low-life like Lenny and hire a couple of drug-addicted babies to satisfy their hunger.

A short, paunchy man in his late fifties who said his name was Paul let us into his home. There was no offer of drinks or food; he acted as if he was in a rush, saying he had a friend waiting in the guest bedroom who had to "catch a flight to L.A."

We entered the bedroom and the friend was lying on the bed with a sheet covering his body up to the waist. He looked somehow familiar, as if I had seen him on television. "They sent two," Paul said.

"I'm only paying for one,"

"I know, but they travel together. Seems the little blond here is still in training."

"Still in diapers, eh?" The man smiled wickedly. "Well, he's perfect. You keep the other one busy."

Paul offered me a Coke. I suggested something a bit stronger He brought out the rum and added it to the Coke and we sat in the living room drinking together. "You sure I couldn't do anything for you?" I suggested, letting my hand drop to his thigh.

"No, I only called the service because of Christopher. He has so little time to find anyone and even now he's rushed."

Just then we heard Christopher hollering from the bedroom. "Paul, get this little shit outta here."

We went to the bedroom to find Matthew already on his way out the door, buttoning up his pants.

Christopher was kneeling on the bed, the sheet wrapped around his waist. "Little shit couldn't come. He said he'd just come on his way over here!"

I looked at Matthew, but he ignored me, heading for the door. "Matthew," I shouted after him, "wait there in the living room with Paul while I take care of Christopher."

Paul shut the door behind me and I advanced toward Christopher.

"You've got a lot more training to do ..." the man said.

"And you're in a hurry," I said, opening my pants. I stood next to the bed and made him lean over to get it. My erection throbbed as he began kissing it.

"Oh," he moaned, "this is such a nice one. This is what I come to New York for."

If what he wanted was for me to come in a hurry, I was not going to disappoint him. It seemed all I had to do now was think of Matthew so willingly spreading his asscheeks and I could come.

Even after I'd shot my load down his throat, Christopher didn't want to give it up. He kept sucking, licking, nibbling. Finally, Paul was pounding on the door saying the limo had arrived. The limo, I thought. It seemed every time I met a john who had a limo he was always in a hurry.

As soon as we were out of the building, I pushed Matthew into the first dark corner I could find. Grabbing him by the throat, I said, "Don't you ever lie to me again."

"I'm sorry. I didn't think it would make any difference whether I came or not. I can come seven times a day if I want. It's just that that man was all teeth and it hurt."

"I don't give a shit. What matters is that you lied to me." I began banging his head against the brick wall. His bag of clothes dropped to the ground and he tried to push me away but I overpowered him.

"Don't hurt me," he cried.

"Sonofabitch!" I backed off, feeling he'd gotten the message. As we continued on, I said, "You've lucked-out so far, but this can't last."

And it didn't. The next night, the man who hired us was not respectable and refined. He said his name was Buck and, after giving me the $200 fee, he brought us to a darkened room at the back of a large loft in the Village. Awaiting us where two other men, even more menacing. When they saw Matthew, they grabbed him and began pawing him. Matthew fought back and they started slapping him. I tried to intervene, but Buck held me. Matthew fell down and tried to crawl away but one of the men put his boot on Matthew's head and held him. Matthew cried out. This was too much even for Buck. "Hey, that's enough. He'll do what ya want,.." He knelt down to Matthew. "Won't ya, boy?"

Matthew, crying now, nodded.

"Good. You two take care of the other one, I'll handle this one.

The two advanced toward me, backing me into the wall. They pushed me down to my knees and hauled out their cocks. One was hard and oozing pre-cum; the other was getting there, but it took some work.. I alternated between them and by the time one had come, the other was ready,

After I swallowed both their loads, they stepped away and I looked across the room to see Buck had Matthew naked and was giving him a standing fuck. Matthew was hanging on to a big chest of drawers; his face was turned away from me and he was sobbing. The two other men walked over to them and began stroking their limp cocks as they watched Buck roughly slam in and out of Matthew. "Tightest damn whore we've had," Buck snarled. "You guys gotta have some of this."

It didn't take long for the two of them to get hard again and they began taking turns. For a few minutes I was ignored, but then they wanted me over there, kneeling, sucking each of them as they pulled out of Matthew and waited their next turn. Finally Buck came and another one came while I was sucking him. The third man finished in Matthew and they left us alone. I helped Matthew get dressed and, without a word, Buck handed me a $100 bill tip as he let us out of the apartment.

"Lenny'll be glad you got a tip," I told Matthew, sliding the bill into my pocket. "It was you, you know. They said they'd never had a tighter ass."

"Why don't we keep it?"

"I'll admit you earned it, but if Lenny ever finds out you're holding back on him, you're finished. I'll tell him it was your tip."

When we got home, Lenny put his hand to Matthew's chin and studied the bruise on his cheek. Matthew stared at his sneakers.

"Rough bunch," Lenny said, going to his desk to prepare our shots. He glanced at me. "How'd he do otherwise?" I shrugged. "Fine. He got a tip."

Lenny counted the bills I had laid on his desk. "Nice. I'll put it away for his college education."

After Lenny shot us up, we settled onto the mattress together. Matthew laid his head on my shoulder and, after asking my permission only with his eyes, he laid his head on my chest and began sucking his thumb, I let him stay that way. I gently brushed the hair from his eyes and kissed the bruise on his cheek. He smiled, then closed his eyes and welcomed sleep.

TWO

"That photographer wants you kids back," Lenny said after he called me into his room. "He was very pleased with you. He said you look good together."

"Lenny," I said softly, "when you gonna send him out on his own?"

"Why?"

I shrugged. "You said I only had to show him around his first week. He's ready to go out on his own." I didn't want to admit to Lenny that what was really bothering me was seeing Matthew getting brutally fucked by someone else.

"Didn't you hear what I said? You work well together. Everyone's happy with the two of you_ And don't you tell me you don't enjoy him."

"Yeah, I enjoy him, but ..."

"No, I'm keepin' you together."

I bowed my head.

"You got a problem with that?"

I shook my head.

He laughed. "Good. You know I'm gettin' damn good money for the two of you together, I'm sellin' you as a package, like the two Jimmys. Guys dig watching them make love to each other, just like they like watchin' you two. It's a good gimmick. Besides, Matthew would fuck up. He'd get lost or something. He looks so fuckin' innocent, someone'd jump him on the streets all alone and I'd never see him again. I need you to watch out for him."

"But -

"You hear?"

"Yes."

"Good," he said, sitting on the bed and pulling me down next to him. He began rubbing the back of my neck. "You're the best, you know that."

"No, I don't."

"Oh yes, you do. You're smarter'n you let on. You're a man in a boy's body; the best combination." I felt his hot breath on my neck, his mouth on my shoulders, licking, kissing, nibbling. Finally he pushed me back on the bed, his sweaty hands all

over me. "I got a prize when I got you."

It was true. I did my best for him; I was strangely fulfilled when I knew he was satisfied because of me.

Now he got into position, straddling my head and undoing his trousers. He cupped my head in his hands and brought it over the massive head of his penis. It was a stubby cock but the head made up for it. I could barely get it in my mouth. Before long he had raised up and was hovering over me, jamming it in my mouth, down my throat. His pubic hairs tickled my nostrils. He was horny and came quickly. I tried to swallow it all so as not to disappoint him.

"Damn you're good," he said, lifting off me, panting. "Nobody sucks a dick like you do. Not even Matthew. Now go take him to the photographer."

As I unlocked the door and stepped out, Matthew was just dropping to the couch, his eyes on the television.

"Come on," I said, "we got our assignment. Let's go."

He got up and came over to me. He lifted a finger to wipe away some cum from the corner of my mouth. He giggled and I realized that he'd been listening at Lenny's door.

Later, as we walked across town, he said, "You're Lenny's favorite, aren't you?"

"No, Jeff is. But sometimes ..."

"You please him."

"I try."

"I want to please him too," he said.

The poor kid was determined to fit in.

Lenny's door opened and he called Matthew and me to come into his room. "Sit," he said, smiling as he shut and locked his door. "Your photographer friend was mighty pleased again." He stood in front of us, sitting at the edge of the bed, and put a hand on each of our heads. "Tell me," he said, "just what the fuck is it that you two do?" Matthew smiled up at Lenny and lifted his hands to settle on Lenny's crotch. "You're a fast learner, Matthew," he said as Matthew unbuckled his belt and unzipped the fly. He smiled at me. "Yeah, Michael's the best damn teacher ..."

"I had nothin' to do with it," I said. "You taught him everything he knows."

"I just need to be reminded every once in awhile," Lenny said as his cock grew stiff in Matthew's grip.

I moved closer and fondled Lenny's hairy balls while Matthew sucked. We alternated, kissing, licking, sucking until Lenny was holding our heads tightly. After awhile, he pulled away and said, "That's not all you do." Matthew and I looked at each other. "Let's see the rest. Show me all of it."

Matthew reached over and touched my hard-on. His eyes half-closed, mouth half-opened. I opened my pants and Matthew took my cock out and began sucking. He spent a few moments applying his tongue to the underside

of my penis, then got it all sopping wet. He stood up, pushed down his pants and bent over. This was the moment Lenny had been waiting for; he stood over us, jerking his semi-flaccid cock as I entered Matthew. Soon he was hard and ready to come again. He stepped closer so that his jism splattered on Matthew's ass and rolled down between the cheeks where my cock was going in and out. I started breathing deeply and Lenny pushed me out of Matthew. "Save it," he said. "You guys have work to do tonight. Don't waste it."

"I can come again," I cried, refusing to stop. My load joined Lenny's on Matthew's backside.

"You better, or there'll be no shot, understand?"

Sliding my cock into my jeans, I nodded.

We left Lenny's room and told the Two Jimmys they were next. "Look out," I said, "Lenny's horny as hell tonight."

"I told you we made a good team," Matthew said as we walked to Shaw's once again.

I smiled coyly.

"Still rather work alone?"

I said nothing.

"I like doin' you, Michael."

"You like doin' everyone," I said, and he hit me playfully. I hit him right back.

When we'd finished our routine at Shaw's, this time with Matthew on his back so the man could get both our loads in one shot, Shaw handed us a large manila envelope.

"Give this to Lenny, will you? He asked me for some prints." He walked us to the door. "See you boys next week," he said, and we left. Up the block we stopped at the corner under a street light and Matthew pulled the envelope out from under my arm.

"What are you doin'?"

He opened the envelope and slid out several 8x10, black and white glossies of us together in several different positions. "Oh, man ..." he gushed, wrenching his neck to get a better look. "I wanna keep one," he said, a gleam in his eye.

"Better not," I warned.

"I want this one, with your cock on my cheek."

"Lenny'll find out and be pissed."

"He won't find out," Matthew said, unable to take his eyes from the pictures,

"Come on, you better not. Anyhow, where'll you keep something like that anyway?"

"I'll find a place." He looked at me defiantly, then returned to the picture of my erection caressing his cheek. "I want this one."

I grimaced. "Come on, let's go."

He slid the photos back into the envelope, hanging on to the one he claimed. "You're gonna get us in trouble."

He held the picture for several minutes, stopping every few feet to look at it again. "Okay," he said finally, handing it to me. I slid it in with the others. "But I'm gonna ask Lenny if I can have one." We picked up our pace for home. "And if he says no, I'm gonna ask the photographer for my own copy."

I just shook my head. "Yeah, well while you're at it you better ask for a smaller size, I don't need this stuff lying around for other boys to see."

He smiled. "Well, we do look good together, don't we?" I didn't bother answering him.

When we got back home, Jeff was at Lenny's closed door and the other boys were trying to sleep.

"Come on, man," Jeff whined, "I can't wait no more please, man." For some reason, Lenny was withholding his shot, teaching him a lesson, Jeff's habit was a bad one, and Lenny let him suffer. Jeff wiped his nose and sweaty face as he shuffled back and forth in front of the locked door, hunching his body forward ever so slightly.

I left Matthew sitting on the couch and approached Lenny's door. I knocked. "Lenny," I said.

I got no answer.

"Hey, Lenny," Jeff said, "it's one of your babies! Yeah, your babies are back."

The door opened slightly and as soon as Lenny saw me, he let me in. Jeff rushed the door, pushing me inside..

"Get the fuck outta here!" Lenny snapped.

"Please, Lenny... please?" Jeff begged.

"You're a fuck-up! You're shit!"

"I'm sorry, man, it was a mistake."

"You're a fuckin' mistake!"

"I won't do it again, I promise," Jeff pleaded.

Lenny slapped him hard and he slumped down on the bed. "Michael!" Lenny shouted.

I tensed.

"Get Matthew in here," he demanded, sliding open a desk drawer. I tilted my head out the door to see Matthew approaching. As Matthew entered the room, he stared at Jeff whimpering and clutching himself; I was certain he'd never seen anything like this before. Lenny eyed Jeff as he wrapped a tourniquet around my upper arm. Jeff moved closer to us, sitting on the bed watching as the shot was administered, longing for it to be his shot. I stepped back, allowing Matthew his turn.

"Please, Lenny, do me next. Please, man..." Jeff cried as he clutched at his stomach and rocked gently back and forth. Lenny shot him a disgusted

look. Matthew stood before Lenny with his arm held out while staring at Jeff. When he was done, I handed him the envelope. "From the photographer," I said, turning on my heels and leaving the room.

Matthew and I stripped and lay down on the mattress. He put his head again on my chest, his thumb in his mouth, his eyes staring up at nothing, and we listened to Jeff crying and pleading in Lenny's room. Eventually we drifted off to sleep.

The next day, Lenny called me into his room and flung a plastic bag on the bed. "Put it on."

"What?"

"Put it on," he repeated sternly.

I opened the bag. "It's a dress, Lenny."

"I always knew you were a smart kid."

"Come on, man, I can't put that on."

"Put it on, Michael, and don't give me a hard time." "I can't..." I gulped. "I'll look stupid."

He'd had enough. He was suddenly at my throat, with one hand shoving my head into the wall behind me. He jerked me hard a few times as he held an opened hand in the air aside my face, ready to hit me. I kept a wide eye on that hand while getting knocked into the wall several more times.

"You do what I say, boy! All right? I don't wanna fuck up that pretty little face of yours." His opened hand pressed into my cheek as a warning. "You got a call to go on,"

"Please, don't send me out wearing that..."

He stared right through me, looking ready to rip me apart. He pulled me off of the wall by my shirt and shoved me into the bed where I lost my balance and fell onto it.

"Put it on," he growled. He heaved me to my feet and pulled my shirt, tearing it right off me. "Come on, come on," he said impatiently, wiggling all the fingers of one hand at my jeans. "Let's go! Move it, move it! Get those fuckin' things off!" He loomed over me as I slowly stepped out of my jeans and stood before him, without looking at him. He gave me some white lace panties and stockings with rosette garter belts. "Put those on," he barked. Then he threw the dress at me. "Put it on.

I put it on and stood wilted before him, still unable to took at him., He pulled at the fabric sharply here and there, straightening it out as a designer might do to a model wearing his creation.

"Please, Lenny," I begged one last time, trying to pull away.

He slapped me again. "Knock off the shit!" he yelled. "Stand right!" He pushed my chin up in the air and pulled at the fabric some more. "There, see?" He looked satisfied. "Turn." He pulled at the back of the dress, then turned me back around to face him. "You look damn good."

"I feel like an idiot."

"Na, you look great."

"I don't look like no fuckin' girl," I grumbled.

"We're not done." He pushed me down to the edge of the bed and I watched him rummage through a dresser in the corner. He came back and dumped the contents of a small bag onto the bed beside me. Cosmetics. I thought surely I'd die. I closed my eyes.

He smeared a beige cream all over my face and neck and then did my eyes with black eyeliner, like Jeff's. After stepping back occasionally to admire his work, he carefully brushed mascara onto my eyelashes. With a fat, soft brush he stroked blush on my cheeks.

"Relax your face," he demanded, but I kept drifting back into a frown. "Open your mouth. Like this." fie concentrated on doing a perfect job with the lipstick and I watched him, thinking how stupid he was and how ridiculous I must look.

"There." He stepped back, tossing the lipstick on the bed. "Where's your earring?" he asked. I retrieved the earring from my jeans on the floor and put it in my ear. "Lean forward," he said, pushing my head down in front of me and I felt a brush go through my hair while he sprayed hairspray in it. fie pushed me back to sit upright and fluffed up the hair on the top of my head, picking out the sides and applying more hair spray.

Finally he stood back. "Get up." I did and he looked me over. "The shoes are in that bag. You look great, Michael, or is it Michelle?" He was quite pleased with himself. He opened the door to his closet and angled the full-length mirror on the back of the door so I could see myself.

I stared at my reflection in disbelief. "Lenny, I can't do this." "Sure you can."

"Why? "

"It's what the john wants."

"But why me?"

"You're the prettiest."

"What about Matthew? He's the prettiest," I said.

Lenny smiled and held up a bag, pulling out the same dress I wore, only in light blue. "He's next. You're goin' out together."

Lenny went to his door and called Matthew in.

Coming into the room, Matthew glanced at me, looked away, then did a double take and started giggling.

"You're next," Lenny said and Matthew whipped his face around to him.

"Really?" Lenny gave him the blue dress and Matthew held it up against his chest. "Why?" he asked like an excited child.

"It's what the guy wants. He wants to fuck two pretty little boy cunts," he roared

I sat silently watching Lenny do Matthew's face and hair, which was pretty long, all one length, resting just on his shoulders, and he skillfully plaited a French Braid down the back of his head. He pushed him in front of the mirror and the boy was completely awed, turning his face from side to side, posing, full of himself. He turned to Lenny with a big smile on his face.

"Can I get an earring?" he asked. Lenny smiled and pulled several earrings from a top dresser drawer, laying them out for Matthew's selection. He headed out of the room and returned with two ice cubes in a towel and proceeded to pierce his ears.

Matthew chose large, gold, dangling earrings and Lenny inserted them. Matthew again posed in front of the mirror, smiling with a silly, gaping grin.

When Lenny handed out the shoes I started my complaining all over again. "They hurt."

"Something's gonna hurt a lot more if you don't start acting like your little buddy here," he threatened me as Matthew paraded back and forth across the room in his new shoes, getting the feel of walking in pumps. "See?" Lenny pointed out to me, "It's all in your frame of mind. Would you ever guess what he's got under there?"

"What's the point?"

Lenny slapped me across the face with the back of his hand. "It's what he wants!" he growled.

"Why don't he just hire some girls?"

"He don't want girls! He wants to fuck boy ass, not pussy." Lenny grabbed a fistful of my hair and pulled, "Walk!" he demanded, pushing me ahead of him.

"I got skinny legs," I whined,

"Walk! Stop moping and stand right! Get into it!" He pushed he hard.

"Lenny," Matthew said, "let me show him. He'll be okay. He'll do it."

"I can't do this," I stressed through clenched teeth.

"You can. What's the big deal, man? So what?" Lenny stood back observing the two of us, quite pleased with his newest boy. Matthew had been able to impress him tonight, with all the right moves and all the right words. "Let me see you walk," Matthew said patiently. "I'll help you. Like this." We walked together, side by side.

"Swish it, Michael," Lenny snickered

He gave Matthew the assignment and, for lack of pockets, Matthew slipped the piece of paper in his shoe. Lenny opened the door for us and now came probably the hardest part for me: walking through that front room past the other boys watching MTV. I tried not to look at them, to rush right past their stares and whistles and wisecracks, following closely behind Matthew.

I walked very carefully clown the stairs, grasping the railing, feeling quite shaky in the pumps, and Matthew waited at the bottom smiling up at me. "Your legs ain't so bad," he teased. "You know, you look pretty hot."

"Fuck you, Matthew," I grumbled, and he giggled. "I'll never do this again. This is the last time." I walked with my eyes lowered beside him.

Strutting with his head held high, he said, "See? This ain't so bad. We're giggin' on everyone! No one knows!"

"You love it, don't you?"

"It ain't so bad. Just relax and enjoy it."

And that's exactly what I did. The john, Chester, a balding, portly man in his fifties, in New York on business, staying at the Hilton, entertained us in his suite with a dinner of prime rib and two bottles of vintage red wine.

The waiter, a rather cute guy in his 20s dressed in a pressed black and white uniform, was standing next to me, going through his elaborate bottle-opening rigmarole, cutting the red seal and inserting the corkscrew and all, paying all the attention to Chester because obviously he was the one who would be signing the bill. But as he was pouring the wine, his eyes locked with mine and I grinned. After getting Chester's signature on the bill, the waiter managed another look at me before he glided out of the suite. None of this was missed by Matthew, who kicked me under the table., "Bitch," I muttered.

Matthew giggled and Chester joined in, perhaps more aware of the little drama than I gave him credit for.

"Now now, ladies," he said, and we burst out laughing.

With all the wine and food and play-acting I was feeling giddy by the time Chester told us to get into bed together and start making love to each other. He went to the bathroom and came out wearing a robe. He turned out the lights and got on the bed with us. As we kissed, Chester removed our pumps and ran his hands up and down our nylon-covered legs. Going from one to the other, he kissed and licked the exposed skin of our thighs and occasionally felt the bulges in our panties. Satisfied we were turned-on, he had us roll over on our stomachs. He lifted our skirts and slid the panties down and off. Kneeling over Matthew's ass, he told me to go to the head of the bed and have Matthew suck my cock. He spit on his fingers and probed Matthew deeply, then parted his robe. He lifted Matthew's ass in the air and his robe obscured the view as he began. At first I figured the man must be very small because Matthew gripped me as if he was in pain and my cock dropped from his mouth.

"Oh, God," Matthew moaned over and over as the fuck continued. Finally, Chester was sweating and he pulled out of Matthew long enough to fling away his robe. I finally saw the incredible cock glistening in the dim light. The monstrous thing was at least a foot long and as thick as my arm. Chester lifted Matthew up so I could watch as he shoved it into him all the way. As inch after inch went in, Matthew became delirious. Chester let him

drop to the mattress and leaned over him, taking my cock in his mouth while he fucked Matthew. Crying out in agony, Matthew gripped my thighs. Seeing Chester's hips move over Matthew excited me and I started to come. This stirred Chester into a frenzy and he took my asscheeks in his hands and drew me closer, sending my cock deep down his throat. When I came, he did too, filling Matthew, who was now flailing his arms and gasping for breath.

Slowly Chester pulled out and I saw that the uncut cock, even limp, was a staggering sight. I scrambled over to take it into my mouth and lick up the jism still dripping from it. Matthew joined me. We shared the sucking of it until it was hard again.

"Oh," Matthew said, 1 want it again."

I blinked. 'What?"

"Oh yeah," Matthew moaned. "Oh yeah!"

This time, he wanted it lying on his back so he could watch as Chester fucked him. I lay beside them, jerking off, watching intently as Chester took his pleasure.

"Oh you girls are good! So good," Chester cried, coming again. He gave us a very generous tip.

As we walked home, I was carrying my shoes in my hand while Matthew was strutting gracefully in his. "How can you walk in those things?" I asked.

"I've had some practice," he told me coyly. "I used to walk around in my mom's heels when she wasn't around."

I stared at him for a second and then cracked a smile and shook my head. "You're weird."

"And you're gonna tell me you never tried on your mom's shoes?"

"No, never!"

He shook his head in disbelief.

"The only thing I ever did with my mother's shoes was drive them around the floor ...like trucks, you know?"

"And you call me weird? Most kids just drive trucks around the floor like trucks."

"Yeah, well, I didn't have any trucks. I didn't have any toys, so I played with her shoes."

He'd stopped smiling. "You didn't have any toys?" I shook my head. "None?"

This seemed to truly sadden him. "Well... like, didn't you get toys on Christmas? And on your birthday?"

I chuckled. "Christmas never happened for me. And my birthday was just a reminder of the biggest mistake she ever made by putting off that abortion."

"You never got anything?"

"Well I can't really say I never got anything. I got beat up and locked in the closet a lot. And she did give me her johns to do."

"A john?" he asked. I nodded. "How old were you?"

"Five." I thought I heard him say "Oh God" under his breath, or maybe I just knew he thought it by the expression on his face.

"Why did she do that to you?"

"Why not? She did it, and her mother did it... why shouldn't I? Right? Just 'cause I wasn't a girl was no reason she couldn't carry on the family tradition." Matthew looked shocked. "You're lookin' at a genuine third-generation whore."

"I thought you only been doin' it since Lenny ..."

"I been doin' it all my life."

"God, Michael."

The minute we got home Lenny had his hand up Matthew's dress. "God, you're a cute boy-cunt," Lenny cooed. And the two of them moved together toward the bed. Shortly Lenny was locking the door behind him. All I wanted was my shot so I could just forget the whole damned night, but now I'd have to wait. I sat on the couch at Danny's feet.

"Rough night?" Danny asked, rubbing his feet up and down my thigh. I didn't stop him; it felt pretty good.

"Shit night."

"But you looked pretty damn good ..."

"I ain't ever doin' that again, man."

"You'll do it again," Jeff, on the couch across from us, said as he pushed himself up on one elbow.

"No fuckin' way, man."

"Yeah, you will," he said smugly, " 'cause Lenny'll tell ya to, and you'll bend just like the rest of us have to do."

Suddenly loud moans came from Lenny's room and we all paused. Then came the unmistakable groaning as Lenny got off. "Sounds like your little girlfriend's coming along nicely," Jeff snickered,

"You shit," I said under my breath. "You don't know the half of it."

THREE

With the weather turning colder and nastier by the day, Lenny finally took Matthew and Ralph and me to buy winter coats. Jacob couldn't get them for us so Lenny relented and said it was a necessity: he was tired of losing money on us when a cold or a cough got so bad we had to miss a night of work.

We thoroughly enjoyed our shopping spree at Alexander's (he said Bloomingdale's was too expensive), often stopping to look at all the Christmas decorations. This was the only time he'd ever taken any of us anywhere and I

felt special, especially when Lenny bought me a black leather jacket. "Somebody will have to take over for Jeff one of these days," he rationalized.

But Christmas Eve was not as happy for us. The phone wasn't ringing. Lenny stayed in his room all day and never went out to get dinner.

"Merry fuckin' Christmas," Jeff sneered. "He gets like this every Christmas."

"Why?" Matthew asked.

"No jobs," Jeff said, "everyone's home with their families 'stead a' lookin' for ass."

"We get a night off?"

"Hell no!"

"So what do we do?" Danny asked.

"What I do," Jeff said. "We all work the streets. That's Christmas at Lenny's."

"I never did the streets before," Matthew said.

"'Bout time you did. Yeah, when he comes outta there, he ain't gonna have nuthin'."

"Jeff!" Lenny loomed in the doorway like the Grinch. "Get your ass over here."

Jeff jumped up and Lenny put an arm around his shoulder, turning him to face Matthew and me on the couch. "Those two are yours tonight."

Jeff nodded and came back to the couch. Lenny called the two Jimmys. "You're doin' Tenth and you got the Square," he told them. I assumed they each knew exactly what he meant, as they nodded and then turned their attention right back to the television and the movie we were watching, "It's A Wonderful Life".

"Ralph!" Lenny called.. Ralph sat up on his mattress, just waking up. "You're workin' the strip near Nobel's place." Ralph nodded sleepily. "You hear me?"

"Yeah," he said,

"Danny!" Lenny looked around the room. "Where the fuck is Danny?" he shouted and Danny carne out of the bathroom. "Get over here!" He ran up to Lenny. 1 want you on the docks."

"Oh man, come on, not the docks ..."

Lenny held a fist to Danny's jaw. "Go on! Give me a hard time, you little fuck! I'm just waitin' to slam someone!" Danny said nothing more.

"Three hundred dollars!" Lenny hollered, looking at us as a group. "You don't make three hundred, don't expect to get fixed."

"Three hundred a on Christmas Eve?" Jeff said after Lenny slammed the door and locked it.

"Fuck him," Danny grumbled, 1 ain't workin' no fuckin' docks." But he knew he would. He knew he had to.

John Patrick

One by one, we reluctantly started going for our coats. The Two Jimmys went out together, one mumbling something about Scrooge.

Matthew stood and looked at Jeff, still relaxing on the couch, finishing his cigarette. We were the last three remaining. "Well?" Matthew said.

"You in some kinda hurry?" Jeff asked, curling his lip.

I got up and turned off the TV. "Anxious little babies," Jeff said under his breath as he stood and dipped his hand in his pocket. "Michael," he said, tossing his eyeliner pencil at me, "Lenny wants that on you:

Oh great," I said.

"Go in the bathroom and put it on."

I did as I was told and when I came back into the room, Matthew was on his knees in front of Jeff. Jeff was rubbing the boy's head into his crotch.

"What are you doin'?" I asked, stepping up to them.

"I'm just havin him warm it up for me. I've heard how good he is,"

"Too good to waste on you if we have to make three hundred tonight,' I said, dragging Matthew away from the bulge that he had always found so fascinating.

"Okay, but there'll be a time. Believe me, there'll be a time."

We sat on the subway, all in a row. Last minute shoppers kept their distance, clinging to their bags and peering over them at us suspiciously. A well-dressed young woman even changed her seat to get away from us.

Matthew started to hum softly to himself and I soon recognized the tune as "White Christmas." I stared out the window across the aisle, watching the occasional subway station whiz by, people standing on the platforms as a blur. I remembered past Christmases. My mother would also go and enjoy herself in some bar, drinking all night, leaving me alone in our tiny apartment to watch the Christmas shows on our portable black and white TV until I'd fall to sleep on the floor.

And even though she said it was her "night off," when she finally came home she'd have a man, usually stinking drunk, with her. I'd have to stay on the couch in the living room, listening to her played-up moans, waiting patiently for that final creak of the bed before I fell asleep.

The snow fell softly on Broadway as we followed Jeff past a Salvation Army band, horns playing "God Rest Ye Merry Gentlemen," and Matthew humming along with it. We huddled together as Jeff instructed us on how to stand, look, think, act and talk, what to say and not say, what to do and not do, what to expect. We watched men pass, listening to Jeff's little asides about each one. "Here comes a potential," he whispered out of the corner of his mouth, and we looked at a man who came slowly toward us, looking us over with a peculiar expression on his face. Jeff pulled a cigarette from his pack and let it dangle from his lips. "Watch," he told us, "and listen." He took a step into the man's path. "Got a light?"

The man smiled at him. "Sure," he said, searching his coat pockets. "You from out of town?"

The man was smiling at Matthew and me. "Yeah," I thought I'd take a stroll. Sad havin' to sit alone in my hotel room on Christmas..." He lit Jeff's cigarette.

"First time in New York?" Jeff asked.

"No, I was here about six years ago, but it was in the summertime. This is a hell of a time to get stranded here, but the job I'm on just didn't get finished and we have to work tomorrow too." The man looked at me, then Matthew.

"You like my friends?" Jeff asked.

"Cute," he said.

"Mmm, they're good too."

"Good?"

"Yeah. Very good, 'cause they're lonely too."

The man squinted at Jeff.

"You want 'em?"

"Want 'em?" He acted as if he didn't seem to know what Jeff meant.

Jeff leaned over and whispered, "You can have both, or you can take just one. Which one you want?"

"For what?"

"To keep you company. Make you feel good. They got no one else to share their Christmas with. They're orphans, you know. But they know how to make you happy, know what I mean?" The man studied him for one more confused moment before he finally caught on.

"Ohhhhhh ..." he said, "Oh, no, I never."

"Come on," Jeff said with a sly smile, "you're lonely, they're lonely. Yeah, you'll be loin' 'em a favor, man. Besides, no one'll know. Go ahead, pick one,"

"Oh but I couldn't ... "

Matthew stepped up to him and smiled innocently. "Hi," he said, and the man smiled at him.

"You got a room around here?" Jeff asked,

"Well, yeah, but ..."

"Good, he's only fifty bucks, okay?"

"Fifty?"

"Yeah, and that's a bargain, 'cause it's Christmas. This kid's good, I'm tellin' ya."

"I'm sure," the man said, "but I don't

"I'm tellin' ya, man, you won't regret it. And next time they send ya to New York, you'll be right back here lookin' for Matthew,"

"Matthew?" the man asked and Matthew nodded. "That's my little nephew's name."

"You ain't gonna regret it, man. Matthew's the best." Jeff held out his hand. "That's fifty," he reminded him, "you can pay me."

"You?"

"Yeah, pay me first and take him." The man gave Jeff fifty dollars. "Half an hour. Thirty minutes."

"That's all?"

"Ah, ya see?" Jeff grinned at him, "You're into it all of a sudden, aye? Havin' fun already! A hundred for an hour."

"Oh, a half hour will be fine," the man said, smiling at Matthew.

"Where you stayin'?' Jeff asked.

"The Grand, on Sixth."

"Thirty minutes," Jeff reminded them as they walked away from us. As I watched them turn the corner, Jeff came to stand next to me.

"That fuckin' little kid's a natural," he said.

"What if he doesn't come back? What if this guy does something to him?"

"Like what? Kill him? Chop him up into little pieces? Hell, that's the chance you take. Just like when you go out on a call. You never know who you're walkin' away with." Jeff's attention was already focused on another approaching figure. "Here comes your shot," he whispered. We both watched as a man in his mid-thirties in a long cashmere coat marched towards us.

Smiling, Jeff stepped up to him. "Like what you see?"

"I like your little brother," the man said in a gruff voice as he eyeballed me. "What's your name, kid?"

I told him and he shook my hand. "Hi, Michael, I'm Rich." "Is that your name or your financial status?" Jeff joked.

"I like that." The wind blew his wispy blond hair and he pushed it back out of his eyes. "How much?"

"Yeah, well, I don't know," Jeff said, puzzling me with his sudden hesitation. "You'd say if you were a cop, right?" The man laughed.

"Well, you a cop?" he asked the man straight out.

"No way," he chuckled. "I'm just a lonely guy looking for a good time."

"He goes for $200." Jeff surprised me with the price "And you pay me upfront."

"I only got a hundred,"

"I don't know," Jeff said, "he goes for two. He's the best." The man slipped a $100 bill from his pocket and handed it to

Jeff. "Take this. If he's really good, I'll give him the rest." "Okay, but only half an hour."

I went with the man around the corner.

"You stayin' somewhere around here?" I asked.

"Na, I live in Brooklyn. Right here's fine by me," He turned into an alleyway, seeming to know exactly what he was doing, "So what do you do?" the man asked.

"Anything you want," I said.

The man put his hands on my shoulders and forced me to my knees. I unbuttoned his coat and massaged his groin. He was already stiff, This wouldn't take but a minute, I thought, and I was right I got him moaning and groaning and then took every drop down my gullet. He leaned back against the wall catching his breath and I stood up. "Was that good enough for the other $100?"

"If I can do you o " he said, bending over and unzipping my jeans, He tried but I just couldn't come. I thought of Matthew with the man at the hotel, I thought of me fucking Matthew. I thought of Matthew and me with this dude in a nice hotel room, fucking our brains out. Nothing worked. "That's okay," I said finally. "Our time's almost up, I better get back,"

When I turned the corner, I saw Matthew was there, standing beside Jeff, smiling at me.

"You okay?" I asked him.

"Fine," he said simply. "The guy was real nice. He told me all about his job back home, He really was just lonely"

1150 ain't bad for a start,' Jeff said. Looking at me, he asked, "Did the guy give you the extra hundred?"

"No, After I did him in the alley, he just ran away " "Figures. The guys cruisin' the streets are assholes, man.' "Little Lenny," Matthew said.

"Speak a` the devil," Jeff muttered as he fixed his eyes across the street, We looked up to see Lenny rushing toward us. He was wearing his black pants and black cape He looked like Dracula

"How much?" he asked, sweeping up next to Jeff.

"One fifty," Jeff told him.

"That's all?"

"We ain't been out an hour yet ..." He handed the cash to Lenny.

"You got one fifty more to go," Lenny said, pocketing the money. "I'm gonna go down and check on Danny."

Just as Lenny left, racing to the subway, we stood huddled together in the doorway of a closed electronics store. Except for an occasional drunk staggering by us, and a guy who was sleeping on the sidewalk up the block from where WE' stood, there was hardly anyone left on the streets at all,

"I'm freezing," Matthew turned up his furry white collar on his new coat and buried his chin into it.

Jeff looked up and down the street. "This is fuckin' ridiculous, man," he mumbled. "We ain't gonna do nothin' else tonight."

"You think Lenny'll let us go back $150 short?" Matthew asked.

"Sure," Jeff grumbled, "but he said no fix. If that's what he says that's what he'll do. And I ain't doin' that gig tonight, man." He sniffed and wiped his nose. "Fuck it, man. Where we gonna get a hundred bucks?" He walked away from us and stood over the sleeping drunk. He squatted down beside the body and felt his way through the layers of clothing. He pulled him by a sleeve and let him roll onto his side so he could go through the back pockets. He came up empty.

"Come on," he hollered when he stood up. We followed him to a theater with a marquee that promised "XXX GIRLS GIRLS GIRLS." He turned to us. "Let's just stand here for a while." One man left the theater, passing us quickly, without even taking any notice. When the second man finally came out, Jeff stood in front of him with an unlit cigarette.

"Hi," he smiled, "got a match?" The man pulled a lighter from his pocket and lit Jeff's cigarette as he cupped his hands around the flame. The man started to move away. Jeff said, "You interested in some?"

"Na," the man said, "I ain't into boys."

"The blond don't know he's a boy." Jeff dragged Matthew over to him.

"He's pretty, all right," the man said. "But Id know he's a boy – know what I mean?"

The man tried to move away again but Jeff persisted: "He's really good. He'll do you better than any girl can. Man, when he's down there and you're feeling good, you ain't gonna know what he is anyway." The man patiently listened to Jeff's pitch while his eyes took Matthew in. "Listen," Jeff said, "I can let him go for $200." The man shook his head and tried to get away, but Jeff stayed on him. "What, too much? Okay, I can do better for ya.. Look, it's Christmas, Only one-fifty." The man looked at Matthew again and Matthew turned on his most dazzling smile.

"I only have a hundred," the man said, still gazing at Matthew.

"Okay. But if you like him, give him an extra fifty, okay? We gotta get $150 for our rent."

The man nodded and I watched them disappear into the night. As Jeff and I trotted down the stairs to the subway, I said, "I hope he'll be okay."

"You'd just better hope he brings back the extra $50. That's what you better hope."

Both Jimmys were already back when we walked in. Lenny was not there.

"Where the fuck is he?" Jeff huffed. The front door opened, getting the attention of each of us. It was Ralph. Jeff rushed him. "You seen Lenny?"

Ralph shook his head. "Not since about 2:30."

Suddenly the door opened again, and this time it was Lenny. He wasn't smiling. "He ain't here?"

"Who?" Jeff asked.

"Danny! He ain't here?"

"No," Jeff said.

"Shit." Lenny went into his room and slammed the door. Jeff pounded on it.. "Hey, don't you want your fuckin' money?"

Lenny opened the door. "Yeah, okay. You two first ..." he motioned to the two Jimmys

When he got around to us and found we were $50 short he threw a fit. 'Matthew's bringin' it," Jeff said.

"Matthew? You let Matthew go off alone with some shithead? Little Matthew?" It suddenly dawned on him that there was more than one boy missing from the nest. He sunk into his chair.

I smiled smugly when Lenny told Jeff, "You better pray that Matthew comes back – fifty bucks or no fifty bucks."

Matthew did come back, about an hour later, with the fifty bucks. "And that guy didn't want a boy!" Jeff screamed.

"You told him I don't know I'm a boy so I proved it," Matthew said, smacking his lips and rolling his eyes.

Lenny opened the door and, seeing Matthew, he shouted, "Hey boy cunt, get in here." Matthew raced to the office and Lenny bolted the door behind them.

It was cold in my bed as I listened to Matthew's groans while Lenny fucked him. Finally the drug kicked in and I slept.

Danny didn't come back. A few days later word got back to Lenny that someone had worked him over and dumped him under a highway overpass. His wrists were bound and he was wearing only his socks. Lenny figured he'd probably died from being left out in the cold in a weakened condition.

The news devastated me. I kept working it over in my mind, the horror Danny must have faced in his last minutes of life. I thought of him, how he'd kept to himself, sitting quietly, like a fixture in the room when we were all there together. He wasn't a bad kid, he did whatever Lenny told him to do. In fact, the last night I saw him was the first time I'd ever known him to complain about anything. He didn't want to work the docks. Maybe he knew he wouldn't be able to survive it. Maybe his fear brought on his death.

FOUR

In contrast to the week before, Lenny said New Year's Eve would a big night, especially on Times Square. Our goal was $600 each.

"If you think you can get away with snatching a wallet or a purse," he said, "go for it. The tourists'll be out in droves. I want you to spread out. You

three stay together in one area and you three work the other end of the crowd," he said, pointing a finger at us. As Lenny talked I quickly multiplied $600 by six boys – Lenny's goal for the night was to earn $3,600 total. Damn, I thought, that was a hell of a lot of money to earn in one night. Lenny had to be salting it away. I often wondered what he did with all of his money. It didn't go into a luxurious place for to live, or for nice clothes for himself or for us, and he didn't even own a car. The only expenses I could see Lenny having were the rent on the apartment and the constant supply of heroin.

"I'll be up to check on you at one," Lenny's voice pulled me from my thoughts. "So make sure you're all out in front of O'Malley's by one, hear? I might need you. I might get some calls."

As we left the apartment, Jeff, dressed in his usual leather jacket, pants and boots, his black hair moussed into a wild, thick mane, his eyes lined in black, and his silver earring dangling, led the way.

Matthew went in drag. Lenny wanted it that way, and that was fine by Matthew. He got such a kick out it that it picked up all our spirits after being depressed about Danny.

The night was fast and wild, but we didn't make anywhere near the $600 each we were instructed to. Still, at ten minutes before one o' clock, we waited in front of O'Malley's just as Lenny had instructed. The Two Jimmys were there first, then Lenny, and soon after came Ralph, barely on time. Lenny led us into the shadows of a quiet side street and collected the money, then folded it all together, burying it deep into one of his back pockets. Next he handed us our assignments; he'd managed to get us each a call. Jeff set off for the East Side alone, the Two Jimmys went toward the West Side and Ralph,

Lenny, Matthew and I took a cab downtown together. We dropped Ralph off on 25th Street and then continued down to the Village where Matthew and I were to go to a party. Lenny said not to worry about the cash, that he knew the guy giving the party and would get the money later.

At the party there were men and women, men dressed as women, women dressed as men, all very fashionably turned-out. I felt out of place with just my jeans and white T-shirt and leather jacket, but Matthew fit right in his silly dress. The people were loud, as was the music from the expensive sound system. They danced, shouted, laughed, and openly snorted coke and smoked joints all around us. Suddenly, a voice cried out, "Hey! Mikey and Matty!" It was Shaw, our photographer friend, very happy to see us, especially Matthew in drag. "Quite fetching," he teased. "I won't tell a soul!" He was without his cameras this time, a guest at the party, and he said he was responsible for our being there. As if we were his old buddies, we shared a joint as he introduced us to some of his pals, rattling off names to faces we'd never remember and really didn't care to.

Finally Shaw sat us down, away from the groups of people, and tapped some white powder out onto a mirror from a small amber glass bottle.

While he was chopping at the powder with a straight-edge razor, Matthew asked him for some wallet-sized prints of the pictures he had given Lenny. Matthew had never screwed up the courage to ask Lenny for a copy.

"Sure, kid," Shaw said, drawing out several lines of coke on the mirror. He pushed the mirror toward us, handing us a straw and Matthew looked at me in puzzlement.

"Like this," I said, and put the straw to one nostril, snorted up one line, switched the straw to the other nostril and then sucked up another line, as Matthew watched and Shaw smiled. I sat back, my eyes tearing a bit, and let the rush come over me. I grinned at Matthew and handed him the straw.

Later we were given drinks and more drugs and finally ended up in a large bedroom. Shaw took charge, as if he was taking our pictures again, instructing us to get on the bed and make love to each other. "That's all. No one will touch you.'

Trouble was, there was already someone in the waterbed, a young blond who resembled Matthew in a way, except he

wasn't in a dress. In fact, he wore nothing at all.

"That's Frederic. He's from Denmark and doesn't speak English. He loves to watch. I hope you don't mind"

Frederic batted his long lashes at me and grinned.

I couldn't help it. My ever-active mind began to spin with fantasies. I saw myself sprawled out on the big waterbed with Matthew to my left and Frederic to my right, all of us naked, both of them pressing close against me, squirming and wriggling. I imagined the sleek texture along the inside of Matthew's thighs and the feel of his hot young cock against my hands while the rest of me was busy with Frederic. And then slipping free of Frederic and turning to Matthew, gliding into him up to the hilt while Frederic hovered above us both, grazing my lips with the tip of his huge, uncut cocks

But back in the real world, things started to go strange. Shaw had left us alone all right but people kept wandering in and out. A guy about twenty-five, slender, pleasant-looking if unspectacular, with horn-rimmed glasses and quick, penetrating eyes, had decided to stay. He said his name was Bob. At first he just stood next to the bed and stared as I lifted Matthew's skirt and began fucking him. But soon his hand passed between my thighs, and he was playing with my balls. He kissed my shoulders and Frederic, who had been content to just sit and watch, joined him.. Before long I was fucking Frederic, working into him slowly, and Bob had gotten Matthew naked and was fucking him. Then another man, older, with long, shaggy hair, climbed on the bed and was fucking Bob while Bob stayed in Matthew. Pretty soon a youngish woman, overweight, with red hair, rolled naked onto the bed and it was getting a little confusing and distracting. The woman was watching me intently as I was developing quite a thing with Frederic. There were all sorts of things to

think about. Bob and Matthew were busy with each other, licking and grappling, slurping away merrily. Finally the man who was fucking Bob wanted to fuck Frederic, so I slid myself between Bob and Matthew to remind them I was there. I peeled them apart and Matthew pulled me into his embrace. I entered him again and he was really heated up and ready, wild even, and as his hips began a frantic triple-time pumping I had to catch him and slow him down or I would've come. The long-haired man wanted to fuck Matthew so I let him. I pulled out and there was the redhead, naked, thighs spread wide, waiting, I hadn't fucked a girl in so long I just had to slide into her. She was so wet, I kept slipping out of her and while I was messing with her, Matthew was moving around in the background somewhere. He was one more thing to worry about, but he could take care of herself, I knew, and would, and did. Bob came up behind me and started playing with my ass as if he was going to try to fuck me. I pulled out of the redhead and let him have here Now Frederic was free again and I entered him. At last I was getting in the rhythm of it, swinging between Frederic and Matthew, and back to the redhead, and on to Bob, who by now was lying on his stomach begging for it. While I was with Bob, Matthew and Frederic kept each other occupied and the long-haired man fucked the redhead.

Our bodies were shiny, with sweat; we were all gasping, dizzy with the craziness of it. I finally came in Matthew and when I pulled out, I rolled off the bed with a thud. I lay on the floor in a stupor for I don't know how long while sounds of men fucking Matthew senseless came from the bed above me.

We didn't make it back to Lenny's that night. I woke up the next morning still on the floor, naked. I opened the bedroom windows to let the place air out, and woke Matthew, who was sleeping peacefully in bed. We showered and dressed and, as we headed for home, Matthew said, "Well, you satisfied?"

"Satisfied?"

"Yeah, you did a girl.'

"Hey, I've done lotsa girls."

"Oh, yeah, I forgot. But it looked like you were havin' more fun with the boys."

I shrugged. "That's what workin' for Lenny can do to you."

"Yeah, Lenny," Matthew giggled. "It's all Lenny's fault."

"Asshole," I said, shoving him so hard he stumbled and broke the heel on one of his little girl pumps. Still, as he hobbled the rest of the way home, he couldn't stop giggling and carrying on about my true sexual nature.

FIVE

"Your habit's too fuckin' big and you're gettin' too old," Lenny yelled at Jeff behind the closed door, "so what the fuck am I supposed to do with you?"

"Come on, man, it ain't that bad, I'm still bringing in a good price. They like me, man, you know that , I ain't so old."

"Yeah well, all I know is I'm not gettin' what I used to for you," Lenny muttered.

"I'm good on the streets, man. I'm good with a hustle. I trained your babies in there. I did good with them, man. You said so yourself. I can train all your new boys, that's earning my keep, ain't it? And none of your boys' got a bigger dick, man."

"A dick that can't stay hard."

"Bullshit. Only once. One time. And the fucker was ugly." "Only once? Bullshit! You aren't getting as many callbacks as you used to."

"Okay, you been lookin' for new kids, I can help you ..." "I don't need you to take over my job."

"I'm not tryin' to take over your job. You'd have more time to spend on the phone."

There were more sounds of flesh hitting flesh and then Jeff whimpering. It was hard for me to imagine Jeff crying, he always came on so strong, so cool. "I'll cut down. Please, man, don't throw me out. I got no place to go..."

"That's not my problem, After you leave here I don't give a shit where you go."

"Please, man, give me a chance. Taper me down."

"Yeah, you'll come in here moaning and begging for another hit." Lenny began playing the scenario in falsetto; "cause you didn't get off on the one 1 gave you, you gotta get high, just one more time...just tonight, which'll be every night."

"Why're you sayin' this, man? I never done that. I'm not like that."

"Yes, you are. You do it all the time."

"I won't. I promise,"

The New Year had started off badly, but in the long, cold weeks that followed, Jeff tried his best to keep his end of the bargain, never once going in to ask Lenny for more. He'd been doing well, not an easy task, and I grudgingly came to admire him. Then one night it was to be Jeff and me, together – and that had never happened before.

"Me too, Lenny?" Matthew interrupted Lenny as he gave Jeff instructions.

"No," he said, "you're going solo tonight."

"But, Lenny ..."

"You did okay Christmas Eve, you'll do okay tonight," Lenny said.

"You'll be okay, Matty," I whispered. I rubbed the back of his neck. Lenny handed him a piece of paper and he took it without bothering to read it.

"Michael," Jeff called, tossing me his eyeliner pencil. "Let's go." I stood up and Jeff came over to the couch. "It's just a fuckin' job, When we get back you can have him all to yourself again. Suckin' his dick – suck, suck, suck all night long."

Matthew pushed him away. "I hate you."

Jeff slapped him lightly. "Cocksucker! Baby cocksucker! I've seen you.

It was true. Even though we were down to six boys and had a mattress for everybody, Matthew still slept with me, and lately that meant letting Matthew suck my cock rather than his thumb. And later he would usually wake up before I would and start sucking. I'd come and then we'd go back to sleep nestled in each others' arms.

"Come on, Jeff," I said, "take it easy on him."

"He's a fuckin' little baby," Jeff taunted.

Matthew started to swing at him and I got between them. "Lay off him, okay?"

"He's a baby all right, but a bigger whore than the rest of us put together."

"Okay, Jeff!" I screamed.

Jeff shrugged and, stepping away from us, said, "Let's go." I stared at Matthew. "I gotta go. I'll see you later."

"I'll miss you," he called after me.

"No, you won't," I said without looking back. "You'll be too busy."

I followed Jeff's long strides westward. When he turned south, I finally caught up with him and asked him where we were going.

"Some leather queen's place."

"You been there before?"

"Yeah. You ain't gonna like it," "Why?"

"Fucked up. And tonight they fuckin' want two of us." He shook his head sadly. "God, I get the fuck-ups."

"You get a lot of 'em...?"

"It's the slot Lenny fit me in." He turned to look at me for the first time during our walk together. "Looks like Lenny's fittin' you into it too. But you'll never replace me, you know that?"

"Yeah. Nobody could replace you, Jeff. Nobody."

He bunched his crotch. "Got that right,"

When we got to the stairway of the building, we separated to walk up the two squeaky flights to the apartment. I watched him walk ahead of me. It was the first time I noticed his ass. It was really a hot-looking ass and I wondered if he ever got fucked. Strangely, the thought of fucking him had

never occurred to me. In fact, I had never thought a lot about Jeff one way or another.

A heavy, bearded man in his thirties, dressed only in a leather jockstrap, answered Jeff's knock_ After the man left us alone in the living room, Jeff's hand reached over to my shoulder, roughly pulling my body close, I was bewildered; what was he doing? But I played along. My arms met his, embracing him back, pulling him toward me, and we began to kiss, slowly and gently at first. With a sweep of his tongue, he took my entire mouth in his, sucking me in and releasing me, over and over, resting his lips against mine, trying to suck my tongue into his mouth. Our tongues darted around each other, slowing down and speeding up, drawing back, then hurrying on for more. He would moan and move to nibble my ear. I opened my eyes to see the other guests, some in black leather harnesses, studded with silver rivets, x-ing big hairy chests like ancient warriors, others in black leather thongs or jeans or jockstraps, or nothing at all, had gathered around us, watching.

Someone had put on heavy, hard-driving rock music. Now it dawned on me: This was a show that Jeff was putting on, it really had nothing to do with me, with us. We moved against each other. I couldn't stop myself from moaning slightly when I felt his erection through the leather pants. Suddenly he grasped me, hands squeezing my shoulders, and pushed me down. "Lick it," he barked.

I sucked on the leather, licked the enormous outline his cock made. I suddenly had never wanted a cock more. As I massaged his groin, he gasped, "Oh, yeah. Yeah!"

Then, grasping my hand firmly by the wrist, he pulled me to walk with him, and led me around the apartment, passing the other men, who reached out to us, touching, pinching, feeling.

Once in the master bedroom, Jeff pushed me slightly so that. I sat down. He pulled off my shirt and began caressing my pecs with increasing firmness as he leaned into me.. Soon we were lying along side of each other, deep kissing. He twisted my erect nipples, then pushed me back on the bed and bent down to nibble and suck each tit and I squirmed in rhythm to the firm pressure of his tongue.

I saw the other men had followed us, their bodies pressed up hard against each other, jacking off and moving their hips in sync with each other. Two of the men began tearing at our clothes, tugging them off. Before the man removed Jeff's pants, I reached over to stroke and kiss again the outline of his erect cock. I leaned forward as Jeff's pants were pulled away and tossed into a corner. I took the cock in my hand. Odd how I had never seen it erect, had never really wanted it before now. I thought of Matthew, how much he would love it, the full nine inches or so of it, the thickness; the heavy veining of it. Jeff got on his knees and shoved it at my face. I opened my mouth and he slid

it in so fast I gagged, but kept it in. Hands reached over to us, stroking my hair, playing with Jeff's ass, while I sucked.

"Now, we will tie you up," the host said to Jeff. He wrapped one piece of rope around Jeff's right wrist, running it like a chain under the mattress until it met his other wrist from the opposite side. Next, he attended to his legs, securing his feet with another rope. He made one loop gently but firmly around an ankle, then put the rope under the mattress to secure the other, spreading his legs far apart but held tightly in position. They wanted to see him struggle, beg to be released. Sweat broke out on Jeff's forehead. I lay down next to him and began to kiss him, caressing his cock. I had one leg slung over the "V his body made on the middle of the double bed. My knee slowly rubbed his penis lightly back and forth. With my free hand, I played with the hair on his chest, occasionally stroking and pinching a nipple until it grew hard, then bending over him to tongue it and suck it until he groaned. I moved myself slowly over him, changing direction on the bed to suck his toes, tickle and rub his feet, making my way to the center of his body, to nibble the inside of his downy thighs, alternately licking, sucking, kissing, and biting him. His cock bobbed up and down as I took his big sweaty balls into my mouth. Some of the men leaned over us, their hands caressing every inch of our bodies while they jacked off.

I nipped at the many tiny folds of skin around the base of Jeff's massive erection, then licked him from base to tip, first hard, then softly, alternating. He was going crazy, tossing his head from side to side, his body shuddering.

I ran my tongue around and around the top of his penis, licking away the pre-cum, taking the big head between my lips, making little thrusting motions with my mouth and tongue. With one hand, I grasped his cock, pressing hard against the ridged area just below its tip that connected the sides. After sweeping my tongue around the head of it, I took him deeply into my mouth, moving my tongue over its full length, while my hand ringed him. When he lifted his hips to stick his cock deeper into my mouth, I slid my hands under his ass, grasped his cheeks and rubbed them as I continued to suck. I moved my fingers back and forth along the crack of his ass until I felt the hairy opening, warm and moist, throb against my gently probing finger. He opened to me and I eased my middle finger into him, feeling his sphincter tighten around my finger, release, then tighten again. I worked it to his rhythm, stopping only when my finger could easily enter him no further. I tried two fingers, then three, moving them inside him, slowly back and forth, pressing up against the front of his rectum, allowing his thrusting to work my hand, setting the pace, all the while my mouth and other hand never leaving his cock, moving over him, in rhythm to my fingers fucking him easily as he pressed his ass against me with each inward motion, allowing me more deeply inside him.

After awhile, I began to think of his cock inside my ass, I couldn't believe it: I wanted it! Men had tried to fuck me but without success; it was just too painful. But tonight, with all these guys cheering me on, I wanted Jeff inside me. I lifted myself up and turned my back to him. I grabbed the shaft and poised the slick head at the entrance. One of the men covered my nose with a rag soaked in poppers. I breathed deeply as I slowly lowered myself over the cock. His body pushed against me hard, sending his erection into me fully. I closed my eyes, letting the pain turn to pleasure as he fucked me and the men pawed us. Once I was used to it, and after a few more hits of the amyl, I leaned back on my hands and took over, fucking his cock while two men played with my dick.

"Oh, God," I cried, rolling my head from side to side as I came, "it's too much."

After one of the men licked my cock clean, I was lifted off the bed by two others and dropped to the floor. They untied Jeff, who still hadn't come, and grabbed me. Dazed, I resisted and one of the men slapped me hard across the face.

"Hey," Jeff said, "take it easy. He's just a baby."

The man grunted and shoved Jeff back into a corner. They began hitting each other. The host pulled them apart and told Jeff's attacker to go into the living room and cool down.

Still, they wanted me on the bed on my stomach. "It's okay," Jeff whispered. After they had tied me up in the same spread-eagle position, but on my stomach. Jeff sat next to me, leaning down to kiss me, tonguing me deeply. Pulling away slightly, he bent over and kissed my back and continued down to my ass. After sliding two fingers in me, he moved them in and out with harder and faster thrusts until I moaned and strained against the ropes, He scrambled on top of me and stuck his cock into me again. I raised my hips as much as I could to meet each quick thrust.

"Oh, fuck it," Jeff moaned. "It's so fuckin' good."

Two of the men leaned over us, kissing and biting our skin, sucking hard on Jeff's bare= shoulders as he fucked me. Jeff finally came, plunging all the way into me until I screamed with pleasure, rocking with him, tightening my ass muscles to grip him when he was deepest inside me, making him gasp. He squeezed his eyes shut, and whispered, "Oh it's just so fuckin' good."

After he pulled out, our host climbed on the bed and jammed his hard, six-inch cut cock into me. Another man shoved his cock in my face and I began sucking while our host finished. Another man quickly took his place and Jeff's cock was suddenly replacing the one at my mouth. Opening to him with a sucking kiss, I could taste his cum. I began licking and moving my mouth over him, taking him all the way into me, then pulling back on him. Before long I was falling into a smooth rhythm of taking him in and wrapping my mouth around him. As Jeff rocked back on each thrust, the man in my ass

came, only to be replaced by another. I looked over my shoulder to see it was the man who had slapped me earlier for resisting him. He stopped for a moment to bend over and untie me. They rolled me over and reached for pillows to slide under my hips. I lifted my legs high. I wrapped my legs tightly around the man's neck. His cock was almost as big as Jeff's and it hurt as I guided it into me. His fucking of me was rough and he kept slapping my ass as he slammed into me until he came. Each man's thrusting had been different. Some moved in and out very fast, with strokes that were close together. Other times their fucking was long and slow, reaching so deeply into me that I would cry out. Sometimes, like the last man, they fucked me with such anger I pleaded for them to stop. At one point, Jeff straddled me again, bringing his cock very near my mouth, then he took my head in his hands and began kissing me again. His sweat mixed with mine as he nuzzled his face against my neck. He reeked of the smell of sex. As the angry man finished inside my ass and no one replaced him, Jeff moved down and took my cock in his hand. Finding it hard, he mounted it and began fucking himself with it. I looked about the room. Everyone had disappeared. It was just Jeff and me, and Jeff, the big stud, was fucking himself with my dick! If someone had told me this would ever have happened, I never would've believed 'em for an instant. I reached up and ran my hands up and down his thighs. There was no need to put on a show anymore. What he was doing was just for his own pleasure – and mine.

"Oh, God, it's so good," he kept moaning over and over until he came.

After he had lifted himself from me, he took my cock in his hand and jerked it until I came, leaning over and lapping up my cum as it spurted in his face.

As I tugged on my jeans, I was again thinking of Matthew and wondering what kind of call he was on and if he was doing all. right without me.

When we reached the street, I said, "No, nobody can replace you, Jeff."

"What?"

"Just what I said: Nobody could ever replace you."

"Yeah, but what goes on on these kinda gigs, that's just between us. Got that?"

"Yeah," I chuckled, patting my still aching ass, "I got it all right."

Our bodies aching, we walked through the streets slowly toward home. Suddenly, Jeff turned the wrong corner, not our street toward home, and I stopped walking while he kept on. "Where're you going?"

"This way," he said, "come this way." I followed.

"Why? Where're you going?"

"Man, I gotta get high tonight. I ain't gonna settle for the measly shot Lenny's gonna give me. We deserve a little treat tonight."

"What are you doin'?"

"I found a connection. I know a guy I can blow for a shot." "But what if Lenny finds out?"

"Well he just better not find out!"

"I ain't gonna say nothin', but what if word gets back to him?"

"Just make sure it don't."

I waited outside for Jeff, smoking one of his cigarettes as I leaned in the darkened doorway, looking up and down the block, anxious someone might see me where I wasn't supposed to be. I wanted no part of this. Finally he came stumbling out of the doorway.

"Shit, man," I looked at him holding himself up by the wall. "You're all fucked up! You ain't gonna be able to hide this from Lenny.."

"I'm fine," he said, grabbing my arm to steady himself,

When we arrived back at the apartment, Matthew was sitting on the couch, arms folded across his bare chest, staring blankly at the TV. His eyes shifted to me, then to Jeff, then back to me. He wasn't smiling.

Lenny came out of his room and saw Jeff.

"What the fuck?"

"The john shot him up," I said, telling him what Jeff had told me to say, then dashed to the bathroom to wash the makeup off my face. When I came out, Matthew had moved to our mattress. I collapsed next to him.

"Are you all right?"

"I'm okay." I let him stroke my hair and rock me in his arms. He cradled and warmed me..

"Did you have an easy call?" I asked him finally,

"Yeah," he said softly, "a nice older dude,"

"That's good," I said, running a finger along his chin. "I thought about you."

"I thought about you, too,"

Suddenly Lenny came out of his room, five prepared syringes in his hands, and did one boy at a time, working his way around the room. He skipped Jeff.

Matthew took care of me, pulling off my sneakers and jeans. He leaned over me, unbuttoned my shirt and slid it off my arms. After covering me with a blanket, he stood, took off his clothes, and slipped in next to me. His skin was warm against mine as he settled his head into my shoulder and rested his face against my chest, the way he'd always done.

He kissed my chest,, moving down to my stomach, gently and slowly, until his head disappeared under the blanket.

I let him continue, throwing off the blanket. I didn't care who saw us or what they thought anymore.

The next night, Matthew and me went to see Shaw. After we posed for him, this time performing a standing fuck in the shower, with plenty of steam, he gave us the wallet-sized prints Matthew had asked for. Matthew was thrilled and we were feeling pretty good until we got back to the apartment

"You're a little lyin' piece a' shit! I warned you!" We heard slapping and thumping sounds coming from Lenny's room. We cringed listening to Lenny slap Jeff around but none of the others knew what had happened.

Then the door was flung open. We sat up, flinching in fear as Jeff came stumbling out of the room, his face bloodied, falling to the floor in a heap before us. Lenny stood in the doorway, eyes wild and frenzied, breathing heavily, looking like a demon possessed. Jeff moved slightly on the floor, making an effort to pull himself up. Matthew jerked forward in response, wanting to go to his aid, but I held him back. It was best not to interfere, everyone knew to make themselves invisible during one of these scenes.

Lenny must've gotten his second wind because all at once he rushed Jeff and began kicking him. I held Matthew back, but at that moment what I really wanted to do was join him and the others in jumping Lenny, beating him the way he had beat us, maybe even killing him.

Jeff crawled across the floor, trying to escape the savage stomping. I closed my eyes, unable to watch anymore, wishing it would be over. Matthew held me close to him.

Ralph came in the front door, walking right into the scene in progress and interrupting Lenny's fit. When he realized what he'd stepped into, he slid his way to a corner of the room. Lenny stood erect, fists clenched at his sides. "This is what you get when you go behind my back." We all sat in wide-eyed silence, too afraid to budge. "You think you can cop a hit on the streets? That's what you'll look like!" Lenny gave Jeff a final push with his boot and went back into his room, slamming the door shut.

I got up, slipping from Matthew's arms, and went to Jeff, who was gasping for breath, blood and saliva hanging from his mouth. "Come on, Jeff," I said softly, turning him by the shoulders. He looked up at me, focused on my face and suddenly threw my hands off of him.

"Get the fuck away from me,"

"Let's clean you up:

"Wait," Lenny said, opening the door to his room wide. "I ain't finished. I still gotta deal with you." He was looking directly at me.

"What did I do?"

"What did you do?" he snapped. "Think! You think of what you did!" He rushed me and pulled me towards his room.. Shaking me, he screamed, "What did you do, you little fuck, huh? What?" It was my turn, and everyone watched round two. He started hitting me in the face as I turned my head in an effort to protect myself. "What? You lied to me?" He slapped either side of my

head alternately. "You lied for this big stud piece of shit? Huh? Isn't that what you did?"

Lenny beat me about the face and head while pulling and pushing me, slamming me against the wall. "You didn't think I was gonna call that john, find out what the fuck was going on? You're a stupid shit, that's what you are. Stupid!" He smashed me in the mouth with the back of his hand, sending me to the floor, then pounced down on me. "You wanna lie for that worthless shit when I'm the one who feeds you?" He stepped over to Jeff and gave him another swift kick in the back. Then he grabbed me and shoved me towards Jeff. "There you go. You stick with the garbage! You fuckin' deserve each other!" He backed away from us, panting. "Two pieces of shit," he ranted. "All I get is shit from every last one of you ungrateful little bastards! That's all! Shit!" Finally he went back to his room and slammed the door behind him. Once again silence surrounded us.

I got up and tried to pull Jeff up. He resisted. He tried to stand on his own, but tumbled back. Finally I yanked him up and he let me walk him to the bathroom to tend to his wounds. I sat him on the toilet seat and ran the cold water in the sink. His head tilted back to rest on my hip, I carefully placed a cold, wet towel on his face, causing him to jump a bit from the pain. We could hear Lenny passing out the doses and we knew we were not going to get any. He burst into tears, his mouth in my groin, and I held him. "It'll be okay," I whispered.

Jeff and I dozed together, restlessly, on the couch and soon, with our growing need to get high, we were up and pacing the in front of Lenny's room. Finally Lenny's door opened and he let us in. Without a word, he shot us up and we were relieved once more, having suffered enough, our punishment ended.

SIX

Jeff was to sneak drugs on several more occasions, but without my being involved. He'd return late from a call completely wasted; bumping into furniture, and Lenny beat him each time. Now I felt Jeff had no one to blame but himself. Finally Jeff got so messed up one night he didn't come home until late the next afternoon. Lenny was furious and, rather than beating him, he simply threw him out.

Over the next few days, Jeff called and called but Lenny always hung up on him. Finally, Jeff redeemed himself by bringing in a new recruit, an Hispanic boy named Hector, who was small for his age, short and fine-boned, and appeared much younger than his years. I could see why Jeff chose this one: he was quite appealing with his big brown cow eyes and long, dark lashes, a tiny nose and full lips. His hair was straight and thick, grown out in long tufts against. his neck and forehead, and his clothes were too large and

quite filthy, giving him the overall appearance of a street urchin. He obviously
was devoted to Jeff, hanging on him as Matthew did on me.

At that point, Lenny needed all the new boys he could get. The two
Jimmys had gone out on a call together and never come back. Lenny tried to
track them down but it was useless. He said they probably went off with the
john, a record promoter from Los Angeles. "They'll be back," Lenny said, but
he still instructed Jeff to "find some more."

And Jeff proved to be quite the recruiter. A couple of days later he
brought Lenny another blond, Ricky.

Ricky's first day out of Lenny's room, Lenny brought him to me at
my bed and woke me. "Wake up, sleepy, Jeff's got a big date tonight so I want
you to take Ricky out."

"Now?" I asked. It was barely noon.

"Yeah, noun"

As Ricky and I walked through the streets of SoHo, making our way
to our assigned address, I thought about how much he reminded me of Danny,
with the same warm brown eyes and wavy hair, only taller and thinner. He
didn't look at you when you spoke to him and. he didn't say very much either,
but his quietness was not peaceful like Danny's; this boy appeared to be even
more tormented than Matthew. Perhaps it was the horror of spending a week
with Lenny. Lenny had cut short Hector's initiation so he could take Ricky in.
Finally I asked, "Where you from?"

"Everywhere."

"Like?"

"Canada, Vermont, Wisconsin, Florida, maybe the moon..." I rolled
my eyes. "How come so many places?"

"My mother." He pointed a finger to his temple. "A real wacko.. We
never stayed no place longer than six months. That was the longest, and that
was Wyoming. She'd meet some guy and off we'd go. She couldn't sit still."

"I don't understand."

"She's a Hippie Gypsie. Mobile. Beep Beep." He grinned. "She don't
know who she is. She's still searchin' – she don't even know what the hell
she's lookin' for."

"Where's she now?"

He shrugged. "Boston, last I knew."

"What you been doin'?"

"Getting fucked."

"Mm," I said softly.

"Yeah, I lived with a guy for about nine months. He kept me. Fed me,
bought me shit, clothes, all the coke I could do... He went to work everyday at
some big bank and I was like his little wife at home. He wanted a nice dinner
all ready for him. After I did the dishes, he'd fuck me. Same old shit every
day. Borin' as hell, man, but it was an easy life."

"So what happened?"

"Got tired of me, found a new boy to take my place. Somebody who could really cook I guess."

"You miss him?"

"Hell no."

"Did he get into any S&M shit?"

"Some, at first, to train me. Why? You into that shit too? Jeff sure as hell loves it. And Lenny, wow!"

"No, not me. Jeff and Lenny, yeah, but not me,"

"Yeah, well, to each his own, I say," he muttered.

We were heading for The Stud, a bar in midtown. Because we were so young, we couldn't have gotten in the front door, but we were there long before it opened anyway, going to the service entrance. The man who let us in introduced himself as Jesse, "the bartender," but he really was the owner because Lenny told me so. Tall, maybe six-two, and muscular, Jesse was a dark-haired guy in his late thirties who looked like he should be punching cows, not serving drinks. He even wore a cowboy skirt stuffed into his tight jeans.

He got us Cokes, put some country-western music on the jukebox, and told us to strip, Ricky first. I wondered if we were being auditioned.

Ricky had a narrow waist, hard belly, and a good four inches of soft cock hanging down over a nice set of balls. Naked except for his socks, he did a little dance and then lowered himself to the bar stool and drank his Coke. I started stripping. Seeing Ricky naked got me hard and I didn't get a chance to do any dancing because Jesse came around the bar and dropped to his knees in front of me. As he began sucking, Ricky stepped over to us and I ran my hands over those nice pees and tweaked his nipples a little. Then I leaned into his crotch. I touched his prick with my lips and then started licking it. It started to grow. I took the head into my mouth and tongued it, then sucked on it His dick kept growing. It was no match for Jeff's but big nonetheless. I swallowed the whole thing, my nose going into his freshly-scrubbed cockhair. I backed off until I had just the head between my lips, and wrapped the fingers of one hand around the base while my other hand went to his big balls. Jesse was keeping his eye on my sucking of Ricky while he played with my balls and sucked my cock.

Jesse eventually left my cock and went back behind the bar. He came out carrying a beer bottle. He began rubbing it against Ricky's butt cheeks. Ricky looked behind him and saw what it was and just groaned. Jesse poured some of the beer on the ass and it ran down and mixed with my saliva. I never cared for beer but I loved it when I could lick it off Ricky.

Before long, Jesse started fucking his ass with the beer bottle, driving the upper part in and out.

"Keep suckin' that big dick and he won't mind this a bit," Jesse said to me,

I stepped up my attack on the prick and could sense when the pain was easing off a little, I started slowly jacking the shaft, and bent my head to work one of his balls into my mouth. As the brutal fucking of Ricky continued, I let the first of his balls slide out of my mouth and went for the other. I tongued it while I continued to stroke him.

At some point, leaving the beer bottle in, Jesse unbuckled his jeans and hauled out his cock, which resembled the beer bottle he'd been using on Ricky. Jesse slid the bottle out and tossed it on the floor. He started fucking, working his cockhead in and out of Ricky. He kept shoving in more cock, the way he had added inches of the bottle, and Ricky cried out. Jesse started fucking. I was glad he'd picked Ricky and not me. I had the tasty, beer-soaked young cock in my mouth and was enjoying it, Ricky was responding, driving his dick in and out of my mouth, putting his hands on my head and gasping. "Get ready, man!" As he shot his load into my throat, I jacked off and my own spunk dropped on the floor with the spilled beer. As if it was a chain reaction, Jesse shoved his big prick deep into Ricky for the last time, shooting his load into him. I kept sucking on Ricky's dick, milking the last of his juice.

Now there were two cocks I knew I would never turn down: Jeff's and Ricky's:

SEVEN

My job as trainer of the new boys had kept me from turning any tricks with Matthew. While we still slept together and he still blew me, he said was missing the other sex we had. One day, when everyone was watching TV, he took me into the bathroom and started kissing me. I hugged him.

"I love you," he said.

"I know you do." I was used to hearing it by then. "Why are you so mean to me?"

"I'm nice to you. Nicer to you than to anybody."

"'Cause you love me too."

"Give it up, Matthew."

"I won't. 'Cause I know."

"You know shit." He started to run his hands around me softly and moved his mouth along the skin of my chest and stomach, heading down. "Don't you ever get tired? You do this shit all night for a living and then you wanna do it some more.

"This isn't the same. This is something I wanna do. It gives me pleasure."

"Everyone gives you pleasure. You love your work."

"No, I love you," he said as he took my cock out and began sucking it.

"You love sex, Matthew," I said as my cock hardened.

"No, what I love is this up my ass," he said, bending over, guiding it in.

As I sunk it all the way in, I realized once more just how much I loved fucking him. I loved fucking him more than anything, probably because nobody enjoyed getting fucked as much as he did.

Hours later, Matthew woke me up, clinging to me and trembling, his eyes wild with fear. "What's wrong?"

"I'm scared. Hold me." I put my arms around him.

"What is it, Matthew?" The room suddenly lit up in a series of bright flashes and thunder cracked loudly and Matthew shot his face down into my armpit, cowering in fear. "Matthew, it's only thunder."

"Hold me, Michael."

As I listened to the rain pounding on the windows, I held him and kissed him. Soon he moved his lips to my chin, then my chest. Eventually his head disappeared beneath the blanket. I stroked his hair as he started sucking my cock. My cock was raw from my trick earlier in the night and then the fucking I gave Matthew, but I let him continue; it pleased him so much to suck it. "It's okay, Matty," I whispered. "Everything's okay."

The next night, I went out on a call and came back to discover that Lenny had finally done it: he had sent Jeff and Matthew out on a call together, and by the time Lenny administered the doses, they had not returned.

I woke at six the next morning to find that Matthew was not beside me. I got up to look around the room and discovered Jeff was not there either. Perhaps they'd had an all-nighter. I wanted to ask Lenny but was reluctant to disturb him and fearful of his ridicule of my concern for Matthew, so I lay back down. I tossed and turned, unable to sleep, and it began to rain, heavy drops hitting the window pane. Soon there were claps of thunder that shook the windows and I wondered if Matthew was afraid wherever he was. Despite myself, I hoped he had Jeff to hold him under the covers and hide his face from the lightning. I fell asleep.

By three in the afternoon, they were still not back and I knew something was terribly wrong. Lenny was still in his room. I knocked on his door.

"You know Matthew didn't come back yet?"

"He'll be back," he called to me. "Go back to bed."

"It's three in the afternoon. Even if they supposed to stay overnight."

"They didn't say nothin' to me 'bout wantin' them all night." "What kinda people are they?"

He opened the door at last. "You takin' a census?"

I looked him straight in the eye and spoke calmly. "Could you tell me the address please?" He studied me in silence. "Please?" I begged.

"Why? You gonna go look for him?"

"Please, Lenny, please?"

Lenny shrugged. 'Take Ricky with you."

It was a warehouse near Canal Street. The door was locked. I rang the buzzer frantically, but not really expecting an answer. Finally, becoming enraged, I kicked the door.

"What are you gonna do?" Ricky asked. There was no alley; the next building was attached. He followed me down the street. "What are you doing?"

I turned into the first alley we came to. It was closed off by a stockade fence. I climbed it and was able to see the back of the warehouse. I pulled Ricky up and we jumped down to the other side. We had to climb four more fences before reaching the warehouse. I tried the only door and it was locked. "Now what?" Ricky asked. "How are we gonna get in?" There was a window above our heads and a fire escape above the window.

"Give me a leg up."

"To where? What are you gonna do? There's no way to – '"

"Just do it!" He laced his fingers together and held his hands down for me to step into. I had to spread myself flat against the building, stretching to reach the window ledge above me. "Push me up, higher." I reached it and pulled myself up onto the ledge. I looked inside but could see nothing , the window was plastered with a thick layer of dirt. All I saw was my own reflection in the late afternoon sun.

"What's in there?" Ricky asked.

I balanced myself on the ledge, trying to reach the bottom rung of the fire escape ladder above me. I could only get it if I jumped. If I missed, I'd fall one and a half stories to the concrete where Ricky waited. I took a breath, leapt, and grabbed hold of the last rung, my weight immediately causing the ladder to roll down with me on it, and jerk to a halt above Ricky's head. I pulled him up and we climbed to the platform portion of the fire escape where there was another clouded window.

"Turn away," I said, leaning back against the fire escape railing, and I heaved a sneakered foot through. the glass. The giant pane shattered, sending a snowstorm of glass to fall over us as we covered our heads under our arms.

Our feet crunched in the broken glass as we looked around the dark, musky room. There were pieces of dusty machinery scattered about, a metal folding chair twisted out of shape and lying on it's side, and discarded Styrofoam food containers from take-out restaurants. "Now what?" Ricky asked, I picked up a pipe and handed it to him.

"Don't be afraid to use it. And use it like you mean it, If we meet anyone, they won't hesitate to kill us." I'd scared him, his eyes were huge as

he stood with the pipe over his shoulder, poised like a baseball bat,, I picked up another piece of heavy pipe for my own weapon, and he followed me toward an inner door. We moved swiftly but cautiously, listening for any sounds, ready to strike. I opened the door. There was a mattress on the floor, a table with a few metal chairs around it, a short piece of kitchen counter with a sink and a stove and unlit, burnt-out candles atop the stove.

I saw a pile of clothes on the floor and poked at them with the end of my pipe. I picked up an aqua and white striped tee shirt and stared at the blood on it. My heart began to races

"What?" Ricky asked.

"Matthew's," I oaid, still staring at the shirt in my hand. My eyes scanned the room for a clue, anything that could tell me what happened and where he was, There was no doubt now, Matthew was in danger. "Come on," I said, tossing the shirt aside, "we have to search the building."

"What do you think happened?" Ricky whispered, trying hard to control his panic..

"Let's just hope they're still here,"

We went upstairs first, searching the rooms of the top floors, all empty but for debris, old office furniture, battered pieces of machinery. Then we searched the lower floors, finding nothing, only the basement left. We went down past the metal door into the darkness; roaches scattered from the walls of the stairwell as we passed, I could hear water dripping and see a dim flickering light coming from within. We went around a turn to find the light coming from a single kerosene lantern hanging from a nail on the cement wall. The smell of mildew filled my nostrils and cobwebs pressed against my face as we crept around a second turn and then we stood dead still. My heart pounded in my ears as I took in what I saw,

I stared at antiquated torture equipment and chains with leather wrist cuffs hanging from the walls. In the far corner there were three tables; and I didn't want to explore what I knew I must, what looked like a body on each of the tables, each covered by a large black cloth. Ricky stood frozen as I approached one of the tables and slowly lifted a corner of the cloth. It was the dead nude body of a young blond boy, not Matthew, but still two more tables to explore. I forced myself to look under each cloth and was relieved to find that none of them was Matthew or Jeff. I looked over at Ricky and shook my head.

"Thank God," he said, letting his shoulders drop.

"Over there," I whispered, one more corner to turn. We crept, very fearful of what we'd next find around that turn.

There on the wall, side by side, two boys hung from their wrists, thin, naked bodies, limp and milky white, their heads covered by black sacks. I knew it was them immediately and it seemed my heart stopped beating for an instant. "NO!" I dropped my pipe and ran to them, hoping to learn I was

wrong. I pulled the hood off. "Oh no!" I yelled in anger, holding Matthew's head. His eyes were closed, he'd been beaten, his face was badly bruised. Ricky was helping Jeff, whose whimpering was a vague, muddled sound in my ears. All of my attention was focused on getting Matthew out of the cuffs. His skin was cold; I didn't know if he was alive. I pushed his body up as I unstrapped the leathers and I laid him down. I put my ear to his chest; he was breathing; he was alive. I ran back to the tables and swiped two black cloths, tossing one to Ricky as he struggled with Jeff's weight.

"Come on," I said, "let's get them outta here before someone comes back."

We struggled with the dead weight of the boys, each of us dragging a black-wrapped body up the cellar stairs and out from the dampness and stench of death. We dragged them down the block and settled just in the narrow alleyway we'd used to reach the back of the building. The sunlight found Matthew's face in my lap. I called his name, trying to summon him back to consciousness. "Come on, Matty, it's me. Matthew... Matthew,.." His eyes opened and I smiled at him but it seemed as if he didn't recognize me. "Matthew, it's me, Michael. Look at me, Matty." His eyes began to focus and soon grew huge with terror and confusion. "Matthew, it's me. You see me? Who am I? Come on, Matty," I said softly, and his lips parted, starting to form the "M" and I waited.

"Michael?"

"Yeah," I said under my breath, grinning.

His bottom lip began to quiver and he started to cry. "You're all right now,"

He raised his arms around my shoulders and I held him close, hiding my own tears from Ricky,

"You saved my life, Michael. I know you love me," he whispered. I didn't look at him. "I know it for sure now. "

EIGHT

After that terrible day, I often caught sight of Matthew across the room, eyeballing Jeff up and down, even more than before. The subtle glow in his face told me they had formed a special bond of some kind and I felt a strange pang inside of me. It was a feeling completely foreign to me; I'd never been jealous of anyone,

Jeff stayed in bed for two days and Matthew would often go to him and stand over him, staring.

I came up behind him and bumped him, as if to wake him up. "So why don't you just go curl up next to him and make it all better," I sneered sarcastically.

"What's with you, man?"

"I've seen the way you've been carrying on about him since that night."

"I can't believe this," he snickered. "You're fuckin' jealous!" "I'm not jealous, don't flatter yourself."

"So what is it then?"

I turned and walked away from him.. I had no answer to his question. Soon I felt his hands on me. "You'll never admit how much you love me," he whispered.

"I don't love anyone. I don't know how. I don't even know what love is."

"This," he said, "the way you feel right now."

"Bullshit," I snapped.

He shrugged.

"So," I said, "did you do him that night, before it got rough?"

He rolled his eyes. "It was business, like you always say, just business"

"You wanna do everyone."

"He's neat, but no one can take your place, Michael. I have something very special with you. I can fuck anyone but I only love you."

"Bullshit," I said, because I was expected to say it. He held me, resting his head on my shoulder, and it felt good to be in his arms,

That night, I woke with a start. Matthew had gotten out of bed and gone to stand over Jeff, who was asleep. I watched him looking down at him for a while, running his hand up and down Jeff s thigh. He bent down and rubbed Jeff's crotch for a few moments, then, shrugging, came back to bed.

"Sure you got the right bed?" I asked, as he settled in next to me under the covers.

"I'm sure," he said, taking my cock in his mouth,

The next night, I again woke up and realized Matthew had left our bed, I looked back to where Jeff had his mattress. Jeff was awake and I saw Matthew slide under the sheet next to him. Jeff wrapped his arms around Matthew and my heart began pounding in my chest. As they lay side-by-side, Jeff reached down under the sheet. Soon he was moving his hips and I knew he was fucking Matthew. Before long, the sheet had fallen off of them and I had a good view of Matthew jacking off while Jeff slammed that big, beautiful cock into him. They tried to muffle their cries as they came. They lay still for a few moments and then Matthew got up and returned to our bed. I rolled over and pretended I was still asleep,

Matthew got in bed and hugged me to him. I pulled away, growling, "Get the fuck away from me!"

"Michael m "

"Next time you're hurting or sad or fuckin' scared of the thunder don't come to me, you little shit. Go to Jeff." "Please, it's not like that."

"Get away from me," He put a hand on my shoulder as he glanced around the room.

"Shhh, Come to the bathroom so we can talk."

"1 just saw him fuck you. I don't wanna talk to you." "Please?" he whispered, pulling at my cock, which, I hate to admit, was erect.

Shrugging, I got up and he followed me to the bathroom, I sat on the toilet lid and he stood before me.

"So talk, I said.

"You know I've always been attracted to him."

I sighed. "Yeah, I know. He's neat. This is what you brought me in here for? To tell me how hot you are for him?"

"No. I., ." he stammered. 1 don't know. I don't expect to get from him what I get from you."

I stared at him. "You're fucked up."

"I know." He bowed his head and stayed like that for a long moment before looking at me again with renewed hope. "All I'm tryin' to say is, I love you. I want to be with you, and only you – even if I do wanna fuck somebody else sometimes. I never hid that from you."

"You never made an effort to hide it, that's for sure," I spat.

He touched my shoulder. "You tell me you don't love me, but then when I show interest in someone you get all bent outta shape." His hand moved down to my crotch. "Like this."

I still had a fierce erection. Matthew grinned and squeezed it. "Yeah, just look how much you love me."

"No, I don't love you. It's just that I'm horny as hell for some reason."

"You need me."

I stood up. "Right this moment I do. Turn around. I'll show you just how much."

"Oh, Michael, I love you," he moaned, tugging at my cock.

After lowering his underpants, I planted my hands on his shoulders and shoved my hips forward, sending my cock deep in the sopping hole where Jeff had just been. It gave me a perverse pleasure screwing Matthew now, being as rough as I could, holding my hands over his mouth, muffling his cries.

As he bit my fingers, delirious with the pleasure I was giving him, I rammed my cock in one last time and any orgasm was the most intense I had felt in months.

NINE

A week later, Ricky, who'd had an afternoon call, came rushing into the apartment, his eyes wild. "Hey, didn't you see him?" he asked us.

"Who?"

"Jeff! He's down there in the doorway!"

"What?" Matthew asked.

"Jeff's down in the foyer, behind the door, with blood all over him!" Matthew and I ran down the stairs, Hector and Ricky right behind us. Jeff had cut both his wrists. He was not yet unconscious, although the stare in his eyes told me he was on his way. He and Lenny had had another argument and Lenny had thrown him out again. Now this.

"Go get Lenny," I told Ricky, who ran back up the stairs. "Squeeze here," I told Matthew, and he held the slice on one wrist closed while I held the other and Lenny came clambering down the stairs followed by Ricky. He put his head to Jeff's chest, then slid his arms underneath Jeff's dead weight and lift him easily.

"That's good," Lenny said to us "Keep pressure on it while I carry him up."

We brought Jeff up to Lenny's room and Lenny called a client, a doctor in the Village, who arrived quickly and sewed up the wounds and bandaged each wrist.

Lenny kept Jeff locked in his room during his recovery, until he was well enough to get beat up for what he tried to do. "It ain't your life to take. You belong to me. I own you. You got no right to try a stunt like that."

The door opened and Jeff stepped out slowly. His face was bruised but Lenny had been pretty easy on him. I felt bad for him, the drug addiction having overtaken him and the tricks fewer and fewer. It got so I didn't even mind when Matthew occasionally went on calls with him; at least Matthew wasn't going to his bed in the middle of the night any more because Hector, who threw a jealous fit when he found Matthew in bed with Jeff, had taken to sleeping with Jeff himself.

Then Jeff went on a call that he didn't want to take. Lenny insisted he go, as the john had specifically asked for him and would have no one else. Jeff gave in after a big argument. In fact, that was the first time I saw him as his old spunky self since his suicide attempt. He just quieted down and gave in after the argument and went out on the call, only he never really went. Days passed without any word and Lenny became increasingly short with us. It was bad enough that Lenny got this way every Christmas, even if everything else was running smoothly, but this was July.

We were all relieved after a busy Fourth of July weekend when Lenny began to calm down. I secretly envied Jeff for being Lenny's obsession. It didn't seem to matter to Matthew that Jeff had probably suffered at Lenny's hands more than any of us due to this obsession; all that Matthew could see was that Lenny wanted Jeff around, and when Jeff left he wanted him back, and when he was gone Lenny was miserable. Matthew said he wished he could matter that much to Lenny.

As life went on without Jeff, it seemed our own addictions were taking us over. We experienced the pains of withdrawal more frequently as we gathered in the front room with the other boys after our calls, our deterioration and growing dependence on the drug what the babies had to look forward to. It got to the point where we had to rush back after work or we'd be sick by a certain hour. Lenny was becoming less tolerant and began treating us with the disgust he'd ended up dishing out on Jeff in his last days.

Then one day Lenny came back to the apartment in a jovial mood. "I got him," he said to us, smashing a fist into his opened palm. "I found Jeff and I got him." Matthew and I looked at each other.

"Where is he?" Matthew asked.

'Dead," Lenny said. "I beat the shit outta that little fuck. That's what he gets for runnin' out on me!" Lenny looked like a crazy man as he went about the room wringing his hands. "You can all learn a lesson from this," he said, looking at each one of us, his fists clenched so tight that his knuckles were white. "Any one of you little pricks decides to walk..." He rammed his fist into his palm, "Pow! You're dead! Just like Jeff. Got that? No one gets away from Lenny and lives!"

After Lenny slammed the door to his room behind him, Matthew and I looked at each other in bewilderment.

"Shit, man," Matthew whispered, "I never thought he'd kill him."

That night, Matthew cried about Jeff for the first time. He went to Hector and the two of them just broke down. I joined them, as much as I fought it. Jeff and his big cock and what he did with it, I could see, had enormous power over everyone: Lenny, Matthew, Hector, Bernie at the deli, countless tricks

even me, To think that he really was gone for good was too much for us to bear alone. Matthew thought of turning on Lenny, having him arrested for murder. "But we don't know the facts," I argued. "Besides, where would we go?"

As the days passed, Lenny began to feel sorry for himself. "Shoulda brought him back," he'd mumble, preoccupied with his thoughts, unaware of our presence. "Shoulda just dragged that fuckin' little bastard's ass right back here. Damn! I woulda had him right here now!" He'd leave the apartment for long periods and we speculated he was probably searching the streets for another big-dicked leatherboy.

Sure enough, he began bringing in boy after boy, but only a few of them lasted through their initiation. For those who passed, Lenny used me as the trainer. Occasionally I would take Matthew with us on a three-way call, once returning to Shaw's place..

Shaw was happy to see us and delighted with the new boy, another blond named Jody. Matthew at first had resisted going on the call because he

knew he would have to share me with Jody, but Lenny told him he either went or he was history.

While Shaw posed Jody in various stages of undress, Matthew and I finished off several glasses of wine. Jody was even more innocent-looking than Matthew, with big eyes that you could get lost in. By the time Jody was naked and his cock was sucked to hardness by Shaw, I was eager to fuck him. Matthew sat in the wicker chair watching us. Shaw poured him another glass of wine and got between his thighs. While Shaw sucked him, Matthew's eyes never left us. I finally had to change position so that Jody was on top of me to avoid Matthew's glare. When Matthew was hard, Shaw told him to climb on the bed and let Jody suck him while he was bouncing up and down on my prick. In this position, Matthew's balls were hanging in my face and I sucked on them while Jody sucked him. My hands moved to Matthew's ass and I began finger-fucking him. Shaw snapped away, now with the hand-held camera, zooming in for close-ups. Eventually he told Matthew and Jody to switch places. Now I got for the first time a bird's eye view of Matthew sucking some other boy's cock. Shaw was so taken with Jody that he took his pants off and climbed on the bed and began fucking him. It was too much – the sight of Matthew sucking, of Jody being fucked, and having Matthew fucking himself with my dick – and I came. This brought them all off and there seemed to be cum everywhere, dripping out of the corners of Matthew's mouth and out of Jody's ass, and Matthew's spunk flying across my belly. I asked to use the shower, and when I came out Matthew had become sick, badly in need of his shot. He sat on the edge of the bed, hunched over in pain, his hair falling forward from his bowed head. Shaw caught that shot, and continued to snap as I went to Matthew to comfort him. I kneeled in front of him and took him in my arms and held him close to me. All my efforts to ease his pain were captured by Shaw in black and white.

"Why doesn't he just give us more?" Matthew grumbled as we waited for Lenny to shoot us up. "I wouldn't have to go through this shit every fuckin' night if he'd just give me a little more..."

"He has been, Matthew," I said, "you've just been needin' more."

"He keeps me on edge," He was getting annoyed. "I just wanna get high!" he whined loudly out of his frustration and pain.

"I know. I don't get high any more. All I get is the pain to stop."

"It's bullshit. Does he think we do this shit for free? He don't even pay us, man. That's our only pay. Least he could do is get us high." We both knew the place we'd finally reached. We'd known right from the start where we were headed but let it go unsaid.

I rubbed his back as he rocked himself, doubled over in pain.

"I can't wait any longer," he cried, shooting to his feet. He went to Lenny's door and knocked. Lenny let him in. I waited outside, my ear to the door:

John Patrick

"You're getting too strung out too fast, kid. Get out there. Learn to wait."

"I can't wait, Lenny. Please, do me now."

"No."

"Why? I'm hurtin', man."

"And tomorrow you won't wait again."

"Please, just give me a little more so I can get off again." "How long since you stopped getting high?"

"Long time. I don't know. It's bad, Lenny. Please. Just get me high tonight." He was saying all the wrong things, he never should have let on how badly he needed it, and he knew that too, but he was desperate.

"You're costing me a lot, Matthew, You crossed the line long ago. `

"What line?" he moaned.

"The profit line. You been ridin' even for months. You're not makin' me any money."

"Please, Lenny... I'll work harder..,."

"I've heard that one before."

"But Lenny..." he whined.

"Look!" Lenny snapped at him, "I been keepin' you on only "cause you do a good job trainin' the little ones and takin' them out. I need someone to do that. But I got Michael. I don't need two of you to do it. Especially if one of you is eatin' up my profits."

"What are you sayin'?"

"I'm gonna have to let you go." There was silence.. I didn't even want to imagine life without him.

"Not now ..."

"No," Lenny said, "but if you continue this way I'll have no other choice."

"But I'm hurtin' real bad, I don't know what ..."

"I'm gonna taper you off."

"Taper me off?"

"Yeah, I'm gonna cut you a little bit every night till you're back down to turnin' me a profit." Matthew looked at me nervously. "It ain't gonna be easy."

"We'll make it."

"You know what happens if you don't make it."

Matthew and I waited, cramped and perspiring, in what seemed an eternal silence until Lenny was ready for us. After our shot, we felt a little better. We reclined on the couch and my fingers idly stroked a lock of his hair as we watched "The Thing" on television.

"We'll be okay, right?"

"Sure." We were not high, but we were not sick either.

As time passed, the doses decreased and our discomfort elevated. "I don't know if I'm gonna be able to do this," Matthew said.

I looked into his eyes and I saw his pain and fear and wished I could do something to take it all away and have those eyes return to the soft, youthful spheres I once knew. But there was nothing I could do. There was nothing anyone could do: Matthew had to do it himself.

The next night, Matthew returned from a call uptown with a big bruise on his face, but he was smiling. Since he didn't seem to be the least bit anxious for Lenny's appearance with our shots, I was suspicious.

"Have a rough call?" I asked.

"Not bad," he said casually as he sat himself down next to me on the couch. I studied him.

"Does it hurt?"

"What?"

"Your face." He shot a hand up to the bruise as if he'd forgotten about it.

'Oh, that," he said, "it's okay."

"You got high," I whispered.

"I couldn't bring you back none..."

"You shouldn't have done it."

"He ain't gonna know."

"I knew," I said,

"Well he won't."

Matthew was lucky; Lenny didn't notice that night and he continued to supplement his habit with regular small, controlled doses he'd get on the street in exchange for sex. He said he'd be smart about it and he was, But one night I watched Lenny hold Matthew's bare arm in his hands as he poked a finger about his swollen veins in search of the best spot to insert the needle. Matthew's arms looked terrible: marred, dotted with red and purple marks, bumps and bruises running up the insides of his arms. Suddenly Lenny stopped and his brow creased as he raised Matthew's hand closer to his face. He poked at the back of Matthew's hand. "What's this?"

"What?"

"This!" Lenny showed him a tiny needle mark on a vein near a knuckle. "I don't hit you there. I never hit my boys in the back of the hand. That's fucked up."

"That ain't from a needle," Matthew rubbed it with a finger and smiled stupidly at Lenny. He looked back down at his hand. "I don't know, guess it's a scratch." Lenny wasn't smiling as he took Matthew's other hand and examined it.

"Stand up," he demanded.

Matthew stood.

"Take down your jeans."

"Here? Now, man?" he laughed nervously.

"Do it!" Lenny snapped.

After Matthew obeyed, Lenny found what he was looking for. Matthew hung his head as Lenny looked over a few needle marks in the veins of his legs. Matthew's fair skin bruised easily and his tracks were obvious. "Okay," Lenny said calmly as Matthew pulled up his jeans. "Now you can leave."

Matthew appeared to be confused.

Lenny went on, "I never hit you with a needle in your hand or your legs. You're fuckin' around behind my back. You sneaky little fuck!"

Matthew cowered, blinking his eyes and leaning away from Lenny who suddenly turned to me and snatched my wrist. "You too! Right?" He pushed up my sleeve to look over my arm and very closely at the back of my hands.

"No, Lenny. Not me."

He wiggled his finger at my jeans and I obeyed his silent command. He checked my legs carefully but found nothing so he went back to inspecting my arms.

"Take your shoes off," he told me.

"Lenny, I'm not doin' any. I swear, man." I was startled with a smack to my face and Lenny began ranting.

"You little fucks think you can get over on me! You'll see! You'll see how it is..." He kept hitting me in the head.

"Lenny! No!" Matthew yelled, "Stop it! He's not doing it! It's only me!"

Lenny stopped smacking me.

"It's just me, He wouldn't do it. He didn't even know."

Lenny began beating Matthew, shrinking under upraised arms. My fingers bristled through the air in a fruitless attempt to catch his arm and stop him, until my arm hooked into one of his, demanding his attention. "Please, Lenny. Stop!"

He looked at me only for a second and simply shook me off of him so he could continue.

"Give him another chance. Please, Lenny, he'll do it this time."

"He's outta here! He's gone!" he screamed as the beating continued.

"Please, Lenny, stop!" I yelled, and was surprised when he actually did stop. He towered over Matthew's folded frame and breathed heavily from the depths of his chest, tears streaming down his face.

"That's what I get. I try to give 'em a chance and I get fucked,"

"I know he won't do it again."

"Damn straight," Lenny said, " 'cause he's outta here."

"Just give him one more chance, Lenny. You need him to train the new kids ..."

"I got you to do that, I don't need him. He blew it."

"But he'll make it this time Keep him with me for a while, I'll make sure he don't go off and do anything. I'll keep an eye on him,"

"Get the fuck out," he ordered Matthew, ignoring my appeal.

"Lenny, please. He can't make it out there. You know he'll never make it alone."

"That's his problem. He shoulda thought of that before. He was warned." He grabbed Matthew and dragged him to the front door.

"You can't! You can't throw him out!"

"Watch me." He dragged Matthew, kicking and screaming, down the stairs to the foyer, He held the front door open and was pushing the boy out onto the sidewalk. When I got to the bottom of the stairs, I knelt down and put an arm around Matthew.

"Let me go too, Lenny. He needs me. He can't be out there alone." I tried to pull my arm free. "I'm not stayin' here without him! We're a package deal."

"That ain't the way I see it," Lenny sneered. "Let's go. You'll get over him." He started pulling me back into the building. "Beat it, Matthew," he said.

"Matthew, wait for me. I'll meet you," I cried as Lenny jerked me around.

"You ain't goin' nowhere," he said, and swung me up and shoved me toward the stairs, slamming the front door in Matthew's face.

"I'm going to him, the first chance I get."

"Yeah, well, I'll find you, and I'll kill the little bastard right in your face!"

Lenny brought me to his room and handcuffed one wrist to the iron headboard of his bed. He continued to beat me until I stopped my hollering, then went out into the front room to fix the rest of the boys. After Lenny finished his business, he came back in with the empty syringes gathered in his hand, He threw them in the waste basket beside his desk, then released me from my cuff.

"You ready?" he asked, stepping back over to the desk where the two remaining syringes lay. "You been doin' good, kid. I know I can depend on you. You'll get over that little piece a' trash."

"He's not trash! You didn't have to let him go," I cried, couldn't you give him another chance?"

"I gave him enough chances."

"He couldn't help it,"

"That's why he's out. He's too far gone and I can't afford him,"

"Give him my share."

"Shut up." He brought a syringe over to me. "See, I knew what was goin' on. I knew you were fucking him every chance you got. I thought putting him with Jeff would end it, but it didn't. No, you were just too wrapped up in that tight little boy-cunt, but you're too good for him. You got a future. He don't have no future. All he wants is the high. He ain't goin' nowhere."

"And where am I going?"

"You'll go places. You'll see. I'm keepin' you with me for a long time," he said, tying the tourniquet around my arm, "you got what it takes. You're not like the rest. You're a pro. Born right into this. Sarah raised you right," he said under his breath, and I froze at the sound of my mother's name. I stared at him. He held my arm in his hands, searching for a vein.

"How come you remember her name, Lenny?"

He squinted. "What's the big deal? I remember lotsa names."

"You knew her. You knew Sarah. Who was she to you?"

He continued poking at my arm, ignoring me. He poised with the needle ready to inject, and frowned. "Sarah was my sister." We stared at each other for a long moment. He chuckled at my expression of shock. "Yeah," he said, "I'm your uncle. You happy now? One big happy fuckin' family, but don't you go gettin' no ideas that maybe you're somethin' special 'round here now that you know, 'cause you're not."

"Where is she?"

"Dead. She knew she was gonna die. That's why she brought you here. It wasn't 'cause she didn't love you. 'Take care of him, Lenny,' she said. She really loved you, more 'n anything, but she was real sick. Shit, I never seen anybody so sick ..." Shaking his head sadly, he turned away from me and returned to his desk.

"What the hell," he said as he looked back at me. He picked up the syringe he'd prepared for Matthew, tossed the yellow plastic cap into the waste basket and smiled. "Bet you'd like to get high tonight." He shot me with it and I felt the effects immediately. I looked up into his eyes and saw he was crying. I started crying again too and he took me in his arms and held me.

The next thing I remember was hearing, "Come on, Michael." Ricky was trying to wake me up. Lenny was already handing out the night's assignments.

TEN

Perhaps I was only imagining it but it seemed that after Lenny told me I was his nephew he was even harder on me than before – and the number of blowjobs I had to give him increased. But of course, he didn't have Matthew to kick around and suck him off so maybe that had something to do with it. Neither of us ever again mentioned our relationship, and I never told anyone about it.

But Lenny did start doing something he hadn't done before – going out and buying the Sunday Times and making me read it. He bought a dozen books and laid them on the coffee table. He'd turn off the TV and make me study them, When I was in his office, after I'd given him a blowjob, he'd point to a locked drawer of his desk and say, "All your tips are in there. I'm savin' 'em for your college education. But first you gotta pass the test and get your GED."

"Sure, Lenny," I would say, not really believing it.

As I went out on my calls, I always kept an eye out for Matthew but I never saw him. Once I thought I had spotted him. I had finished an afternoon call and was starting down the stairs to catch the subway at Sheridan Square. A long-haired blond boy was stretched out lazily on a park bench and he very obviously cruised me. I stopped; actually I froze. "Hi," he said, smiling slightly. As I stepped closer, I saw it really wasn't Matthew, just a cheap imitation, but I wanted him just the same.

"Hi," I said as he looked me up and down.

There was a long silence and I was about to turn away to catch my train when he said, "I live over there," pointing to a building on the Square.

"Oh?"

Looking directly at my crotch, he said, "Shall we go?"

I looked to one side, then the other. "I don't know. I haven't got much time."

"Okay."

What was okay was the head he gave me once we were naked. Almost as good as Matthew. At one point, he pulled it out and told me how big and beautiful my cock was. He went back to sucking it, then got some Vaseline and prepared himself. He rolled over and lifted his ass to meet my cock. He wasn't as tight as Matthew but it felt good, fucking this person with no name. It occurred to me that he was the only person I'd had sex with on my own in over two years, ever since my mother brought me to Lenny.

After I got it all the way in and was settling into a rhythm, he was crying out desperately.

"Do you want me to stop?" I asked.

"No! Oh, no. Fuck me. Keep fuckin' me."

And so I did, for at least a half an hour. I was hot and sweaty by the time he came, collapsing under me. I pulled out. "Did you come?"

"Yeah," I lied, breathing very hard. I still had an erection but I also still had the evening's calls to live through.

He lay back on the bed watching me dress. "You're really good."

'Thanks. I get a hundred dollars for what I just did to you." He smiled. "I had a hunch you did. That makes it even better. Please come back some time."

"Sure," I said, hurrying to the door.

When I got home, I couldn't help it: I went to the bathroom and pulled out Matthew's photos from his secret hiding place under the behind the toilet. A shot of me standing beside Matthew as he sat on the edge of the bed, my hard cock pressed against his cheek, was my favorite. I recalled the moment it was taken. His head was bowed slightly forward, as if he was anxious to take my cock into his mouth, and his hair cascaded down his bare shoulders and neck like a glistening curtain which back dropped his soft profile. The left portion of the background in the photo was pitch black, the light coming from the right side only, creating sharp contrasts on our bodies. Matthew's eyes were gleaming then as he was about to do what he enjoyed most, making other guys happy. Matthew's favorite picture showed him on his back, me over him, my dick in his ass. We are smiling at each other before I lowered myself to kiss him on the lips. It is a portrait of our passion at its most intense. I jacked off to the images and, even when I was finished, I still ached from wanting him.

Ricky had taken Jeff's bed, at the very back of the main room, and after he had returned from an afternoon call he told me he was going to take a nap. There was gleam in his eyes that made me come over to him.

"Room for me?"

"Sure," he said, lifting the sheet. He was nude. We hadn't had sex since that time at The Stud and I felt like making up for lost time. The other boys were watching television and Lenny had gone out to look for some new talent – we were down to only five now – so we had plenty of time.

As usual, Ricky said nothing as I slipped off my underpants and snuggled behind him. I kissed his bare shoulders and rolled him over on his back. I began to move slowly down over his stomach, surrounded by powerful abdominal muscles. It took some time to cover the whole surface. His navel stood out, a small white ball outlined by the rounded mass, and I kissed it, swirled my tongue around it. I knelt down to massage his abdomen. He moved towards me and I raised my head and saw his swelling balls, his taut cock, incredibly large, straight above my eyes. I skirted around it towards the inside of the thick thighs. He was now lying back, his arms spread. He was groaning, his cock throbbing. I felt he was going to come before I even touched him.

I kissed, licked and nibbled his solid legs and got between his thighs. His cock sprang up to meet my lips. I moved my hand over his balls, back up to their base near his ass. His cock stood up again, more violently. I held it in my other hand, squeezed it, began slowly pulling it up and down. I spit on it and continued until the spunk spurted out in bursts, splashing my face.

He lifted up and licked the cum from my face. His tips caressed mine and he pulled back, looking deep into my eyes. His eyelids were heavy as if under the effect of a drug. At this point, Matthew would have said something crazy like, "I love you," but not Ricky. He just sighed and fell back on the bed.

As I rolled him over, he relaxed completely. I kissed his asscheeks, then stuck my tongue between them.

"The john just fucked me, Michael," he murmured, "He was just gettin' it ready for you."

I began eating his ass.

"What took you so long, Michael?"

I raised my head, What a time for him to become talkative. "It's been a rough time."

"I can do everything Matty can do."

"I know." I lifted his hips with both hands, then firmly thrust two fingers into him. He tensed at first but finally, with several thrusts, the tension slackened and he let me finger-fuck him for several minutes. Then he rolled over.

"Make love to me, Michael. No one ever really makes love to me."

I drew him close, raised up a little, put my arms around him. I took his head in my hand and thrust my tongue in his mouth all at once. I wiggled it at the back of his throat, wrapped it and rolled it over mine. I began biting his lips till I tasted blood. Then I opened his thighs wider and, guiding my hard cock to his ass, I pushed it into him. He bent his legs around me as I rode him vigorously. Occasionally my cock slipped from him, glistening and red, and he held it and rose up to watch it as I put it back in.

But I was going too fast. He calmed me down gently. He would wait as long as I wanted to make the pleasure last – and the pain. He unfolded his legs and I lay on top of him just moving quietly within him, kissing his face. He lay motionless, contracting the muscles of his ass around my cock. As I chewed at the great expanse of his chest, it seemed an electric charge was flowing through my tongue. He was trembling. I was squinting with pleasure, ready to come. But he wanted it to last even longer, so he rolled over onto his side. My hard cock nearly filled him again. As I dug my nails into his pecs, he breathed more heavily, jacking himself off.

I suddenly became aware we had gathered a crowd. As if they had been given permission to do whatever they wanted, the other boys crowded around the bed watching us, jacking off as I fucked Ricky,. It had never happened before in the many months I'd been at Lenny's. Most of the time, we were either too tired from tricking or we were doped up or Lenny was in his office. None of that applied now. Jody ran his hand through my hair as he jerked his cock. Erect, Hector's long, uncut slab of meat was an incredible sight, irresistible to Ralph, who sat on the bed and took it in his mouth. I turned my head so that I could take Jody's erection between my lips. He knelt on the bed and began to fuck my face with it while I fucked Ricky.

After a few minutes, we came, one after the other, on and on, our groans mingled, coming from the very depths of our chests, sounds of satisfaction so long denied us.

ELEVEN

Around the first of October, just after we'd finished our dinner from the deli and Lenny was getting the evening's assignments ready, I was reclining on the couch watching the Movie of the Week when there was a knock on the door. Ricky got up and let the caller in. I sat up, staring at Matthew, thrilled and shocked at the same time. I was happy to see that he was alive, but he was in really bad shape. His clothes were dirty and hung off his narrow frame like drapes. His hair was dirty and greasy, and lay limply against his neck and shoulders, parting in stiff sections of gold and yellow and light brown streaks. His eyes were sunken and no longer sparkled.

I rushed to his side. "I missed you. I've been looking for you all over. I was hoping you'd ..."

"Couldn't," he said, sniffling and running a knuckle under his nose. "Lenny in there?" He looked beyond me to Lenny's door.

"Yeah. But are you all right? I've been worried about you.

"Yeah, I'm okay. I'm just kinda hurtin' a little right now, you know?" He spoke softly. "I can't get nothin' at the moment. I owe this guy some money and he won't give me nothin' 'till I pay him." He looked beyond me again. "I gotta see Lenny." He stumbled past me and knocked on Lenny's door. I didn't think Lenny would see him but he told him to wait.

I came up beside him. "What you been doin'?"

"Ohhh, a little bit of everything. I stayed with some guy for a coupla weeks, then he threw me out. Mostly I work in a club."

"A club?"

"Yeah, a members-only kinda place. I do a number there."' "What do you mean? What kind of number?"

"A live show. I dance and end up, well, you know, on my knees and shit." He looked away. "I meet a lot a nice guys that way."

"I've been worried about you..."

"Hey," he said, turning his face back to me again, .don't you worry 'bout me!" He moved away from me. "I've gotta take a piss."

I followed him to the bathroom. He left the door slightly open. I went in, closed it behind me.

"Can't anybody have any privacy around here?" Matthew said, mocking me. "Let me pee." He unzipped his jeans, started a stream of piss into the toilet.

"I've missed you."

"No, you've just missed my ass. 'That's what you mean."

I took his asscheeks in my hands and squeezed them. "Yes, more every day. But I miss holding you at night, going with you on tricks."

Dangerous Boys, Rent Boys

He stopped pissing and leaned over, lifted the file and took out the pictures. 1 forgot these."

"I'm glad you did. I look at them every day."

He smiled, gazing at the photos. "We were good together, weren't we?"

I put my arms around his waist, hugging him to me. "Fuck me Michael,"

"What?"

He tugged his jeans down, exposing his ass. "Fuck it." "Here?"

"We've done it before."

Even if it was bruised and reddened, his ass looked as wonderful as ever. I licked the hairless crack until he started moaning and turning on my every move, I spit on my hard-on and slowly put it into his ass.

"Ohhh," he moaned as my balls finally began slamming against his asscheeks. Even with all the fucking he'd been getting, he was still tight. Watching my cock slide in and out of him brought back memories of all the times we'd done this in front of other guys for money and on our own. It was true: I never enjoyed fucking anyone more than Matthew.

He began clamping hard on my cock, as if demanding I come. He reached back and grabbed my ass, trying to push me deeper into him, I pumped for several minutes and we were kissing when, suddenly, the door opened.. Lenny said, "Well, just like old times," he chuckled. "When you can pull yourself away, I'll see you in my office, Matthew."

As he slammed the door, I carne,

"Oh, yeah," Matthew groaned. "Just like old times."

After I pulled out, he turned around and I reached for his semi-hard cock, but his fingers brushed me away. "No," he said. "Have to see Lenny," he said.

He wanted to keep the pictures. I let him have his favorite one and I stashed the others back behind the tile.

While Matthew was with Lenny, I sat at the edge of the couch waiting for that door to open again, trying to hear whatever I could without being too obvious in front of the other boys. I heard some rumbling from beyond the door, but no yelling, no arguing, and no pleading from Matthew.

Finally the door opened and Matthew came out carrying a piece of paper in his hand. Lenny had made a deal with him. Perhaps a chance to come back, I didn't know. Matthew ignored me and went out the front door without a word. I ran down the stairs and caught up with him out on the sidewalk.

"Where are you goin'?' I puffed.

He looked at me as if he didn't know me.

"Matthew, what's wrong with you?"

"Nothin'. Lenny gave me this guy's name. Fie said he'd fix me up." He smacked his lips. "I had to blow the fucker to get it, but it was worth it."

"Matthew!" I pulled at his arm. He glared at me.

"You got what you wanted, Michael. A piece of my ass. That's all you wanted and you got it."

"Please stay." I tugged at his arm.

"Can't."

"Come on, we'll talk to Lenny and ..."

"He won't take me back, blowjob or no blowjob."

I hugged him. "Oh, Matthew."

He whispered, "I think about you all the time, if that's what you want to know` only I have to stop myself."

"Why?"

"'Cause ..." He rolled his eyes.

"'Cause?"

"'Cause I can't afford to think about you." Fie pushed me away and wiped his eyes. "I gotta go."

"No."

"Yeah, I do.''

"Then I'm going with you."

"No! Go back to Lenny. You're what he wants."

"But I want you."

"You wanna take care of me all the time, but I'm fine. I can look out for myself." He started backing down the street and I moved with him. "Uh-oho" he yelled, pointing past me. "Your ass is in trouble now!"

I looked over my shoulder and saw Lenny rushing toward me. When I looked back to Matthew, he was gone.

I stood still on the sidewalk in the middle of the block. I could have outrun Lenny easily, taken after Matthew, found him. But it seemed as if my feet were stuck; I just couldn't move.

"You done?" Lenny asked, grabbing me by the shoulder.

I nodded and, my eyes brimming with tears, I followed Lenny home.

CONTRIBUTORS

Ken Anderson

The author lives in Georgia and is a frequent contributor to Iris, the gay literary magazine.

Keith Banner

The author is editor of the Oxford Magazine, the literary review at Miami University, Oxford, Ohio, and is a frequent contributor to gay literary publications, including Christopher Street.

William "Bill" Barber

The author, who passed away of complications from AIDS in late 1992, was a frequent contributor to STARbooks' anthologies. The story included in this book is an expanded version of a story which previously appeared in Tarnished Angels. He was the author of the novel Marty, now included complete in the best-selling anthology, A Natural Beauty.

David Patrick Beavers

The author's first novel, jackal in the Dark, about Los Angeles in the 70s, was recently published by Millivres Books, London. The author lives in Los Angeles.

Michael C. Botkin

The author writes for Bay Area Reporter, Diseased Pariah News, and Processed World, but when it comes to sex, he's stricty an amateur these days. His confession originally appeared in Black Sheets.

Lawrence Benjamin

The author lives in Philadelphia where, when not dodging hostilities, he is at work on a novel. Several of his short tales have appeared in STARbooks' anthologies, including Seduced and RunawayslKid Stuff:

Frank Brooks

The author is a regular contributor to gay magazines. In addition to boys and writing, his passions are figure drawing from the live model and mountain hiking.

Leo Cardin

Author of the best-selling book, Mineshaft Nights, Mr. Cardini's stories and theater-related articles have appeared in a variety of magazines. He is the co-author of a musical now being fine-tuned for Broadway.

William Cozad

The author is a regular contributor to gay magazines and a collection of his work, Lover Boys, will be published soon by STARbooks Press.

Terry Cross

The author's "career" spans the Golden Age of Homosexuality (as Boyd McDonald put it) from 1946 until he became a born-again virgin a few years ago. He is a frequent contributor to STARbooks' anthologies.

John C. Douglas

The author has an enviable track record, having some thirty novels published, and more than twenty screenplays produced. A former Alabamian, now living in Florida, Douglas has a number of works in progress. "Most of the time," he admits, "I don't have a firm plot in mind. I prefer to create the characters and let them do whatever they like. Sometimes, they surprise even me!" A full-length novel, "The Young and the Flawless," will appear in STARbooks Press' Barely Legal.

Dirk Hannam

A California-based writer, Dirk's work has appeared in many gaymale publications, including In Touch and Guys. He can attest to the fact that the fields and backwoods of America are amply populated with gays, "they are just more reclusive than city folk. There are few gay pride parades on country back roads."

Bert McKenzie

A free lance writer and drama critic, the Kansan writes a column for a major midwestern newspaper and has contributed erotic fiction to magazines such as Torso, Mandate, and Playguy. He is a frequent contributor to STARbooks' anthologies and will soon have an anthology of his work published by Badboy.

Jesse Monteagudo

The author is a columnist for the Community Voice in Miami and is noted for his non-fiction writing, including a passage in John Preston's highly-acclaimed Hometowns.

Thom Nickels

The Cliffs of Aries, the author's first novel, was published in 1988 by Aegina Press. His second book, Two Novellas: Walking Water & After All This, was published in 1989 by Banned Books and was a Lambda Literary Award finalist in 1990 in the Science Fiction/Fantasy category. A regular columnist for an alternative weekly in Philadelphia, Thom has contributed feature articles, book reviews and celebrity interviews to several gay publications. A collection of his best writing was published by STARbooks Press under the title, The Boy on the Bicycle.

Sean Michael O'Day

The author is a frequent contributor to gay publications and his novel, Firestorm, was published by Alyson in 1984. He lives in Ohio and recently completed the mystery novel, The Eighth Deadly Sin.

Peter Z. Pan

A first-generation American of Cuban descent, this twentysomething author calls himself a "quintessential jack-of-all-trades: multimedia writer, theatrical director, and sometime actor-singer." Peter says he resides in Miami, "physically anyway." Spiritually, he says he will always live where Lost Boys forever frolic: "_second star to the right, and straight on till morning."

Adam Starchild

The author, an entrepreneur, has written a number of books on business and finance. He has written for a variety of gay publications, including Advocate Men, In Touch, Gay Community News, Drummer, Holy Titclamps, Mandate, and First Hand.

Tony Stephenson

This story originally appreared in The Gay Review, Vol. II, No. 4. The author, a University Professor, is widely published and lives in Toronto.

Michael Taylor

The author is a frequent contributor to STARbooks Press' anthologies and resides in New York.

Christopher Thomas

The poet has had his work published in many literary journals including Deviance, The James White Review, Michigan Quarterly Review, Poetry Motel, Chiron Review, Duckabush Review, Evergreen Review, New Voice, RFD and Gay Sunshine Review. He makes his living as a Gentleman Farmer and will soon publish a collection of his best work: as The Smell of Carnal Knowledge.

Don Valpo

This memoir originally appeared in The Gay Review, Vol. II, No. 3. The author lives in Chicago.

P.K. Warren

The author is currently "on retreat," courtesy of the State of New York. This is his first published story.

James Wilton

The author, who resides in Connecticut, has contributed stories to various gay magazines. The story in this collection has been adapted from material originally appearing in Manscape..

ABOUT THE EDITOR

JOHN PATRICK was a prolific, prize-winning author of fiction and non-fiction. One of his short stories, "The Well," was honored by PEN American Center as one of the best of 1987. His novels and anthologies, as well as his non-fiction works, including Legends and The Best of the Superstars series, continue to gain him new fans every day. One of his most famous short stories appears in the Badboy collection Southern Comfort and another appears in the collection The Mammoth Book of Gay Short Stories.

A divorced father of two, the author was a longtime member of the American Booksellers Association, the Publishing Triangle, the Florida Publishers' Association, American Civil Liberties Union, and the Adult Video Association. He lived in Florida, where he passed away on October 31, 2001.

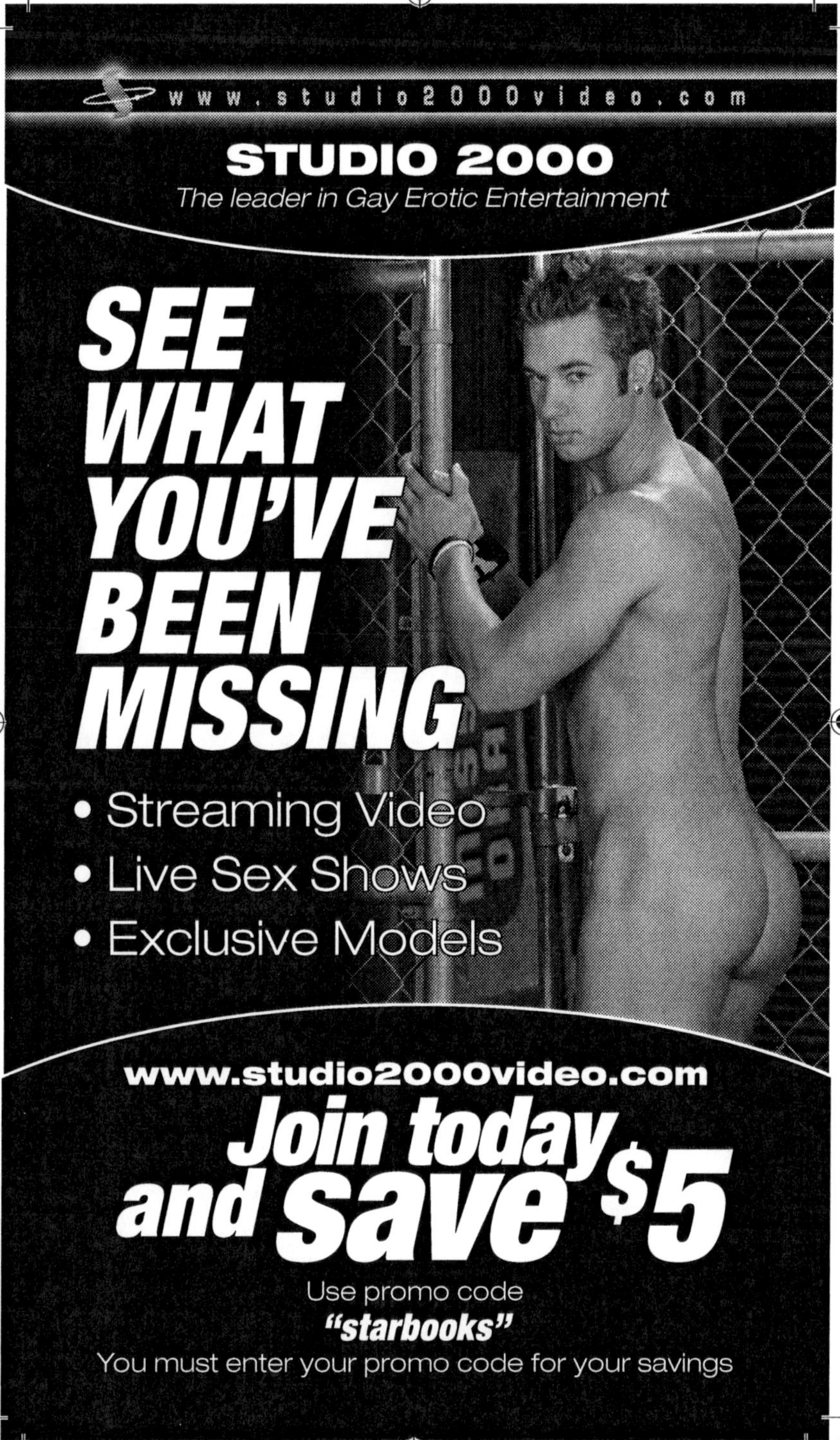

OTICFICTION4.25x7.25v2.indd   1   5/16/06   7:19:28 PM